Phantom

Barbara Meyers

This edition published by Barbara Meyers, LLC and Sandalstring Productions
Copyright © 2019 by Barbara Meyers

Cover by Steven Novak, Novak Illustration

Digital ISBN: 978-0-9836772-8-4
Print ISBN: 978-1-951286-02-6

1. Action/Adventure – Fiction
2. Contemporary Romance – Fiction
3. Covert Operations – Fiction
4. Central America – Fiction
5. Emerald Mines – Fiction

Prologue

"He's heading north past the park. Try to cut him off." Aaron spoke aloud, knowing the tiny microphone beneath his shirt collar picked up every word and transmitted it to his fellow agents.

They'd had Eli Carzoui boxed in, had cut off all chance of escape when he tried to blend into a crowded line outside a Starbucks. But he'd bolted into the street, yanked a commuter out of a black BMW and commandeered the car.

Aaron and his fellow agents scrambled to pursue him. For a terrorist recently transplanted from the Middle East, Carzoui drove like a native New Yorker. Aaron wrenched the wheel, tires squealing, as he followed his quarry into a hard right turn.

Everything after that happened in slow motion as it always does when tragedy strikes.

Aaron, close behind, saw a man and a young boy holding hands as they crossed the street. The BMW hurtled toward them. Aaron saw the man's first hint of horrified awareness, his attempt to clutch the child closer as if to shield him from harm, his instinct to run, to escape. But there was no escape.

Aaron slammed on his brakes and watched in horror as the BMW hit the pedestrians and kept going. Both bodies catapulted through the air to land with sickening thuds that could be heard even through the closed car windows.

Aaron jammed his car into park and vaulted out. Carzoui swerved erratically when he looked back over his shoulder, his dark, crazed eyes fixed on the destruction he'd wrought. He overcorrected then slammed the BMW into a garbage truck. The car burst into flame and three explosions in quick succession rocked the neighborhood.

Aaron knelt next to the man who'd been hit, knowing before he got there it was too late. The man's eyes fluttered, his lips moved. "Zoe?"

Chapter One

An Uber driver in a white compact will be idling in front of your building. Zoe laid the letter in her lap. She'd read it so many times she had the instructions memorized. The driver silently navigated the nearly empty streets and parked in a loading zone. She perused the building as best she could from the glow of security lights and the car's headlights. Industrial green blank brick walls gave away nothing.

She caught the driver's eye in the rearview mirror. "Can you drive around the corner? Slowly?" He shifted into reverse and did as she asked while she peered at the façade, searching for some clue as to what type of building it was, or had once been. But the mystery held, for she saw nothing but more of the same old brick covered in the same shade of green and no other entrance. Sections of what might have been windows in an earlier era had been sealed with stucco giving the structure even more of a blank look.

Zoe instructed the driver to circle the block only to find it filled with more of the same type of industrial warehouses, some with signs and windows, but all as nondescript as her destination.

When he returned to the original parking place, she wondered why she wasn't more nervous. All of her senses were on high alert, but she didn't feel as afraid as she thought she would. She didn't feel the threat of imminent danger. But of course she hadn't yet set foot outside the car. She could leave now. She still had that option. But even as the reminder flashed through her mind, she knew she wouldn't leave. She'd made her decision.

Before stepping out, she withdrew the black-handled paring knife from her purse and carefully tucked it inside the sleeve of her sweater. At the top of a short flight of stairs the heavy metal door opened easily.

Two flights up, first door on the left.

The utilitarian shades of green, the white-globed ceiling lights hanging from chains in the hallway, the walls painted a sickly cream and doors with ancient, tarnished knobs reminded her of the antiquated courthouses and social services offices she'd regularly visited as a child.

Once inside the room, she slowly toured the space, though there wasn't much to it. No window. No video cameras hidden in corners either, as far as she could determine, though she was hardly a surveillance expert. A bed, little more than a wide army cot, took precedence, its tubular metal frame painted the same hue as the walls and doors, made up with regulation issue white sheets and an army-green blanket. Two under-stuffed pillows lay side by side near the headrail. An empty metal cabinet next to the bed and a plain wooden chair completed the furnishings.

The heat had obviously been turned on, but it hadn't dispensed the pervading chill or the slightly musty smell of the old building.

A door in one corner opened into a small bathroom, sink and toilet circa 1940, Zoe figured.

So what? She asked herself again. Her fatalistic attitude had seen her through a year of hell. How much worse could it get?

She set her purse on the chair and slipped out of her coat draping it over the chair back. Then she toed off her shoes and left them next to the chair.

She wished she was getting some dreadful negative vibes from her surroundings, something that would make every instinct she had scream at her to get out of there now. Not that she'd ever considered herself to be a highly intuitive person. But even the most obtuse individual could sense danger approaching. She sensed nothing. No dread. No evil presence lurking, watching perhaps, waiting to make a move.

You will not be harmed.

We'll see, she thought with what she hoped was a healthy enough dose of skepticism. What if *I know what you've lost* meant *I know you've lost your brother*? What if this mysterious letter writer could help her find and rescue Ben? But he certainly wouldn't pay her to have sex with him as well.

Zoe had already admitted to herself that such a scenario seemed farfetched in the extreme. Trading sex for information made sense. Being paid for sex and receiving information on top of it made no sense. Then again, the letter hadn't exactly stated that sex was mandatory. Expected, but optional was how she'd interpreted it. Yet she couldn't fool herself. That money was payment for something other than the overnight pleasure of her silent company.

She turned out the light, not quite prepared for total darkness. But when she flipped the switch near the door which controlled the ceiling light in the room, the ones in the outer hallway went out as well. She flipped them back on, then turned them out again.

Please, she prayed, as she shuffled in the direction of the bed, please God, let this be a way to save Ben. She said the same half-assed help-me-save-Ben prayer every night. Maybe tonight Ben's God had decided to grant her wish.

In the dark she padded carefully back across the cracked linoleum to the bed. She dislodged the tightly tucked blanket from beneath the mattress and lay down. She released the knife from her sleeve and placed it under the pillow, with the handle in easy reach.

She had read and reread the letter since she'd found it after returning from the restaurant the previous night. Apparently it had been slipped under her apartment door during her absence.

Money and a similarly typed note had been slipped under her door over a year ago, right after the accident. *I'm sorry for your loss* that note had said. No signature, no card. Just hundred dollar bills. She'd needed money badly then, too. Funerals were expensive.

This latest precisely typed missive on plain white paper outlined a business deal pure and simple. Spend the night with an anonymous male. A male with a supposedly clean bill of health.

Nothing kinky. Nothing to be afraid of.

Enclosed with the letter was a small stack of hundred-dollar bills. She'd counted them, weighed them in her hand for a long time and imagined doubling the amount. By selling herself. How could she do such a thing?

How could she not? She'd exhausted every resource she had in her efforts to find and free Ben. Her credit cards were maxed out. She had no assets. She was barely getting by.

The call from Julio, as she stood there with the letter in one hand and the cash in the other, strengthened Zoe's resolve.

In his heavily accented, but surprisingly good English, Julio, calling from somewhere in

Central America, painted the image of Ben, shackled, beaten and half-starved being dragged to an even more remote location.

"But I don't understand what they want, Julio. They haven't asked for a ransom from the church or the government or—or me." She supposed it was possible her brother's kidnappers knew that she had nothing, so there was no point in asking.

"I do not know, Senora Zoe," Julio replied. "But if you offer them money, I cannot say for certain, but maybe they let Father Ben go."

This wasn't the first time that Julio had intimated that perhaps a large amount of cold hard American cash would free Ben. There'd never been a reason to consider it before. *If our first meeting is successful, others may be requested at the same rate of exchange.* "How much money, Julio?"

Static crackled before Julio said, "I do not know, Senora Zoe."

Her stack of unpaid bills swam before her eyes. On top lay the final notice for her phone bill. Her phone. Her only link to Julio. Her only connection to Ben. She couldn't lose it. She stared at the cash in her hand. The bizarre proposition outlined in the letter might be her one chance to save him.

If the situation were reversed, she knew Ben would do whatever he had to in order to save her.

But he wouldn't sell himself! Her subconscious scolded her.

Would he?

She clenched the cash in her hand harder, feeling hope race through her along with a bravado she'd never felt before. "Julio, is there any way you can get word to the people holding Ben? Tell them I'm getting money for them. It might take a little while. But tell them I'll pay to get Ben back."

A long silence ensued. Zoe wondered if they'd lost the connection. Julio's calls were infrequent. She knew he had to travel a good distance from the mountain village of Santa Rosaro to access a working telephone. Then Julio's voice came through again, as if he'd been contemplating her words. "I can try, Senora Zoe. I will do my best. I will help you save Father Ben."

Zoe hadn't realized she'd been holding her breath waiting for Julio's response. She released it, thinking fast. "Tell them a healthy hostage will be worth more to me than one who's been starved and mistreated."

Again there came that pause as Julio seemed to consider her words. "If I can get word to them, I will tell them."

Julio promised to call again when he had news.

Zoe had given herself a long hard look in the bathroom mirror before she stumbled into bed. She tossed and turned most of the night knowing that if she didn't do everything in her power to save Ben, she'd never forgive herself.

But trepidation filled her as she lay waiting.

Waiting in the dark.

Chapter Two

Somehow Zoe had dozed off, but woke abruptly when an unmistakably male body pressed up close behind her. She sucked in a breath as a hand slid around her waist and down across her belly. Wide awake now she remembered the letter just as words of objection formed on her tongue. *You must not speak.*

Every nerve ending in her body screamed in panic. *No! No! No!* Her muscles tensed in silent protest of a stranger's touch.

An uncontrollable tremor started deep inside her and spread outward. She couldn't do this. She'd experienced a temporary lapse in sanity to believe she could. She remembered her grandmother's words from long, long ago telling Zoe's mother, "Anything that sounds too good to be true usually is."

Something like this. Cash. Lots of it. So some healthy anonymous male could spend the night with her. *With her?* It made no sense. Sex wasn't that hard to come by. No pun intended, she told herself now. Especially for a man with money. Her mind seemed to be splitting in a million directions as she tried to decide what to do.

If she screamed only he would hear her. She could try to escape from the bed and find the light switch before he caught her. There'd be a face-to-face confrontation. She could simply run screaming out of the building. Assuming she could find her way back out before he caught her. Her coat was on the chair. Her shoes right next to it. She'd have to locate the light switch to find them. She had no way out.

The knife under the pillow! She gripped the handle. He could have a gun, of course, somewhere within easy reach. Or an even bigger knife. Her attempt to have a defense weapon close at hand seemed laughable now. Still, it was better than nothing.

Zoe forced herself to swallow her instinctive whimpers of fear and sent her mind to another place. All of those hundred dollar bills, she reminded herself. For one night.

All she had to do was have sex with a stranger and she'd have a healthy start on Ben's rescue fund. She'd pay off whoever she had to in that god-forsaken Central American jungle to find him and bring him home. That's why she'd come here. It was a chance she had to take. If she survived the night, she'd be that much closer to saving Ben.

But she couldn't stop shaking. She couldn't turn her mind off. Her heart beat triple time as the stranger's fingers brushed her jaw then slid down to her throat. Long fingers lay heavily against her neck.

He's going to kill me. That was how she would die. Strangled in the dark by an unseen force. He'd dump her body somewhere. Her fragmented mind fed her visions of a dumpster. A river. He could leave her here, in this bed in this room, to be found only God knew when.

And if she died no one would care. Ben wouldn't even know she'd been trying to save him. Ben might die too. Maybe she'd meet him in heaven. A place she no longer believed in.

Drew. Drew would care. The thought thundered through Zoe's head as she remembered the one other precaution she'd taken so that if she didn't return from this...encounter, at least there'd be a trail for Drew to follow. She'd photocopied the letter and left it with the envelope of cash in plain sight near the door of her apartment. If she mysteriously disappeared, she knew Drew would leave no stone unturned until he found out what had happened to her.

The pressure from the stranger's fingers increased slightly, pressing against the side of her neck, and Zoe gathered a breath to scream. She wouldn't give up without a fight, she decided. She'd at least leave a mark on him, gouge his eyes out if she could, though her nails were pitifully short. The paring knife was small but surely she could do some sort of damage, leave some kind of forensic evidence so maybe her killer could be caught.

As she readied herself to roll over and strike out, she felt pressure from his thumbs against the base of her neck. Her scream came out a sigh instead as he found a pressure point she hadn't known was there. Tension seeped out of her body as his thumbs moved lower between the tops of her shoulders. Of its own accord, her grip on the knife relaxed. She held her breath and fumbled to hold onto the knife handle, waiting to see if this was some kind of trick, if his hands would tighten around her throat now, cutting off her air. Instead his hands moved across her shoulders, massaging her, encouraging her to relax even further.

As the tight ball of tension in her stomach eased, it occurred to her that he hadn't undressed. Right behind that revelation came the one that so far he'd made no effort to remove her long-sleeved sweater or slacks.

The trembling stopped as her mind continued to race. She shoved several fingers in her mouth, for words were against the rules. If he wasn't going to hurt her, if this was for real, she wanted the rest of the money he'd promised.

Somehow, she was on her stomach, her head turned to one side as his hands worked their magic, finding knots of tension down her back before they returned to her shoulders, her neck.

Heat seeped into her skin as his hands roved over her. His fingers slid into her hair massaging her scalp, a touch so intimate it brought tears to her eyes.

No one touched her this way anymore. For over a year she'd deprived herself of any but the most casual physical contact such as a handshake or peck on the cheek.

His touch unlocked something painful deep inside her, tapping into her loneliness and sorrow. Tears seeped from her eyes and she couldn't make them stop.

I'm sorry for your loss.

Clearly, that first note had been in reference to the deaths of Tim and Zach.

I know what you've lost. Maybe I can help you find it.

Maybe those words had nothing to do with Ben. She'd lost so much the past year, the stranger could be referring to any number of things. One of the things she'd lost was her ability to feel anything. Feeling *hurt.* Caring was too painful. Much better to insulate herself from everyone and everything and remain numb.

He worked his way down one arm and then the other, circling the backs of her hands and between her knuckles with his fingers, and then he came back to where he started, cupping her below the jaw, his thumbs at the base of her skull.

Tears continued to leak from her eyes of their own volition. From an early age Zoe had trained herself to cry quietly, to keep pain private. He lifted her hair, and she could feel his breath, warm against the back of her neck. His lips made contact with her skin in the curve where shoulder joined spine.

She felt the heat of his body pressed up against hers, but she didn't feel sexual heat. She felt strangely comforted and secure. She didn't understand what was happening to her. Her emotions and her mind were going haywire all at once. Temporary insanity perhaps. At least she hoped it was temporary.

Her nose started to run and she sniffed. She felt him motionless behind her, listening perhaps. She could almost sense him peering down at her in the dark as he moved damp strands of hair away from her face. A finger touched her wet cheek.

He eased back on the bed and drew her head to his shoulder. He held her and stroked her hair.

At one point he shifted away from her. Seconds later he pressed something soft and cottony into her hands. It felt like a man's tee shirt. It was his tee shirt, she realized. He'd removed it and given it to her. She raised up on an elbow to wipe at her damp face and caught a fleeting scent of laundry soap or fabric softener, gone almost as quickly as it registered.

Pain seemed to seep out of her. She didn't know where it was going, unless he was absorbing it. Was this all she'd needed this last year? To be held, comforted, allowed to cry on someone's shoulder with no judgment, no recriminations. The silence he insisted on became a blessing in disguise. She couldn't speak to him, but neither could he ask about her tears, thereby alleviating her of the obligation to explain, to acknowledge her deep sense of guilt over Tim and Zach's deaths.

Somehow her mind seemed to have reconnected itself enough to make her aware of how surreal this experience had been so far. Confident she wasn't going to die, she lay back down. If he'd planned to kill her he'd have done it by now. He took the damp shirt from her, and he must have dropped it on the floor.

He repositioned them front to front, his arms wrapped securely around her. One hand brushed up and down her back, the other resumed stroking her hair.

She stretched her fingers across his chest, taking note of a light covering of chest hair over taut muscle. She moved her hand in an exploratory manner up over his collar bone to his throat and along his jaw. Like a blind person, she slid her fingers across his cheek, her thumb brushed his lip, his nose, his brow. Her fingers feathered back into the close-cropped hair on his head.

She frowned when he removed her hand and pressed a kiss to her palm. Whatever mental image of him her brain had tried to create from her exploration evaporated.

He resumed stroking her back, his lips brushed against her temple, his hand played idly with her hair. He seemed disinclined to do anything else at the moment. She found his behavior puzzling. Who *is* this? *What* is this? She hadn't known exactly what to expect, but it wasn't this. This *caring.* Or merely an attempt to lull her into a false sense of security?

She was lulled, for sure, and that heightened her suspicion threshold. This man, whoever he was, wasn't a threat to her. Somehow he'd communicated that to her in the short time they'd been together.

He tugged her closer, cradling her against him, her head tucked under his chin. She breathed in the scent of him, absorbed the warmth of his skin beneath her cheek and fingers. She turned her head slightly, brushing her lips against his collar bone. If he could communicate silently, then so could she. The message she hoped she sent was: I'm okay now. I know you're not going to hurt me.

Her mind fell back into her body when she realized her nipples had puckered and tightened through her bra and sweater. As if he were aware of it at the same instant, he brushed light kisses along her temple, taking his time, past her ear where she felt his breath tickle that sensitive place, to her throat.

While she'd imagined the worst, none of her fears were founded. Based on what she could tell, from every sense other than sight, her phantom lover was not overweight or especially aged. His touch aroused rather than repelled, and Zoe could detect no particular scent, on his breath or anywhere else, other than that of human male.

He was in no hurry. Zoe drew in a shaky breath as he ran the palm of his hand back and forth beneath the hem of her sweater. His fingers fanned out across her ribcage and midriff, but as if content with such a caress, he made no move to explore further.

She felt a flutter of excitement in the pit of her stomach. Heat pooled between her thighs.

This wasn't rape. It was seduction. Wasn't it? And God forgive her, it felt so good, to have this stranger touching her.

His hands roamed over her as if he'd never encountered female flesh beneath his fingertips. Yet his reverent touch spoke of experience.

He touched her as if by doing so he could absorb her very essence.

Zoe trembled involuntarily at the purely tactile sensation of his skin against hers. Dear God, it had been so long since anyone had touched her.

Every part of him seemed to touch every part of her. He used his mouth to explore the sensitive flesh below her ear, his tongue delved into the curve where throat met collarbone. Eventually the palms of his hands grazed her back as well as her belly, yet he made no move to undress her.

Male musculature lay beneath smooth heated skin and the rough curly hair on his chest and arms. From her own exploration she'd determined he wore lightweight sweatpants with a drawstring waistband. Impossible to ignore, the heavy weight of his arousal branded her each time it brushed against the fabric of her slacks.

Physical desire, surprising in its intensity, spread like wildfire as her body readied itself for mating.

Beneath the stranger's touch Zoe came alive. She caressed his shoulders, ran the palms of her hands across every bit of flesh she could reach.

One of his hands slid between her thighs and her breath hitched. Heated wetness pooled in her panties as he cupped her, his hand moving back and forth in a slow rhythm.

Zoe wanted to laugh and cry at the same time. The fact that she was still dressed, reminded her of a clumsy back seat encounter in high school. But this man was no awkward teenager. His touch awakened and aroused.

Zoe yanked off her sweater. He made a low sound in his throat when he realized what she'd done. With his lips against her throat, his fingers brushed against the snap of her bra and then moved away, as if asking permission for access.

At that silent gesture, something came undone inside Zoe. Clearly, he had no intention of forcing her to do anything she didn't want to do. She'd bet all the money in that envelope that if she got up and got dressed and walked out right now he wouldn't stop her. As long as she made no attempt to discover his identity, that is.

He trailed a string of kisses along the tops of her breasts above her bra. His hands, where they touched her waist and belly and back were warm and strong and sure. He moved lower, using his mouth and tongue on the bare skin of her midriff. All the while he caressed her thighs and bottom, and between her legs as if in silent promise of what she could have. If she decided.

Zoe wanted time to analyze her reactions, but her brain refused to function in its normal capacity. And apparently, so did her body. Having been dormant for the past year, it seemed to have suddenly sprung to life, physical responses overriding mental ones.

She unsnapped her bra, the tiny click of plastic against plastic loud in the darkness. Again she heard that almost inaudible sound from him. He wasted no time finding her breasts with his mouth, pushing the bra off and helping her shrug out of it completely. He suckled and licked and teased until Zoe writhed in a pleasure so intense it was almost painful.

She moved his hands to the waistband of her slacks. When she unbuttoned them and slid the zipper down, he drew them off, then peeled her panties off as well. And lastly her socks. She sucked in a breath as he caressed an ankle and pressed a kiss to the bottom of her foot.

Then he came back to her. His fingers touched and explored the flesh they'd uncovered, easily discerning her preferences through every nuance of reaction.

Zoe wanted to scream, to cry out, to tell him, yes, there, right there, but words were outlawed. And unnecessary. He found her quickly, easily. Eagerly, wantonly, she spread her legs further, hitched her knees higher.

His tongue grazed a nipple, then his mouth closed around it to suckle greedily.

Zoe went over the edge, hands clamped over her mouth as she cried out with pleasure at the release he'd brought to her.

In the disorienting darkness, she heard a slight rustle, sensed the momentary waver of his attention. Part of the agreement: *A condom will be used during any sexual encounters.* Although the copy of a recent medical report included with the letter showed him to be free of disease, Zoe knew she'd be putting herself at risk. For money. She'd calculated the risk to the best of her ability. Reread the letter. Weighed the odds. Blew the dust off her diaphragm. By morning she'd either be dead or have her dreary existence enriched by all those lovely hundred dollar bills.

Tiny tentacles of trust had already formed and now ran rampant through her mind. She'd imagined the worst. Yet everything had happened exactly as spelled out in that perfectly printed letter. Well, not everything. Surely he hadn't planned on her earlier tears. And she hadn't expected an almost professional massage as part of the encounter or to have her fears so quickly allayed.

Zoe closed her eyes against the impenetrable darkness as he came to her. He kissed her everywhere except on the mouth. His hot breath rushed against her ear. Braced above her, he entered her, filling her quickly and then he waited, lodged deeply inside her, for her to relax once again.

Thoughts and emotions collided within Zoe, but she had no time to process any of them. She arched beneath him, moved in conjunction with his rhythm, urging him on. Beneath her lips, his skin tasted salty from a thin sheen of perspiration. Her hands slid down his back to cup rock hard glutes. She nearly drowned in sensation overload as she breathed in the musky scent of their joined bodies.

Gently he rearranged her hands so one lay on either side of her head. His fingers twined between hers as he rocked back and forth, his pace quickening. Zoe fought the urge to disentangle her hands from his so she could cover her mouth once again to stifle her natural vocal reaction. Instead she bit her bottom lip as he slammed into her, against her, flattening her knees almost to her chest.

She buried her cries of ecstasy at the back of her throat, wondering if he also held himself in check as he came.

For long seconds he stayed inside her, his forehead bowed against hers as they listened to each other breathe.

Zoe didn't move. Much to her surprise she didn't want to break contact with him. Degree by degree they both relaxed. He moved to her side, and she supposed, removed the used condom from the immediate vicinity. Zoe prepared herself for his departure. She turned to her side, turned her head away, even though she couldn't see him.

But he didn't leave. In a repeat of the move which had initially awakened her, he pressed close behind her, one arm draped around her waist. He lifted a lock of her hair and kissed her shoulder.

Hard as she tried not to, Zoe fell asleep in a stranger's arms.

Chapter Three

Zoe woke up alone.

These days she always woke up alone.

Except for last night.

Tentatively she stretched. The disorienting darkness remained. But she was alive. Physically unharmed. And free to go.

More secure now in navigating her way between bed and door, she threw back the covers and padded across the cracked linoleum, feeling along the wall. In seconds she found the switch and blinked against the relatively bright light from the single fixture in the ceiling.

The room hadn't changed, except for the rumpled bedding. Her attention shot to the chair where she'd left her coat and purse. A plain white envelope sat atop her things. She crossed to it quickly. Inside were more hundred dollar bills.

She fumbled through her purse for her phone. Five-thirty a.m.

She gathered her clothes and sat on the bed as she dressed and tried to ignore the whispers flitting through her mind. *Whore. Prostitute.*

She'd sold her body for cold hard cash. How often had she seen high-priced call girls being wined and dined at the restaurant? She'd always been curious, had wished she could ask one of them, what's it like? How did you come to be in this line of work?

What if the answer was as simple as her own? She needed money and no one got hurt.

You needed the connection too, came a whisper from another corner of her mind. *You took a chance maybe he'd rape you and kill you and leave you for dead. But he didn't.*

Once dressed, Zoe availed herself of the bathroom facilities trying to shut off her thoughts. She'd been doing it for over a year. No reason that ability should fail her now.

The bathroom light switch didn't work, so Zoe located the toilet and pulled the door closed behind her. The light came on. She opened the door. The light went out.

More insurance to protect his identity.

The mirror over the sink had cracked and the finish flaked in several strategic places. It made her think of the way her mind and emotions had ricocheted and collided with each other last night, leaving her vulnerable and out of control. She stared at her incomplete reflection. "I hate you," she whispered.

Swallowing an unidentified lump of emotion, walking on legs that felt quivery and unsure, she made her way back down the flights of stairs to the door. Bitter cold greeted her as the metal door clanged shut behind her. The same white car with the same driver sat in the same space as last night. The driver didn't look in her direction. He was like an automaton. If she'd told him to turn around and take her back home after they'd circled the block last night, she was sure he would have.

She stood on the landing debating. The narrow street was deserted at this early hour, the pavement damp from the few snow flurries blown about by the January wind.

A gust of frigid air propelled her down the steps to the car. She got into the back seat, savoring the warmth. The driver flipped the heater to high.

She sat shivering, scanning the vicinity, the blank walls of the building, the street in both directions. Maybe he was there watching her.

She saw no one. Not even a stray cat.

"Who cares?" she asked aloud.

The driver accelerated down the street.

But he didn't answer her.

Weak wintry rays of the rising sun tried to make their presence known as the car turned onto her street.

The clang of church bells penetrated her scattered thoughts. "Stop!" The driver hit the brakes in front of St. Mary's.

Zoe stared at the old redbrick structure, the stained glass windows, the faded oak double doors.

An old woman, leaning heavily on a cane, grasped the handrail and labored up the concrete steps. She paused halfway up as if to rest.

Without thinking, Zoe exited the vehicle and followed her.

She grasped the woman's elbow. "Here, let me help you."

The woman peered out from beneath the wool scarf tied under her chin. Her dark eyes were almost buried under heavy gray eyebrows and drooping lids. "Thank you, dear."

Zoe offered her a polite smile in return, for the first time wondering what had propelled her forward to assist the old lady. Zoe couldn't help but notice the way the woman's back curved so she was half bent over. Ancient black galoshes were buckled around her ankles and a black cloth coat covered the woman from neck to calf. The only hint of color was the plaid scarf she wore over her head and the tinge of pink in her cheeks and the tip of her nose caused by the frigid winter air.

Zoe pulled the heavy door open and wondered how the woman could have done so without help. Though she may have been strong once, she was no more.

"Thank you, dear." The old woman's lips twitched in a semblance of a smile as she hobbled inside.

Still holding the door open, Zoe watched her slow progress down the aisle. Another gust of biting wind pushed the door against Zoe, even as she fought to hold it open. She found her feet on the other side of the threshold as the door banged shut behind her.

Zoe had never set foot inside St. Mary's, though she'd passed it often enough. She hadn't been in church since...since when? She had no use for churches. God had given up on her long before she'd given up on Him. *The Lord giveth and the Lord taketh away.* She remembered that verse from some long ago religious education class, but she'd discovered the truth early in life. God took. He took and took and took. Everything and everyone she'd ever cared about. Her mother, her grandmother. Her husband, her child. And then her brother. She didn't have much left for him to take. Her dignity, her pride, maybe. Her self-respect. Herself.

After last night it seemed like He was pretty intent on taking those as well. Or maybe she simply had no use for them any longer.

She glanced back at the door, the memory of the cold outside fresh in her mind. She took a few steps forward engulfed by the scent of old incense and ancient prayers.

Wood arches soared and crisscrossed high above the rows of pews. Stained glass windows depicted various Biblical scenes along the outside walls.

"Good morning," whispered a priest, as she moved into the church proper. He indicated for her to pass to the rows of pews. An altar boy holding a cross with the image of Jesus nailed to the top eyed her with sleepy curiosity.

The church was nearly deserted. Zoe counted thirteen parishioners sprinkled about as she took a seat in the last pew.

The old woman knelt alone midway up the aisle, her rosary beads clacking against the back of the wooden pew in front of her.

The priest, the altar boy and a man holding a thick red book aloft made a humble procession to the front of the church.

Zoe's mind went blank as she observed the proceedings. Peace, if it could be called that, enveloped her as she listened to the formulaic prayers and the rote responses of the parishioners.

One of the parishioners, acting as usher, offered her a basket attached to the end of a long-handled pole. She stared at him blankly until he moved up the aisle. Only then, when she saw the old woman drop something into the basket, did it occur to her that a donation was expected.

Zoe blushed in embarrassment though there was no one to see.

No one but me.

Zoe looked around. Where had that voice come from? It wasn't her internal voice. Maybe it was God. She tried not to smile at the thought of God talking to her. She hadn't heard from him in a long time.

Zoe remained seated when everyone else approached the priest as he descended the few steps from the altar. His voice carried even to the back of the church as he spoke to each of them. "The body of Christ. The body of Christ. The body of Christ."

Thirteen times. Zoe felt her own exclusion from the proceedings. She hadn't contributed. She wasn't a member of the scraggly congregation assembled this morning. She didn't belong. She wasn't worthy.

She could leave. No one would notice if she left now.

I'll notice, came that voice again. *I want you to be here.*

A shiver shot down Zoe's spine.

God? Is that you?

Silence.

Zoe didn't move. The service ended. The priest, the altar boy, and the man with the big red book passed her. The other parishioners followed until only she and the old woman remained.

Finally the old woman got to her feet. She pocketed her rosary and retrieved her cane from where she'd hooked it over the back of the pew.

Teetering slightly from side to side, but not exactly limping, she came toward Zoe. Zoe nodded gravely and followed her. The old woman paused at a small font filled with water, dipped a finger into it and crossed herself. Next to the holy water Zoe saw a poor box.

She slid her hand into her coat pocket and grasped the wad of cash. Closing her eyes she withdrew a single bill and crumpled it in her palm. Without looking at it, she dropped it into the box.

Chapter Four

Safely inside her tiny apartment with the door locked behind her, Zoe pulled the letter from her purse and read it through again. She'd sensed the sincerity of the author the first time she'd read it and became more convinced after each subsequent reading. That feeling returned in full force, for everything had occurred exactly as the letter stated. Well, not everything, but only because she hadn't exactly followed all of the instructions.

She'd received the promised payment. No words had been spoken. She'd arrived home unharmed.

When she tried to analyze how she felt now, two words floated across her mind. Bereft. Vulnerable.

She dropped the letter on the table. Her eye caught the copy of the letter she'd left for Drew to find...just in case. The envelope with the down payment lay next to it. She pulled the second envelope of hundred dollar bills from her purse and laid it on top of the first. She stared at the letters and the envelopes until her vision began to blur. Then slowly she tore the copy she had made into tiny bits, the individual words no longer readable. She tucked the original letter into one of the envelopes and went into the bathroom to undress.

She tried to ignore the languorous feeling in her limbs, the ultra-sensitivity of her skin. The feeling that she'd been well and truly made love to, *loved* by a man.

He doesn't love you, she reminded herself viciously as she turned on the hot water in the shower.

But he had made love to her. That was the unavoidable truth. More than that, he had made her feel, had touched something inside her. She didn't want to regret her decision now.

The warm water trickled across her skin, touching every place he had touched, making her nerve endings hum in remembrance. She removed the diaphragm, cleaned it, then returned it to its case.

Wrapped in a towel, Zoe stared at herself in the mirror and wondered how her body could have betrayed her. How she could have betrayed herself. Warring with the sense of physical satisfaction was a hollow feeling in the pit of her stomach. As though she'd given a part of herself away, lost it forever. Sadness enveloped her. But she refused to cry.

Drew Warner tossed his fork onto the plate where a few remnants of moo shu pork and fried rice remained. "Okay, I give up. What's with you tonight?"

Drew sent Zoe a penetrating look and for the first time in the five years of their friendship, Zoe could not meet his eyes. Instead she toyed with her own food, picking apart the half-eaten spring roll with her fingers and dropping the pieces onto her plate. "Did you ever do something you knew was going to be a mistake before you did it, but you did it anyway? And even though you know you shouldn't have, you're not exactly sorry you did it? And you justify it to yourself, even though you know it's wrong?"

When Drew didn't answer, Zoe looked up to find him studying her intently, his bright blue eyes that never missed anything, clear and knowing behind the lenses of his round wire-frame glasses. This time Zoe couldn't look away. Although she could never admit to Drew what she'd done last night or explain exactly why she'd done it, she almost hoped Drew would guess so they could get it out in the open.

"I take it this isn't a rhetorical question." Drew pushed back from the table and wheeled to the stove where he turned the gas up under the tea kettle. Dropping Chinese tea bags into two mugs he took from a rack on the counter, he turned back to Zoe and waited.

After her shower this morning, Zoe slept until early afternoon. She'd spent the rest of the day alternately reliving the purely sensual sensations she'd experienced last night and berating herself for what she'd done. She'd endangered herself, thereby endangering Ben's rescue. She'd prostituted herself. She'd enjoyed sex with a stranger. And hoped against hope it would happen again soon.

She couldn't admit any of this to Drew. Drew, too intelligent for his own good who embodied father, brother and best friend rolled up into one. Zoe couldn't risk losing Drew's respect, his love, or his friendship by telling him the truth.

When Zoe remained silent, Drew spoke. "The answer to your first question is yes. I knew going after the Bio-Tech story was going to be a mistake. But I went after it anyway. Even after I'd been warned off."

There was no bitterness in Drew's response. As an investigative reporter for a national news magazine he'd continued to pursue a story on illegal dumping of hazardous chemical waste by a major corporation. He'd been threatened and beaten. When that didn't work, he'd been the target of a hit and run "accident" which had nearly killed him and left his legs mangled and paralyzed. He'd written the story while undergoing grueling rehabilitation and physical therapy. When the magazine published it, the EPA launched a probe into Bio-Tech's disposal practices. It took years, but each of Drew's allegations had been proven; Bio-Tech had recently been slapped with millions in fines, and Drew was now a legend in the world of investigative reporting.

He accepted his paralysis as the natural consequence for his own dogged determination and stubbornness. But he'd never, as far as Zoe knew, second-guessed himself or regretted pursuing the story.

"I can't answer the other two questions. I wasn't wrong. And even though I risked my own safety, I can't say I regret it."

The whistle on the tea kettle blew. Drew turned off the gas and poured water over the tea bags. Placing a tray in his lap he set the mugs on it and wheeled back to the table. He slid one mug across to Zoe, put the other one at his place and set the tray aside. "Lots of people make personal sacrifices for something they believe in, Zoe. Sometimes with unexpected and unpleasant results."

Compared to the consequences of Drew's actions, her current dilemma seemed ridiculously insignificant. He'd made a sacrifice yes, but his sacrifice had far-reaching benefits to humanity. All Zoe wanted to do was save her brother. Zoe stared down into the steamy brew wishing she had one-tenth of Drew's strength and determination. "I don't know what to do," she confessed, speaking to her mug of tea.

"About what?" Drew spooned sugar into his mug and stirred. "About Ben?"

Zoe's head came up. "That's part of it."

"Not quite ready for another assault on the State Department?"

Zoe tried to smile. "Not quite."

She and Drew had flown to Washington a week ago when all contact from the Deputy Director's office had ceased. Zoe needed answers about Ben, his whereabouts, his chances for being set free.

"I should be hearing from my contacts in the next day or two," Drew reminded her.

"Julio called yesterday. He saw Ben."

"He saw him? Why didn't you tell me? He knows where he is then?"

Zoe shook her head. "No. He said they were moving him to another location. Julio doesn't know where exactly. He said—he said—" Zoe choked up as she struggled to hold back the tears. "Sorry," she gasped as she tried to get control of herself.

Drew reached across the table and covered her hand with his. "It's okay."

She curled her fingers around Drew's. She wanted to be more like him. Tough. Matter of fact. Instead of confused all the time. Couldn't somebody else save Ben? The church or the federal government? It shouldn't be left up to her.

Because the church's official position was that Ben had gone missing. There had been no ransom demand. No verification of his whereabouts. They were looking into the matter. Even Julio's firsthand account of Ben's capture had not convinced them.

Various U.S. government agencies were of little help. Zoe and Drew had contacted every department they could think of, the embassy, the State Department, the CIA. Sympathetic noises were made, but a lot of countries in Central America were unstable. Any American traveling or residing there was apprised of the risks before leaving U.S. soil. Ben, it seemed, was on his own. And so was Zoe.

Bitter anger at the unfairness of it all burned in Zoe's gut and dried her tears. She would not let Ben perish at the hands of drug lords or militant guerillas or whatever extremist faction had kidnapped him. With Julio's help, and Drew's, and now with her phantom lover's cash, if it kept coming, she would figure out a way to free Ben and bring him home.

She squeezed Drew's hand and let go, brushing the tears aside with her fingertips. "Julio says it looks like Ben's been mistreated. Beaten."

Drew kept his expression neutral. She knew they were thinking the same thing.

She shrugged, allowing the possibility to take shape in her mind before speaking it aloud. "Tortured, maybe. I don't know."

Drew cleared his throat and Zoe once again gave voice to his unspoken thoughts.

"They could kill him. I don't understand why they're keeping him alive. They don't want a ransom. I can't imagine what they have to gain by torturing a missionary."

"Zoe, you know we've been over this a hundred times. Ben could have stumbled onto something he'd have been better off not knowing. A mine of some sort. Cocaine fields. A guerilla training camp."

"Exactly." Zoe slammed her open palm down on the table. "So the expedient thing would be to kill him."

"But he's being kept alive for a reason. Otherwise, as you say, killing him would be the logical step."

Zoe wrapped her arms around her waist and leaned forward as if feeling real, physical pain. "I have this terrible feeling that I have to move faster, I have to do something. Before it's too late. And yet I can't. I don't have the money, for one thing. I don't have enough information. I feel paralyzed." Her hands flew to her mouth. "Oh, Drew. I'm sorry. What a thoughtless thing to say."

He waved off her concern. "Don't be ridiculous. I know exactly how you feel." He gave her a crooked smile and Zoe returned it with a weak one of her own.

"About the money—"

Zoe held up a hand. "No. Don't even go there." If she'd learned one thing growing up in the foster care system, it was that nothing was ever as simple as it seemed. Beware an offer that looked as if no strings were attached. Repayment, in one form or another, was always expected.

"Zoe, I can get the money. You know I'd gladly do it to help you. And Ben."

"No. Drew, please. I can't let you do that. I can't. Please try to understand."

It was a bone of contention between them. Drew was currently involved in a lawsuit against Bio-Tech and expected to receive a significant monetary settlement because of his "accident." Zoe knew he could borrow against the anticipated settlement and single-handedly finance a rescue attempt. But she also knew the suit could drag on indefinitely and the settlement amount could be hard to collect. A huge conglomerate like Bio-Tech had deep pockets and battalions of lawyers. She refused to sacrifice Drew's financial future, even if he was willing.

That was the argument she used with Drew, but she valued Drew's friendship more than he probably knew. She strongly suspected that Drew's feelings for her went far beyond friendship, though he'd never said anything. She felt bad enough about not being able to return the kind of love she saw in his eyes on the rare occasions when he didn't try to hide it.

As it was, she'd been forced to accept some of Drew's generosity the past few months, when she'd blown the credit limit on her charge cards with plane tickets and hotel bills and missing work. He'd helped pay the rent on her apartment for a couple of months.

She didn't want to owe him any more than that, though he was too noble to expect repayment in any way other than monetary. At the time, Zoe hadn't thought she'd ever be able to repay him in any way. Not with her love or with cold hard cash. *What about with your body?* came the unbidden question. *You're selling yourself anyway. To the phantom. Why not to Drew?*

The thought sickened her and she winced. *Is it because Drew's not a whole man?* her conscience niggled. No. That wasn't it. Her friendship with Drew was the one clean, pure thing she had left in her life. And she didn't want to taint it or ruin it the way she had everything else.

She'd earn every nickel she needed if possible, if her anonymous benefactor was willing. At least she earned it honestly. She knew the rules.

It was cut and dried. A business proposition, plain and simple. There was no hidden agenda. Sex for money. It wouldn't be so simple with Drew.

"I wouldn't expect anything in return," Drew reminded her as he did every time her precarious financial situation came up.

"I know." Zoe stood and came around the table to hug Drew from behind. "That's what I love about you." She kissed his cheek, but straightened quickly. She carried her mug and the empty plates to the sink.

She had to leave. "I'm lousy company tonight." She smiled to soften the blow. Still she saw the brief flash of disappointment in Drew's expression. On her nights off work, she and Drew would share a meal, watch a movie, play cards or a board game. But she felt fragile tonight. Vulnerable. She didn't want to give herself an opportunity, in a weak moment, to tell Drew about the phantom. About what she'd done. "I'm going to go, okay?"

"Sure, okay." Drew forced a smile. "Be careful driving home."

Zoe chuckled as she waved and went to the door. His admonition was their shared joke. She didn't have to drive home, even if she'd had a car. Drew lived two floors below her.

Chapter Five

The disillusioned expressions on the faces of some of the younger village women was what Father Ben Dumont noticed, and what first aroused his suspicion that something was terribly wrong in Santa Rosaro and the surrounding villages. The clink of coins in the pockets of the men. The rumblings of disapproval by the older generation that stopped whenever he came within hearing range.

For three months his repeated attempts to draw out his people met with resistance. Julio, his assistant at the rectory, remained mum when Ben questioned him. Which was even more suspicious because Julio seemed to know everyone in Santa Rosaro. In fact, his network and knowledge extended to the other nearby villages. Ben wouldn't have been surprised to learn that Julio knew about everything that went on within a hundred-mile radius.

Ben decided to find out for himself what was going on. He followed a group of men early one morning as they left the village on foot. About a mile outside of the tiny town, an ancient mini bus awaited them. They climbed aboard and the vehicle rattled and bumped across the dusty trail, leaving Ben to stare after it. Next time, he would bring the Jeep. Julio would object, but he would be overruled.

The ever vigilant Julio discovered him two mornings later before he could make a clean getaway and follow the men as they left the village.

"Father Ben, do not do this," Julio begged, agitation apparent in every gesture, from the crease between his dark eyes to his stance in front of the Jeep.

"Then tell me what's going on. Tell me where the men are going and why they come back with pockets full of pesos."

Julio said nothing. His eyes were sad, but he didn't move.

"Then get out of the way," Ben told him.

Ben inched the Jeep forward. "Either get out of the way or come with me."

Still Julio didn't budge. The front fender of the ancient vehicle nudged his knees. Ben knew he couldn't run Julio over, and he hoped it wouldn't come to that.

Inspiration struck. He relaxed, kept the engine running, sat back in the seat and made the Sign of the Cross. Closing his eyes, he prayed, softly murmuring, his lips moving. Through the veil of his lashes he saw Julio's shoulders slump in defeat, and felt rather than witnessed him come around the side and slip into the passenger seat.

Ben continued his pose of prayer a few seconds longer, blessed himself once more, and put the Jeep in gear.

Julio, for all of his nineteen years, had a larger-than-life faith. Previous missionaries had taught him English and in return he'd made himself indispensable to them, becoming a jack of all trades. If the Jeep broke down, replacement parts mysteriously appeared within days. He knew every road, every inhabitant, human and otherwise, of the mountainous jungle area. Had he been in Hollywood he'd have been a major player. On Wall Street, he'd have made a killing. In the mountains of Guatemala, the children looked up to him. The women came to him for aid. The men were proud to claim him as one of their own.

And Ben, well Ben didn't know what he'd have done if Julio hadn't climbed into the Jeep beside him.

"You must be careful," Julio stated after they'd gone nearly a mile.

Ben slowed the Jeep and then stopped. The trees and vines seemed to close in on them on either side of what passed for a road. "Where are we going?"

Julio looked away. A parrot screeched as it flew overhead. The rustle of leaves in the crisp morning breeze and the sense of moving, living things all around pervaded Ben's senses, but he kept his gaze on his companion.

Julio took a deep breath and seemed to sink in on himself in defeat. "The mine," he said simply.

"What mine?"

"You'll see." He indicated for Ben to drive on.

After another hour, Julio told Ben to pull over. They hid the Jeep off the track in a section of forest overhung with vines.

"You must be very careful," Julio warned. "It is dangerous."

"Why is it dangerous?" They'd driven higher into a more remote area of the mountains, but they'd seen no guerillas this morning.

"The men at the mine," Julio paused and looked away for a moment, before once again fixing his dark gaze on Ben. "They are evil. They are dangerous."

"Guards?"

Julio nodded. "Many guards. Many guns."

"What's in the mine?"

"Emeralds."

"You never told me about this."

"It is not for you to know. There is nothing you can do." Julio paused. "You should not be here."

"Why? What do you think will happen?"

Julio's shoulders slumped. Sadness clouded his eyes. "I should not have brought you here."

Ben would find out what Julio wasn't telling him later. "Which way?"

Ben followed as Julio picked his way through trees, dodging vines and plowing through the thick carpet of leaves underfoot. The dank, humid air caused sweat to pour off his body, only to be chilled in the shade of the trees. Ben began to regret his curiosity when Julio stopped and held up a hand. He turned, his finger pressed to his lips, his eyes deadly serious.

Ben froze in place. Fear washed over him, followed by a sense of pervading evil. Julio crooked a finger and Ben stepped forward.

From their vantage point, still hidden by jungle, Ben could see a makeshift camp set up outside the mouth of a cave. The cave itself was more of a huge crevice with steep sides, a split in the rock, as if someone had partially ripped a seam open at the base of the mountain, leaving it wider at the bottom, narrow at the top. An open pit had been scooped out of the mountain in an almost perfect circular shape. Julio had led them to the perimeter above the bowl, so that they could look down without being seen. Watchful men with weapons slung across their chests, their fingers never far from the triggers, clustered in groups in the muddy gravel around the mouth of the cave.

Several military-style tents huddled close together a slight distance away. The flap of one opened and a man ducked out through the opening, then straightened to his full height. Shouldering a weapon, he joined the others. Good-natured jeering and rowdy taunts greeted his appearance. Ben tried to follow the Spanish dialogue and gleaned the comments were sexual in nature.

Minutes later the tent flap moved again. This time a woman appeared. A young woman, her dark hair in a long braid that fell over one shoulder. She buttoned the jacket she wore and adjusted a full gauzy skirt that fell to below her knees. Her bearing was tall for a native woman and almost haughty, but even from this distance Ben could sense the sadness in her stance.

She approached the coffeepot which sat atop a small cook fire and poured steaming liquid into a metal cup. As she raised it to her lips one of the other men detached himself from the group and approached her. Ben could not hear the conversation, but he saw the woman nod. Money exchanged hands. She set the cup down and they both disappeared inside the tent.

Ben's hands clenched at his sides. He recognized the woman as from one of the neighboring villages. The eldest of nine children. He must have moved or Julio sensed he was about to, for he felt Julio's fingers clench painfully around his bicep. Julio's eyes sent the same message. Ben forced himself to relax and nod imperceptibly at his companion before turning back to watch.

Two men appeared from behind one of the tents and joined the others. They spoke clearly in the kind of Spanish Ben was used to. Spanish learned as a second language in an American schoolroom. He zeroed in on the newcomers. Though dressed like the others in military-type fatigues, they stood out. Clearly, they were in charge. But they didn't appear to be native to the area. One was tall and sported a blond crew cut. The other, slightly shorter and squatter, reminded Ben of a wrestler.

They were giving orders. The guards, who had been lounging around, divided into groups of two and melted into the trees, taking up posts as instructed.

Julio signaled Ben and they began their retreat. But not before Ben saw the tent flap open and a guard adjusting his fly. The American in charge spoke to him, the words carried away by the wind.

Dread washed over Ben. Despair filled his insides. He had a job to do. But he didn't know how he could help these people.

Chapter Six

Aaron Manning stepped into the shower ducking his head under the wall of water. He couldn't stop thinking about last night. Couldn't stop thinking about Zoe Bradford.

That's your problem, Manning. You think too much. He'd been told that by his superiors at Level One too many times to count. Bitterness twisted his smile into a grimace. If it weren't for the agency, he wouldn't be thinking about Zoe Bradford at all. He wouldn't have recurring dreams about her. He'd probably never have met her. Correction. He'd probably never have spent the night with her. He had to keep reminding himself that he *hadn't* met her. And he probably never would.

But he didn't have to meet her to have her in his bed. Okay, technically not *his* bed. A bed. And the memory of her last night, the scent of her skin, her gasp as he slid into her, the way she'd smothered her cry when she came. He'd be thinking about those things whether he wanted to or not.

In a hundred years he couldn't have prepared himself for what happened with Zoe last night. He didn't know what he'd expected. He supposed he hadn't expected anything. Because he hadn't expected her to accept his offer. He could hardly believe he'd made the offer.

Ten days ago Aaron had been bone tired, when he'd unlocked the door of his apartment, dropped his duffel bag and headed to the kitchen. The call light on the landline blinked maddeningly, which could only mean he had a ton of messages. All of them, he'd be willing to bet were from Lauren Page. The first few would be calls of concern, worry. The next set would be annoyance. And the final ones would be hurt, outrage and disgust. From similar past experiences he knew that on the very last message he would hear such words as "I'm sorry I ever met you!" "You're a pig." And most definitely, "I hope I never see you again."

He opened the refrigerator and gave the contents a quick perusal. Not much there. A few condiments. The dried remains of a pepperoni pizza still in the cardboard box. A bottle of white wine and one of Spanish sangria. A couple of Kieran Lights. The bottle of water he chose would do little to fortify him as he played back the messages, but he punched in the code for the voice mail and drank as Lauren's voice came through.

"Aaron? Aaron are you there? I thought we had plans for this evening. Call me."

Wednesday, 7:30 p.m. relayed the machine's mechanical voice. Aaron hit the delete button.

Wednesday. 10:30 p.m. "Aaron, I hope you're all right. Why haven't you called? I'm imagining you in the hospital somewhere or something. Call me."

There were more calls on Thursday, starting first thing in the morning.

By Friday, Lauren sounded not only frantic, but annoyed. Aaron had heard the mixture of those tones in women's voices numerous times.

On Saturday morning's message he could hear the tears in her voice. "I can't believe you're doing this to me," she wailed. "Bridget's wedding is this afternoon. You promised me, Aaron. You promised. My mother is going to have a fit if I show up at another family wedding without a date. If you don't want to see me anymore, I understand. But could you please go to the wedding with me? Please?"

The last message came late Saturday night. Lauren sounded a little drunk and a lot unhappy as she let loose with a string of insults about his character, his family tree and his performance as a lover. Her parting "I'm sorry I ever met you" was a foregone conclusion.

Aaron hit the delete button one final time, drained the last of the water from the bottle and tossed it in the trash. Another relationship down the tubes.

Relationship. Yeah, right. He'd known Lauren all of what? Three weeks? A month? Before he'd been yanked overseas again, with no notice. For five days this time.

He understood first-hand why James Bond only indulged in one-night stands and why each movie featured a different woman.

At the start, he tried to warn women about his unpredictable schedule. Usually, they cooed their understanding.

But he'd quickly learned women didn't like men who disappeared without warning. Who didn't call or show up when they were expected. Women became extremely suspicious when a man surfaced after five days or two weeks unable to adequately or honestly explain why he'd been missing in action.

Give it up, Manning, Aaron told himself as he stripped and fell onto his rumpled bed. But he couldn't give up the fairy tale fantasy of a home in the suburbs surrounded by a white picket fence, a couple of kids who played on soccer and Little League teams. There was no such thing as a nine-to-five job in his world. No such thing as a home and a family. A normal life. Working for Level One destroyed any hope of that happening.

He closed his eyes trying to shut out the sound of Lauren's distress which continued to reverberate through his head. He had another assignment starting tonight and he needed some sleep. A couple of hours at least. And maybe for once, God willing, he wouldn't be haunted by dreams of Zoe Bradford.

The following evening Aaron followed a mid-level Defense Department employee suspected of leaking information to a couple of well-known Middle East arms dealers into a restaurant on Manhattan's Lower East side. He seated himself at the bar close enough to the booth to eavesdrop on the conversation. One of his gifts, the ability to blend in. That's part of what made him such a successful operative. Aaron Manning, master of disguise.

The place was another posh upscale eatery with exotic, often unrecognizable food combinations never before attempted by chefs anywhere else in the world.

His seat gave him a clear view into the narrow prep lane connecting the kitchen to the dining room. It was there he saw her. She stood alone as if she were lost. As isolated from the rest of the world as he was. Like she'd been encased in a clear bubble or a force field of some sort. No one could get in. And she couldn't get out. Her expression and posture perfectly mirrored his own plight. Trapped, he often thought, in a web of his own making.

He knew he shouldn't stare because it might attract her attention, but he had to convince himself this wasn't another of his many dreams. No. He was here, awake, alive. This was reality.

She was Zoe Bradford.

Another server appeared in the lane, exchanged words with Zoe and the two disappeared into the kitchen. Aaron's mind divided itself as he kept track of the conversation behind him, easily translating the occasional Arabic dialect into English, and on Zoe as she moved from dining room to kitchen to bar and back.

He observed her, absorbed nuances of behavior, her quick but vacant smile, the sadness in the soft blue of her eyes, the continual movement to tuck a stray strand of silky blond hair behind her ear. Not once did she look in his direction or notice him, which meant the persona he'd chosen for this evening worked. The wire-rimmed aviator glasses not only made him look older than his 36 years, they gave him a studious look. A poorly fitted, ten-year-old suit, along with some padding to add a slight paunch, and the slouch he'd perfected over time spoke of the defeat of a businessman stuck in middle management and going no further.

Beneath the disguise, however, the tug of recognition, of *connection* he'd felt with Zoe the first time he'd seen her a year ago, came back even stronger. He'd barely spoken to her then, had worked hard to make himself invisible on that occasion as well. But then, as now, he'd been inexplicably drawn to her, and he'd understood why the last word on Tim Bradford's lips had been his wife's name.

For a year he'd been tormented by dreams of her, memories of his part in her family's deaths. In the dreams he implored her to trust him, not to leave him. He couldn't explain it, didn't understand it. And always in the dreams she disappeared, escaped his grasp, leaving him bereft and alone.

And now, here she was, in this particular restaurant, waiting on the table where his quarry sat. What were the odds, he wondered, feeling a bit like Rick in Casablanca. "Out of all the bars and gin joints in the world, she walks into mine..."

Aaron didn't believe in coincidence. His suspicion rose each time she approached the table. She could be passing a coded message along with the wine list. Or perhaps a microchip with sensitive data enclosed with the check.

Ridiculous, he assured himself. A year ago the background check had revealed nothing untoward in Zoe Bradford's life. Although he'd only scanned the file, anything unusual would have been red-flagged. At the time, the only issue of concern was Zoe Bradford's close relationship with the maverick investigative journalist, Drew Warner. Still, he could always check her out again tomorrow, although if there'd been the slightest hint she was a player or even a contact for the arms dealer, he'd be aware of it.

He sipped his scotch and followed every word exchanged at the table, admitting to himself that Zoe Bradford behaved like a professional member of the wait staff and nothing more. Even when one of the Arabs detained her and whispered in her ear, she maintained her professional demeanor, shaking her head and clearing his plate.

"That guy hitting on you?" the bartender, a young guy named Marco, asked her as she waited for a drink order.

Aaron's ears perked up, waiting for her answer, though he continued to stare down at the amber liquid in his glass.

"Not hitting on me. Offering me money to, ahem, spend the night with him."

"Oh, yeah?" Marco's eyes lit up in amusement. "What's your going rate these days?"

"We didn't get into dollar figures," she returned, loading drinks on a tray as he set them before her. "But if business doesn't pick up in here tonight, I might have to start negotiations."

"I hear ya, babe," Marco agreed.

She spun away with her tray of drinks.

From the corner of his eye, Aaron watched her approach a table in the corner. He had the distinct impression that in her conversation with Marco, she was only half joking.

He forced himself to focus on his assignment as his objective rose to leave. Aaron waited a few beats, then reluctantly followed.

After he filed his report and returned to his apartment, he was too keyed up to sleep. Seeing Zoe Bradford again had to mean something. In a city of over four million individuals, the chances that he'd randomly run into her defied calculation. He'd never been in that restaurant before, hadn't known she worked there. He'd been forced to take that particular assignment tonight to cover for another agent.

Aaron paced in front of the bank of windows that offered a view of nighttime city lights. He thought about the odds of creating a relationship with Zoe Bradford. Something real. Not the short-term disasters he'd been settling for all these years. He wouldn't risk a two- or three-week hit and run with her.

No. She'd become too important to him. Ridiculous, he thought. He didn't even know her. But you do know her, his subconscious answered him.

His work with Level One made normal relationships impossible. But there had to be a way to achieve the impossible with Zoe Bradford.

His sudden disappearances and erratic schedule destroyed his previous attempts at relationships. His inability to truthfully explain what he did for a living was a death knell to any kind of future with a woman.

If only the woman wasn't in a position to question his absences. If she had no expectations of him. And he never had to explain himself or his whereabouts or his job.

He couldn't imagine how he could make that happen. If he never spoke to her and she wasn't allowed to speak to him, there wouldn't be any questions, any need for explanation.

Aaron almost laughed out loud at the thought of a woman who doesn't ask questions.

What if she were paid not to?

Aaron shied away from the thought. He might as well approach a hooker on 47th Street, if he wanted to pay a woman who wouldn't ask questions. He couldn't do that to Zoe.

He took a Kieran Light from the refrigerator and sipped it while he paced and turned the problem over and over in his mind.

He'd be paying her for her silence. It seemed wrong, somehow.

But if he'd interpreted her conversation with Marco correctly, she probably needed the money. Restaurant servers could make a decent living, but life in New York City didn't come cheap.

Money, at least, Aaron had. He had a lot of it. Level One paid well. And he'd been with Level One for a lot of years. And what was he supposed to do with his money when he had virtually no life outside his work?

He'd have to think of a way to spend time with Zoe, no questions asked.

He could do it anonymously.

No. That couldn't possibly work. Could it?

Could it?

Aaron set his half-finished beer on the table and opened his laptop. Fingers poised over the keyboard, he thought for a moment then started to type.

For reasons I cannot explain I must approach you anonymously. We've never met and you don't know me.

Now what? I want you? I need you? I know you? What could he say that wouldn't freak her out?

I know what you've lost.

Her husband. Her son. How well he knew.

Maybe we can help each other.

There had to be a reason why he kept dreaming about her, why he'd been in that restaurant tonight, why he'd seen her again when he'd told himself a thousand times in the past year that he never would.

I don't mean to insult you and I will not hurt you. I ask only that you consider my offer.

I will pay you to spend the night with me.

Aaron's mind raced as he typed, developing a time and a place and even transportation arrangements.

No conversation.

It sounded less harsh than "no questions please."

We will meet under cover of darkness.

If our first meeting is successful, others may be requested at the same rate of exchange. Should you attempt to discover my identity or should you disclose the contents of this letter or share details of our meetings with others, I will be forced to terminate the offer.

The enclosed cash is yours whether you agree to the meeting or not. Should you choose not to, there will be no further contact.

Aaron sat back and read what he'd written making a few changes here and there. It was simple. Straightforward. Almost businesslike. He had no intention of harming her. But she probably wouldn't risk it anyway.

Aaron pondered the possibility and the longer he pondered it, the more he became convinced that he had nothing to lose. If Zoe didn't meet him as dictated in the terms of the letter he'd be out some cash, but that was all.

No guts, no glory. The thought popped into his head, but Aaron knew it had come from Bill Matthews, his commander and mentor back in his Delta Force days. He and his squad had survived many a mission by playing the odds and often using unconventional methods. Bill had a hundred stories of harrowing missions and narrow escapes, but none was better than the one where he'd rescued a young woman and her family from a Cambodian prison camp.

In the aftermath of the Vietnam War, Bill had encountered Mai Su only briefly in a village market in Cambodia. To hear Bill tell it, he'd fallen fast for the sloe-eyed Mai Su when she'd smiled shyly at him as her hand brushed his when he took his purchase of peas and cabbage from her. Three weeks later, when his tour of duty ended, he returned to Mai Su's village to discover that many of the local farmers had been rounded up and imprisoned, and were being questioned and often murdered by the local militia.

Mai Su and her parents were being held in a makeshift prison in the jungle.

Bill recruited a couple of buddies and some of the locals to raid the prison, freeing all of the detainees, and suffering a bullet to the shoulder in the process. He then somehow smuggled Mai Su and her parents into Thailand and from there to the States. He'd become fuzzy with those particular details, but Aaron could still see him smile across the room at Mai Su as he ended the tale at his retirement dinner. "No guts, no glory, kid," he told Aaron, his eyes softening as he winked at his wife.

Bill had died two years ago after a bout with colon cancer. At his funeral, Aaron hugged Mai Su and shook hands with their two sons and daughter. Bill's family were truly in mourning. He would be missed by people who had loved him.

Perhaps that was when it started, Aaron reflected now. His sick yearning for something more, something permanent, someone who would miss him if he was gone.

He stared at the envelope he'd prepared before he then turned back to his laptop to access a directory database to make sure Zoe hadn't changed addresses, gambling that she wouldn't be home from the restaurant yet. It won't matter, he told himself, as he sealed the letter and the cash inside the envelope along with a copy of the results of his most recent physical giving him a clean bill of health. She's not going to take you up on this.

So what? He asked himself as he hailed a cab and gave the driver her address. He gained access to the building the same way he had a year ago, retraced his steps to her apartment, slid the envelope under the door.

Feeling almost foolish but also lighthearted, something he never felt, he returned to the cab and then to his apartment. Bill would approve, he thought.

Last night he'd watched and waited. People rarely surprised him, but Zoe Bradford did. He saw the white car slide into the loading zone as he'd instructed. Then he watched it back out and his insides plummeted in disappointment. She'd changed her mind. He should have known her appearance was too good to be true. *Zoe, don't leave. Come back*, he signaled her silently. And miraculously, after a minute or two she did. Aaron had held his breath as she opened the metal door and disappeared inside the building.

He'd seen enough genuine fear up close and personal, had experienced it himself on occasion to know she'd been petrified at his initial touch. He'd done the only thing he could think of to reassure her, force her to relax.

He'd used every bit of experience and wisdom he'd gained about the art of sensual touch, much of it gleaned from skilled Japanese women during a brief assignment in that country. Almost immediately Zoe's tremors ceased, the tension eased out of her. Still, Aaron hadn't counted on her falling apart emotionally. Not that he'd minded.

Because Zoe had given him a piece of what he was looking for. Part of what he thought would be a normal relationship between a man and a woman. Comforting each other in a time of need.

Though he had no personal experience on which to draw. Sexual encounters were plentiful. Emotional connections were rare.

Even now, he felt an almost equal satisfaction from that interlude as he did from the sexual contact. Zoe had clung to him and he'd done nothing more than hold her, stroke her hair and offer the use of his clothes as a handkerchief.

She'd needed him. Well, maybe not him, but she'd needed someone. Another human being. Comfort. And he'd been the one to provide it, even though making such a gesture was foreign to him. Displays of emotion were discouraged within the agency and therefore relatively rare in his world. Odd that something so simple could give him such pleasure.

He smiled again. Zoe hadn't undressed as he'd suggested. He'd gotten into the bed to discover her completely clothed except for her coat and shoes. He chuckled. Zoe Bradford was no pushover. The clothes sent a clear message. Or maybe an unclear one. She'd shown up, but she hadn't entirely committed to a course of action. He wouldn't have been surprised if she'd bolted the minute he arrived. In fact, he'd picked up on that fight or flight response building in her. God, he hadn't wanted her to leave. To reassure her, he'd started massaging her, trying to relay without words that he truly had no intention of harming her.

Nothing had gone exactly according to his plan last night, thanks to Zoe.

Good thing she wasn't an agent with Level One. She'd throw a wrench in every mission. That was one thing they had in common, he supposed. Neither of them were terribly good at following orders to the letter. In his case, it hadn't compromised any of his missions. Yet. Zoe, however, was another matter.

Aaron punched the faucet to turn it and his memories off.

She's not a mission, he reminded himself. He knew that of course, but he wondered sometimes if he even had the capability or the humanity to approach another human being without making it a mission. He was used to *conquering*. To having a plan, being in control, overseeing every detail, improvising when necessary to achieve the objective.

That's what he'd done last night. And maybe that was part of the thrill. He hadn't known exactly what to expect, although he'd reasonably expected that once Zoe showed up at the appointed place and time she'd do as instructed. She hadn't. She hadn't undressed. And he hadn't expected to start things off with a massage, but it had worked. He hadn't expected her to fall apart, either. He didn't know why she had started crying. Fear most likely. Or sadness over her husband and son. Even though it had been a whole year. What if, the thought suddenly occurred to him, there was another man in her life? Then she wouldn't have considered his outlandish offer. Would she? Aaron wished he could ask her, he wished he knew her better, but that wasn't likely to happen. He could have part of a relationship with her. He'd never have the whole thing. But he'd learned early in life to settle for what he could have instead of everything he wanted.

Her tears affected him deeply, as if they'd been dripping into his very soul. He hoped what he'd done hadn't caused them. Probably they weren't even about him. He didn't know, but it had changed things between them before they'd even begun.

He could have held her all night and done nothing more if she'd been resistant. Except he couldn't keep from touching her. Even through her clothes, he craved getting to know every inch of her, inside and out, as much as he could within the confines of the arrangement he'd created.

Zoe probably didn't realize how titillating it was for a sexually experienced adult male to be made to work at getting a woman out of her clothes. Too many women, in his experience, took sex for granted. They gave in too easily.

Zoe at least had made it a challenge. He'd already decided he wasn't going to be the one to take her clothes off. He wouldn't force himself on her. The very thought left a bad taste in his mouth.

But she'd responded. The touch of her hand against his skin drove him wild, though he'd held himself in check. Until she yanked the sweater off over her head. A sure signal that told him she was ready.

He sighed in satisfaction at the memory of being inside her, feeling her response to him. He wished he could have stayed longer afterward, held her while she slept, but he didn't dare.

Once she left he returned to dispose of the evidence of their meeting, stripping the bed and remaking it. A smile quirked at the corners of his mouth as he recalled the paring knife he'd discovered under the pillow. It was a pitiful excuse for a weapon. He'd have disarmed her in a split second had she attempted to use it. But the fact that she'd had it there within easy reach, more proof that she hadn't approached the situation blindly, intrigued him. He'd replaced the knife beneath her pillow.

His morning ritual of showering and shaving complete, he yanked a starched white dress shirt off a hanger and shrugged into it. He didn't understand this weird connection to Zoe Bradford. But apparently, she needed cash. And he needed...a relationship.

He looked at himself in the mirror as he buttoned the shirt. "Asshole," he commented to his reflected image. He'd set Zoe up, and their arrangement hardly qualified as a relationship.

"Didn't want a prostitute, huh?" he asked his reflection as he knotted a geometric patterned maroon tie. He *had* paid a woman money in exchange for sex.

Okay, he cajoled his conscience. But *she* isn't a prostitute. And it wasn't just sex, either, was it?

The glint went out of his eye and he faced himself in the mirror. "No," he told his image. "It wasn't just sex." And it wasn't just any woman, either.

You took advantage of her, his conscience niggled him. He slid his feet into black loafers and reached for a belt. No, I didn't, he argued. She wasn't obligated. She could have ignored the letter and kept the cash he'd enclosed with it. Showing up last night had been entirely her choice.

Apparently his conscience had no answer for that argument.

Last night he'd wanted to touch and savor, absorb and possess. And in the anonymous darkness, he'd done all of those things.

Zoe had no expectations, either. She couldn't. He could have been a lousy lover, could have taken his pleasure and left.

He couldn't do that. Hadn't wanted to do that. He wanted Zoe to enjoy being with him. He wanted to please her. Because, he thought, in some way maybe that could make up for what he was taking from her.

Doesn't the money do that?

"Not entirely," he answered out loud.

So making love with you is like an added bonus?

Aaron looked at his reflection in the mirror, the dark blue suit, the government-issued tie. He smiled and winked at the mirror. "Sort of."

As he left his apartment he brushed aside the sense that perhaps he'd gotten much more than he bargained for with Zoe Bradford. At the same time his pulse quickened at the thought of arranging another anonymous meeting with her.

He planned to create a real relationship with a woman, or something that closely resembled a real relationship, which he'd wanted and been denied for a very long time.

And Level One be damned.

He arrived at the compound even earlier than usual, nodding to the guard on duty before using the fingerprint scanner to enter the agency offices. Using his security clearance and access to federal government databases made it easy to do some personal research.

Zoe Dawn Dumont Bradford. Age 29. Widowed. Former elementary school teacher. Now a server at Mathilde's.

Nothing new there, except he hadn't known her exact age.

Aaron's eyebrows rose when he saw the amount of debt Zoe had. He let out a low whistle. She'd exceeded the limit on each of her credit cards. She had no assets. Unless he missed his mark, he guessed Zoe was barely keeping her head above water.

He was glad then of the amount he'd offered her to meet with him.

He scanned the charges on her credit cards. It appeared she'd made three trips to Guatemala in the past few months. Why?

He switched databases looking for a reason for those trips and came upon State Department encrypted files. A red flag of alarm shot through him and gave him pause.

His telephone intercom buzzed a specific code summoning him to his superior's office. He exited the Zoe files. This particular research would have to wait.

Chapter Seven

"Father Coughlan?" Ben had to be hallucinating, surely, from exhaustion and lack of food. Father Reece Coughlan, couldn't possibly be in this armed camp. Unless he'd come to rescue him.

But...Coughlan had disappeared from his missionary post over a year ago. The same post Ben had subsequently been assigned.

Ben sat up too suddenly and his surroundings spun in a dizzying whirl. He covered his face with his bound hands, trying to regain his equilibrium, tamping down the nausea that rose to the back of his throat.

Slowly, carefully he opened his eyes. Still the image of Father Coughlan stayed before him.

"Father?" he queried again, his voice hoarse from dehydration and the recent coating of bile.

Coughlan folded his arms over his chest and shook his head sadly. His shock of white hair ruffled in the early morning breeze. The brilliant blue of his eyes dimmed with sadness and disappointment. "I prayed it wasn't you," he said. "Ah, Ben. What are we to do with you now?"

One of the guards standing nearby spoke in gutteral Spanish and Coughlan replied. Slowly Ben translated the words into English. He hadn't been in Central America long enough to think in Spanish nor was he familiar with all of the various dialects. "Kill him," the guard had said. "Not so fast," was Coughlan's reply.

Ben held his bound hands out toward Coughlan. Surely he'd come to secure Ben's freedom. Coughlan frowned. "They've been mistreating you."

Ben lowered his arms. His brain felt sluggish, his mind dull. Coughlan had walked into the camp unarmed. Approached a prisoner freely. Conversed with the guards as if they were old friends.

"Water," Ben replied. He dreamt of it. Prayed for it. Fresh, clean water. Not the foul stuff he'd been forced to drink because his body was desperate for even the few drops the guards offered him.

"Agua," Coughlan ordered the guard. Reluctantly the man handed him a canteen. Coughlan placed it in Ben's bound hands. "Slowly, now. Not too much," he warned as if Ben were a child. Ben forced himself to take only a couple of sips. He clenched the canteen tightly between his fingers, afraid Coughlan or the guard would take it away. The tepid, gritty fluid trickled down his throat and tears gathered in Ben's eyes.

"Thank you, Jesus," he said aloud.

He thought he heard Father Coughlan chuckle, but he couldn't be sure, and he didn't care. He tipped the canteen to his lips and took a couple more sips.

His mind cleared a bit. He lowered the container and gazed at Coughlan. "You're not here to see that I'm released."

This time Coughlan did chuckle. The sound he made and the look in his eyes frightened Ben.

"Give me strength, Lord," Ben prayed silently.

"Ben, Ben, Ben." Coughlan shook his head. He lowered himself to a fallen log nearby, clasping his hands between his knees. "If only I could set you free. But I'm afraid it's not possible. You involved yourself in things that are none of your business. I'm afraid you must suffer the consequences."

"The welfare of the villagers is my business."

"Ah yes, but the mine operation we have here. That is none of your business. You should have stayed away as Julio suggested."

"I couldn't. I see the village women returning with sadness in their eyes. The men with unexplained pesos in their pockets. And no one would talk."

Coughlan shook his head sadly. "Because they knew better. As you should have. How quickly you forgot the lectures in the seminary.

79

Lectures I gave. Offering you the experience of my wisdom. Not to involve yourself in activities outside your jurisdiction."

"You're a part of this. You had me captured. You're the one holding me against my will."

Coughlan shook his head. "You gave us no choice in the matter. Trust me, Ben, it's better than the alternative."

"But you were a missionary. You devoted your life to helping these people—"

"I'm still helping them," Coughlan shouted. He gained his feet and began to pace, gesturing wildly with his arms. "I'm helping them more now than ever. Do you know how many years I toiled alongside these peasants, telling them God would provide? All they had to do was believe. You have no idea how many children I watched die in their mothers' arms. How many crops were washed away in storms. How many men lost hope.

"The suffering, they endured. My God, Ben, what you've seen in your short time here is only the tip of the iceberg.

"And after twenty years, it got no better. Their government doesn't care and can't cope. Our government doesn't care. Their lives were no better than they were when I first arrived. All that time, all those prayers. Wasted."

"Prayer is never wasted," Ben said.

"You're a fool if you believe that. Like I was a fool."

"You taught at the seminary!" Ben cried.

"I taught fools to believe in something that doesn't exist. Faith alone will save you. Pah! Money is the only thing that will save these people. And that's what I give them."

"You're corrupting their souls, encouraging them to sell out their faith."

"You fool!" Coughlan glared at Ben. Dribbles of foamy saliva had gathered at the corners of Coughlan's mouth. Ben clasped his hands together, resting his elbows on his bent knees, and lowered his head, trying to think, trying to pray. Coughlan roared at the guard in Spanish and the man slunk away.

Ben could feel Coughlan staring down at him. "Are you working for them?"

Ben raised his head. The other priest towered over him, his eyes wild. "Them?"

"The government. The CIA."

Ben shook his head.

"Don't lie to me!" Coughlan roared. "I know how they operate. Who better to spy for them than missionaries? The innocent and the righteous."

Coughlan cuffed him open-handed on the side of the head. Unprepared for it, Ben toppled over. He closed his eyes, making no effort to right himself. Tired. He was so tired.

He slipped into unconsciousness while Coughlan paced nearby, muttering to himself in Latin.

Ben came to slowly, keeping his eyes closed. He ached, oh, God, how he ached. His head pounded from Coughlan's blow, but he refused to groan. He held his breath to keep from expressing his pain. *Oh, Lord, give me strength.* He exhaled, counting seconds to distract himself.

He listened as best he could, with one ear pressed to the cold wet leaves beneath him. Voices murmured, low and indistinct, some in English. He thought he heard more than one American accent. Coughlan and who else? Snatches of Spanish drifted through the trees to where he lay. Smoke from a fire tickled his nostrils. They were cooking. Maybe they would feed him.

As if to add to his discomfort, his empty stomach growled in anticipation. He knew better than to hope for a decent scrap of food. A strong prisoner, a well-fed prisoner presented more of a threat than a weak, incapacitated one.

And water. Oh, God, what he wouldn't do for water. *Please, God, please, have mercy. Even a sip. A couple of drops.* He tried to lick his dry lips with an even drier tongue. Tears filled his eyes. Perhaps, if he sat up at just the right angle, the tears would drip into his mouth. He would have something to drink.

He struggled to a sitting position and then stood. His bones and what remained of his muscles protested the movement. Hobbled by the chains around his ankles, one of which was attached to the trunk of a tree, he couldn't move very far or very fast.

He squinted through the cover of foliage and trees to where a small group was gathered near the fire. Heat. Warmth. He tried not to shiver as the cold mountain breeze found every tear in his clothing.

Several of the guards milled around the fire. Coughlan and another man stood with the burly American guard, heads together, deep in conversation. Ben studied the other man. He looked American. More importantly, he looked familiar to Ben. A memory teased the outskirts of Ben's mind.

Some of the stiffness in his joints eased as he paced in the limitation forced by his bonds. As he returned to a sitting position a guard stepped forward. Seeing him awake and upright, the guard scowled and turned back to the group. He addressed one of the others.

Presently, Coughlan himself appeared holding two stainless steel cups. He handed one to Ben and held the other.

"Soup," he said, as the aroma of vegetables and meat tickled Ben's nostrils.

"And water." Coughlan carefully set the other cup near Ben's feet.

Ben's wariness rose a degree if that were possible. Saliva pooled in his mouth as he stared up at the older priest. Coughlan's behavior aroused Ben's suspicion. He was being provided decent food. And water. One last meal before they killed him?

Coughlan waved a hand at him, indicating he should eat. Hunger won over suspicion. Ben sipped the broth and nearly groaned with pleasure at the bland concoction of something both warm and edible.

Coughlan clasped his hands behind his back and began pacing before Ben as if he were at the front of a lecture hall. "I lost my temper before. I apologize, Ben. But patience, formally a virtue of mine, is no longer. My eyes were opened, Ben, as yours will be some day. Someday soon, I hope. Before—well, we won't go into that. I feel confident you, too, will see the light.

"My associates," he waved vaguely in the direction of the fire, "aren't so sure. If it were up to them—frankly, Ben," he paused and gave Ben another of those searching looks with his keen eyes, "you wouldn't be here now. They consider you dispensable. It is only through my— intervention—that you are still with us. I've made them see the value, for now at least, of converting you to the cause."

"What cause is that?" Ben wanted to be careful. More than that, he wanted to stay alive. After Coughlan's earlier outburst, he knew it best to pretend Coughlan was a reasonable man.

"Our cause. My cause." He thumped himself on the chest. "Helping the poor in a very tangible way. Don't be obtuse, Ben. Surely you see the benefit of what we're doing."

Casually, Ben lowered the cup of soup and replaced it with the water. Coughlan had asked if he'd been recruited by the CIA and Ben had been truthful when he'd said no. Coughlan hadn't asked about any other government agency, however. Level One must know about Coughlan's operation. Russell Gannett had hinted at it during their meeting last fall. This had to be why Corbridge recruited Ben.

"I'm still not clear on exactly what you're doing." He swallowed some of the water. It tasted cleaner and fresher than any he'd been given thus far. He hoped it had been boiled and tried not to think about what bacteria and parasites could do to his already weakened immune system.

"I explained this to you earlier," Coughlan reminded him a bit testily.

"Providing money to the peasants."

Coughlan beamed as if Ben were his star pupil and had given the correct answer.

"I know you've seen their lives improve, Ben, in the short time you've been here. They now have decent clothes for their children. They can afford a pair of shoes. Or a few chickens. Surely you've seen the benefit to them."

"They're sacrificing their souls for money, and you're encouraging it."

Coughlan gave him a disappointed look. "Ben, Ben, Ben. I'm feeding their souls by allowing them the opportunity to feed themselves and their families."

Ben snorted in disbelief at Coughlan's twisted justification. "And what do you get out of it, *Father*?"

Coughlan's head snapped back as if Ben had slapped him. His eyes narrowed in shrewd assessment. A chill shot up Ben's spine, his tenuous grip on life and freedom held in this man's hands. Insulting him was not wise and Ben knew it. He silently prayed for the strength to hide his disgust and contempt.

"Perhaps my associates were correct. Perhaps I should have allowed them to eliminate you as they planned."

"Forgive me, Father," Ben said, schooling his features into an expression of remorse. "I'm a slow learner."

Coughlan's expression did not change, except for an almost imperceptible hardening of his already stern features. "Perhaps," he agreed. He turned and made his way back to the others.

Chapter Eight

Marcus Sydell tapped on the open door of the agency director's office and stuck his head in. "Sir? Do you have a minute?"

Russell Gannett glanced up from the mountain of paperwork and reports surrounding him and motioned Marcus into the room. Marcus closed the door behind him and stood waiting until Russell glanced up again and motioned him into one of two wingback chairs. He tossed down his pen and folded his hands across the file he'd been working on. "What is it?"

Marcus crossed the thick burgundy carpet, conscious as always of his awkward gait, lowering himself to the chair, shifting slightly in the glossy leather seat. "We have a situation, sir."

Russell Gannett's ears perked and his nostrils flared. Marcus sometimes thought his reactions resembled those of a stallion, sensing danger in the wind. For at Level One, the word "situation" often substituted for "danger."

"Go on."

Assured he had his superior's complete attention, Marcus spoke. "It's Agent Manning, sir."

"Again?" Gannett blew out a breath that was half sigh/half groan. Why, he wondered, as he'd wondered at least a hundred times since taking the position of director at Level One, why his best operative caused him the biggest headaches. Aaron Manning had been taken to task numerous times during his tenure with L.O. Unfortunately, his work in the field was so exemplary, his leadership skills and experience so necessary to his missions, his penchant for unorthodox methods and risk taking had thus far been mere footnotes in his file.

"It's a woman, sir," Marcus supplied. He'd learned, on unofficial business at least, it was often best to offer Russell Gannett bad news in small pieces, one at a time. Sort of like hand feeding a finicky Schnauzer.

Gannett fixed Marcus with a look. "Again?" he repeated.

Marcus had the presence of mind to look chagrined. Out of all the operatives, Aaron Manning gave them the most trouble with personal relationships.

"This is a bit different, than his other...transgressions, sir."

"In what way?" Gannett looked intrigued.

"It appears he's arranged to meet with a woman anonymously. It's our belief he's paying her."

Gannett shrugged. "So? What's the problem?" Paying for sex and remaining anonymous were behaviors not only approved for Level One operatives, they were encouraged.

"He's using one of our facilities for the meetings," Marcus answered.

Gannett frowned. "Which one?"

Marcus told him, adding, "The woman isn't a prostitute, either, sir."

Gannett raised his eyebrows, silent encouragement for the other man to continue.

"She's a waitress, sir."

"A waitress?" Gannett thought for a moment. "Other than the fact he's using one of our sites without authorization, I really don't see the problem. We're not currently using that facility for any of our operations are we?"

"No sir, but—"

"Keep him under light surveillance. Document his encounters with this woman. Unless you have reason to believe she can compromise him in some way, don't do anything else for now."

"Yes, sir." Marcus stood to go.

"Oh, and Marcus?"

He turned back to Gannett.

"Yes, sir?"

"You'll keep me informed if anything untoward develops?"

"Yes, sir. Of course, sir."

Russell Gannett stared at the multitude of files on his desk, but his concentration was shot.

He removed his wire-rimmed glasses and rubbed his eyes with thumb and forefinger.

Was it his imagination or did Marcus seem to keep a closer eye on and report on Agent Manning more often than the other agents?

He'd watched both men closely the past couple of years, ever since Marcus had been put on desk duty after a field operation gone wrong. Agent Manning had been in charge of the mission, demolition of an unstable weapons cache along a disputed Afghani border. All of the other agents had no problem following Aaron's lead, even when he didn't exactly follow protocol, but Marcus— Marcus had a competitive streak that proved to be his undoing that day.

The charges were set, Aaron had given the command to clear out, but Marcus insisted on setting one more charge. Aaron had literally gone in and dragged Marcus out, but not soon enough. The explosions had already begun, debris had started to fall, including a concrete support post which had crushed Marcus's ankle and foot, leaving him partially crippled.

The ensuing investigation had shown Aaron had, for once, thank God, mostly followed procedure. Marcus had been at fault. Gannett had ordered a complete psych work-up on Marcus when he'd expressed interest in continuing to work with Level One, albeit in a less active capacity. Marcus had shown no resentment or animosity toward Aaron, nor had the psychologist picked up on anything unusual which would prevent him from continuing work with the agency.

But there had been moments over the past couple of years when Gannett sensed something in Marcus Sydell's manner when discussing Agent Manning, something in his behavior whenever the two of them crossed paths. Marcus was too smart to do anything obvious, but the same worrisome itch surfaced from time to time with Gannett. Like Sydell's report on Manning just now.

Manning had been a wild card from the day he'd joined the organization, and Russell had only himself to blame. He'd been given carte blanche to staff this unofficial section of the Defense Department, allowed to pick and choose from top candidates in the military, CIA and FBI.

Manning's file had arrived on his desk as a recommendation from the commander of Delta Force. He tested off the charts for intelligence, was in superb physical condition, and had received awards on more than one occasion for outstanding performance and bravery in the field. Aaron's only flaw was that he had a slight problem following orders.

Still, Russell had been in covert operations long enough to know that occasionally that could be a good thing. He'd taken a chance on Aaron and had rarely been disappointed. When Aaron took matters into his own hands in the field, the outcome, so far at least, had been positive.

Aaron's successful performances outweighed the occasional lapse in obedience. They were noted, of course. He'd been reprimanded on occasion, but Russell and Aaron had reached an understanding. They were both results-oriented, and as long as Aaron got the results, his sins were forgiven. If he ever stepped over the line, if the outcome was less than desirable, both he and Gannett would be booted out of Level One. If they were lucky, that's all that would happen.

Gannett tapped his pen nervously on top of a report outlining a Central American guerilla force's latest movements. There would be no getting around it. Sooner or later, he'd have to have another "talk" with Agent Manning.

Aaron sat at the bar of Matilde's, as he had weeks earlier, keeping an eye on Zoe. This time he had no official reason to be there, no DD employees leaking information, no terrorist plots to unravel, no surveillance devices to plant. This time he was there for himself.

He sipped Dewar's on the rocks while he fiddled with a swizzle stick he'd snatched from the bartender's ample supply. Upending it on the bar, sliding his fingers down the length of it, flipping it over and repeating the movement. He adopted an outward appearance of casual boredom, the play with the swizzle stick the only indication of his nervousness.

Ridiculous to be nervous, he told himself. Any casual observer would think the fiddling was because he was bored. But Aaron could remain perfectly still for hours at a time. No, playing with the swizzle stick was definitely due to nerves.

He had that same buzz in the pit of his stomach he always got when embarking on a new assignment. The more dangerous the assignment, the steadier the buzz.

Zoe had yet to glance his way, though she'd approached the bar several times to place drink orders.

Aaron glanced in the mirror behind the bar from time to time, satisfied that he hadn't lost his ability to make himself virtually invisible.

A monotone voice, bland facial expressions, nondescript clothes. A certain posture, an adopted attitude of low self-esteem, never making eye contact, guaranteed he'd be ignored by waiters and witnesses alike. Sometimes he added one of several pairs of glasses to give himself a more studious look. Minor adjustments to hair and clothes, and he could be mistaken for a computer geek.

Not that I'm not a good-looking guy, he thought to himself and had to catch the smile before it arrived at his lips. Close-cropped dark blond hair, unique hazel eyes, and a taller than average physique could easily make him stand out in a crowd. Added to that, he was in top physical shape, every muscle honed to perfection and maintained by vigorous workouts.

Without appearing to, he focused his attention solely on Zoe, watching her move from table to table.

Again he noticed the way she held herself apart from those around her. It wasn't his imagination, but he seemed to be the only one aware of it, besides, perhaps, Zoe herself. She took orders, disappeared into the kitchen, brought food, served drinks, interacted with the customers and her co-workers. But she wasn't really there. He wondered where she was.

Was her mind constantly drawn, as his was, back to the time they'd spent together two nights ago? The taste and scent of her was still fresh in his mind; he could still feel the touch of her skin against his.

Aaron blinked. He tossed back the rest of his Dewar's, knowing he was close to doing something he'd regret. He waved off the bartender and waited until Zoe was out of sight. Then he went out into the cold New York night and reminded himself for the hundredth time that Zoe

Bradford wasn't an assignment. Zoe Bradford was a choice. He couldn't get attached to her. Couldn't get attached to anyone. Level One couldn't allow it.

"Oh, no." Zoe groaned when she spied the white envelope on the floor inside the door.

She'd barely survived her shift at the restaurant last night before coming home, downing numerous ibuprofen and falling into bed.

Her period had begun yesterday which meant today would be the heaviest flow.

She bent to pick up the envelope before stumbling into the kitchen area. As she did every morning, she ran her fingers over the drawings covering the refrigerator. She smiled at Zach's kindergarten photo. Kissed her index finger and pressed it against the picture. She wondered if Zach knew of her regrets. If he'd forgiven her for her shortcomings as a mother. If he blamed her for his untimely death.

Ben would tell her Zach was at peace. The guilt was a human emotion, not an ethereal one. That Zach was looking down on her with nothing but love. Zoe wanted to believe that was true.

While coffee brewed she opened the envelope. The sight of all that lovely cash still had the ability to lift her spirits. Soon, Ben, soon.

She'd been stashing the money in a safe deposit box in her bank on a regular basis. After only a few months she had accumulated a sizable amount of cash. She'd almost stopped feeling guilty about her clandestine meetings with her generous, anonymous lover. Certainly guilt wasn't among the many emotions he evoked during their time together.

She poured a mug full of coffee and stared at the bills peeping out of the envelope. So far she hadn't had her period when she was with him. Probably the inconsistency of their time together was the reason. But she was a healthy adult woman. It was bound to happen sooner or later.

She had no way to notify him that she was...indisposed. Perhaps he wouldn't mind. Some men didn't. Besides, it wasn't like they had any set schedule. Some weeks they were together three or four nights in a row. But she'd also gone for days without finding an envelope waiting for her. Each time, she panicked, both at the thought of being unable to increase her nest egg, but also of not being with her phantom lover. That was how she thought of him. A nameless, faceless phantom. Was he even real? She knew she wasn't dreaming their encounters, and certainly she hadn't imagined the growing amount of cash squirreled away in a safe deposit box at the local Bank One branch. But somehow in the light of day, those nights seemed the stuff of pure fantasy, distant and unreal.

Yet she'd become sickly dependent on being with her phantom, whoever he was, whatever he looked like, what name he had, none of it mattered. He made love to her with power and passion, and she'd begun to convince herself they were silently communicating on more than a physical level. She wasn't sure exactly what messages they were sending each other. She only knew she felt connected to him and she didn't want to lose the connection.

Zoe spent the better part of the day pondering her dilemma. She hated the idea of missing an opportunity, thereby forgoing the addition to Ben's rescue fund.

Yet what if her secret lover were turned off, disgusted by female biology? He could terminate their meetings altogether.

Zoe, she scolded herself, you're being silly. He wouldn't do that.

Would he?

It drove her nuts sometimes wondering who her phantom lover could be. A part of her desperately wanted to know. She found herself studying men on the street, in the restaurant, on the subway. Mentally she dissected their build, their hair, the shape of their nose and lips, the length of their fingers. He could be anyone. He could be a regular patron of the restaurant. Maybe she'd seen him there.

One thing she knew for sure, he had money at his disposal. Plenty of it. And he paid her in cash.

Another part of her didn't want to know who he was, what he looked like or where he got his money. He could be a drug dealer, a terrorist, a serial killer.

No, she told herself, he was none of those things. For to be so, he'd have to be ruthless and cruel. And she sensed none of those traits in him. He was sensuous, giving and loving.

Zoe's mind rebelled at the direction her thoughts were taking. Love had nothing to do with their encounters. She'd told herself that from the first. And reminded herself of it after each and every encounter since.

Then what does it have to do with?

Sex, she told herself. Nothing more.

Liar, came the internal answer. He doesn't have sex with you. He makes love with you. And you with him.

Stop it, she commanded herself. She couldn't care about him, couldn't be in love with him, because she didn't know who he was. All she knew was the way he made her feel.

Loved. Okay, there she'd admitted it. When she was with him she *felt* loved whether he loved her or not. She felt cherished and special. Like you're the only woman alive? Yes! Yes. That's it, exactly. And maybe for him, she was.

But still she'd have to figure out how to handle tonight.

Curled on her side, Zoe felt warm and drowsy and barely came awake when he slid into bed behind her.

His hand began its now familiar exploration, sliding around her waist, moving up to cup a breast and tease the nipple, then gliding down to her hip where he hesitated only momentarily.

Zoe opened her eyes. She felt the pressure of his palm as he explored the covering he couldn't see. When he encountered the pad securely tucked inside the crotch of her panties he slid his hand back up, letting his arm rest across her waist.

She felt his lips on her shoulder. He pushed her hair aside so he could kiss the back of her neck and below her ear before he pulled her closer.

Within minutes she could feel his slow even breathing. He'd fallen asleep. His silent understanding and quiet tenderness broke apart something inside her.

Zoe snuggled back against the warmth of him and dozed off.

When she woke it was to find her arms and legs entangled with his, and her nose pressed up against his ribcage.

Her cramps were gone and she felt wonderful.

She pressed her face against the smooth skin of his side and curled her fingers into the sprinkles of hair on his chest.

She drank in the scent of his skin and dropped a kiss there before burying her nose in his chest. Zoe sighed in contentment, loving the way he smelled, the way the curly hair tickled her nostrils and fingertips.

She kissed and explored every inch of his chest, moved up to his throat then straddled him to kiss her way back down.

He was awake now, probably wide awake, but Zoe was intent on what she was doing and she hardly noticed. Excitement tingled through her.

With her tongue, she delved into his navel, an innie, and let her hands drift down over the hard bones of his pelvis to his thighs. Her body followed her hands and she slid over his erection slowly, feeling the pressure of him between her legs even through the layer of protection.

Her downward trek continued, the tip of him skimming along her stomach and between her breasts.

In the pitch black room he couldn't see the glint in her eyes, but Zoe knew exactly what she was going to do. What she wanted to do.

She positioned herself between his legs continuing to stroke the tops of his thighs with smooth, firm pressure. Lightly she let her thumbs drop to the inside of his thighs, smoothing them up from knee to crotch where they lightly brushed against his scrotum each time.

He was submitting to her, Zoe thought with delight. She could hear him breathing, could imagine him watching her in the dark.

She slid her hands up slowly one last time along the length of his thighs and with her right hand cupped his balls. Gently she nudged his thighs further apart.

Zoe sucked in her breath, not quite prepared for how her seduction was making her feel. Powerful and vulnerable at the same time.

She circled the base of his penis with her thumb and forefinger and with firm pressure slid them up to the tip. He jerked in reaction to this treatment and Zoe smiled, rubbing the tiny drop of moisture with her thumb as she bent forward.

She closed her lips around him and took him in her mouth, feeling him fill her until the tip of him felt as if it were halfway down her throat.

Using her tongue and her lips and her fingers, she pleasured him. His fingers tangled in her hair, and she knew he was suppressing more than the few gutteral noises that escaped.

Zoe didn't care. She wanted to do this. She reveled in it, perhaps in some way paying him back for the all the pleasure he'd given her.

He surged into her mouth one last time, his fingers tightening against her scalp, her mouth jammed against him, her tongue swirling as he came. Semen squirted down her throat. Zoe fought not to gag and won, swallowing successfully as she caught her breath.

Like a cat, she crawled back up his body, dragging her tongue along the flat, hard angles of his abdomen and chest, dropping kisses as she went. He yanked her to him, wrapped an arm around her shoulders and cradled her head in one hand. He kissed her throat, her face, her eyes, before pulling her closer still, holding her on top of him. She could feel his heart beating beneath her. Knew he wanted to express something that could only be said in words. Knew also that he wouldn't.

She put her lips to his ear and breathed the words. "I know." It wasn't even a whisper. Maybe he hadn't heard her. But Zoe thought he did. She thought he nodded once in response, before they both fell asleep.

Chapter Nine

Aaron liked some of the New Jersey suburbs. Lots of families, nice homes, pretty parks. He liked neighborhoods where it was safe for the kids to play outside without constant adult supervision. Riding bicycles on sidewalks, tossing footballs in front yards. Building snow forts and sledding in winter.

Today he'd taken a drive to Ridgefield. It was the first of April, sunny and unseasonably warm. He drove aimlessly, gazing at the carefully tended lawns where leaves were beginning to bud on old trees. Minivans sat in driveways. He hoped to have one of his own.

He knew the life he wanted was impossible. Yet this longing, which had surfaced a couple of years ago, simply wouldn't go away. And lately, he'd begun some dangerous thinking along the lines of, "Why not me?"

If any of his...associates...knew of his sick, secret habit of driving through suburban streets, stopping at ball parks and wandering the sidewalks of residential neighborhoods, he'd take all kinds of grief for it.

But there was something inside him that was helplessly drawn to those family scenes, to the dream of having a wife and children, and all the problems and dysfunction that went with it.

He was *lonely*, dammit. In spite of everything he had, the things he longed for eluded him.

If he didn't return from one of his missions, no one would care. No one would notice. Death was commonplace in his line of work. The other agents, his superiors, perhaps a few of the underlings would be informed of his demise. Some of them would attend the memorial service the agency would arrange. But there'd be no tears. No one's life altered forever by his permanent departure. He'd be merely a disappearing blip on the radar screen of the agency and lately the thought galled him. He did important work, valuable work, work which, for the most part, went unnoticed except in the highest levels of covert government operations. And even then, his name wasn't always attached to the missions. Names weren't important. Objectives were the priority. As long as he accomplished the objective, completed the assignment, succeeded in the mission, that's all that mattered. The best way to get noticed was to fail. That's when those in command learned your name and remembered it.

He didn't want to be remembered for failure. He wanted to be remembered for the stupid and sappy reason that someone loved him. Really knew him and loved him anyway.

He stopped at an intersection. A family on bicycles walked their bikes across the street in front of him. They all wore protective helmets and had small orange flags flying from the backs of their bikes. Like goslings following the mother goose, three young children dutifully traipsed after a woman in the lead, while a man, presumably the children's father, brought up the rear.

I want that, he thought as he watched them reach the end of the crosswalk, mount their bikes and start down the sidewalk. A car horn beeped behind him, and he realized the light had turned green while he'd watched the family disappear into the distance.

Surely there was a way he could have what they had. There had to be a way out of Level One that would leave him alive and intact.

At the last minute he turned in the same direction the family had. For a time he cruised slowly, keeping an eye on them as they made their way along the sidewalk. The kids' legs pumped double time on the smaller bikes as the parents set a comfortable pace. All five of them veered off the sidewalk. He drove on, glancing at their destination. A park. Across the expanse of greenish brown grass he could see a soccer game in progress. He circled the park and found an empty parking place then made his way toward the bleachers.

A pink and green banner over a makeshift concession stand announced today as the annual Spring Sports Day. Registration desks were set up nearby. Tee shirts were being handed out and training clinics for soccer and baseball were in session.

He was anonymous in the crowd. He couldn't afford to strike up conversations with any of these people. The last thing he wanted was for someone to remember him. He thought he'd done well copying the suburban dad weekend outfit of polo shirt and khaki slacks. He kept a lightweight jacket in the car in case the weather was cool. But the sun shone brightly, and he didn't need it.

He wandered casually, taking in the scene as he would any other, making note of potential alternative exits, anything or anyone out of place or suspicious. *More suspicious or out of place than you?* Did he expect a terrorist with an AK47 to pop out of the oversized trash barrel and start shooting? He'd learned to expect the unexpected so he never ruled out those kinds of possibilities. He'd learned to take every precaution, to guarantee his personal safety and that of his team, to minimize risks. After years in his line of work, it was a habit.

Knots of parents and children were gathered here and there along the perimeters of the field. He took the bleachers two at a time and found a place mid-way up along the outside. He could jump to the ground from here if he needed to. A breeze with a hint of warmer weather soon to come blew across the field. He watched the referees in their black and white striped shirts trot along with the kids as they moved back and forth from one goal to the other. The coaches strode along the sidelines, shouting orders and encouragement.

A small girl of perhaps five, smiled shyly up at him from where she'd been digging in the moist dirt at the bottom of the bleachers. He smiled back, though it'd be better if he ignored her. She quickly cast her eyes back down to her endeavor of creating piles of soil, sprinkling bits of grass on top.

Had he done things like that as a child? He couldn't remember. His childhood had been cut painfully short. Maybe he'd never had the opportunity to dig in the dirt.

This little girl had wispy brown curls that framed her face as she bent her head forward. She wore a pair of jeans with pink butterflies on the pockets, a long-sleeved pink shirt and pink sneakers. If he had a daughter he'd go shopping for her. He'd find pink clothes like this little girl wore.

Catching him off-guard, she glanced up at him again. He didn't look away as he should. Instead he smiled, encouraging her to do the same. She did. Her already rosy cheeks turned a deeper shade of pink and she returned once again to fussing over her dirt piles. His heart warmed at the simple innocence on display in front of him.

She cocked her head as he watched, her gaze fixed on something on the ground underneath the bleachers. What was it? A bomb with a timer? Plastique and wires waiting for the push of a button from a remote control? That's what *he'd* expect to find. He leaned forward involuntarily, trying to see what she saw. She reached under the bleachers and he wanted to say, *Don't do that, honey. You'll get your hand blown off.* But when she withdrew her hand it was still intact and she held a bunch of tiny yellow flowers. She sniffed them experimentally, and then her gaze locked with his again.

This time she grinned first as if they were playing some sort of game, taking turns making eye contact with each other and smiling first. *She's a little flirt!* The very idea broadened his smile. He'd no idea feminine wiles developed at such a tender age. As if his bigger smile had made her decision for her, she clambered up the bleachers toward him. Once she reached the riser one step below his, she looked down at the bouquet in her grubby hand, her brows furrowed in concentration. Aaron took in every detail of, her sturdy body, the gold glints in the brown hair, the smear of dirt on her elbow, the long dark lashes framing the chestnut of her eyes.

After some seconds, she extracted one of the tiny flowers on its frail stem and presented it to him. Touched to his core, he accepted it solemnly. "Thank you," he managed, every other word he might have uttered stuck around the lump in his throat.

She smiled at him as if delighted with her decision and his reaction.

"Katie, come on," called a woman at the bottom of the bleachers. She held her hand out and the girl backed down the steps keeping her gaze on him until she reached the bottom. The woman took her hand and, with the one holding the flowers, the girl waved to him. He raised the flower in silent salute.

His heart heavy, he made his way down the bleachers and back across the park to his car. He laid the delicate flower, probably a weed, but now very precious to him, across the dashboard.

He sat in the car for a long time, the chatter from the soccer field still audible, but at a comfortable distance. The sun shone down as he watched families come and go, loading and unloading equipment, listened to sliding van doors open to dispense children. He wasn't a part of any of this. It was almost as if he was watching a movie. It wasn't real. He couldn't reach out and touch it, interact with it, be a part of it.

He drummed his fingers on the dashboard, and his thoughts turned, as they often did, to Zoe. He knew much more about her than he had a couple of months ago. She'd taught kindergarten before her husband and son had died. Growing up she'd spent a lot of time in foster care along with an older brother named Ben. A brother who was now a missionary in Central America and who had disappeared three months ago. That fact explained the trips she'd financed with credit cards. She'd been trying to find out what happened to her brother. She'd enlisted Drew Warner's help and insisted to the State Department and every other governmental authority she'd contacted that he'd been kidnapped, but no ransom demand had been received. Father Ben Dumont had simply disappeared.

He wondered if Zoe's brother was one of Corbridge's recruits. Even if he was, there was nothing Aaron could do about it. But he wished he'd done more research into Zoe's family before he'd approached her with his payment plan for secret meetings. No wonder she'd put herself on the line for the kind of cash he'd offered. She desperately needed that money to find out what happened to her brother. She probably thought he was still alive. Maybe she had some idea that he could be rescued. Anyone who watched news magazines would know rescues of kidnap victims didn't come cheap. If that's what Zoe was planning, he hoped she also knew they were rarely successful.

Zoe was becoming a problem for him. He usually figured out all the details of every op beforehand, planned for contingencies, made sure he had more than one escape route available.

Zoe's not an op!

What had he been thinking when he'd approached her with his anonymous letter and his idea for these clandestine meetings? He couldn't remember now, he'd been so intent on making that connection with her. Since then everything had blurred. He'd told himself then the same thing he told himself now. He couldn't have a normal relationship with a normal woman. *This is not normal!* his brain pointed out. *This is bizarre.*

How long could he keep up the anonymous meetings when he wanted more? He fantasized regularly about a life with Zoe. A real life. A normal life. With kids and a house and minivan. She'd proven she could live that life. She'd married and had a child.

The what ifs started again. What if he met Zoe in the light of day? What if they had a regular relationship or as close to one as he could get without compromising his job? What if he could somehow escape the agency in one piece? What if Zoe fell in love with him and wanted to marry him? He almost laughed out loud because the possibility seemed so remote. He knew of only one way to find out.

Mind made up, he started the car. A man jogged by with a Golden Retriever trotting along beside him. The dog's easy gait and flag-like tail drew Aaron's eye. Its golden brown fur glinted in the sun. *I want a dog like that.* He wanted to be the guy jogging along with his dog on a spring afternoon. Romping in the yard with his kids and the dog when he got home. Throwing a ball or a stick for the dog to fetch. He'd name it Butch or Spike, something that sounded tough. Even though inside the dog would be a big marshmallow.

Yeah, right, he reminded himself. His current lifestyle didn't even allow him to keep a goldfish alive for more than a week. He watched the man and his dog until they turned the corner.

Then he turned the car in the opposite direction and drove back to his life.

Chapter Ten

"Agent Manning?"

Russell Gannet cleared his throat and gazed briefly at the other faces gathered around the small conference table before returning his attention to Aaron.

His best agent was absently tapping a pencil, eraser side down on top of the unopened report in front of him.

"Agent Manning?" Russell queried once more.

The pencil tapping stopped. "Yes, sir?"

Aaron opened the report and sat up straighter.

"What do you think of the proposal to infiltrate the ISIS underground here in the U.S.?"

Aaron did his best imitation of being relaxed as he waited in Russell Gannett's office. Level One's director of operations had detained him after the meeting earlier and insisted he needed a word.

Aaron had no illusions what "the word" would be about. Zoe. He and Gannett had had differences of opinion before about Aaron's often unorthodox method of getting a job done. Usually Gannett deferred to his judgment, being that he was the one actually out in the field making quick decisions as circumstances warranted.

But this was different. This was personal. It had nothing to do with Level One. Except that Aaron chose to thumb his nose at the agency by using one of its own facilities for his clandestine meetings. Operation Zoe, he thought, smiling grimly to himself, was about to blow up in his face.

The door behind him opened, and he heard Russell's familiar step as he came across the room and took a seat behind the desk. He regarded Aaron for a minute, tapping his fingers on the edge of the dark mahogany, a frown forming between his eyes.

"It's come to my attention," he began.

"I want out," Aaron said.

Russell's eyebrows shot up. "Excuse me?"

"I want out. Of the agency. For good."

The frown returned. "That's not possible and you know it. We've got too big of an investment in you. You're too valuable, too knowledgeable—"

"What are you saying, Russell? That I'll never get out? At least not alive?" Aaron's mild tone belied his frustration. This was nothing he hadn't expected. He wondered if he could make a man like Russell Gannett understand.

"Let's not even go there," Russell warned.

Aaron stood, shoved his hands deep into the pockets of his trousers and paced to the window and back. "I can't do this anymore. More than that, I don't want to. I want a life, Russell. Can you understand that I want a normal life?"

"A wife?" Russell quizzed, not completely sarcastically. "Kids and a house with a white picket fence?"

Thinking of that bright-eyed retriever he'd seen yesterday, Aaron slouched back into the chair and eyed Russell with resentment. "Yes, dammit."

"And we're supposed to let you go?" he asked mildly. "Just like that?"

Aaron shrugged. He hadn't thought this through. Hadn't thought exactly how to approach the director with his resignation. No agent had resigned from the agency. Ever. They didn't have to. They didn't live that long.

"Is this about that woman?" Russell asked point blank, eyeing Aaron from beneath his brows. He shuffled through several file folders and pulled one out of the pile. Opening it, he said, "This, er, waitress? Zoe Bradford?"

Aaron wasn't surprised by the file or Gannett's knowledge of Zoe. But it didn't change anything. "Leave her out of it. This has nothing to do with her."

Gannett probably knew about Aaron's drives through residential neighborhoods on weekend afternoons. That he watched children play in parks, families gather in front yards, couples working together in their gardens.

His own childhood had been snatched away by his parents' unsavory choices. Those few years after the Mannings adopted him had given him a taste of home and stability, but his choices had propelled him away from that kind of life and into the life he had now. A life he'd come to abhor.

The niggling need he'd denied for years refused to be silenced any longer. He had to get out of Level One, out of covert operations altogether. There had to be a way out. One that would leave him alive. Russell Gannett was going to help him find it whether he wanted to or not.

Surprising Aaron, Russell suddenly relaxed back into his chair, pushing the file he'd been holding away from him. "You know, this is the first time I've ever had a request such as this from an active agent."

Aaron shrugged and glanced out the window again before returning to Gannett once again.

"You can make it happen," he informed the director. "Can't you?"

It was Gannett's turn to shrug. "Possibly. Perhaps." His expression changed. Aaron had seen that look before. Gannett was plotting, strategizing, the wheels of his mind turning as he examined a problem from all possible angles. Known for his creative solutions, many of which involved Aaron as the lead executor of his plans, if there was a way for Aaron to leave Level One alive, it might be unpleasant, but Russell Gannet would find it.

"You do realize you're not exactly marriage material."

"Let me worry about that."

Gannett cleared his throat. "You've been meeting this woman. Regularly." When Aaron made no response, he continued. "And using one of our facilities for the meetings."

Still Aaron said nothing. He knew Gannett knew about his meetings with Zoe. He probably had a big fat dossier on her by now, each of their meetings carefully documented by the surveillance team. If Gannett had something to say, he could damn well say it, Aaron thought. At the same time he knew that while Gannett might be displeased, the assignations he'd arranged which took place on agency property were not, in and of themselves, enough to get him booted out of Level One. *Damn.*

"I'd like you to explain your actions," Gannett said. He laid the pen down and sat up straight in his chair, pulling it close to his desk and folding his hands in front of him.

Aaron shrugged. "She can't identify me."

Gannett tilted his head to one side and studied Aaron. "How is that possible?"

"That's why I'm using the Warren Street location. She's never seen me. She doesn't know who I am."

"But you've met with her. On numerous occasions. According to the—"

Aaron waved away Gannett's explanation. The surveillance team could only know so much. "I'm with her only in the dark. I've remained anonymous. She has no idea who I am or what I look like. She has no way of identifying me."

Clearly perplexed, Gannett lifted a hand, expecting further explanation. When none came, he said, "May I ask why?"

Aaron shifted in his seat. The last thing he wanted to do was discuss his "relationship" with Zoe with his boss. "Because I arranged it that way."

"You're paying her." It was a statement which meant that Gannett knew.

"Yes."

"But she's never seen you?"

"No."

"Yet you're sleeping with her."

"Yes," Aaron gritted out. A nerve worked in his jaw. What he did with Zoe went beyond "sleeping with her." And it was none of Gannett's business.

"And you're using that location because?"

"It suited my purposes. I had access. We haven't used it since 9/11." Aaron shrugged. He and Gannett knew the real ownership of the building was virtually untraceable should anyone attempt to try. It was one of many facilities under the agency's aegis, used when necessary, abandoned when it wasn't needed, maintained at all times.

"Are you aware that Ms. Bradford's brother is or was a missionary in Central America?"

Aaron was used to Gannett's abrupt change in subjects during questioning. "I knew he was a missionary. He disappeared a few months ago," Aaron acknowledged.

"Ms. Bradford believes he was kidnapped."

"There's been no ransom demand."

"True."

Gannett continued to regard Aaron. If Gannett had something to say about him and Zoe, about the location of his meetings with Zoe, or about Zoe's brother, he could damn well come out and say it.

"How long have you known Ms. Bradford?"

"I don't know her. I've never met her." Aaron glared at Gannett, for the question reminded him once again that if not for the agency, he would have had that opportunity by now.

Gannett mulled over that information for a moment but did not press for details. "You're aware she's a widow?"

Aaron slammed his hand down on Gannett's desk. "For God's sake Russell, if you've got something to say, spit it out. Quit playing Twenty Questions with me."

Gannett's eyes narrowed. "Her husband and son were victims of a hit-and-run accident over a year ago. You were running the op to trap Carzoui when he mowed them down."

"Yes."

"But you didn't know her before that?"

"I don't know her now. I've never met her. I told you, our arrangement keeps me anonymous.

Gannett looked as if he wanted to say more but thought better of it. He raised a hand indicating acceptance of Aaron's explanation.

"Give me some time," he said, fixing Aaron with another of his stern expressions. "And don't do anything rash in the meantime."

For the first time since he'd walked into Russell's office, Aaron smiled. "You know me, Russell. Always the picture of decorum."

Russell waved him out as the phone on his desk shrilled.

Aaron was still smiling as he strode down the hall back to his own much smaller office. Marcus Sydell was headed his way. He nodded to the other man who was limping more than usual today.

A flicker of recognition crossed Marcus's face but quickly became a glower. Aaron was used to it. Marcus had never forgiven him for the accident that had resulted in the partial loss his right foot, even though an extensive internal investigation had cleared Aaron of any wrongdoing.

Marcus's problem was that he hadn't followed Aaron's orders, but instead had followed agency protocol even when it was apparent that protocol wasn't necessary to get the job done. A company man to the end, Marcus had ended up injuring himself and jeopardizing other agents in the process. It had been Aaron who had saved the day, pulling Marcus to safety, making sure the rest of the team got out alive.

Aaron's star rose with Level One while Marcus's seemed to be permanently tarnished. No longer fit for active assignments, Marcus had been relocated to the support team, overseeing requests for Level One assistance from other government agencies.

That was one way out of active duty, Aaron knew, to injure oneself and opt for a behind-the-scenes desk job. But it wasn't for him. What little time he spent behind his desk now was too much. Aaron needed action, movement, engagement. He wanted out of Level One completely and permanently.

Marcus had a certain amount of power, as Russell Gannett's right-hand man, but bitterness had taken root and grown over the years. Marcus rarely sought Aaron out unless he was given no choice. When they met within the agency walls, such as today, Aaron followed Marcus's lead, nodding in acknowledgment and going about his business.

A time or two Aaron thought he'd caught Marcus gazing at him with pure hatred in his eyes. There had been moments shortly after that long ago assignment had gone awry that animosity radiated off the other man in such strong waves it surprised Aaron that no one else seemed to notice it. Perhaps it had been his imagination, and his own feelings of guilt over Marcus's handicap. But with time, whatever sense of responsibility Aaron had felt for Marcus's injury had dissipated. It had happened. It was over. Marcus blamed him, hated him. There was nothing he could do about that.

Aaron took a seat behind his desk and tapped his password into his computer. As the screen came up, filled with the messages about the latest hotspots, Aaron continued to smile as he read the various reports.

He was scheduled to see Zoe tonight.

A new message came up on the screen, highlighted in neon green which meant it was from Russell Gannett. For his eyes only.

Aaron opened the message and the attached file, his smile slowly fading. There was suspicion of a rogue agent within Level One. Pieces of the puzzle were still being assembled. Reports from Central and South America were being sifted through, more clues were being gathered. Several members of the agency were being watched.

Chapter Eleven

The sun shone brightly on a late April morning, and Zoe woke up feeling almost hopeful. She decided to treat herself, something she rarely did. Wrapped in a baggy sweater with a red scarf wound around her neck, she planned a trek to Kemp's Bookstore where she would bury herself among the shelves and force her mind off her phantom lover.

Easier said than done, she found, as she navigated the city streets, feeling, as she often did, isolated from the rest of the world. Was it the city that made her feel estranged? No, she decided, it was her. She had few friends, except for Drew. She'd never been particularly good at relationships, always having the feeling she was standing on the outside looking in at other people's lives, not really able to identify with them. She wasn't sure why Drew was the exception, except he was single. Alone. And, as she looked back on the years of their relationship, she'd been better able to identify with him after his injury and the ensuing paralysis. Physically, Drew was no longer complete. He'd lost part of himself when he lost the use of his legs. Just as she had always seemed to feel something was missing about herself. Only her missing part was internal, invisible to the naked eye. Outwardly she looked normal. Most of the time she behaved as if there was nothing wrong. But there was an indefinable something that set her apart, that made her hold herself back, unable to relate.

Her family, such as it had been, was non-existent. Except for Ben.

If they'd been twins, she doubted they could have been closer. Two years older, Ben had fought time and time again to protect her during their childhood. First from their unstable mother and later as they both wound their way through the foster care system. Never had there been a time when Ben hadn't looked out for her.

Even when she'd married Tim, and later when Zach came along, Ben had been a constant. She'd always known where he was, how to reach him, and that he cared.

The thought of Ben starved and beaten, of him being the one in need clawed at her soul. It was now her turn to save Ben. *Soon*, she promised him silently. *Just hang on*. She allowed herself a bitter smile, remembering the years of reassurances he'd given her as they'd shuffled from one foster home to another. "When you're 18, you're free. Hang in there." Ben, being two years older, was cut loose from the system before she was. Zoe didn't know how he did it. He must have worked his ass off, but by the time she turned 18, he had a tiny apartment, a full-time job, and a place for her to stay.

He arranged college scholarships for her, and she waitressed to pay the bills. Through sheer determination, somehow they both survived.

Ben's desire to become a priest came to fruition. Zoe didn't understand his faith in such a cruel God. It became the one bone of contention in their otherwise close relationship, and finally they agreed to disagree.

Shortly before Tim and Zachary were killed, Ben left for his assignment as a missionary in Central America. Zoe hid her dismay and wished him well. She wrote to him weekly and he to her, though the mail system in certain regions of Central America was notoriously irregular and unreliable. Then the first call came from Julio and her nightmare began.

As Zoe headed out, she couldn't prevent herself from searching the faces of the men she passed. It had become a habit and today was no different. Any man who seemed to be the right age, the right shape, the right height, caught her attention.

Her phantom lover was tall, but it was hard to determine how tall. He had short hair, and he was in excellent physical condition. That described a lot of men. He seemed neither old nor young to her, so she estimated his age to be within close range of her own. Mid-thirties, maybe.

She could drive herself crazy, wondering who he was and why he had chosen her. Why must his identity remain a secret? As near as she could tell under cover of complete darkness, he wasn't maimed or disfigured in any way. She'd explored every inch of his body including his face to the extent he'd allowed her, and determined no scarring, no abnormalities.

More than once she'd been tempted during their nights together to leap from the bed, race across the room and turn on the light. Or to bring a small flashlight with her, hidden in her purse, and wait until he fell asleep to use it.

She'd done none of those things. Yet.

Should you attempt to discover my identity, the arrangement will be terminated.

Zoe kept the original letter in the safe deposit box with the cash she'd earned. She'd read it a hundred times, fixating on those words. Discovering the phantom's identity meant terminating their arrangement. It meant no more money for Ben's rescue fund. That's why she didn't do it.

Bullshit, her subconscious scoffed. *That's only part of the reason and you know it.*

Zoe lifted her chin as she crossed the street to the bookstore. True, she acknowledged. That is only part of the reason.

But for today, for at least an hour or two, she wasn't going to think about it. She opened the door to Kemp's, immediately embraced by the warmth, the scent of paper, the aroma of freshly brewed coffee.

Near the entrance her attention was snared by a poster above a pile of flyers advertising a self-defense class at a nearby gym. She picked up one of the flyers which also outlined the other services available at the facility. Not a bad idea, she thought, as she headed toward the shelves, still studying the paper. If she was going to rescue Ben, she needed to take better care of herself, maybe work on physical endurance and strength as well as self-defense tactics. Perhaps she should use some of her accumulated cash to pay for a membership.

She dived into the racks, selecting several books in a matter of minutes, shoving the flyer into the first book she chose. Maybe she would even treat herself to a new book. But first, she planned to spend the rest of the morning perusing them each in turn, at one of the tables in the coffee café, before making that all important decision.

As she turned the corner at the end of the shelves she collided with another customer. Her books went flying and she couldn't contain her automatic cry of dismay.

"Sorry," he said, as he stooped to gather the volumes. Zoe joined him, reaching for the ones closest at hand.

"Awfully clumsy of me." He smiled at her as they straightened, holding the rescued books out to her.

She gathered them back into a sloppy stack. "It's okay," she assured him automatically.

He had hazel eyes and close-cropped dark blond hair. "No, it's not. I'm an oaf. Let me buy you a cup of coffee to make up for it."

"That's not necessary." Zoe's suspicion level rose. This guy was trying to pick her up. Possibly he'd bumped into her on purpose. Recalling her reflection in the mirror this morning she thought that highly unlikely. With her wisps of hair framing a cleanly scrubbed, too-thin face, dressed in her shabby sweater and ancient jeans, she wasn't likely to attract much male attention. This stranger, on the other hand, looked like a healthy specimen in tip-top condition. He wore a dark blue jacket, a white button-down shirt, and jeans.

"Okay." He agreed easily to her rejection and Zoe experienced a twinge of regret. "I was going to have a cup anyway. I thought maybe we could discuss the finer points of Elliot Mason's latest." He tapped the book uppermost in her stack.

"You've read it?"

He turned in the direction of the café and Zoe followed his lead.

"I've read most of it," he replied. "It's a bit ponderous, if you ask me. Doesn't have that same capricious tone his other stuff did."

"Would you recommend it?" Other than Drew, few of Zoe's acquaintances were book readers.

The stranger shrugged. "Depends. What else have you got there?"

They'd reached the café and he indicated a table. Zoe unloaded her stack and he set them aside one by one. "If you want a recommendation, it will cost you. Have a cup of coffee with me." He held up his hands as if reading her mind. "No ulterior motives. Promise."

Zoe planned to have coffee anyway. "Fine. Coffee." She pulled out a chair and sat.

"How about a muffin? Or a cinnamon scone?"

"Pushing your luck, aren't you?"

"Cinnamon scone it is."

She watched him order at the counter. He carried himself with a sort of subtle command. He'd never take the direct route, and make demands Zoe decided. He'd use that quiet authority of his and expect everyone to fall in line.

You did, her subconscious pointed out.

It's coffee, for heaven's sake! She wished she could turn her internal warning system off for good. *It's only coffee.*

He returned and unloaded a tray bearing two scones, two cups of coffee and napkins.

He sat opposite her and picked up another of her selections, a non-fiction tome on Central American politics. And another written by a former CIA director on the inner workings of the agency.

His eyebrows rose. "Pretty heavy stuff."

He flipped through the pages of a survivalist manual, glancing briefly at the yellow flyer she'd stuck inside.

Zoe took a sip of coffee. She studied his hands as he rearranged the books from one stack to another. Long, blunt fingers and wide palms gave his hands a heavy, capable appearance. A narrow scar ran across the knuckles of his left hand. She wondered if it was true large hands were an indication of the size of a man's equipment. As soon as the thought crossed her mind she blushed.

Her companion glanced up at that moment. He studied her intently. She had the feeling he could see right through her and somehow knew exactly what she was thinking. She broke off a corner of the scone and looked out the window to the street and beyond, pretending she hadn't been wondering about the length and breadth of his equipment.

Stop it! she silently warned her wayward thoughts.

"I'm Aaron, by the way," he said and reached a hand across the table to her.

Zoe returned her attention to him, wiped her sugary fingers on a napkin, hastily swallowed the bite of scone, and shook his hand. "Zoe."

He held her hand longer than necessary. Or possibly it seemed that way to her because she'd been reluctant to let go. An odd sense of security washed over her which she found unsettling. She knew for a fact there was no security in her world. People she loved could be taken from her in the blink of an eye. Her future, which just over a year ago had seemed set and certain, was shaky and unpredictable. The only thing she'd come to count on was her phantom lover and the steady growth of her cash fund. Great, Zoe, she thought. The one person you rely on is someone you don't even know. A man you've never seen.

But she did know him. That was the weird thing. She knew him intimately and not just in the physical sense. She'd convinced herself she understood his thought process when he was with her. That he wanted more of her than occasional nights in a bed. But for some reason he wasn't able to have what he wanted.

"You're very pretty," Aaron said.

Zoe, lost in thoughts of her phantom lover once again, had to mentally shake herself. "No. I don't think so."

Aaron nodded, then reached over and lifted her chin with a forefinger. "Great bone structure." He feathered his thumb across her jawline as he turned her head to one side. Zoe shivered. "Classic profile."

"Were you an anatomy major?" she asked when he removed his hand.

He chuckled. "No. But I know beauty when I see it."

Zoe swallowed the lump in her throat. It had been a long time since anyone had complimented her for anything. Especially a male compliment on her looks. Tim had. Ages ago. Most often during or after they made love. She could still hear those whispers in the dark, remember how it felt to have a man appreciate her for the woman she was.

Before she'd sold herself to her phantom lover.

"I have to go." Abruptly she scooted her chair back nearly knocking it over. Coffee sloshed over the rim of her mug. She left her books on the table and hightailed it out the door.

"Zoe!" She heard Aaron call from behind her, but she didn't turn around or slow down. Tears pressed against her eyelids and the chilly wind did nothing to dissuade them. People passed by, uncaring, not noticing. She was invisible to them.

"Zoe." He was next to her, easily keeping pace with his long stride.

"Sorry. Thanks for the coffee." She tried to ignore him and turned a corner without warning.

"Are we going somewhere specific?"

"We are not going anywhere."

"Hmm." Still he stayed with her.

A stoplight halted their progress. She glared up at him. "Can't you take a hint?"

"What sort of hint?" He grinned at her.

Zoe wasn't in the mood to be amused by him, but she couldn't help it. She tapped her foot in imitation annoyance. "A woman bolts after you graciously buy her coffee—"

"And a scone." The light turned. Aaron took her elbow and guided her across the street.

"The hell with the scone," Zoe responded crossly. She wanted to jerk her elbow out of his grasp almost as much as she wanted to maintain the connection to him. She stopped on the other side, ignoring the grumbling of passers-by who were forced to flow around them.

"Go away. Leave me alone."

"Why should I?" Aaron challenged.

Zoe yanked her elbow out of his grasp. "Because I said so!" She started walking again, and damn it, he was still next to her.

"It was the 'beautiful' remark. You thought I was coming on to you."

That wasn't exactly what she'd been thinking but it was close enough. "Weren't you?"

Aaron shrugged. "Not exactly. I was stating a fact."

"You do realize what you're doing falls into the category of harassment? Why is it the normal-looking guys usually turn out be stalkers?" That got a laugh out of Aaron. They were passing a park. Zoe stopped again and sank onto the nearest bench. Suddenly she felt exhausted. Drained. She rubbed her hands over her face and looked at him. "Why me?" she asked wearily. Vaguely it occurred to her that she had that same thought about the phantom. Why had he chosen her?

Aaron sat next to her. A frown creased his brow. "You read. Not fluff, either. I noticed you in the current events section first. The inner workings of the CIA? Central American politics? Not too many people of my acquaintance reading that kind of stuff. I thought, now here's a woman with a brain, if she's going to tackle that. And she's beautiful, too. I'd like to meet her."

His assessment was so far off the mark, Zoe didn't even consider trying to correct him. "So you bumped into me."

"It seemed the most expedient way."

It was her turn to study him. He had to have an ulterior motive, but damn if she knew what it was.

"In my line of work, it's tough to meet people. Normal people. I thought maybe you were someone, hell, I don't know what I thought. We could hang out. Talk. See a movie. Drink coffee."

"Eat scones." Zoe smiled against all odds. "What kind of work do you do that makes it hard to meet *normal* people?"

"Mostly government work."

"What kind of government work?"

"You could say I'm sort of a trouble shooter."

"Sounds intriguing."

"It's not. Trust me, it's boring. But I do travel a lot, sometimes on short notice, which makes it tough to maintain relationships. If you know what I mean."

Zoe nodded, though she wasn't a hundred percent sure she knew what he meant.

"Can I call you? Or I could give you my number and you could call me sometime when you're in the mood for coffee. Or you need a book review."

Danger and security seemed to swirl around Aaron, but not in a way Zoe could discern which was the stronger of the two. She recalled the way she'd felt just shaking his hand. His touch on her face. Scary and good all at the same time.

And he was offering her control, leaving it up to her whether to contact him. She hadn't told him her last name. She knew she wouldn't be that easy to trace. Not unless he followed her home.

She wouldn't go directly home, she decided. If she made several stops along the way, she could check around, see if he was following her.

"If you want to give me your number, maybe I'll call." She looked into the gold-flecked depths of his eyes and did her best to control the shiver of excitement and fear that ran down her spine. "Then again, maybe I won't." But taking his number seemed the best way to placate him.

He took a small notebook and pen from his pocket and scribbled his name and phone number. He handed the slip of paper to her, and she rose to leave. He stayed on the bench. "Just for the record," she said, "there's no such thing as normal."

Aaron groaned. If he hadn't been walking along a street crowded with pedestrians, he'd have kicked himself.

He'd promised himself one chance to meet Zoe in the light of day and he'd almost blown it. He still couldn't believe it. He was a master of covert operations. He'd set up more scenarios, worked undercover long enough to know the first rule was never to let your opponent get the upper hand.

Yet he'd allowed it to happen. Zoe had all the control and he had none. If she didn't call him, he'd have lost his one and only shot at being with her as himself. He'd have to resign himself to being anonymous forever. He wasn't sure he could do that.

So clever, Manning, he berated himself. You thought you had it all figured out. The perfect relationship, with a normal woman, under cover of darkness.

What he hadn't counted on was his own feelings. Feelings he'd kept under wraps for years. Cool and controlled. In the service. Then Delta Force. And especially after Level One recruited him. His focus was always on the job. He thrived under pressure, did his best work, experienced startling moments of clarity, right when things seemed about to go haywire.

Yet this particular woman had him bumbling about, tormenting himself with questions, like some inept adolescent.

Aaron clenched his fists, so angry with himself he could hardly contain it. He hated this churning, upside-down feeling in the pit of his stomach. He hated the uncertainty. Zoe might never call him. He might never see her. He'd be left to imagine what she looked like when she was lying in his arms in the dark.

Zoe thought he was a stalker. But also that he at least looked normal. That was something, wasn't it?

No. It definitely wasn't.

Aaron hailed a cab and scowled during the short ride to Level One's operations office.

Chapter Twelve

Zoe picked up the phone and held it until her palm grew slick with perspiration. She set it down and stepped back, wiping her hand on the leg of her jeans.

She glanced down at the now crumpled slip of paper clutched in her other hand. Aaron Manning's phone number.

Stupid, she told herself. You're a grown woman. What is wrong with you?

A week had gone by. The memory of Aaron constantly teased at the corners of her mind. She had no plans to contact him. There would be no point. Yet she'd held onto his phone number. He seemed like a decent enough guy. He didn't know anything about her. Not her last name or where she lived. It wasn't unlike meeting someone online or at one of those speed dating events. She could choose a neutral location for a meeting.

Coffee. Conversation. A cinnamon scone.

In spite of herself she smiled at the memory. What would be so terrible about seeing him again? Casually. As a friend. Someone to hang out with. There was nothing wrong with wanting to see him again. She tried to assure herself that her reaction to him and his open invitation was perfectly normal, even as she realized she'd never been quite sure what "normal" was. At any rate, right now she could use a dose of anything close to normal to balance the arrangement she had with the phantom.

Before she picked up the phone again, she opened the refrigerator and gazed at the unopened bottle of Pinot Grigio. She picked it up, smoothed her fingers down the cool neck of the bottle, rubbed her thumb across the label. The bottle had been in the refrigerator over a year, a constant reminder of her choices. Nothing in her life would be as hard as losing Tim and Zach. The wine reminded her every day of her part in their deaths. There'd been no meetings for Zoe. No rehab. No hitting bottom and crying out for help. Just cold determination and the realization that everything she did involved choice. Every impulse she'd ever followed was a choice. A conscious choice. And every choice she made had consequences.

She grabbed up the phone and punched in the numbers.

"Hello?"

Oh, God. It was him. Aaron. He'd answered his phone.

"Hello?"

Zoe froze. It wasn't too late to hang up. He'd never know she called.

"555-6748, are you there?"

Shit! Caller I.D. Maybe her name had come up as well. Maybe he knew it was her. Shit! Shit! Shit!

She heard him clear his throat. Any second he'd hang up, irritated with a caller who stayed on the line but wouldn't speak.

"A-Aaron?"

"Yes?"

"It's Zoe. I don't know if you remember me from the—"

"Bookstore. Cinnamon scone. Walk in the park."

Zoe smiled at his less than accurate description of their first meeting.

"How are you?" he asked.

"I'm—I'm good." *Liar.* "How are you?"

"Truthfully? I'm lonely as hell. I was hoping you'd call. Are you going to let me buy you another cinnamon scone?"

"I'd like that."

"When? Where?"

"I could meet you at Kemp's again."

"Tonight?"

"Um, no. I have to work tonight." *And then I have to meet my phantom lover.* "How about Saturday?"

"That will work. What time?"

Her first self-defense class was in the morning. Followed by a session with a personal trainer. "I don't go to work until five tomorrow. How would two o'clock be?"

"Odd hours," Aaron commented. "What do you do?"

"I wait tables at a restaurant on the West Side."

"Ah. Two o'clock tomorrow. I'll see you then." He paused. "Oh, and Zoe?"

"Yes?"

"If by chance I don't make it, it won't be because I stood you up. It'll be because I had to travel on short notice."

"Oh. Right."

"I'm glad you called."

"Me too."

Aaron seemed pleased to hear from her, and it made her feel good. She'd be careful. As he'd said, they could hang out together, assuming he showed tomorrow. Go to a movie now and then. Meet for coffee. No big deal.

Aaron did something he hadn't done before. He made arrangements to meet Zoe Saturday night by the convenient method of slipping the instructions in with her Friday night payment. He didn't care how their book store meeting went. He wanted to prolong his time with her. Even if it was broken up by her shift at the restaurant. He'd see her twice in one day. Okay, he wouldn't actually see her both times. But he'd be with her. Twice in one day. It was almost like a real relationship. An outing during the day. Sharing the same bed that night.

He craved every moment with her. Wanted more of her. Not just under the cover of darkness. He wanted to see her. Really see her. Do everyday things, like a regular couple. Hold hands. Go for a walk. Watch a movie. Have a conversation.

Longing gnawed at his soul. He'd spent his entire life being different. Isolated. Disconnected.

Maybe, through these wild arrangements he'd made with Zoe, he'd have the chance to be something he'd never been. Something she'd told him didn't exist.

Something approaching normal.

Chapter Thirteen

"I can eliminate him now." Nick Sheppard took a drag on his Marlboro and regarded Coughlan. At one time nothing would have given him greater pleasure than to put a bullet into the meddling missionary's head. He'd seen Father Ben Dumont as an unwanted thorn in the otherwise perfect paw of the mine operation. Coughlan's insistence on keeping him alive was increasingly irritating.

But Nick had changed his tune, though Coughlan didn't know that. No, after some consideration, Nick had every interest in keeping Father Ben alive. Because if he played his cards right, the starving missionary priest was going to serve as the perfect bait to lure one specific Level One agent into Central America and onto Nick's own private playing field. And when that happened he'd extract the price from Aaron Manning for leaving him for dead on that ill-fated mission.

"Soon perhaps," Coughlan replied. "Not yet." He signaled to one of the men nearby to bring him coffee.

In the meantime, Nick entertained himself by baiting Coughlan. "It's a mistake, Father. He can't be converted and you know it."

"Some sacrifices are unavoidable. Some aren't." Coughlan replied philosophically, as he accepted a tin cup of bitter brew with a nod. "Gracias."

"He's an unwanted headache," Nick, in the mood for an argument, continued. "I say we make an example out of him right now."

"Killing the local priest will not bring the cooperation of the peasants," Coughlan snapped, his nerves already frayed by the encounter with Ben. He'd seen the contempt in Ben's eyes. It mirrored his own when he looked in the mirror each morning. But Coughlan was in too deep to turn back now. He'd set his destiny on a course long ago, believing he'd found an easy way to make a tangible change in the lives of the poor people he'd come to serve. But time had eroded that belief and though he tried not to, he saw the truth. He had not improved their lives, but he had, as Ben pointed out, encouraged them to sacrifice their souls, and in the case of some of the young women, their bodies. He saw the disillusionment in their eyes, the weight of internal conflict on their shoulders. The people were no happier and no better off than before. He'd accomplished nothing. At times he wondered if he hadn't made their lot in life worse by taking away their simple pleasures.

He'd allowed Nick to make examples out of a few of the more defiant villagers, believing at the time that it was necessary to keep the others in line, to make them understand the importance of what he was doing for them. But could he allow the execution of a fellow priest? He could no longer find that line between good and evil he used to see so clearly. In the sacrifice of the peasants' souls, had he lost his own?

"We don't need him. He's a liability. The workers are suspicious. They're getting spooked."

"They don't know what happened to him. As far as they're concerned, he walked into the jungle one day and never returned. They all know how dangerous it is outside the village."

"What about the sister Julio told us about?"

Coughlan shook his head. "Not a problem. She and Dumont grew up in foster care. They've got no resources, no family, no money, no power. She's a waitress. Julio can string her along all he wants, but she'll never come up with ransom money even if we demanded it."

"You don't know that. Maybe she's got friends. Maybe she'll borrow it. She could show up tomorrow ready to make a deal."

Coughlan gazed at Sheppard through narrowed eyes, giving him the look that used to make seminary students quake in terror. "I'm telling you it's not going to happen." He put up a hand to forestall Nick's interruption. "And if it does, by some miracle, and trust me, it *will* be a miracle, we'll let Julio and his friends deal with her."

"I still don't like it. I say let's get rid of Dumont. Permanently. So the villagers never find out. And his sister never shows up."

"When I say so," Coughlan replied firmly. "We have an agreement."

Nick frowned. They did. Fifty/fifty. One did not make a decision of major importance without the other's approval. Nick was in charge of security and mining operations. Coughlan oversaw recruitment and shipping. It was his job to keep the workers in line, to keep them content and to keep emeralds flowing out of the mine. And profits into both his and Sheppard's pockets.

They'd clashed before and Nick always backed down. He owed Coughlan his life. He never forgot that, and he knew Coughlan hadn't either. Nick's mouth twisted into a familiar bitter line as it did each and every time he recalled his abandonment by the U.S. government. More specifically, the covert operation known as Level One. That bullshit about "should a mission fail they would disavow any knowledge of an agent's involvement" turned out to be true. His team had been sent to take out a guerilla leader wreaking havoc in Honduras and threatening to topple the newly elected parliament.

Nick had strayed from protocol during the operation. He'd seen other agents do it often and get away with it. Most notably, his old buddy Aaron Manning. Yep. Aaron broke rules when it suited him, when it was in the best interests of the operation, and he had never once failed to achieve the objective. Russell Gannett let his disapproval be known, but Aaron blew off the reprimands time and time again.

There'd been no reason for Nick to think that he couldn't do the same. Except in his case, straying from protocol had spelled disaster. His team had been forced into a street fight with the guerilla security force and they barely got out of the city alive. Nick, taking one chance too many to take out as many of the enemy as possible, had been wounded. Rather than sacrifice any more of the team, Aaron gave orders to retreat without him. Retreat they had, leaving him there to die and the guerilla leader no worse for the wear.

Nick managed to crawl into a church, narrowly avoiding being picked up by the guerilla forces. He'd planned to die, huddled and bleeding in the dark on the dirt floor of the confessional.

Instead, he woke days later, his wounds bound and healing, a dark-skinned nun wiping his face with a damp cloth. She'd cried out in alarm

153

when he'd instinctively grabbed her wrist and twisted it. Coughlan had appeared then, sending the nun away and assuring Nick he was among friends.

It amazed Nick still, how he'd conveniently fallen into Coughlan's lap. The priest happened to have need of someone who possessed Nick's unique skills. For all intents and purposes, his old life was dead, as dead as the U.S. and Level One were to him. He couldn't return. Not only had his mission failed, by now his team would have been debriefed. He had no illusions. His men were loyal, not necessarily to him, but to Level One. They were all ambitious, eager, as he'd once been, to prove themselves capable of commanding their own teams. They wouldn't cover for him. He'd taken a chance and it had literally blown up in his face. He couldn't go back. And until he was ambulatory, he had no choice but to listen to and consider Coughlan's proposal.

Coughlan had discovered the mine when he'd been a missionary in one of the mountain villages. An earthquake had rocked the region, followed by the torrential seasonal rains. As he'd traveled with some of the villagers in search of food, trees and thatch to rebuild the ruined huts, he'd noticed the deep valley between two steep mountains, a cave really, more of a wide-jawed crack visible at the base where the mountainsides touched. Gravel and sandy silt had been dislodged as the earth had shifted during the quake and washed out by the rain. A small stream fueled by an underground spring washed rock and mica out of the cave in a slow dribble.

Coughlan had taken a brief look, studied the gravel, much of it buried in the thick silt. Geology had been a pet interest of Coughlan's since adolescence. He'd often explored caves near his home in North Carolina collecting mineral specimens to add to his collection. He made a note of the location of the cave, picked up several of the rough pieces, studying them covertly, hiding his growing excitement before pocketing them.

He was almost sure two of the pieces he'd pocketed held a glint of emeralds. What if, he wondered, and the rest of that day was consumed with thoughts of the discovery of an emerald mine, what it would mean to his people, the money and prosperity it would bring to them. He fantasized about building a real church to replace the mud walls and thatched roof that barely covered the altar.

He considered whether the church could claim possession of the mine. His face clouded. No. Of course not. The Honduran government would claim ownership, with its corrupt bureaucracy and faint understanding of distribution of wealth. For that matter, the governments of both Guatemala and El Salvador might get into the act for the mountainous area in question had, in years past, been claimed by all three, the border still in dispute by various rebel factions. The peasants, good, hard-working, devout, would see little or nothing of the profits of such a mine. In fact, they might be edged out of their homes to make way for housing for the government officials who'd be put in charge.

There had to be another way, Coughlan thought. His mind already working even before he knew what he had. That night, in the dim light of a single light bulb and using the crude tools available, he'd carefully chipped the mica away from the most promising looking specimen until it broke into two perfect pieces. Coughlan gasped as he held one half up to the light, marveling at the perfection of the green color of the gem.

He tried to calculate the retail value of this one piece, were it faceted and sold on the open market, and couldn't. Perfect emeralds simply didn't exist. Most were riddled with cracks and imperfections. They were heated and filled with synthetic fillings to give the impression of perfection before they were sold. Even so, the imperfect gems were worth more than diamonds.

Amazing, Coughlan thought as he turned the specimen this way and that, watching the light reflect off the green depths. Although Columbian emeralds were widely available, the rest of Latin America was hardly known for its gemstones, except for Brazil, with its deposits of tourmaline, topaz and aquamarine.

He thought of the hundreds of thousands of years the pressure of the mountains had exerted on this particular vein to create such beauty, such depth and color and clarity. Had the earthquake not occurred, another hundred thousand years might have passed with no one the wiser.

"And no one is the wiser," Coughlan had breathed as he related the story to Nick, "except me."

The phrase "sitting on a gold mine" had never had quite as much meaning as it did at that moment.

For months, Coughlan had considered how to extract the emeralds from the mine without drawing the attention of unwanted parties, either guerilla factions or government bureaucrats. The remote location of the mine was a plus in that regard, but it also made it difficult to recruit workers. Who could he trust? The villagers were fairly isolated, but would they understand the need for secrecy, for discretion? Would they talk?

Coughlan made two trips back to the area alone, bringing along a high-powered lantern and investigating the cave, taking note of the narrow interior, his hands feeling along the rough walls, searching for a vein. It wouldn't be easy, he thought, as he ducked lower through a small tunnel, to extract emeralds from this location without a professional mining operation. It would be slow work. And yet the rewards might be worth it. He thought of the money to be made. Money he would share with the poor people of the area. Money that would improve their lives, that would feed and clothe them, provide medical care, give them hope. Money that could wipe out the hopeless poverty in which they lived generation after generation.

During a brief sojourn home, he brought one of the rough stones to an old acquaintance, John Sargent, now a gem dealer in Albuquerque. As expected, the man was overwhelmed as he examined the stone beneath a large magnified light, turning it this way and that.

"Where did you get this?" he asked, his crafty gaze shifting from the stone to Coughlan and back, his tone suspicious.

Coughlan shrugged. He'd prepared an answer for this. He'd rehearsed it, decided it was plausible and shared it now. "One of the villagers gave it to me to thank me for helping his family with some government paperwork." Coughlan smiled. "I don't think he knew what he had."

"Hmm," Sargent responded, giving little indication as to whether he bought Coughlan's story or not. He turned off the high powered, magnifying light under which he'd been examining the piece, and set his loupe aside. "I'll tell you what you've got there, my friend. An emerald. Looks to be about six carats. No occlusions, which as you know is rare. If you had documentation as to the source, retail would be about quarter million."

"But without source documentation?"

Sargent handed the piece back to Coughlan who returned it to the small leather pouch he carried it in along with two slightly smaller stones. "No reputable dealer will touch them. Not without authentication papers."

"And if I can't get authentication?"

Sargent shrugged. "Then you'd be looking at the black market."

Coughlan pushed his hands deep into his pants pockets, burying the small leather pouch in the right one. "And if I were to go that route, how would I locate a dealer?"

Sargent held up his hands and took a step back from the counter. "You're asking the wrong guy, Reese." He dropped his hands and eyed the priest. "We go back a long way, so I feel I have to say this: Don't do it. The kind of people involved in the black market are not the kind of people you want to get involved with."

Coughlan knew enough to quit while he was ahead. "Perhaps you're, right. It was just a thought." He held out his hand to Sargent. "Thanks for your help, John." They shook. "I'll keep you in my prayers."

If Sargent wouldn't help him, he'd find someone who could. He'd pray for a way to help the poor, for God to bring someone into his life who would help him help them. For Coughlan knew one thing. Eventually, he could bring God around to his way of doing things.

Chapter Fourteen

"You're off on Wednesday nights, right?"

"Mmhmm."

Aaron and Zoe were strolling through Greenwich Village looking in shop windows, wandering aimlessly, enjoying the day and each other's company.

"Let me take you to dinner. Somewhere nice. Somewhere special."

"Wow, like a date?" Zoe glanced up at Aaron from beneath her lashes. The time they'd spent together the past few weeks didn't fall into the category of dating. At least not as far as Zoe was concerned. They met for coffee. Often at the bookstore. They talked. They'd gone to a movie. And talked. Strolled through Central Park one morning then had brunch. And talked.

They were companions. Occasionally, Aaron took her arm as they crossed the street. Or guided her with a hand on the small of her back when they jockeyed for space in a crowded café. But there was nothing romantic in the gestures. Aaron was a gentlemen. They were friends. Until now.

Aaron didn't smile at Zoe's teasing tone. "Yes," he said. "Like a date."

Zoe sobered. Dating meant the beginning of a relationship of some sort. A physical relationship. One she wasn't ready for. One she couldn't have. Not with Aaron. Not while she was involved with the phantom.

"I can't." She resumed her stroll and sensed Aaron reluctantly follow.

"Why?"

She'd known Aaron's presence in her life was too good to be true. It was impossible to be friends with a man. She thought of Drew. She considered him her dearest friend, but she sensed Drew's feelings for her went beyond friendship. And Aaron's might if she gave him half a chance.

She said. "I'm involved with someone."

"Involved?" Aaron was at her side now, his hands shoved in the pockets of his pants. He didn't seem angry exactly. He seemed curious. Interested. As if she'd told him her middle name.

"It's complicated, and I'd rather not explain it to you. I'm not attached. Nothing permanent will ever come of the relationship I'm involved in now. I know that. But I'm still..."

"Involved."

Zoe nodded.

"So involved that you can't have dinner with me?"

Zoe gave him a sideways glance. "I'm surprised you'd still want to."

"Why not? It's dinner. I enjoy your company. I'd like to have a meal in a nice restaurant and not eat alone."

"And it doesn't bother you that there's someone else?"

"You just explained that there's no future in that relationship."

Zoe couldn't admit to Aaron that she wished for more from her phantom lover.

"We can eat a meal together. It doesn't change anything."

Zoe stopped and faced him. She backed out of the stream of passers-by and up against a section of storefront. "Aaron, what do you want?"

"To take you to dinner."

"No. I mean where do you see this going?"

"I don't know. I like spending time with you. I like talking to you. It doesn't have to be more than that."

"Do you want it to be?"

"I can't answer that. Have dinner with me." He smiled.

Zoe turned and started to walk again. "Usually I have dinner with a friend on Wednesdays."

"A friend?"

"It's the only time I see him."

"Him?"

Zoe gave Aaron another sideways look. "He's a friend," she repeated as if he were a particularly slow child.

"A friend like I'm a friend?" Aaron asked.

"You know, usually I find it easy to be with you. Today, you're exhausting."

Aaron put an arm around her waist and tickled her until she darted away.

"I'd like to meet your friend. And I'd also like to be your friend."

Zoe sighed. She had four significant men in her life. Her brother who was missing. Drew, who had feelings for her she couldn't return. The phantom for whom she had feelings that would never amount to anything. And Aaron. She stole a glance at him. Aaron. The unknown quantity. Who claimed not to know what he wanted. She didn't believe him. Aaron was the kind of man who always knew what he wanted. And he probably got what he wanted most of the time. What she couldn't figure out was what he could possibly want from her.

"Why me?" she asked aloud. Before Aaron could become important to her, she could lose him, alienate him now, while it didn't matter.

"Why you what?"

"Why did you pick me? You bumped into me. Arranged to meet me."

"Why not you?"

He wasn't going to give her a straight answer. "I'm going home." Zoe crossed in front of Aaron and stepped off the curb to hail a cab. She hated to spend money on cab fare, but what she wanted right at this moment was to get as far away as possible from Aaron.

As usual, Aaron was right behind her. He lightly grasped her elbow as she raised her arm to signal a passing cab.

She fixed him with a look as the taxi continued past. He said nothing, but studied her for a split second before he spoke.

"Why is it so hard for you to believe that a man might be interested in you? Attracted to you?"

"We're not talking about 'a man.' We're talking about you specifically. Look around, Aaron. This is New York City. Filled with beautiful women. You could have your pick. But you chose me. You bumped into me. And I want to know why."

Aaron steered her away from the curb. There was no privacy on the street. Nowhere they could go and be alone so he could somehow attempt to answer her questions. He had to settle for escaping the passers-by as best he could and facing her next to the windows of a stationery shop.

"I thought I'd already explained this to you. The day we met in the bookstore."

Zoe shook her head. "Not good enough. Why not make your pitch to someone else, somewhere else? There are hundreds, thousands of women in this city who would be perfectly happy to spend time with you, sit in a restaurant with you and not expect anything more, and have you expect nothing more from them."

"I could ask you the same question," Aaron countered. "Why'd you call me if you weren't interested?"

Zoe had no answer for that, at least none that she wanted to share with Aaron. Her gaze stayed on his for long moments, until it seemed as if something shifted between them. Some indefinable change in the air around them, a softening of their stances, an unspoken compromise to their impasse.

Aaron reached out and cupped her cheek, his fingers sliding back into her hair. "Zoe, it's dinner."

She hadn't realized how much she craved being touched by a man she could see until that moment. She told herself it didn't matter what Aaron wanted from her or what continuing a relationship with him might bring. It was enough to feel the palm of his hand on her skin, to feel the warmth of his fingers in her hair and on her ear. But at the same time little warning bells went off inside her. She'd thrown caution to the wind when she'd taken up with the phantom. She'd created a genuine fantasy life of sorts with him. But this was her reality, the life she'd have when the phantom vanished. And she needed to take more care with it now.

"Let me think about it, okay?"

Aaron didn't quite hide the disappointment her answer brought, but he tried. He found a smile for her and said, "Sure," before dropping his hand back to his side.

Zoe felt the loss of contact and hated herself for wanting it, needing it. "I need to go home now."

Without a word Aaron stepped to the curb and hailed a cab. Handing some bills to the driver he gave him the address then opened the door for her. "I'll see you later," he said, his gaze intent, before he closed it.

Zoe stared at the back of the driver's head. How she wished she knew what she was doing. And she wished she knew why she felt so desolate at the moment. She wished she weren't going home alone. She wished she were still strolling with Aaron, things simple and easy between them. *Things are never simple and easy. When are you going to get used to it?*

She had asked Aaron the question she couldn't ask of the phantom. Why me? She didn't want to project her feelings for the phantom onto

Aaron. Or for him to bear the brunt of her frustration over a situation of her own choosing. But maybe she'd solved that problem. After her behavior just now maybe she'd never hear from him again.

Aaron was waiting for her when she got off work that night. She wasn't expecting him and tamped down that voice inside that told her she was glad to see him. When she started toward the bus stop, Aaron fell into step beside her.

He didn't say anything. Zoe didn't know what to say, even though questions flitted across her mind.

The bus arrived and Zoe got on. Aaron did, too. That struck her as funny, but she didn't know why. She hadn't realized until that moment that Aaron didn't seem like the type to take a bus.

He sat on the bench next to her, looking around in that interested, observant way he had. She wondered if anyone noticed it but her. Aaron was always very much aware of his surroundings.

He slid his hand beneath hers, sliding his fingers between hers and clasping their hands together lightly as if it were the most natural thing in the world. He didn't look at her. Skitters of deja vu rattled along the nerve endings edging her spine. She stared at their clasped hands. The phantom did that. He'd done it the first night they'd made love. And other times since, sometimes during, sometimes after. He'd link his fingers through hers. Just like this.

No. Not *just* like this. She told herself she was being ridiculous. But she couldn't stop staring at her hand linked with Aaron's. Hundreds of couples held hands this way. It was nothing unusual. It was nothing. Was it the *same* hand? The phantom's hand?

She flexed her fingers, and Aaron responded by squeezing hers more tightly. He looked at her then, at the same moment she turned to him. Their gazes connected, held. Zoe's dropped to his mouth. And even as she did it, she wondered what led her to lean forward, lift her head, touch her lips to his. And why she didn't stop after that. The simple answer was she couldn't. She hadn't guessed until that moment how much she wanted to kiss Aaron. Maybe it was because the phantom never kissed her. He made love to her until they were both sated, but he never, ever kissed her. Not on the mouth.

But Aaron did and Zoe drank it in. Tasted his lips and his tongue against hers. With her free hand she cradled his jaw.

Oh, yes, she thought. *Kiss me. Water me. Feed me.*

Passion welled up inside her. But was it for Aaron? Or would it be for any man who kissed her like this? Who gave her what the phantom deprived her of? The bus stopped. One passenger departed. Two got on.

Their kiss ended. Aaron bowed his head against hers. "Zoe," he breathed.

She wondered if he could hear her heart hammering over the sound of his breathing. She put her hand on his chest. His heart was beating faster than normal.

She giggled. He pulled back and half grinned/half scowled at her. "Witch," he whispered.

At Zoe's stop, they got off and paused in front of Zoe's building, hands still clasped.

She started to let go of his hand, but he wouldn't let her. "Dinner? Wednesday?"

"I don't know." *Can't you see I don't know what I'm doing? I don't know who I am. I don't know who you are.* One thing she knew for sure. She liked kissing him. She wanted to do it again. "I'll call you." Half-heartedly she tried to disengage her hand. She wasn't surprised when he tugged her forward.

He let go so he could hold her closer. In silent agreement they kissed, like before only better. A deep, slow exploration, a silent communication.

Chapter Fifteen

"Are you sure you don't mind?" Zoe asked again.

Drew frowned. "Zoe, it's fine. What's with you tonight?"

"I don't know." Zoe got up to pace, wringing her hands, something she never did, but couldn't seem to help. She didn't know what she'd been thinking to invite Aaron to her Wednesday night dinner with Drew, even though Drew himself had insisted. Afraid to trust her own instincts perhaps, she wanted a second opinion. Drew was more worldly. Drew radiated skepticism. He knew how to ask questions, how to trap people.

Was it because she didn't trust Aaron? No, it wasn't that. It was the feeling that there was more to Aaron, much more, than met the eye. He was always alert, on edge, almost. More highly aware of his surroundings than even the most vigilant New Yorker needed to be. At the same time, she always felt safe with him.

Oh, face it, Zoe, she scolded herself. You don't know what you're doing. Between agonizing over Ben, running herself ragged at the restaurant most nights and juggling meetings with the phantom, she couldn't seem to think straight.

Maybe she wanted Drew to do her thinking for her. Gather impressions of Aaron, and tell her what he thought, so she could compare it against her own inadequate yardstick.

The intercom buzzed. Zoe whirled around. Her eyes shot to Drew. "That's him."

"Yes," he responded dryly, watching her. "I imagine it is."

Zoe stepped outside Drew's apartment after she buzzed to let Aaron in. Her insides tingled, perhaps because of the memory of Aaron's kiss the other night. Somehow that seemed to change everything.

Aaron stepped off the elevator, one arm wrapped around a large paper sack from which tantalizing food scents escaped. His other hand clutched both the neck of a wine bottle encased in a brown paper bag and a bouquet of flowers.

Zoe was already smiling at the sight of him, but when she saw the flowers she beamed. He grinned at her as he stepped closer.

"Here, let me carry something," she insisted, automatically reaching for the bouquet.

He held out the wine bottle, twisting his wrist so that the flowers were away from her. "You can carry this. The flowers are for Drew."

She froze in surprise, her gaze returning to his. He was trying not to laugh at her startled expression. "Come here," he whispered. He bent his head and kissed her, lightly, once and then again. "Just kidding," he said softly. "The flowers are for you."

"People are starving here." They both looked around, to find Drew framed in the door to his apartment, arms across his chest, a witness to their brief exchange.

Zoe forced herself to relax. Aaron followed her and Drew rolled back into his apartment. "Drew Warner, Aaron—Aaron—" Zoe frowned as she blanked out on Aaron's last name.

"Manning," he supplied, handing Zoe both the flowers and the wine so he and Drew could shake hands. "Thank you for including me."

"Don't thank me. It was Zoe's idea." And then, as if realizing how that might have sounded, Drew added in a jovial tone, "Of course, when she said you offered to buy dinner, I was all for it."

Both men chuckled politely. Maybe Zoe's idea to have Drew and Aaron meet was nothing more than a prelude to disaster. She indicated the bag of food Aaron still held. "What is this? It smells wonderful."

"Thai," Aaron said. "I hope that's okay."

Both men followed her to the kitchen. She rummaged in a drawer for a corkscrew and handed it to Drew. She found glasses in his cupboard and set three on the table. She filled a tall pitcher with water and fussed with arranging the flowers, then began to set the food out.

"Sit, Aaron. Otherwise you're in the way."

Aaron took one of the two chairs and Drew slid a glass of wine in his direction. Their eyes met, while Zoe, oblivious, set out plates and silverware. Drew wheeled himself to his place and Zoe sat.

Drew regarded Aaron from behind his glasses, his gaze intense and inquisitive. He tilted his head to one side. "Have we met before?"

Aaron scrutinized Drew. "No. I'm sure I'd remember."

"Hmm." Drew remained non-committal. Then, as if realizing he was being rude to Zoe's guest, he relaxed and smiled. "Sorry. For some reason, you look familiar."

"Drew, you meet so many people. You couldn't possibly remember them all," Zoe interjected. "After a while I bet everyone looks familiar to you."

She softened her words with a smile, hoping to set both men at ease.

"Aaron, Zoe tells me you're a consultant doing work for the federal government."

"I think the word I used was trouble-shooter," Aaron said easily.

Drew helped himself to noodles in peanut sauce. "In what way?"

"Any way that's needed. I pretty much go where they send me, try to diffuse potentially troubling situations."

"What department do you work with most often?"

Aaron met Drew's gaze head-on. "Defense."

"Hmm."

"Here, try the vegetables," Zoe said to Drew passing the container his way. She stared hard at her glass of wine, twirling the stem of the glass with her fingers. "The wine looks wonderful."

"Where are you from originally?" Drew asked Aaron.

"The Midwest."

"Drew, you don't have to interview him," Zoe said, patting his hand to once again soften the words.

"No, not at all. He's your friend. I'm interested."

"To tell you the truth, my life is pretty boring," Aaron said. "Not really that much to tell." He sent Zoe a look. "Although it's getting more interesting all the time."

She smiled, pleased, then concentrated on her food.

"How did the two of you meet?" Aaron asked, directing the question to both Zoe and Drew.

"In the elevator, actually." It was Drew's turn to smile. "Zoe was trying to hang onto Zach, her purse, and about six bags of groceries."

"I still had use of my legs, then," Drew informed Aaron.

"He offered to help me carry something."

"I ended up with Zach. Squirmy little thing he was."

Zoe sent Aaron a weak smile. She hadn't exactly told him that she was widowed, that both her husband and son were dead.

"We kept running into each other after that. Started hanging out. And then, well, when I was in the hospital, Zoe was a lifesaver. I don't know what I would have done without her."

Drew turned in Zoe's direction, his eyes warm, his smile affectionate.

"And now it's Wednesday night dinners," Aaron said into the momentary quiet.

Drew's head whipped around at that. "It's more than that, actually." His tone held a hint of steel.

Aaron said nothing, but sent Drew a look, as if to say, *Is it? Then why am I here?*

Zoe wanted to dissolve into her seat, ooze down the legs of the chair and disappear into the floor. This had been such a bad, bad idea. She felt like a choice hen being plucked by two rival chefs. Whoever ended up with the most feathers would win.

She gazed at the glass of wine, feeling her appetite dwindle. She hadn't wanted to let Drew down by canceling Wednesday dinner with him.

But she'd also wanted to see Aaron again. She wanted Drew's impression of Aaron. And maybe she wanted to send Drew a clear message. Letting him witness her interest in Aaron would perhaps dissolve his hope that one day their friendship would become something more. She'd been selfish and now was paying the price. It was a thoughtless and cruel thing to do to Drew.

Aaron and Drew were addressing their plates, eating in silence, making no attempt at further conversation. In another life, Zoe thought, these two might have been friends. She poured the last of the wine from the bottle into Aaron's glass and added the contents of her glass to Drew's. Then she held her empty glass up in silent toast to the two of them.

She remembered well the days of drinking herself into the warm fuzzy solace too much alcohol provided so she wouldn't have to deal with her life. She'd sought an easy escape, where all her questions had simple answers. Too much wine hadn't provided an escape. It simply made her existence more solitary.

Abruptly, she set the glass down, and pushed it away. The glass hit the table harder than she'd intended, and both men looked up. Her gaze shot to Drew. Then she looked at Aaron. "I don't drink."

She got up, opened the refrigerator and uncapped a bottle of mineral water trying to hide her distress. Typical Zoe, she told herself. She hadn't had a drink in over a year. But oh how she'd wanted that glass of wine tonight. She could blame it on Aaron's presence. The distraction of having him here, when it had been just her and Drew every Wednesday for over a year. *No, Zoe, it isn't Aaron's fault. You can't drink and you know it. It always ends badly. For everyone. Remember that.*

She sat back down and looked around wildly. She couldn't look at Drew. Didn't want to look at Aaron. "This was a bad idea," she said to no one in particular.

Dead silence reigned and then both men burst into laughter. Just like that the tension evaporated. Zoe had no idea how it happened.

"What are you working on these days?" Aaron asked Drew once they'd stopped chuckling.

"A couple of things. One you might find interesting."

"Oh?"

"I started looking into the disappearances of missionaries in Central and South America."

"Really?"

Drew nonchalantly swallowed a bite of shrimp before continuing. "In the past five years, a dozen priests have disappeared or been murdered. One has to wonder why the church continues to send them into those areas, knowing the danger. Especially in light of the shortage of priests. Most of the factions responsible for either kidnapping or killing them are of the belief they're not there to improve the spiritual lives of the faithful, but rather to spy for the U.S. Government."

Aaron sat back, arms crossed over his chest. Even Zoe picked up on his defensive posture. Her ears pricked, alert for any reaction. "And you think this would interest me because?"

Zoe had heard Drew's theories before, although she'd found it hard to believe that Ben might be a spy. Drew seemed to think it was possible, but Zoe knew subterfuge wasn't Ben's style. She'd never known him to have a hidden agenda. What you saw was what you got with Ben. His only desire in becoming a missionary was to help souls less fortunate that he. And Drew couldn't come up with a reason why Ben was being kept alive, either. His capture didn't seem to fit any particular pattern. If he'd been caught spying, surely he'd have been killed.

But tonight she saw a twinkle in Drew's eye. Something was going on with him as he purposely dangled the bits and pieces of research he'd strung together for Aaron's perusal. She had the feeling he was toying with Aaron and wondered if Drew had any idea how dangerous that might be. Dangerous? Her head swiveled back to Aaron.

Aaron had never seemed threatening before. He seemed...capable. Excessively capable. Of handling anything. Or anyone.

"Well, as a *trouble-shooter* for the U.S. government, I thought you'd be aware that this is a problem."

"Surely not all the priests or missionaries are American?"

"Not all, but most. And most have affiliations with orders based in the U.S. What's even more surprising is that a rather high percentage, eight out of the twelve, had links to organizations suspected to be fronts for the CIA."

"Are you saying the priests really are sent there to spy?"

Zoe noticed Aaron didn't seem too surprised by Drew's revelation. He seemed annoyed that Drew had figured it out, however.

"Weren't they?" Drew asked.

Aaron spread his hands in a gesture of innocence. "Hey, you're the investigative reporter. You tell me."

"I will. As soon as I'm done digging. What's even more interesting is the church's apparent lack of concern over the disappearance of its priests."

"The church is setting them up?" Aaron's tone held a note of disbelief.

Zoe's head bopped between the two of them as she tried to pick up on what they weren't saying to each other. There was a swirl of silent communication between these two. Drew was telling Aaron something without using words and Aaron was sending a signal that sounded like "message received."

Drew twirled the base of his nearly empty wineglass. "Setting them up might not be the right term. It's no secret the Catholic Church has been battered from all sides recently. They've had to pay out some huge settlements in a number of abuse cases at a time when revenues have dropped considerably. Coinciding with that is a great deal of unrest, and terrorist groups and pockets of insurrectionists in just about every corner of the globe. What better way for the CIA or any other branch of the U.S. government to gather information, especially in Third World countries than by sending in what look like missionaries. Especially Catholic priests. Recruit the priests, make a large donation to the church in exchange. Priests are exceedingly loyal. They probably see it as their duty to help Mother Church and themselves as instigators of peace by sending information back about anything they pick up in the course of their mission. Illegal arms. Drug shipments. Secret mining operations."

"Mining operations?"

"I've uncovered what looks like at least one. Emeralds, my friend. Sold on the black market.

Some of the best in the world. The government of the country knows nothing about it and those in charge want to keep it that way."

"You're saying if a missionary happened to stumble across an illegal mine—"

"Possibly guarded and/or operated by individuals who are clearly not native to that particular country—"

"They'd do anything to silence the priest."

"The priest, the villagers, their own people." Drew maneuvered around the table to the counter and filled the kettle with water. Setting it on the stove he lit the flame beneath.

"Interesting theory," Aaron said, relaxing back into his chair.

"I think it's more than a theory," Drew informed him. "Too much evidence points in the same direction. You know the old saying, 'where there's smoke—'"

Aaron's gaze snagged Zoe's. "There's fire."

The rest of the evening passed pleasantly enough. Zoe and Aaron offered to clean up but Drew's strenuous objection prevented it. Before they left, Zoe leaned down to embrace Drew and kiss his cheek. "Thank you," she whispered. Drew trailed his hands down her arms as she rose and squeezed her hands in his. Over Drew's shoulder she caught Aaron watching the two of them with unabashed interest. But he smiled easily enough when Zoe caught his eye.

Drew closed the door behind Aaron and Zoe and wheeled back into the kitchen. As always, he imagined the scent of Zoe hung in the air, clung to his senses. It wasn't a definitive scent, either, not flowery or spicy or even especially aromatic. He wasn't even sure it was perfume. Maybe it was the combination of her shampoo and soap, or whatever toiletries she used. Drew had no idea, but the combination always left him feeling a little high.

Normally, after their Wednesday night dinners together, Zoe insisted on cleaning up, but tonight he had shooed her away. Straightening the kitchen would give him something to do. Otherwise he'd dwell on the fact that Zoe had found someone else.

He'd always known she would, but he couldn't help being in love with her. He'd fallen hard and fast, the first time he'd seen her, nearly tripping in her haste to get to the elevator before the door closed, juggling a toddler, an oversized handbag and several plastic grocery sacks.

He remembered everything about that day. She'd been wearing a baggy fisherman's sweater and black jeans. The blue of the sweater made the light blue of her eyes look like the ocean. Wisps of hair had escaped from the clip that held a topknot in place. She'd looked young and defenseless, trying to keep it all together.

Zach had been no help at all. He'd wanted down. He wanted to push the button. He'd fought her hold and grabbed at her sweater before Drew had the presence of mind to say, "Here, let me help." Not normally comfortable with small children, he'd lifted Zach out of Zoe's arms and into his own.

"Hey, sport, what are you doing?"

Zach had regarded him with his own set of blue eyes from beneath dark blond bangs. He'd reached for Drew's glasses. Before he could damage the expensive frames, Drew carefully removed them and set them on Zach's nose, then turned to show Zach what he looked like in the speckled mirror wall of the elevator.

Zach had chortled with laughter and when Drew turned back to Zoe, she was smiling. His heart, with a mind of its own, shot straight to her, and there it had stayed all these years. He'd introduced himself then, followed her up to her apartment that day until she got Zach safely inside. Later, of course, he'd met Tim. The four of them had spent time together on occasion. Zoe would invite Drew up for pizza or if Tim was working late or at class, sometimes they'd watch a movie with Zach.

Drew kept his feelings for Zoe to himself. When he'd been hospitalized the first time, she had visited, fussing over him. The second time, when he'd lost the use of his legs, she'd been distraught on his behalf. Somehow, her care and concern made what happened easier to deal with.

After Tim and Zach had been killed, it was Drew's turn to do his best to comfort Zoe. He'd helped her with funeral arrangements, been there through it all, then he'd watched her withdraw, powerless to help her. She'd given up her teaching job and began working at the restaurant. Even he could see she was just going through the motions of her life, mourning in her own way. She'd shown no signs of moving on from the tragedy.

Until tonight, he thought sadly. He wasn't blind. In a matter of weeks, Aaron had gotten through to Zoe in a way Drew couldn't. They were more than 'friends.' Or they would be soon. Even Drew could see that.

He loaded the plates and utensils on a tray and transported them to the sink. Then he went back to the table and with a heavy sigh, gathered the leftover food cartons, discarding some and storing others in the refrigerator.

Loving Zoe had never been easy. Lately, he'd taken less care to hide his feelings from her, but it made no difference. Either she didn't want to know, or she simply wasn't interested. Maybe both, he thought sadly. He wasn't man enough for her. He was a cripple.

He turned back to the table and did something he rarely allowed himself to do. He put his head down on his arms and cried, letting the pain and disappointment and loneliness he usually kept at bay wash over him.

There was one thing he could do for Zoe, that maybe no one else could do. He could help her save Ben. Her beloved brother. She wouldn't accept his financial help, but maybe there was something else he could do, another way he could contribute.

He pulled off his glasses and wiped his eyes. If he couldn't have her love, maybe he could have her gratitude. Maybe that would be enough.

Chapter Sixteen

"Do you want to come up?" Zoe asked Aaron as they waited for the elevator. It seemed rude not to invite him, even as she tried to decide if she wanted him in her personal space. What if there was a white envelope filled with cash lying beyond her door?

Aaron glanced at his watch, one of those chunky utilitarian ones with lots of inset dials and buttons along the side. "I'd like that, but I can't stay long," Aaron said as the elevator arrived.

"Sure." Zoe stepped on with him, trying to decide if she was disappointed or relieved that he'd made it clear he wouldn't be there long.

Never had Zoe felt so torn. She wanted Aaron to leave almost as much as she wished he'd stay. She craved his kiss even as she felt like she was cheating on the phantom. Maybe if she split herself in half she wouldn't feel disloyal to either of them.

At her door she said, "I don't know why I wanted you to meet Drew. It seemed important, somehow. I'm not sure exactly why."

Aaron took the key from her, unlocked the door and stepped inside. She'd left the light in the small living room on. Aaron did a quick visual sweep of the room, before stepping aside so she could enter, picking up the thread of conversation as if there'd been no interruption. "Hey, I enjoyed it. He seems like an okay guy. Even if he does have a thing for you."

"No, he doesn't." The denial came automatically to Zoe's lips. Then she looked into Aaron's eyes. "Okay. He does."

"It's pretty obvious."

Zoe sighed. "I know. Drew's friendship is really important to me. I don't want to hurt him."

"So you pretend you don't know how he feels." Aaron slid his arms around Zoe's waist.

"I don't know what else to do."

"Sometimes you have to be cruel to be kind." He kissed her and she forgot about Drew and the phantom and Ben. She forgot everything as she wrapped her arms around Aaron's neck and gave herself up to the kiss. God, she had missed this. So simple. A kiss. But even though the phantom's lovemaking left her physically sated, simply kissing Aaron was somehow more satisfying. She relished the sense of safety she found in his arms. The way he explored her, absorbed her. Completed her in some way she couldn't quite define.

She liked the way he made her feel, like he was constantly guarding her, although from what or whom she couldn't have said. She knew next to nothing about him, but she felt safe with him.

Nothing bad was going to happen while Aaron Manning was around. She didn't quite understand why the feeling of safety he gave her also made her suspicious of him. She couldn't see the whole picture, couldn't get a complete view of Aaron. He showed her what he wanted her to see, and though she hadn't made much of an effort to dig deeper, on some level she wanted to. She could see why he had a hard time connecting with people, why relationships never lasted long. He kept parts of himself well hidden. She eased out of his embrace.

"Would you like coffee?" She started toward the kitchen to make some, not because she wanted any, but because her thoughts made her fidgety and she needed something to do.

"Not particularly," Aaron replied, following her. "But if you do, don't let that stop you."

Zoe held up at the counter and turned. "No, I wanted to give myself something to do." Her gaze met his and he stepped closer.

"Why?" He asked, his voice low and filled with humor. "Do I make you nervous?" He gave her a quick light kiss on the lips.

Zoe's confusion mounted. "Yes. No. I don't know."

He placed a hand on either side of her, blocking her in, his body squarely planted in front of hers. "Well, that's definite."

She tilted her head back to look up at him. "I feel safe with you," she admitted. "Though that makes no sense, since I hardly know you."

"And I hardly know you," Aaron reminded her, conveniently turning the conversation in her direction. "You don't drink?"

Zoe's eyes clouded and she dropped her gaze for a moment before meeting his once again.

"You don't have to tell me if you don't want to," Aaron assured her, though in truth he was wildly curious.

"No, it's okay." Zoe eased out of his stance and he followed her to the sofa. She curled on one end, a leg tucked beneath her. Aaron settled on the other end, his body turned toward her.

"I'm surprised you didn't ask before. When Drew mentioned Zach. I used to teach kindergarten. Seems like another life, but it's only been about a year since I quit. I—uh, I was married and I had a son."

"Zach," Aaron acknowledged.

He reached for her hand, rubbing his thumb over the back of it. "It's okay, Zoe, whatever it is."

Zoe fought for control. Hadn't she cried all the tears she could for Tim? And especially for Zach, her baby still, in spite of everything.

She cleared her throat. "It wasn't easy for me and Tim. We hadn't exactly planned on starting a family so soon. Money was tight, Tim was still in school, and we were wedged into this apartment." She gestured at the tiny space. "The three of us. I was teaching and taking care of Zach. Tim was going to school and waiting tables. We were hardly ever together. I was exhausted all the time, felt like I couldn't keep up. I found a glass of wine in the evenings soothed me, I didn't feel so tense and frustrated. Sometimes I had two glasses. During the week, anyway.

"But on Friday nights, the longest night, because of course, Tim worked every Friday night, I'd tuck Zach into bed and finish the bottle. Sometimes I'd start another bottle."

She shrugged. "It seems stupid now. But at the time, what I knew was that I was alone a lot. I taught small children all day and came home to a small demanding child, and I hardly ever saw my child's father. I only had to hang on for another year, and Tim would be through school, he'd get a good job, and things would be easier. I told myself that, but in the meantime, I thought I needed to drink to get through it. So I did.

"One Saturday morning, Zach had a birthday party to attend. He was up and excited about the party, and I was so hungover I could barely move. I told Tim he had to take Zach to the party. Of course, Tim was exhausted and he didn't want to do it. But he wasn't hungover. We had a huge fight. I yelled at him about it being the least he could do for his own child since he never did anything else.

"They left and I went back to sleep. The next thing I knew someone was pounding on my door." Zoe's bottom lip quivered. Her words came out in a rush. "It was the police. They said Tim and Zach were dead. Killed by a hit and run driver."

"Oh, Zoe." Aaron pulled her onto his lap, into his arms, bowing his head over hers, stroking her back.

"That's the last thing I did. I yelled at my husband that he was a lousy father, and I refused to take my son to a birthday party. Because I drank too much the night before." Her words were muffled and tear-filled, though she wasn't crying.

"That's why you don't drink," Aaron said with a sad smile, easing his hold on her a bit. Her declaration was what had broken the icy tension between him and Drew earlier.

He continued to hold Zoe, stroking her back. She was pliant in his arms and he marveled at how good it felt to be able to hold her, listen to her, talk to her, comfort her. He feathered his fingers through the silky strands of her hair, breathing in her scent.

"I'm sorry about Tim and Zach," he told her. She couldn't know he was apologizing on a much deeper level. The level where he felt responsible for their deaths. But it still felt good to say the words to her.

She nodded but said nothing. She wished she could confess her guilt, but it didn't seem appropriate to do so with Aaron. She'd been a lousy wife and an even lousier mother. That was the truth she'd had to face when she'd surfaced from her alcohol-induced haze to face the police at her door. She'd loved Tim and she'd loved Zach, but she hadn't appreciated them. She'd been too bogged down in her own needs to take proper care of anyone else. Guilt gnawed at her. She couldn't ask Tim and Zach to forgive her, and no one else was going to.

Aaron wondered how long she'd let him hold her, how long they could stay like this. It wasn't quiet. There were muffled sounds of movement and conversation from the neighboring apartments. Car noises from the street below. The hum of the refrigerator and the tick of the wall clock. But it was like being inside a cocoon, just him and Zoe, locked together.

His gaze strayed to a nearby book shelf scattered with pictures and what looked like mementos of some sort. A framed photo of a young boy stared back at him, an impish look in his eyes. Next to it was an infant's pacifier and a small pair of sneakers. A tattered copy of a Dr. Seuss book lay next to a toy truck.

A shrine of sorts. For her son.

He glanced to the shelf above, which was similarly laden with pictures and mementos. Tim Bradford looked much as Aaron recalled he had.

Medium build, dark hair and glasses, a boyish, studious look to him. On his shelf were books, an autographed baseball, a set of keys, a diploma and other bits and pieces of a life. Small things, insignificant things, perhaps. But Zoe had kept them, displayed them, refused to let herself forget.

Her telephone rang, shattering the relative peace. She jumped as if she'd never heard the sound before, her head bumping Aaron's chin. "Sorry," she whispered, her eyes worried as she scrambled away from him and snatched up the phone.

"Hello?" she said. "Yes. Yes. Julio, thank God. Hang on one second.

She held the phone to her chest. "Aaron, I'm sorry, I have to take this."

He took the hint and stood, taking the few steps that were necessary to reach her. She stared up at him, her eyes huge and questioning. He framed her face in his hands and kissed her thoroughly, feeling her relax into the kiss before it ended.

Then he left.

Before she turned her attention back to the phone, Zoe stared at the space he had occupied before the door closed, registering the fact that her earlier mix of dread and anticipation had been for naught.

There was no envelope.

Chapter Seventeen

Zoe.

Ben came awake from a brief, fitful sleep trying to hang onto the edges of another troubling dream. Like smoke, the dream escaped, leaving him only with troubling thoughts of his sister.

He thought about her constantly, and wondered how she was doing. He'd written to her often when he'd first arrived in Santa Rosaro. He'd been excited about his work, had sent her long rambling letters about the village, the accommodations, Julio and the other villagers, especially the children, the culture. The news of Tim and Zach's death had hit him hard. He'd felt all right about leaving the States knowing Zoe was surrounded by her family. But after the accident, she was alone again, and that worried him. Zoe had always been much too isolated. And she had no faith. That troubled him, too.

They'd both endured painful childhoods, but Ben had found God, who cared about him and who took all his troubles as his own. Ben had found the peace and comfort he sought in a higher power. He'd tried to share it with Zoe, but her bitterness ran too deep. The hurt and abuse she'd suffered at an early age, especially the abandonment, first by their parents and then by the juvenile system had left her in a place Ben couldn't seem to reach. It saddened him, that while he could touch the lives of strangers in his congregation and now in this remote mountain village, he couldn't bring God into the life of the one person he loved more than anything on earth.

Nightly he prayed for Zoe, that someone would come into her life, help her to find her way to God, help her to have faith. He wanted peace and happiness for Zoe, because each letter he received spoke to him of her sadness and isolation. He knew Zoe better than anyone. What she didn't say was as telling as what she did. She'd abandoned her teaching career for a job as a waitress. Being around young children had been too painful. She holed up in her apartment when she wasn't working, and except for Drew Warner, whom Ben had met on a couple of occasions, she had no close friends.

Unbeknownst to Zoe, Ben had taken it upon himself to write to Drew once, shortly after Tim and Zach died, asking him to look out for her and to contact him if anything unusual occurred. Then he'd written to Drew a second time, more recently, after he and Julio had first spied on the mine. He'd debated the wisdom of doing such a thing. Had waited to mail the letter until he'd been able to arrange a rare visit to Chiquimula.

Even now, as he laid here cramped and uncomfortable on the hard ground, the cool mountain mist edging around him, sinking into his bones and making them ache, he wondered if Drew had received that letter. Perhaps it had been intercepted. Perhaps his captors had been privy to it. What if they knew he'd tried to get information about their operation to the outside world?

Then why am I still here? He asked himself, as he did several times a day, since his capture. Why haven't they killed me yet? What good am I to them? Ben had no answers. The mind-numbing fight for survival kept him from going over the questions too often. The rest of the time he spent in prayer. For himself. For his captors. For Drew. For Zoe. And for that other nameless, faceless person God would use to save them all.

Aaron was more keyed up than usual as he waited for Zoe to arrive. This is how it would be, if only he could have what he wanted, the one thing that seemed to elude him. A life. Like tens of thousands of other men. A simple life. A wife, a home, a family.

He'd have Zoe. Every night. Fixing dinner. Smiling at him over the heads of their children. After bath time, they'd read stories to the little ones and tuck them in bed. They'd have a life together, all the time. Not the way it was now. In bits and pieces, surrounded by secrets and darkness.

He'd come to hate setting Zoe up with these clandestine meetings almost as much as he craved it. The simple act of being with her, touching her, pleasing her, making love to her. What he didn't know was if she knew it was him whether she'd react the same way. What if he never found out? That was the thought that tore him apart. If he told Zoe the truth, impossible as the likelihood of that was, she might hate him forever, banish him from her life, never forgive him. He wasn't sure he'd ever be ready to take that chance. As difficult as the current situation was, it was better than nothing. Better, much better, than losing Zoe for all time.

She arrived at the appointed time as always. He watched her exit the car and hurry up the steps. He hoped she was as keyed up as he was because their encounter earlier had whetted her appetite the same as his.

He didn't wait as long as usual to join her. It didn't matter if she was awake or not when he arrived since she couldn't see him.

A half hour later, he was next to the bed. He thought she had fallen asleep, but he heard her shift positions, felt her waiting for him to join her. He shucked his clothes, already rock hard. She slid into his arms, her breasts pressed against his chest. He kissed her throat, raked his fingers through the silk of her hair, held her tight against him. More than anything he wanted to kiss her mouth, as a prelude to making love to her. Wanted to mimic the exploration of her body with his tongue. Exerting his iron will he fought the urge. This is all you can have of her. Right here. Right now. He groaned silently.

He wanted more.

He lost track of how long he held her, his erection pulsing between her thighs as they caressed each other with hands and lips and tongues, always carefully avoiding each other's mouth. He'd thought he'd have to have her immediately, without foreplay, but once in her arms, that was enough. For the moment at least. Touching in the dark was their way of communicating in silence. Aaron soaked up every nuance of Zoe's exploring fingertips, the way the palms of her hands glided across his skin as if she were memorizing him.

He was being pushed, like a hapless swimmer in waves too big for him. Desperate now, Aaron sensed that soon everything would come crashing down on him. Hadn't he been clever setting Zoe up, paying her to meet him this way? He'd found his soulmate, but he'd never have her. Not the way he wanted. Not completely. Not forever.

Clever, clever Aaron Manning, who never needed anyone, had refused to need anyone since childhood. He'd toyed with women in the past, used them and discarded them without a second thought. Karma. That's what it was. Coming back to haunt him. Just as he deserved. He now stood to lose the one woman he wanted. He had the connection he'd sought for so long with another human being, and through his own doing, he'd lose her.

Sadness settled over him as he held her. He buried his face in her shoulder, drank in the scent of her skin, drew her even tighter, if that were possible, against him.

She shifted, rubbing herself along the length of him, her mouth open against his shoulder. She kissed and licked her way toward his neck, moving up to explore the curve of his ear, nipping the lobe. Offering him her breast. He took the distended nipple into his mouth, sucking hard, sinking his teeth into it, sharing his pain with her. She gasped and he became relentless, waiting until she whimpered before moving to the other one, giving it the same treatment, handling her rougher than he ever had, angry at himself even as he did so.

He had no illusions. He could tell by her reaction, she was as turned on as he was. He got her on her back and used his tongue and his teeth on her everywhere, suckling and nipping at her, mixing pain with pleasure. Between her legs she was hot and wet. He spread them wide, pushing her knees up, opening her, then jabbing the tip of his tongue against her repeatedly, feeling her pulsing with arousal. Then wanting only to please her, he did that, too, gentling his touch, flattening his tongue, teasing her, letting the sensations build and build, bringing her higher and higher until she came wildly, violently beneath him.

He could tell she'd covered her mouth with both hands, forcing back the cries of ecstasy. Revulsion washed over him. He kept her from being herself. He kept himself from having all of her. Even here and now, he only had part of her. He forced her to contain herself, to hold back.

Manning, you think too much.

Almost resignedly, he reached for the condom, opened it. Zoe's hand covered his and his movements stilled. She deliberately removed the package from his grasp and dropped it over the side of the bed. She tugged on his arm, her message clear.

Aaron hesitated, hardly able to believe what she was offering, what she was telling him. Her hand slid down, she grasped his cock firmly. And finally, thankfully, his mind shut down. He stopped thinking and gave himself up to pure physical sensation. Consequences be damned. If Zoe wanted him, no barriers between them, he'd let her have him. Burying himself inside her was like a form of sweet torture. He wanted it to last forever almost as much as he craved immediate release. He forced himself to slow down, savor this once-in-a-lifetime opportunity.

He rolled to his back, the one surefire way to slow the pace.

If only.

Zoe picked up her own rhythm, moving slowly, sensuously, tantalizingly against him, even while she continued to use her hands and mouth on him, caressing his chest, kissing his neck, his shoulders, sweeping her tongue across him, dropping sweet kisses on his face, everywhere but his mouth.

Aaron stood it as long as he could before rolling her beneath him and fucking her hard, slamming into her, wondering who he wanted to punish more, her or himself. He bit his lip, drawing blood as he came. Pain kept him silent.

Chapter Eighteen

Zoe wobbled home in the morning trying to discern what had happened between her and the phantom last night. She felt raw and achy both inside and out. More than anything she wanted to curl up into a ball and cry, to alleviate an almost overwhelming sense of sadness.

She'd had unprotected sex with him. She couldn't quite come to grips with that, even though she knew full well it had been her own doing. What had happened between them? There had been a few tiny drops of blood on the pillow. Dried now, but she knew it hadn't been there last night. It wasn't hers. She'd been marked, but he hadn't drawn blood.

She closed her apartment door behind her. Her whole body drooped with exhaustion.

Who am I? What am I doing? She sniffed, fighting back tears. In her bedroom she stripped off her clothes and examined her reflection in the mirror. Her body wore the marks of a rather brutal encounter. Her nipples were rose red and ultrasensitive. Tiny bruises dotted her here and there. Between her legs she felt swollen, but in a good way. If the phantom were here right now, she knew without a doubt she'd do it all over again.

That was the most shaming part of it all. She turned on the shower and sat on the toilet, her head in her hands.

She had no shame when it came to the phantom. She was completely at his mercy, completely under his spell, and she didn't care. He'd aroused some part of her she hadn't known existed. Some wanton, sensual creature appeared in the all-encompassing darkness. There she existed only for his pleasure. No, that wasn't quite true. She existed for her own pleasure as well.

It's more than sex.

No, it isn't, she argued with herself as she stepped under the spray. She had to stop imagining that the phantom felt something for her. That they were somehow communicating through their physical encounters. It didn't matter what she felt. Women were always more emotional when it came to sex. For men it was just sex. With a faceless, nameless female. Easily forgotten. It meant nothing to him. As often as she told herself this, she couldn't quite believe it was actually true.

Who is he? Last night, after they'd made love, she'd been tempted to chuck it all, race across the room and hit the light switch. Finally, she'd have her answers.

But then she considered what she stood to lose by discovering the phantom's identity. For one thing, the money. She didn't fool herself. Life had vastly improved as she built her nest egg. Ben's rescue fund. She felt more confident than ever that she could find Ben on her own and bring him home. Julio stayed in touch with her, phoning at least once a week, sometimes more. Ben was still alive. Captive, starved, beaten, but alive. That's all that mattered. Julio knew where he was. Grateful for his help, she'd wired money to him, knowing his life couldn't be any easier than that of the other villagers.

The kidnappers had agreed to negotiate Ben's release for American dollars. Julio assured her this was so. But each time he called there was a subtle question. How much longer? How long would they continue to hold Ben, to keep him alive? How much money was enough? Julio refused to give her a dollar figure, claiming that would be negotiated with Ben's captors when she arrived.

Soon. Very soon, with Julio's help, she would find a way to get Ben back to safety. Back to civilization. And everything she'd done, every sacrifice she'd made would be worth it. She'd let Tim and Zach down and she'd lost them. She wouldn't make that mistake again.

But there were other reasons she didn't pursue discovering the phantom's identity. A part of her wanted to cling to the fantasy. A part of her didn't want to know, didn't want to be disappointed.

How could he disappoint you?

She rinsed shampoo from her hair. She had no idea. Except that he'd be a flesh and blood man like any other. And right now, he was much more than that.

Even with the emotional highs and lows of the roller coaster she was on, she recalled only too well her existence before the phantom. She'd gone through the motions, but she had been dead inside. She'd died the day Zach and Tim had. And a little more when Ben had disappeared. Guilt had eroded what life was left.

That's what the phantom had done for her. He'd given her hope. He'd made her feel. Made her remember she was alive. If she discovered his identity, she might lose all she'd gained.

Always at the back of her mind she could hear Ben's voice, the words he'd spoken to her over the years about how God existed, that he answered prayers. She'd never believed it, but she'd been so desperate and scared for Ben, that she'd prayed anyway, to that God she swore to Ben she didn't believe in. Justifying it to herself. What could it hurt? If there was no God, she was the only one who knew she was praying to him. And if he did exist he'd either help or he'd ignore her. Turn his back on her the way she'd turned hers on him all these years.

And that was the biggest part of the reason she avoided pursuing the phantom's identity. He was the answer to her prayers. She was sure of it. She'd prayed for a way to save Ben. A way to finance a rescue. With no hope, she'd prayed to a nameless, faceless God. And into her life had entered the nameless, faceless phantom. He'd exacted a high price, but God had given her what she requested. Money. A lot of it. Sent through the phantom.

So she kept praying. For God to keep Ben alive until she could get to him. For her relationship with the phantom to continue until she had enough money. For God to help her find a way, people to help her, to actually go in and get Ben out. And slowly, somehow, she'd begun to believe in that God Ben had been preaching about to her for years. For if it wasn't God, what other explanation was there?

The one thing she never asked God for was forgiveness. Even though Ben had assured her there was no sin God wouldn't forgive if the sinner were truly penitent, Zoe didn't buy it. How could God forgive her when she couldn't forgive herself?

She toweled off and wrapped herself in her bathrobe just as she heard a knock. Belting the robe tightly she padded to the door and peeked through the peephole. It was Drew. Maybe he'd seen her come in this morning. He kept odd hours. His apartment faced the street.

Oh, God, she had no idea how often he had seen her dragging herself home at dawn. What must he think?

Still feeling a little confused and vulnerable, she undid the locks and opened the door.

Drew gazed at her from behind his glasses, his perceptive eyes taking in every detail from head to toe.

"I was about to make coffee," she lied. "Want some?"

She turned away from him, afraid of what he might see or guess if he looked at her too long, and headed into the kitchen. He closed the door and wheeled into the room behind her, stopping at the opening to the narrow galley kitchen where she was measuring coffee into the filter.

"You okay?"

She glanced at him for a second before concentrating once again on coffee preparation. "Of course. Why wouldn't I be?"

"I was up this morning, working on a story that's been driving me crazy. I saw you come in." He hesitated. "You looked like you had a rough night, like you got beat up or something."

He was fishing for information, Zoe knew, in his subtle, tell-me-what-I-want-to-know, investigative reporter style.

Zoe shrugged, afraid if she tried to answer she'd lose the fragile hold she had over her self-control. She simply couldn't break down and tell Drew the truth, couldn't bear the disgust and disappointment she'd see in his eyes.

She busied herself pretending to look for specific coffee mugs, though Drew knew she only had a few.

"Is it Aaron?"

She swung around, surprise making her speak without thinking. "No! Of course not. Why would you think that?"

Drew looked uncomfortable but he plowed on stubbornly. "Because he's the only guy you've brought around since—since—the accident. And the two of you seemed—"

Drew's gaze slid away and Zoe's heart turned over. He was hurting. For her. Because of her. Whatever she did these days seemed to be the wrong thing. The last person on earth she wanted to wound was Drew. Yet he seemed to be her unintended target at every turn.

"Seemed what?" she asked gently, genuinely curious to learn how she and Aaron appeared to be.

"I don't know. Close. Chummy. Like you're," again he hesitated. "Involved," he finished, never taking his gaze off her.

Zoe shook her head. "We're not. Not like that."

"Then what—"

Zoe shot him a warning look.

"I know. It's none of my business."

She turned to pour the coffee and brought it out to the living room. Drew wheeled close to the table and she handed him a mug.

"Drew, I'm a big girl. I can take care of myself."

"I can't help it. I see you dragging in at all hours. I know something's going on. You've changed."

She took a sip of coffee, wary of continuing the conversation but curious nonetheless. "Have I? In what way?"

Drew's keen eyes studied her for a minute. "I'm not sure. You're more sure of yourself, maybe. More definite."

"Definite." She chuckled, loving that description. It made her think of a fuzzy picture on a television that needed adjustment. The right amount of tweaking resulted in a sharp, clear image. Is that what the phantom had done for her? Put everything into sharper focus, made her more defined? More sure of herself?

"Well, I've been working out, you know. She raised her arm and flexed her bicep, though it was covered by the sleeve of her robe. "Maybe that's it."

"It's more than that, and you know it."

Drew didn't like the way she was evading his questions, but she had no intention of satisfying his curiosity, either. She leaned forward. "Drew, please don't worry. I'm not endangering myself. No one's abusing me. Maybe someday I'll be able to explain it to you, but I can't right now. You have to trust me."

Drew nodded and sipped his coffee, but he didn't look convinced.

Chapter Nineteen

"Come up with me. I'll make coffee."

Since the night they'd had dinner with Drew, Zoe hadn't invited Aaron back to her apartment. Their dates normally concluded with some intense kissing outside the door to her building.

Nonchalantly, he loosened Zoe's arms from around his neck, much as he loved the feel of her body pressed up against his, the way she hugged him when they parted.

He'd spent years honing his instincts and learning to trust his gut. Every nerve ending he possessed was sending him a message. He was in trouble.

Zoe dug through her bag for her keys. The hair on the back of Aaron's neck stood up.

Someone was getting ready to make a move. While he stood a better chance of survival inside the building than out in the open, if he went inside with Zoe, she would be in harm's way. But what if he tried to draw them away and they went after Zoe anyway? Was she safer with him or without him? He knew the answer to that. He needed to determine the strength of the threat.

"I can't stay long." He needed to know who was after him and how many there were before he figured out how to elude them. And he'd rather make that determination with a wall between him and them.

He had no time now to contemplate how being with Zoe was making him less vigilant. She was a distraction he welcomed, but if he wasn't careful, she'd be a deadly distraction.

He stepped behind her, trying without seeming to, to look around, study the street, plan an escape route.

Outside her apartment, Zoe paused and flipped through her key ring for the apartment key.

Once inside, Aaron closed the door, then slid the chain across and opened it a tiny bit, watching and listening. Zoe went into the kitchen. He could hear the sounds of coffee preparation.

He was about to close the door when he caught sight of a shadow creeping up the stairs. His heartbeat quickened, the familiar rush of adrenaline poured into his veins. He'd learned to control his fight or flight response long ago, waiting until the last minute, making the surprise move, catching his opponents off guard.

The shadow turned into a dark-eyed, dark-skinned male dressed American style in jeans and a leather jacket. He heard the man whisper in

Arabic to a cohort on the landing below and quickly translated their intent.

Noiselessly, he closed the door, and held it in place as he slid the dead bolt home with barely a sound.

"What are you—"

He spun around and clamped a hand over Zoe's mouth, holding her close to him. He maneuvered her into the bedroom. She didn't resist and he didn't know whether to be pleased that she trusted him so much, or disappointed when she didn't put up more of a fight to his manhandling.

He put a finger across his lips and removed his hand from her mouth. "What?" she queried silently.

He put his mouth to her ear. "Trouble. We need to get out of here. The fire escape."

Aaron locked the bedroom door then moved the curtain aside, quickly looking up and down though he could see little from this angle. Doubtful they'd be covering the fire escape, but he couldn't be sure. Zoe's chest of drawers sported small wheels and was situated next to the door. It was an old trick, but Aaron shoved it in front of the door. At the very least it would slow down his pursuers. Already he imagined running feet as his would-be assassins amassed in the stairwell, ready to storm Zoe's apartment door.

He could see only a slim wedge of the street from the bedroom window. He'd cursorily cased Zoe's place weeks ago, just in case. He had a pretty good idea how to get away. He couldn't risk leaving Zoe here.

He drew back the curtains and removed the bar that held the wrought iron gate in place over the window. Unlocking the window, he lifted it. It protested mightily and loudly. He heard a knock on the door and motioned for Zoe to step out onto the fire escape ahead of him.

She did and he followed, just as he heard the unmistakable whoosh of a bullet sent from a gun sporting a suppressor aimed at the apartment door lock.

"Up," he urged. "Hurry."

Zoe did as he told her and he was grateful she didn't question him.

He withdrew a Sig Sauer from an ankle holster and clambered up behind her.

They reached the roof of the building. Aaron could hear the voices of their pursuers, their feet on the metal grates as he and Zoe ran to the far side. A three foot gap separated them from the roof of the building next door.

"Jump," he told Zoe.

She jumped, stumbling when she landed. Aaron hauled her up and hustled her to the building's fire escape which he knew let down into the alley below.

This time he went first, let the last rungs down and caught Zoe as she lost her footing. Shouts and curses rained down, along with the sound of feet on metal.

Aaron didn't look back. He kept Zoe close to him, wishing her legs were longer, wishing she could run faster. Down the alley they ran, splashing through puddles and dodging garbage cans and dumpsters.

A bullet whizzed by, spurring Aaron to move even faster. They reached the end of the alley. Once around the corner, Aaron dared a glance back. Their pursuers, at least six of them, were racing down the fire escape. When they reached the ground they would probably separate, fan out, try to cut off escape routes. At least two of them would take the route Zoe and Aaron had.

Aaron thought quickly. The street was deserted at the moment. He grabbed Zoe's hand and positioned her in the corner of a recessed doorway. "Stay here. Don't scream."

He pressed himself back into the corner furthest from the mouth of the alley. He listened and waited, slowing his breathing, calming himself in preparation.

He heard the footsteps, knew there were two of them. When they stepped out of the alley he'd have but a split second to take them both out as they paused and decided which way to go. His finger flexed against the trigger.

One more second.

One more.

Now.

He stepped out. They saw him and raised their weapons. Amateurs, Aaron, thought, as they stood close together, making them easy targets.

Ping. Ping. Two shots. Even in the murky light afforded by the nearest streetlight, his aim was perfect.

Before the two dropped with a thud, their guns clattering on the sidewalk, Aaron put another bullet in each.

He turned back to Zoe. Her hands were clamped over her mouth, her eyes wide with terror and a million questions. But when he held out his hand to her she took it without hesitation.

Zoe's panic receded after she and Aaron zigzagged several blocks at what was, for her, full speed. His steps slowed to a brisk walk, and Zoe, panting beside him, had no doubt he knew exactly where he was going.

He hailed a passing cab and after a last glance around the street they were on, followed her inside. He gave the driver an address. Zoe sat back trying to catch her breath. Aaron showed barely any sign of exertion.

By the time her heart rate had returned to some semblance of normal, the cab stopped.

Aaron paid the driver and opened the door. "Come on."

She followed him a short distance down the block where he stopped next to a black sedan. He punched in a code on the number pad next to the door handle to unlock the car. "Get in."

Zoe complied even though questions pummeled her brain like a boxer using a speed bag. First, she wanted to feel safe. Then she'd ask her questions. Not that she didn't feel safe with Aaron. She'd witnessed his competence at escaping even when outnumbered by armed thugs. Rather, Aaron's sense of urgency communicated to her that now was not the time for conversation.

From beneath the console next to the steering wheel, Aaron produced a set of keys. He started the car and drove in silence out of the city. He zigzagged through lanes of light traffic, took several exits and doubled back through side streets. Zoe had seen enough movies to know he was making sure he wasn't being followed. For a while she watched through the back window to see if any other cars made the same moves, but none did. Exhaustion seeped into her bones as the rush of adrenaline receded. She glanced Aaron's way several times to see him concentrating on his driving. He appeared deep in thought.

Her questions tumbled out all at once. "Where are we going? Who were those people?"

As they left the city behind, Aaron looked at her for the first time, the glow of lights from the dashboard illuminating only half of his face, as if he'd been split in two. "You okay?" he asked.

Zoe nodded. A lump formed in her throat because more of the questions she wanted to ask had congregated there but none could get through. It occurred to her that she didn't want him to answer the questions, too afraid she wouldn't like the answers.

Aaron picked up one of her hands and slid his fingers through hers. He raised their joined hands and kissed the back of hers. The breath caught in her throat. She stared at their clasped hands. A jolt of warning shot through her. Or was it recognition?

She thought of the phantom. He hadn't contacted her for a few days. Had he tired of her? Was he away? It wasn't unusual for several days to go by without hearing from him. The longest had been ten. And then it seemed he made up for lost time, arranging to meet several nights in a row.

She covered the top of Aaron's hand with her other one and leaned back in the seat. Suddenly she felt so weary. Tired of her life. The constant questions that never seemed to have satisfactory answers. As they continued to drive, she fought to stay alert, but the white lines they passed on the dark road lulled her. She closed her eyes. Just for a minute, she told herself. He still hadn't answered her questions.

When she woke Aaron was pulling the car into a darkened garage. He killed the engine and except for the quiet tick of it cooling, they were surrounded by silence and darkness

Zoe jumped when Aaron opened his door and the interior lights of the car came on. "We're okay. It's safe now," he said.

She opened her door and he came around to help her out. She leaned against him. Her eyes were gritty and her mouth was dry. The warmth of his body infused her with a sense of security, however. For now, for a little while at least, she could relax.

Aaron fumbled in the drawers of a small cabinet nearby and extracted a key which he fit into a door. Fingers to his lips, he indicated to Zoe to stay put before he opened the door and disappeared inside. The night air was cool, and Zoe rubbed her upper arms while she waited.

Her earlier questions resurfaced. She yawned, knowing as tired as she was, she needed some answers before she'd be able to sleep again.

Aaron returned and held the door open for her. She stepped inside an old-fashioned kitchen. Metal cabinets lined the walls except where they were broken up by a porcelain sink, refrigerator and stove. A chrome and speckled turquoise table and matching vinyl-covered padded chairs occupied the middle of the room. A small light burned over the stove. The room smelled old and slightly musty from a decided lack of fresh air.

"Hungry?" Aaron asked as he opened the refrigerator door and peered inside.

"Thirsty," Zoe replied.

He opened a cupboard door and found a glass, ran water from the tap and handed it to her. She drank, then set the glass on the counter. "What is this place?"

Aaron removed an old-fashioned set of metal ice cube trays from the freezer, ran water over them and pulled back the lever to snap them apart. He rummaged in the cupboards until he found a bowl and dumped the ice cubes into it. "Want some ice?"

Zoe declined.

He put ice in a glass and returned the rest to the freezer. Into the glass he poured from a bottle of lemon-lime flavored sports drink he'd extracted from the refrigerator. He drank half the glass before he answered her.

"It's a farmhouse. A place where we'll be safe."

He picked up his glass again.

"You mean like a safe house?"

He drained his drink and set it on the counter. "Yes," he said. "It's a safe house."

"Wow." In spite of herself, Zoe was impressed. "Like in the movies."

Aaron chuckled without humor at her comment.

"Why do we need a safe house? And who were those men—those men." It was as if she'd erased the better part of their narrow escape earlier in the evening. But the memories flooded back in full force. "You—you shot those two men."

Aaron's gaze never left her face.

"You killed them."

"If I hadn't we wouldn't be here," he said dryly.

"But—I don't understand." She rubbed her eyes. "None of this makes sense."

"I need some rest. So do you. Come on." He started down the hallway to the left of the kitchen.

"I need some answers," Zoe told him. "And a bathroom," she added as an afterthought.

"Right here," he answered. He pushed open a door halfway down the hall and flicked on a light. Zoe watched him open another door and go in. She assumed it was a bedroom.

She darted into the bathroom and closed the door. A chipped basin stood on a pedestal, a plug dangling from a chain. The old toilet was spotted with stains, but otherwise functioned fine. A claw footed tub took place of honor in the small room, its porcelain faded and scratched. A more modern hand-held shower had been quite obviously added at a later date along with a shower curtain on a circular rod.

Zoe flushed the toilet then splashed cold water on her face and washed her hands. She stared at her reflection in the mirror as she dried off. Her hair hung in thin strands. The skin beneath her eyes looked bruised and her eyes were bloodshot.

She turned out the light and went down the hall to the room she'd seen Aaron enter. A small light burned on a nightstand by the bed. Aaron was lying face down on top of the covers, his head turned toward the door. He patted the empty area next to him.

Zoe crossed to the bed and nudged her shoes off. She laid down on her side and faced Aaron. "I need to know—"

He put a finger against her lips. "You need to know what's going on. I'll tell you. I'll answer all your questions. But not tonight."

"But—" she spoke against his fingers.

He smoothed the lank strands of hair back from her face. "Not tonight." His tone told her she wouldn't get any straight answers out of him if she pursued it right now. "Get some sleep. Tomorrow I'll explain everything."

Her eyes locked with his. God help her, she believed him. "Promise?"

She saw the flash of his smile in the dim light. "Promise." He leaned forward and pressed a kiss against her forehead. "Go to sleep."

Chapter Twenty

Zoe came awake to a familiar pressure across her side. *The phantom*. But it couldn't be. There was light in the room, the misty gray light of early morning. And she was fully clothed.

Cautiously she glanced over her shoulder. Aaron. Of course it was Aaron.

But he was lying on his side behind her, his arm draped across her waist. *Like the phantom*. Don't be ridiculous, Zoe, she told herself. Lots of people slept on their sides with their arm flung out next to them.

She turned to face him. He in turn shifted to his back. He was no longer touching her. She studied him in the dim light. His closely cropped hair was slightly mussed. Though his features were as relaxed as she'd ever seen him, she wondered if he every truly relaxed. He was overly observant, always watchful, constantly alert. Was that because incidents similar to last night happened often?

She feathered her fingers through his hair. Was Aaron the phantom? The phantom had short hair. Was the texture and the length the same? Frustration nibbled at Zoe. Millions of men could have a hairstyle similar to Aaron's. Maybe the

Phantom's hair was black, or red instead of dark blond like Aaron's. How would she ever know?

She scooted closer and laid her head on his chest. His heart thudded steadily in reassurance beneath her ear. I'm here. I'm here, it seemed to tell her with every beat.

"What are you doing?"

Zoe wasn't startled by his voice. "Listening to your heart beat."

She picked her head up and looked into his eyes. Were those the phantom's eyes? The greenish gray flecked with golden brown? She could ask him: *Are you the man I've been sleeping with anonymously for the past couple of months? And if so, oh, by the way, I'm in love with you.*

How could she ever explain the phantom to Aaron? Or to anyone for that matter.

There were no answers in his eyes, that's for sure. He gazed back at her as if he had nothing to hide. But surely he had lots to hide. He'd killed two men last night. Outside she could hear rain begin to fall, a light pitter patter which quickly built into a steady downpour.

She laid her head on Aaron's shoulder. Idly he lifted a lock of her hair and let it fall, just like the ph—

No. She wasn't going to think about that.

"Do you think there's any coffee here?"

"I'm almost sure there is."

"I could make some."

"Mmm. Later." He pulled her closer to him. Zoe buried her face in his neck. She could fall in love with Aaron. If not for the phantom. She had to think about something else. "Those men. You shot those men," she choked out.

"I know. But if I hadn't, they'd have killed me. And you, probably." Aaron sounded bleak.

She chanced a glance up at him, but his eyes were closed, his expression blank.

"You're not really a consultant, are you?"

"Not really."

"You're a...spy?"

He laughed dryly without humor. "Not exactly."

"Then what do you do?"

"I fix things."

"Computers? Refrigerators?"

"Situations," Aaron replied.

"Situations? Like international incidents? Those men were not from around here. From what little I saw I'd say they were from somewhere in the Middle East. Part of a terrorist cell?"

"Hand the lady her prize."

Aaron shifted so that they were face to face. He tucked a stray strand of Zoe's hair behind her ear. "You're so damn smart."

She smiled at the surprise compliment. "It wouldn't take much of a genius to figure out those guys were foreigners with one glimpse like I got."

"Don't sell yourself short," he replied intently.

She stilled the motion of his wrist with one hand. "Aaron, what's this all about?"

"Coffee first." He sat up, swung his legs off the bed and scrubbed his hands over his face.

"You're avoiding answering my questions even though you promised you would," she reminded him.

He turned. "And I will."

With that he left the room. She listened to a door close and the unmistakable sounds of bathroom use. Within minutes the door opened and she heard his tread recede toward the kitchen. How odd, she thought. He slept all night without taking off his shoes.

Aaron measured out coffee and filled the carafe with water while trying not to think about anything, which was next to impossible. In a small corner of his mind lurked the thought that he'd spent the entire night in bed with Zoe. He'd woke up next to her this morning. The memory of the experience filled him with pleasure.

Her head on his chest or buried in his neck was such an intimate gesture, something a wife might do with a husband. His heart twisted painfully at the thought. He didn't see how he could ever have a marriage like that, with a woman who trusted him. A woman who loved him. A woman who *knew* him.

He planted his hands on either side of the counter and stared out at the dismal weather while the coffeemaker gurgled and dripped. Zoe wanted answers. Somehow he'd have to give them to her.

When he heard her exit the bathroom minutes later he poured coffee into two mugs. The earlier bedroom intimacy had evaporated. He saw her hesitate before sliding out a chair at the table and accepting one of the mugs. She wrapped her hands around it and sipped.

"Hmmm. Strong. Good." She tried to smile at him when he took the seat adjacent to her, but her smile faltered.

He didn't know how to begin. That wasn't true. He didn't want to begin. He wished he and Zoe could stay here together forever, insulated from the outside world, protected by a veil of bad weather. Untouchable, that's what he wished they were.

Abruptly he shoved back his chair, opened the freezer, and surveyed the contents. "Want some toast or a bagel? There are waffles in here."

"I'm okay for now," she replied. "I want to know who you are."

Aaron wished he were on a game show. Beep. Next question please. "Can you start with something easier?"

"You promised to answer my questions. You promised to tell me the truth," Zoe reminded him mildly.

You can't handle the truth. Jack Nicholson in A Few Good Men. Completely appropriate.

"I don't know who I am. That's the truth. So ask me something else."

"You're angry."

You're damn right I am. Jack, Jack, where are you when I need you, Aaron thought desperately. "I'm angry because I put you in danger. And now I've put myself in the position of explaining to you why that happened. And somehow I have to do that without compromising the people I work for."

"Who do you work for?"

Why had he promised to answer her questions? *Because you want to*, came that niggling of his sub-conscious. *You need to. You need to tell somebody. And you trust Zoe. Admit it.*

"I work for a branch of the federal government," he told her carefully.

"The United States government?"

He nodded.

"The Department of Defense?"

"Does it matter?"

"I guess not. But that's what you told Drew. I'd like to know if that was the truth."

Of course she'd like to know. And he'd like nothing more than to tell her. But he couldn't.

"The men last night..."

At last. Something he *could* answer.

"I'm pretty sure they were part of a splinter group fashioned after ISIS. A bunch of loose cannons who tried to make a statement a year ago by blowing a hole in the side of one of our destroyers while it was docked in Yemen. I had an unpleasant encounter with their leader which ultimately led to his death. His followers, the men last night, were looking to even the score."

"How did they find you?"

"That's a very good question."

"What do we do now?"

"Another excellent question." Zoe frowned and that made Aaron smile. "It's raining. We could go back to bed."

"What would be the point?"

"Another excellent question."

He got up and opened the freezer again and withdrew a box of waffles. "Want one?"

Zoe still didn't look too happy. "If there's syrup."

"I'll check." He found a bottle in the third cupboard he opened and set it on the table.

"I'll have one."

Aaron set four waffles in the toaster oven and pushed the lever.

"Why do I still feel like you haven't told me anything?" she groused.

"I've told you the important stuff."

"Unh-uh. Not about what you do. Not about who you are."

He found utensils in a drawer and put them on the table. He braced himself on the table and leaned toward Zoe. "Tell you what. Let's eat and have our coffee. And then we'll go back to bed and talk."

Zoe didn't like Aaron's evasiveness. Or the way he tried to distract her to avoid answering her questions with any real concrete answers. But she wouldn't know if he was telling her the truth anyway. Maybe he was making everything up. But she had this overwhelming urge to trust him, to believe him. Zoe looked into the depths of his eyes and capitulated. "Okay."

He leaned closer, touched his lips to hers, closed his eyes. He wanted, oh, how much he wanted this domestic scene. A simple breakfast without who he was or what he did coming between them.

He eased out of the kiss to find that Zoe'd closed her eyes, too.

Aaron wanted to immerse himself in domesticity and forget about everything else. But everything else continued to tease at the edges of his mind while he set the table with plates and utensils and poured more coffee. The refrigerator held a tub of margarine and he put that out, too.

He figured he had until about six o'clock tonight before the alarm went out that a Level One agent was missing. After the bodies of his pursuers were identified, it wouldn't take long for the agency to put two and two together. They knew about his arrangement with Zoe, which meant they knew where she lived. They'd know conclusively that he was involved in the shooting as soon as they ran ballistics tests on the bullets. He'd disappeared and so had Zoe.

He had to contact them whether he wanted to or not. If he didn't they'd be checking every safe house in the system and they'd locate him within 24 hours anyway.

The toaster oven dinged and he removed the waffles to a plate and set it on the table.

After they'd eaten and straightened the kitchen, Aaron took Zoe's hand. She gave him another one of her questioning expressions, but she followed him back to the bedroom.

Rain continued to pour from sad gray clouds. A damp chill pervaded the farm house. Fully clothed with the exception of shoes they buried themselves beneath the quilts. When Aaron drew Zoe to him she came willingly, snuggling close and putting her head on his shoulder. A lump swelled in his throat, but he tamped it down. He couldn't afford to be emotional about any of this.

"Tell me," she said softly.

"Tell you what?" He picked up her hand and idly played with her fingers.

"Anything. About you. Your childhood. Anything."

"Well." He traced his index finger between and around each of hers from thumb to pinkie and then began to do it in reverse. "I was ten when the state took me from my parents. Technically, they took me away from my mother, who was a heroin addict by then. My father was already in prison for armed robbery and manslaughter."

He released her hand and tried to slant a look down at her. "Are you sure you want to hear this?"

"Mmhmm." She wiggled closer and hugged him.

"I got lucky. I got adopted by a couple old enough to be my grandparents. Good people who'd already raised four kids of their own who were grown and gone. They didn't want a baby. They wanted someone to love. Iris and Sam Manning. Good people." Aaron cleared his throat. He hardly ever thought about his adoptive parents any more. They'd died within a couple of years of each other more than ten years ago. He hadn't realized how much he missed them until now.

"I was too smart for my own good. School wasn't much of a challenge, so I began looking for other diversions. Building things, fooling with my chemistry set. I blew the door off the garage when I was fifteen using an explosive device I'd made from instructions in a book.

"That's when Sam and Iris decided to take some action. Put me in another school, where I'd supposedly be more challenged."

Zoe chuckled. She angled a look up at him. "Were you?"

"Yes and no. Socially, yes. I never fit in with the other kids, so that was a challenge. Even though I played sports and was good at them, and I was making good grades, I never felt like I belonged. Know what I mean?"

"I know what you mean."

"Academically, that school was probably the best thing that ever happened to me. Good teachers, college prep atmosphere.

"After West Point, I went into the Army Rangers and then Delta Force. And then I was recruited by—for my current position."

He paused but when Zoe said nothing, he went on. "We go into situations that wouldn't be sanctioned publicly by the federal government."

Zoe repositioned herself with her head on her pillow, still close to him, but no longer touching. "But didn't you say you work for the federal government?"

"Yes."

Aaron turned on his side to face her.

"You're part of something that pretends you don't exist?"

"That's one way of putting it."

"Like *Mission Impossible*? If you're caught they disavow any knowledge of your mission?"

"Kind of like that." *Exactly like that.*

"Hmm." Zoe considered this for a moment. "So what kind of things do you do?"

"I'd rather not answer that."

"Spying?"

Aaron shrugged. "Sometimes."

"Stealing sensitive documents from foreign governments?"

Aaron said nothing, but stared unblinking into Zoe's eyes.

"Assassinating unpopular dictators? Toppling undesirable governments? Infiltrating insurgent factions? Rescuing hostages?"

Aaron didn't answer. As he knew it would, his silence spoke for itself.

Suddenly Zoe's eyes widened. She covered her mouth with her hands. "Oh, my God," she whispered. Then louder, "Oh, my God!"

"What?"

"You can help me. I can't believe it. You can help me!"

"Help you what?"
"Rescue my brother."

Chapter Twenty-One

"Rescue your brother?"

"He's being held in Central America. Honduras or Guatemala, I'm not sure which. In the mountains along the border. He's a priest. His name's Ben."

"And what makes you think I can help?"

"Because that's what you do."

"I'm not a mercenary, Zoe. I don't act alone. I go where I'm told and do what I'm told to do. I don't pick my assignments."

"Oh. Of course. I don't know what I was thinking." Zoe's disappointment was almost too much for Aaron. He saw tears gather in her eyes, and he wished he could rescue her brother. Anything to give her back even a small part of what she'd already given him.

He slid an index finger beneath the palm of her hand where it was curled on top of the quilt and caressed the back of her hand with his thumb. "Tell me about it."

When she looked at him her eyes were bright with unshed tears. "When you said before that you never felt like you belonged, I knew exactly what you meant. That's what foster care does to a kid, I think. Except I wasn't as lucky as you and neither was Ben. Ben was twelve and I was nine when we went into the system. Our grandmother had custody of us before that. I don't even know whatever happened to my parents. My mother was—unstable to say the least. She had no sense of responsibility. I don't know if she knew who fathered the two of us. She disappeared when I was five. Then my grandmother got cancer and she couldn't take care of us. It was only supposed to be for a little while, so she could undergo chemotherapy, and then she'd get stronger and take us back."

"But it didn't happen that way?" Aaron squeezed her fingers.

Zoe shook her head. "No. She died about two years later. She'd come and see us when she could, but it was almost worse when she did because it would get our hopes up that she'd take us with her."

Zoe sighed. "I hated foster care. If it hadn't been for Ben looking out for me." Zoe shuddered. "I don't know what would have happened. He was always there, protecting me.

"We both got jobs as soon as we turned sixteen, saved our money. When Ben turned eighteen he started working full-time and got an apartment and became my legal guardian." She sniffed. "He was so good to me.

"Somehow we got into college. Eventually Ben went into the seminary and I got married.

"I met Tim in college. For the first time I felt like I belonged somewhere. I belonged with him. I started teaching kindergarten when I got out of college. Tim was getting his master's and working full-time. We had Zach."

She looked past Aaron or through him maybe and her voice took on a distant tone. "They were both killed. By a hit and run driver over a year ago."

"I know," Aaron said softly. "You told me." He smoothed his hand over her hair.

At the comforting gesture, Zoe cleared her throat and forced back the tears that wanted to fill her eyes. She'd cried for too long over things she could do nothing about. "I couldn't go back to work. I couldn't face other people's children. I got the job in the restaurant instead." She shrugged. "The money's okay and I only have to deal with adults most of the time."

"And Ben?" Aaron asked.

"Ben wanted to be a missionary. After he saved me, he wanted to save the rest of the world. I couldn't believe they'd send him on a mission so soon after he became a priest, but they did. He was so happy. So excited. Spreading God's word. Helping the poor." She shook her head. "I never understood it. I still don't. God wasn't there when we needed help.

"But Ben had more faith than I did. Almost as soon as he got there he started sending me letters hinting that something wasn't right in the village. I think he started to investigate whatever was going on."

"Drugs?" Aaron suggested.

"I don't know for sure. I stopped getting letters over six months ago. And then, Julio, who was Ben's assistant called me to say Ben had been captured and was being held."

"As a hostage?"

"No. Whoever is holding Ben never contacted anyone about a ransom. Not the church, not me, not the U.S. government."

"Are you sure—never mind."

"What?" Zoe asked. "That he's still alive?"

Aaron nodded, his gaze locked with Zoe's.

"Julio believes he is. He's seen him a couple of times since he was taken, but they move him around a lot." Zoe gazed over Aaron's shoulder as she had before, her voice changed. "I think I'd know, somehow, if Ben were dead. I'd feel it. I'd sense it." Her gaze came back to Aaron. "Like how twins sense things about each other."

"But you're not a twin."

"I know, but Ben and I, we're connected. I can't explain it. Maybe it's because of how close we were growing up. After we went our separate ways, I'd think I needed to call him and he'd call me or vice versa. If he was having a tough time, somehow, I'd know it and he'd be the same with me. We think alike. We'd finish each other's sentences. Have you ever had that kind of connection with someone?"

"No."

"I know he's still alive. I have to get to him before it's too late. I have money. I've saved a lot of money—"

"How much?"

"Thirty thousand."

"How'd you do that?"

Zoe couldn't tell Aaron about the phantom. She couldn't explain her decision to sleep with an anonymous male for money. She wanted Aaron's respect. Almost more than she wanted his help.

"Why does that matter?" she asked, as Aaron had before in answer to one of her questions.

"I guess it doesn't."

Zoe folded her hands under her cheek. "What about women?"

Aaron grinned. "What about them?"

"I was married. What about you? Girlfriends? Wives?"

"No wives."

"But girlfriends?"

Aaron turned onto his back and stared up at the ceiling his hands under his head. "It never works out. I'm not cut out for the long haul, I guess."

"Never? What about before me? No one special?"

"There is this one woman. But it's— complicated."

He turned his head to look at her. "Did you ever feel like you were with someone, but they don't really know you? The real you? Like they only know part of you?"

It took Zoe a moment to start breathing again. Aaron had so neatly defined her relationship with the phantom, for a moment it took her breath away. But he'd also described the way she felt about Aaron. She didn't know who he was. Not really. She only knew a part of him. She stared at the flecks of brown and gold in Aaron's eyes, mesmerized by them. "And you wonder if they knew everything about you, whether they'd be able to accept it?"

"Yes."

"And maybe it's better that they don't know, because otherwise you might lose them?"

"Yes." Zoe had the strongest sensation that Aaron was trying to tell her something. He was sending her a message, but she couldn't decipher the code. Was Aaron the phantom? "Aaron—are we talking about the same—"

"This woman, I think she knows me better than she thinks she does. And when I'm with her, it's the only time I feel at peace, you know?"

"But she doesn't know about your line of work?"

"Not really. Sometimes I don't think she's ever really seen me. She sees only what she wants to see."

"Oh, Aaron." Zoe moved closer and pressed her lips to his. "If she only knew." His arms came around her to hold her tightly against him. He nudged her lips apart and Zoe responded the way she always did, as if she couldn't get enough of him kissing her.

This is what he wanted. To be with Zoe, in the light, not in the darkness. To see the look in her eyes, to not only feel her beneath him but to see what she looked like, how she was, how they were together.

He rolled her to her back. She locked her arms around his neck. He was ready, fully aroused, and by her response, so was she. He slid his hands beneath her sweater, electrified by the feel of her warm bare skin beneath his fingertips. He wanted her. God, how he wanted her.

He covered her breasts with his hands. He grazed his thumbs lightly over her erect nipples through the thin material of her bra, heard the breath catch in her throat.

He held back the groan of longing that swelled inside him. He opened his eyes, ruining the magic of the kiss, but he had to see her, see how she looked when she wanted him.

As if he'd been doused with cold water, the moment he broke the kiss, he knew he couldn't make love to her. Even as she opened passion-filled eyes and gave him one of her questioning looks, her brow puckered in non-comprehension, he knew somehow, he had to gracefully back off.

"I can't do this," she whispered.

He hadn't heard right. *She couldn't do this?* "What?"

She scooted away. "I can't. There's—a man. A relationship. Sort of. I can't do this."

Aaron was stunned. "You're that involved with the guy you said you had no future with?"

"It's—I can't explain it, except to say it wouldn't be right. With you. Here. Now."

Well, hell. She had to be talking about *him*. Her anonymous lover. Unless there was someone else. Either way this was turning into a complicated lover's triangle.

Beyond the bedroom an alarm began to beep, short shrill blasts, over and over and over.

Aaron shoved back the quilts, grabbed his shoes and raced down the hallway.

"What is it?" He could hear Zoe behind him.

He opened a barely discernible box near a door in the kitchen and punched in a series of numbers. The bleeping stopped.

"What's that?"

"It's an alert, sort of a coded message. My employers are looking for me. They send out a signal to see if I'll respond." He said this while punching in more numbers.

While Zoe watched, the lock on the door next to the panel clicked. Aaron opened it and hustled down a flight of stairs. He flicked a switch and lights came on. Zoe followed more slowly, unsure of her welcome. But Aaron hadn't told her not to follow.

She blinked as she turned the corner after the last step. A room that looked like command central of a space launch on a much smaller scale greeted her. Computer screens, rows of switches and dials, communications equipment, phones, fax machines and the like covered the walls and a long counter/desktop.

Aaron was already at a chair, a live computer screen before him. He tapped the keyboard and a line of jumbled letters appeared on the screen.

Like Alice in Wonderland, she had unknowingly followed the White Rabbit down his hole.

Chapter Twenty-Two

Zoe watched Aaron communicate via e-mail—was it e-mail—or a more sophisticated and technical method? It was hard to imagine a secret agent, that's what'd she'd decided to categorize Aaron as, for lack of a better description, logging into a Gmail account and checking the inbox for new messages.

Whatever he was doing, he was doing it in some sort of code, because Zoe couldn't make heads or tails of the screen he was looking at.

She investigated the other equipment in the room more closely while Aaron's back was turned. What looked like some sort of radar screen surrounded by dials and meters was set into one corner of the elaborate network above the counter. Several ordinary looking wall unit telephones were placed at various locations between the other pieces of equipment.

More computer screens, and complicated-looking devices unlike any she'd ever seen complemented the more ordinary and mundane items she could identify.

She slid out a secretary-style desk chair and sat, her eyes on Aaron. He continued to type, the screen before him filled with unrecognizable gibberish. Zoe could sense tension building in the set of his shoulders and the tightening of his jaw.

Something was wrong. Something bad had happened. Or was about to happen. She knew it as sure as she knew her own name. Should she try to escape the farmhouse and Aaron? How long would this last? She could scream and yell. "I have a life, you know!"

But as the thought crossed her mind, it suddenly hit her that she didn't. Her life consisted of work at the restaurant and rendezvous with the phantom. Wednesday dinners with Drew. She waitressed to earn money to survive. She slept with the phantom to rescue Ben. And Drew— Drew was her stable, supportive friend who kept her sane.

She studied Aaron's back, her eyes boring into him, starting at the point where his hair met his shirt collar. Had she purposely thrown her lot in with his? Did sticking with him give her a better chance of rescuing Ben? He had the ability and probably the ways and means to locate and extricate Ben from his captors. If not Aaron, then who? Could she talk him into it and what could she offer him in exchange?

Herself. She sucked in a breath as the powerful thought hit her. She'd learned so much about herself *sexually*, courtesy of her trysts with the phantom. She'd stopped being afraid of letting go, of being passionate, of being herself.

Why hadn't she learned that with Tim? She'd loved him so much. He'd been her best friend and husband rolled into one. Their lovemaking had been more playful than passionate, though, and on some level she knew she'd been holding back, afraid of overwhelming Tim with her desire for more intensity, more sensuality.

With the phantom, every encounter was sensual and intense. Focused. That was it. He was totally focused on her and she was definitely, after that first time when she'd been terrified of what might happen, focused completely and totally on him. There were no outside distractions. Nothing to see, nothing to hear. Surrounded by silence and darkness, her sense of touch and taste had awakened. She'd been given the freedom to explore and experiment. She'd found a part of herself she hadn't known existed. And even though it frightened her at times, she wondered now if it could be used to her advantage.

She stared hard at Aaron remembering the times he'd kissed her, as recently as this morning. His hands covering her breasts, his thumbs feathering across her nipples through her bra. She shivered. She'd almost forgotten about the phantom. Aaron had been holding back, but he wanted her. Her sick sense of loyalty to the phantom was the only thing standing in their way.

Another revelation almost toppled her. The phantom had given her a way to rescue Ben. The money and her newfound abilities in the bedroom. Aaron was the means. She'd give him all of the money. She'd give him herself for as long as he wanted her. All he had to do was find Ben, with Julio's help, and bring him home.

Aaron suddenly punched the off button on the computer screen and shoved the keyboard on its sliding rack away from him. It banged against the desk and rolled forward again. He shoved it back harder and by the time it popped back toward him he was already out of his chair coming toward her. The look in his eyes was murderous and for the first time, Zoe shrank away from him.

He took her elbow and practically dragged her up. "Come on. We've got to get out of here."

He turned off the light and ushered her up the stairs.

"What's going on? Where are we going?"

"I'll explain later." He escorted her into one of the other bedrooms and opened the closet. The basement had been warmer than the house. The rain still came down and the temperature inside had dropped further. Aaron rifled through clothing that hung on the closet rod. He glanced over his shoulder at her and narrowed his eyes as if judging her size.

He pulled a jacket off a hanger and tossed it to her. "See if that fits."

Zoe put the brown corduroy jacket on, while Aaron pulled a thick beige sweater over his head.

The jacket was too big, the sleeves fell past her wrists. "Good enough," he pronounced, giving her a once-over. "Let's go." Zoe noticed Aaron's sweater fit him perfectly.

"Where are we going?" she asked again.

Aaron didn't answer. In the garage, he put the overhead door up. Rain fell and Zoe snuggled deeper into the oversized jacket, bunching her fingers up under the sleeves.

"Wait here." He dodged out of the garage and disappeared around the side of the house. Zoe was scared. Something wasn't right. Was she a sheep to be led around by Aaron? One who went blindly along with everything he said? Aaron had always made her feel safe. Up until now, that is. Now she wondered what was going on. Where had he come from and why had she become involved in his intrigue? Why wasn't she putting up more resistance?

He'd killed two men. Shot them in cold blood and hustled her away from the scene of the crime. He'd given her an explanation, but she didn't know if it was true. He could be a terrorist. Part of one of those massive underground networks that popped up in the news ever since 9/11.

All she knew about Aaron was what he'd told her and what she'd witnessed with her own eyes.

She shivered again, but not from the cold. This time from fear and uncertainty.

An old Chevy Blazer that had seen its share of wear and tear appeared in front of her. Through the tinted glass she could see Aaron at the wheel. The engine idled while she stared. He was waiting for her to get in. To go with him. When she didn't, he lowered the window. His eyes locked with hers. He looked grim, but determined. She had the thought that if she didn't get in of her own accord, he'd get out and make sure she did.

"What's wrong?" he finally asked.

"You tell me," she challenged.

His expression changed. It had dawned on him that she didn't trust him. He seemed surprised. "Zoe, you have to come with me. It isn't safe for you if you don't."

"How do I know I'm any safer with you?"

"You don't. But I give you my word."

A word from a stranger. Someone she didn't know. Just like the phantom. But you do know him, came that voice in her head. *You know him.* She closed her eyes. Her gut reaction was to go with Aaron. To believe him. She opened her eyes. Through the rain, she could see Aaron still watching her, though after the way he'd hustled her out of the house he must be impatient to leave.

She stepped out into the wall of water and he leaned over to open the door. She closed it and he raised her window. Without another word, he accelerated, leaving the farmhouse behind.

Aaron drove the country roads like he knew exactly where he was going. He probably did, Zoe thought. Maybe he had a global positioning system wired into his head.

Zoe imagined she could see a computer-like brain hard at work beneath his skull, processing information, creating possible solutions to the current problem. For there was a problem of some sort, she was convinced of that by the way he'd hustled her out of the farmhouse. By his silence now. A slight frown creased between his brows and he seemed deep in thought.

As they drove south the rain lessened though the skies were still overcast with a thick mantle of gray clouds. Zoe's stomach growled at the same time her eyelids drooped. Her single waffle this morning was long gone. The stress of the day combined with the weather and the moving vehicle made her sleepy. She yawned, covering her mouth, and knew there was no way she was going to stay awake much longer.

Aaron glanced at her and patted his thigh. Made before center consoles were popular, the Blazer sported a front bench seat.

Zoe stared at Aaron while he concentrated on his driving on a winding stretch of road. She had a million more questions to ask him. She didn't want to trust him, but she did. And if she'd learned anything from the past 24 hours it was that Aaron would answer her questions in his own way and in his own time.

She yawned again. The bench seat with its worn leather upholstery and Aaron's khaki covered thigh were too much to resist. She rearranged herself, using Aaron for a pillow. She closed her eyes. The last thing she remembered before she fell asleep was Aaron's hand on her head, his fingers tracing a path through her hair.

She woke when she sensed the Blazer slowing down and turning. She sat up and blinked in the bright lights of a Denny's parking lot. Like a weary traveler she felt only slightly refreshed from her nap.

Aaron looked none the worse for wear, though he'd been driving for at least four hours.

"Where are we?" Zoe wondered aloud. She finger-combed her hair.

"Just outside the city," Aaron answered. He watched as she tried to make herself more presentable. "I like your hair."

"Huh," Zoe said. Her stick straight and fine hair had always defied any attempt at styling. "What's to like?"

"It's on your head."

Zoe blinked and turned to give him a questioning look, but he'd opened his door and was getting out. Zoe followed and he escorted her into the restaurant. A washed-out looking hostess led them to a booth in the back near the restrooms.

After they'd ordered and availed themselves of the restrooms, Aaron folded his hands together and leaned across the table. "We have to talk."

Chapter Twenty-Three

"About your brother—"

"You'll help me?"

The hope in Zoe's eyes was almost too much for Aaron to take.

"I'll do anything. I have money." She reached across the table and covered his hand with hers. "Anything, Aaron. Anything you want."

Her meaning was unmistakable. Aaron's head immediately filled with memories of what "anything" encompassed. She'd already done everything with him. She just didn't know it. Therein lay the irony and Aaron knew he surely deserved some kind of unending punishment for what he'd done. He'd created the web that now had him trapped. If Zoe had been desperate enough to save her brother before, she was doubly desperate now. As he well knew, she had every right to be. Individuals in Ben's situation were not known for their long-term survival rate.

Level One stood in his way. He knew he could rescue Ben from his Central American captors. But Level One wouldn't sanction such an operation. Of course not. They'd never approve of their top agent taking on such a dangerous mission. Ben's rescue was not a matter of national security. He posed no threat to anyone, except his captors. He was insignificant.

Aaron withdrew his hand from Zoe's and scrubbed his hands across his face. His eyes were gritty and dry. He knew there was an answer here somewhere. A way to get everything he wanted, everything Zoe wanted. A way out of Level One. His brain, which normally worked at lightning speed seemed to be stuck in neutral. He needed to eat and sleep.

The waitress set down plates and refilled coffee cups. Zoe glanced at him, a wounded look in her eyes.

Aaron picked up his utensils and leaned toward her. "Zoe." She looked up from her plate.

He didn't know what to say or how to say it. He communicated with her better in silent darkness. "Trust me," he finally told her. "It will all work out."

She nodded quickly and dropped her gaze back to her plate. He didn't think he'd convinced her. Which meant he'd have to find a way to make good on his word.

Aaron found the light switch once they entered the motel room. The room was standard fare with two double beds, cheap furniture and a television.

"I want to go home," Zoe said.

She'd halted a few feet beyond the door, her gaze riveted on Aaron as he switched on another light and shed his sweater.

He turned to look at her. "You can't. It's not safe."

Zoe rubbed her upper arms through the sleeves of her too big jacket. "You can't keep me here. I'm not your prisoner."

Aaron came toward her. She watched him, wariness in her eyes. He lifted strands of her hair and rearranged them back over her shoulders. "I'm asking you to trust me."

"You've given me no reason to."

"Have I given you a reason not to?" Aaron countered.

"Those men—"

"Are exactly who I said they were."

"Are you going to help me rescue Ben?"

"Maybe, I—" He saw Zoe withdraw into herself expecting his refusal and suddenly it all became clear to him. A way he could make everything right. He could rescue Zoe's brother. Extricate himself from service to Level One. Gain Zoe's trust. Maybe even her love. The future he'd dreamed of seemed obtainable for the first time. Zoe was the key.

He didn't give himself time to analyze or question his decision. "Yes. I'll find your brother and I'll bring him home."

Suspicion returned to her eyes. "Why the sudden about face?"

"Did anyone ever tell you you ask too many questions?"

"Did anyone ever tell you you're lousy at answering questions?"

"Trust me, Zoe. That's all I ask. If you can't, I can't help you."

Aaron asked a lot. She couldn't trust him completely. But if he could save Ben, and it seemed likely to Zoe that he could, she would do whatever he asked.

"I need to sleep," he said. He cupped her head in his hands. "Promise me you won't try to leave."

She stared into the hazel green of his eyes. "I promise," she said solemnly.

He kissed her. "I promise," he whispered. He kissed her again. "I promise, I'll make it all right. I'll make it all up to you."

Make what up to me? Zoe wanted to ask. But instead of asking she kissed him back.

Aaron insisted Zoe use the bathroom first and then he took a quick shower and reappeared fully dressed in his shirt and slacks. He yanked the covers back on the bed nearest the door, laid back, sighed and closed his eyes. He hadn't shaved in two days and the short growth of beard made him look reckless and sexy. "Let me sleep with you," Zoe said.

At her words his eyes popped back open. She crawled onto the bed next to him.

"It's too distracting," he told her. "When I said sleep, I meant it."

"I won't distract you."

Aaron watched as she discarded her jacket and toed off her shoes. He turned on his side away from her as she slid between the sheets. "I'm going to sleep now."

"Okay."

She kneaded his shoulder, her thumb working against a knot of tension she found there.

Aaron groaned. He hadn't realized how tightly wound he was. Gently she pushed him forward to lie on his stomach.

She used both hands to massage his shoulders, neck and upper back. "Tim used to love this," she told him. She smoothed his shirt down where it had bunched up beneath her probing fingers.

"Feels good," Aaron told her gruffly. That was a massive understatement. He could feel himself relaxing, his problems dissolving away, the tension leaving him as Zoe worked her magic.

He didn't even feel himself falling asleep.

Zoe did though. She laid her head on his back, listened to the slow steady rhythm of his breathing and felt oddly reassured. She trusted Aaron whether she wanted to or not. If anyone could make things right, she knew in her heart, he could.

Chapter Twenty-Four

When they returned to the city, Aaron checked Zoe into a hotel room on the Upper West Side insisting she stay there until he made sure her apartment was safe. She argued with him but she finally agreed to wait there until he returned. As he made his way to Level One headquarters, Aaron had to trust that she would keep her word.

Upon his arrival he was debriefed about the shooting of his pursuers and then sent to cool his heels until the powers that be were ready to see him.

Aaron turned from the window with the view as the director entered the room. Russell Gannet nodded at Aaron before taking a seat behind his desk. He indicated for Aaron to take one of the two seats across from him, but instead Aaron leaned against the windowsill, hands thrust in his pockets, one ankle crossed over the other.

Gannett sighed, either in annoyance or resignation. Aaron smiled inwardly at the director's consternation. He should be in the catbird seat. Gannett needed him and they both knew it. Aaron didn't necessarily need Gannett. At least not to the same degree. Yet Aaron's brain had been working overtime trying to figure out a scenario where Gannett would be happy to see him leave the agency's service. Alive.

"We have a situation," Gannett began, pulling a report encased in blue binding toward him. He scanned the contents of the document before tossing it to the side of the desk in Aaron's direction. Obligingly, Aaron stepped forward to pick it up and began leafing through it. By the second page his brow furrowed.

He glanced up at Gannett. "Central America. Again." He continued to peruse the contents.

"But with a new twist," Gannett pointed out, then waited until Aaron looked up.

"Are you thinking what I'm thinking?" Aaron asked. The two men locked gazes. Whatever their differences, when it came to the job, analyzing intelligence data, planning missions, achieving objectives, the two were eerily in tune with each other.

"All indications are that it's Sheppard."

"He's alive then," Aaron stated.

"Yes, apparently," Gannett agreed. "Against all odds, and all indications to the contrary, one of our agents may be using the profits from a black market emerald mine to fund a guerilla movement along the borders of Honduras and Guatemala. How he's managed to the keep the mine a secret from the government of either country is a mystery. How he discovered it, how he's manning such an operation in secret, we don't know. Yet."

"It's a pretty remote location," Aaron pointed out. He took the seat Gannett had indicated earlier and studied the map in the file. "And the borders in those mountains are disputed territory.

"True," Gannett agreed. Clearly, he had more he wanted to say,

Aaron looked up from the file and waited.

Gannett chose his words carefully. "I'm sure you understand the unique delicacy of this particular situation. An American citizen, a former agent with a covert and highly classified department within the U.S. federal government, is not only stealing a fortune in emeralds from two of our allies, but is funding the types of insurrectionists who are looking to topple the governments of both countries."

"And you're sure it's Nick?"

"Not a hundred percent, as you can see for yourself. We're still gathering intelligence. But all indicators point to Sheppard as the party behind the mine and the arming of the guerilla forces in the area. High quality emeralds have periodically flooded the market recently. And each time there's a surge in the guerilla warfare along those borders. We think whoever's controlling the mine is funding both sides enough to keep them active as a distraction to the governments of both countries, so they won't go looking too hard for a covert mining operation in a region as remote as this one."

"But this area, there's never been any gem stone mining to speak of. Parts of South America, yes. Especially Brazil. And Columbia, of course. But never before in either of these countries."

Gannett nodded. "It's in the geological report. Do you remember that earthquake a few years ago, 7.8 on the Richter scale? Almost off the charts. The geologists think that could have opened up a section of mountain. If there was a cave already there along the fault line, it's possible the earthquake hit at exactly the right point for the vein to be accessible."

Aaron shook his head. "Seems like a long shot that anyone would find it, though."

Gannett shrugged. "There are a few villages nearby. Some of which are served by missionaries. Of course there are other non-natives in the area, scientists, biologists, environmentalists and the like. It may not be as unlikely that the mine would be discovered as we would like to think.

"At any rate, go through that report. You'll be receiving an update later today when we determine for certain Sheppard is behind this. If so, we'll have no choice but to terminate his involvement."

Again their eyes met. Both knew what 'terminate' entailed in this instant.

"Anything else?" Aaron asked mildly.

Gannett picked up a pen and tapped it on the edge of his desk. He frowned at Aaron as if he found the subject matter he was about to broach mildly distasteful. "Yes, as a matter of fact, there is something else I need to address with you."

Again Aaron felt that inward smile. Here it comes, he thought. But when Gannett spoke, his words were not what Aaron expected.

"Your friend, Zoe Bradford has a brother, Ben Dumont."

"The missing missionary," Aaron replied cautiously.

Gannett cleared his throat, his gaze locking with Aaron's. "He's a Corbridge recruit."

That means Drew Warner is on the right track. Aaron schooled his features into a mask of casual attentiveness, showing no real surprise or interest.

"You already knew?"

Aaron shrugged. "I wondered if it was a possibility, but no, I didn't know for certain. You know I'm not privy to Corbridge's recruitment list."

Gannet nodded then turned his gaze to a red file folder centered in the middle of his desk. He seemed to debate for a moment as to whether to share the contents with Aaron, but then he tapped it and looked up. "We have another potential problem." He opened the file which Aaron could see contained only a few sheets of paper. "An investigative reporter by the name of Drew Warner. It seems he's made some interesting connections between some government agencies and groups sponsoring missionaries in Third World countries."

Aaron forced himself to control his respiration and heart rate, both of which had shot up at the mention of Drew's name. He took the file when Gannett passed it to him and perused the contents quickly. Inside was a draft of an article slated for publication in Global Report magazine's next issue.

"This looks like a lot of conjecture with no definitive conclusions," he said after he read it and handed it back to Gannett.

Gannett leaned back in his swivel chair and steepled his fingers in front of him, tapping them against his lips before he spoke. "True. That's Warner's style. He operates on the "where there's smoke there's fire" premise, and he's got a reputation as a bulldog. Once he thinks he's on to something he won't let it go until he uncovers every fact there is to uncover. There are some very influential people who find Drew Warner very worrisome due to this current situation."

Gannett dropped his hands and leaned forward, his gaze intense. "I want to make certain I've conveyed to you the seriousness of the situation. We are dealing with a scenario, which, if mishandled, will have far-reaching and potentially devastating repercussions not only for this agency, but for the entire U.S. intelligence community.

"I understand, Russell."

"I want you to assemble your team, prepare the P.O.P. I'll have confirmation later today on Sheppard's identity. If this thing falls apart, if we don't terminate Sheppard, retrieve Father Dumont and close down that mine, you won't have to worry about leaving the agency. This agency will cease to exist. As will the Corbridge operation."

Although Aaron had some misgivings about The Corbridge Group's agenda, he knew that while Level One's methods were often unorthodox, its goals were in line with the greater good and protection of the American people. He had no desire to see the entire agency at risk, even if he made his exodus a foregone conclusion.

He placed his hands on Gannett's desk and leaned forward, eye to eye, man to man. "I'll make you a deal. I'll prepare a Preliminary Operations Profile. I'll go in with a team. You give me carte blanche to run the op my way. I take out Sheppard, retrieve Dumont, destroy the mine. Corbridge's little group is still operational. Life at Level One goes on business as usual. With one exception. I'm out. You cut me loose. Early retirement. Full benefits. I disappear."

Gannett held his gaze as seconds ticked by. "And if I refuse?"

"You can find someone else to run your op."

Gannett didn't like the deal, but Aaron wasn't backing down. This was his one and only chance. There was too much at stake for him to walk away. And they both knew there was too much at stake for Gannett to refuse.

Still Gannett stared him down, drumming his fingertips on the desk as seconds slipped by while he swallowed an agreement he clearly disliked. His fingers stilled and after another few seconds he spoke, his voice filled with resignation. "All right, Agent Manning. You accomplish all three objectives and return to U.S. soil alive. Your identity as an agent has already been compromised, so you can't go back to active duty. But instead of retirement I'd like you to consider another position in recruitment and training."

"A desk job?" Aaron let his distaste show.

"Partly," Gannett agreed. "But you'd be in the field most of the time, planning and supervising training ops and doing assessments. There'd also be times where your expertise in designing actual missions would be required."

"But if I decide I want out, I'm out," Aaron insisted.

Gannett hesitated, but finally nodded. "If that's what you want."

Chapter Twenty-Five

When Aaron returned to the hotel Zoe had availed herself of room service and taken a shower. She was chomping at the bit, inquiring when they were leaving for Central America.

"You can't go with me."

"Of course I'm going with you. Ben is my brother. It's my money. I'm the one who has the most invested in seeing him rescued."

Aaron gently grasped her upper arms and looked directly into her eyes. "Zoe, listen to me. It's too risky for you to be there. This is what I do. You have to trust me."

Zoe shook her head. "No. This is too important. I have to make sure..."

"Have to make sure of what?"

"That you'll do what you said you'd do!" Zoe burst out, throwing his hands off and turning away. "How do I know you won't take my money and pretend you tried to rescue Ben? You could take a trip to the Bahamas and I wouldn't know. You could come back and tell me something, anything. You couldn't find Ben. That the rescue operation failed. That Ben is—Ben is dead."

Zoe's voice broke and she choked back a sob. Aaron wrapped his arms around her from behind. "I wouldn't do that," he told her solemnly. "If there's any way to get Ben out of there alive and in one piece, I'll do it. I promise."

Zoe broke the embrace and turned to face him. "I don't know anything about you. Not who you work for or where you live—or—or even how you live. You could disappear and I'd never find you. It's too much to ask. For me to trust you that much. You don't know what I had to do to get this money, to save what I needed. I can't lose Ben now. Not after—after everything."

Aaron frowned. Of course he knew exactly what Zoe had done to get the money to save Ben. He'd unwittingly supplied her with Ben's rescue fund. Who better than he could understand how high the cost, how important it was for her to make sure every effort was made to bring Ben home?

"Then I won't take the money."

Zoe turned to stare at him eyes wide and disbelieving. "You have to take the money. That's the whole point. Otherwise—otherwise everything I did to get it is pointless."

Aaron shook his head. "No. You keep the money. If I bring Ben back, you can pay me then. If I don't, you keep it."

"No!" Zoe's eyes flashed. "Then where's your motivation for doing any of this? How do you know you won't need to pay Ben's captors for his release?"

"That won't be necessary."

"How do you *know?*" Zoe shouted.

"I don't bargain with terrorists or kidnappers."

"Oh, great," Zoe scoffed. "The federal government's favorite line. Well, this is my brother we're talking about. And since it's my money, I get a say in how Ben is rescued."

"No, Zoe, you don't."

"Wanna bet?"

Zoe turned and gathered her coat and purse and headed for the door.

Aaron stepped toward her. "Where are you going?"

"To rescue my brother."

Aaron reached her before she wrenched the door open. He grasped her elbow, but she shook him off. "You said you'd help me," she reminded him.

"I will. But I can't take you with me. You have to understand. You have to trust me."

Zoe shook her head. "I can't. Not with this. It's too important. I'm sorry, but I can't."

Aaron held her gaze for a long time. She didn't blink and she didn't turn away. She wasn't going to give in on this. Finally, he nodded, reached behind her and opened the door. "Goodbye, Zoe."

Zoe hesitated a fraction of second. Perhaps he had succeeded in surprising her for once. She lifted her chin, flashed those eyes at him one more time, turned around, and walked through the door.

He closed it behind her and leaned his forehead against it for a minute. He'd hated doing that to her, hated fighting with her and not giving her what she wanted. But there was no way he was going to risk her safety or the success of the mission by allowing her to tag along. He couldn't compromise Level One's involvement, either.

He moved away from the door and back into the room, checking to see that they'd left nothing behind. If he played his cards right, he'd be on a plane to Central America tonight, planning the mission tomorrow, destroying Nick Sheppard's operation and rescuing Ben Dumont. In three or four days, if all went as he planned, he'd return to New York a hero, deliver Zoe's brother into her arms, ask her to marry him, escape the clutches of Level One and live happily ever after.

Chapter Twenty-Six

"My God, where have you been?"

Zoe looked up to find Drew wheeling off the elevator toward her. Seeing the concern on his face, knowing what was ahead of her, what she'd have to do alone, she felt weariness envelope her.

"Are you all right?" Drew asked as his chair halted in front of her.

She tried to smile, but knew how weak the effort must appear. "I'm fine."

Drew frowned. He reached up to her with both arms. Zoe hesitated, hating herself for doing it, hating what her reaction did to him. But she knew if she allowed him to comfort her now, when she was emotionally vulnerable, when all her reserves were gone, she'd fall apart. She'd tell him everything. *Everything.* And she couldn't do that. Couldn't bear for him to know how low she'd sunk, didn't want to see the hatred and disgust in his eyes.

She grasped both his hands in hers instead, nearly choking with the effort to contain herself. "Please. Don't." She squeezed his hands and let go, turning to study her apartment door. She'd let him come in with her if he wanted, ask his questions.

As long as he didn't touch her, she wouldn't break down. She promised herself she wouldn't.

She was glad to see her apartment door was intact, though there was some obvious effort to repair the damage to the surrounding woodwork and there was a new lock on the door.

Drew handed her a key and she opened the door.

Without waiting for an invitation, Drew wheeled in behind her, the whoosh of the chair wheels the only sound.

Once inside, he wasted no time. "What happened?"

Zoe shrugged out of her coat and hung it up. She suddenly desperately thought of the bottle of wine in her refrigerator. In her mind's eye she saw herself uncorking it and drinking it all straight from the bottle, feeling relaxation wash over her, all her problems and fears drifting away. Drew's voice would become a mild buzz in the background, his face a blur and she'd sink slowly into oblivion.

Coward. The last year had taught her she didn't need that crutch. Wanted it, yes. Craved it often. But she refused to give in. Refused to give up.

"Coffee?" she asked as she headed for the tiny kitchen.

Drew followed her, his gaze boring into her as she stubbornly set about brewing coffee in silence.

"Aren't we friends anymore?"

Her head whipped around in surprise at his question, spoken in a soft voice filled with hurt.

"Of course we are."

"Why won't you let me help you? Why won't you talk to me?"

Zoe stared at the brown liquid drizzling into the carafe. "You can't help me, Drew. Not with this. And if I try to explain..." she sighed. "You won't understand."

"I would."

Zoe locked her gaze with his. "You can't."

"You can't tell me what happened here the other night?"

"We were attacked."

"You and—you and Aaron Manning?" he asked carefully.

"Yes. Armed men followed us into the building, or maybe they were already inside when we got here. They came after us. We escaped."

"They came after both of you? Or they were after Aaron?"

Zoe shrugged. "I don't know." She didn't, she comforted herself. Not for sure. It wasn't exactly a lie.

"Who were they?"

"I don't know."

"What happened?"

"We got out, we got away. We had to wait until we were sure it was safe for me to come back here."

"Where's Aaron?"

"I don't know." That was the absolute truth. The coffeemaker finished sputtering and dripping. She poured two cups.

Drew moved back so she could carry the cups to the table near the sofa. She picked hers up and sipped, cupping the mug with both hands.

"That's it, then? You're back. Aaron's gone. End of story."

"I'm leaving. As soon as I can. I'm going to bring Ben home."

"Alone? How—What—?"

"I don't know how exactly. With Julio's help I'll find him. I'll pay off his kidnappers. I'll do whatever it takes."

"Pay them off? With what? Do you have any idea—"

"I have money."

"How much? From where?"

"It doesn't matter, does it? I have it and I plan to use it."

"It's Aaron isn't it? He's helping you. You wouldn't let me help you, but you let him. You wouldn't take my money, but you'll take his."

"Aaron isn't helping me. Aaron isn't doing anything for me. He's gone. It's my money. I earned it. I'm doing this alone." Zoe felt her resolve strengthen as she reaffirmed everything she'd told herself after she'd left the hotel. The hurt and disappointment she'd felt at Aaron's abandonment had transformed into angry determination. She'd show him. She'd show Drew. And she'd show those damn assholes who'd been holding Ben, torturing him, starving him. She'd get Ben back or die trying. And no one was going to stop her.

"Then I wish you luck," Drew said quietly. He put his coffee mug down on the table. Zoe watched him wheel to the door, open it and disappear through it, closing it with a soft click behind him. Two for two she thought, hating to see him go, but knowing she couldn't call him back.

She poured herself more coffee and went into the bedroom to start packing. Next she'd go to the bank, get her money and make travel arrangements. She'd have to try to contact Julio or pray that he called before she left. But if not, she'd track him down in Santa Rosaro.

One way or another, she repeated under her breath, *Ben I'm coming for you. Just hang in there.*

Zoe had plenty of time to think on the flight to Miami, the layover stop there and the next flight to Guatemala. Her weary mind refused to turn itself off between catnaps, but each time she turned her choices over in her mind, she became more convinced she was doing the right thing, the only thing, where Ben was concerned.

She was through depending on others to rescue her. Her entire life, like a kaleidoscope filled with helpless images, ran on a constant reel she couldn't shut off. After her unstable mother abandoned her children, her grandmother had stepped in, but her illness had cut her care of them short. Zoe had depended on Ben to look out for her and after her marriage, she'd expected Tim to fulfill that role. In retrospect, she realized Tim had done the best he could, but he had his own issues, his own agenda to fulfill. She shouldn't have expected him to be her savior on top of everything else.

Then there was Drew. She'd leaned on him an awful lot, especially the past year, but instinctively she'd known there was a limit to how much she could allow herself to become beholden to him. She hoped she hadn't completely destroyed their friendship with her refusals to explain her behavior and accept his assistance. But deep inside, she knew rescuing Ben was something she had to do alone.

She closed her eyes, resting her head against the seatback, hoping the drone of the airplane's engine would soothe her, but she still felt that stabbing ache of disappointment and hurt every time she thought of Aaron.

Like a fool she'd wanted to trust him. She had trusted him. Trusted him with her life. Trusted him when he promised to help her rescue Ben. But he too had abandoned her, and that, more than anything else, had opened her eyes, pushed her into action and strengthened her resolve to depend on no one but herself.

But what about the phantom? How ironic that the one person she felt she could trust was her nameless, faceless lover. From the moment she'd read that letter, held that first batch of hundred dollar bills in her hand, her phantom lover had stayed true, held fast to every line of that letter. *Him* she trusted. She'd wanted to trust Aaron in the same way, but she had no idea why he should inspire such an inclination. He'd backed out of his agreement to help her with Ben's rescue, proving he wasn't a man of his word.

But from the first she'd sensed his ability to protect her. He wouldn't let anyone or anything hurt her. He'd proven that, hadn't he? She'd escaped without harm that night when they'd come under attack. She'd been on the verge of falling in love with him, wanting, needing to trust him. But the phantom had held her back. And then Aaron himself had killed whatever feelings she'd been nurturing for him.

Now she had herself and no one else to depend on or help her, and she was, to her amazement, quite unafraid of this new state. Whatever lay ahead she would see it through, she would do her best and she would take responsibility for her choices.

When she arrived in Santa Rosaro she would locate Julio. She would pay him to lead her to Ben's captors, but she wouldn't allow him to be involved in Ben's rescue. She would conduct a business transaction with him, but she wouldn't depend on him to help her. If she had to, she'd confront Ben's captors face to face, offer to buy Ben's freedom. She looked down at her backpack which she'd wedged under the seat in front of her. A small portion of her cash supply was buried at the bottom of the pack. The rest of it, she'd secured in a money belt around her waist. Hundred dollar bills, even when there were lots of them, took up surprisingly little room.

She'd chosen loose, comfortable clothing for her trip, and currently wore a black warm-up suit over a gray tee shirt which thoroughly concealed her waistline.

She kept her eyes closed, trying to convince her body to rest, to relax. She'd been falling asleep at odd times lately, catnapping during the day, her eyelids drooping without her consent. Even if she couldn't sleep, she needed to rest as much as possible. She wiggled her toes inside the sturdy hiking boots while mentally reviewing the preparations she'd made, the self-defense classes, the hours at the gym, the survival gear. She was as ready as she'd ever be.

Chapter Twenty-Seven

Twenty-six hours later, Zoe found herself on a rough mountain path following Julio's sure steps as he wound his way through the trees and jungle-like ground cover. He had left the rectory earlier to make arrangements or run errands, the details of which he did not share with her. She spent his absence going over her gear and supplies and counting her cash, putting the majority of it in her backpack and a smaller amount in her money belt. If Ben's captors agreed to release him, she didn't want to waste any time handing over the cash or asking for privacy to retrieve it from under her shirt.

She'd brought fresh water and a few granola bars as well as some medical supplies, extra socks and tee shirts and a hunting knife. She wasn't sure what she'd use it for, but it seemed reasonable to have a knife out here in the jungle.

The sun was going down and the shadows lengthened quickly due to the trees and vines that seemed to overhang them like a canopy. It was relatively quiet, no raucous bird noises or chattering monkeys. Julio explained that at this elevation, there were fewer of those types of creatures. Zoe could hear only the sound of their footsteps and her own breathing. She focused strictly on following Julio, keeping her gaze on his back, stepping where he stepped. Julio had driven them in an old Jeep on a rutted uphill track for several miles and then had pulled the vehicle off into the trees and covered it with vines and branches. The rest of the journey would have to be made on foot, he told her, because the engine noise would alert Ben's captors to their approach. Zoe thought perhaps it was more because the Jeep wouldn't make it up the steep inclines they were traveling now, but she kept that thought to herself.

Zoe tried not to think about what would happen when she and Julio arrived at their destination. She hoped Julio could negotiate Ben's release while she hung back. Once Ben was free, she and Julio would work together to get him back to the village, and from there to the U.S. She knew they'd be dealing with ruthless men who could simply kill all of them and take her money. Or worse. She shied away from considering the worse-case scenarios her imagination conjured up.

Maybe Ben's capture had nothing to do with money. Which meant money wouldn't buy his freedom. All Zoe knew was she had money, she had no one else to help her, no one she could trust, and she had to try. And if she died trying? A chill ran up Zoe's spine. She didn't want to consider her own death. Ben's death. Anyone's death.

I'm not dead yet.

She turned her grim thoughts aside and silently chanted her mantra as she followed Julio. *Rescue Ben. Rescue Ben. Rescue Ben. God help me. Rescue Ben.* Every once in a while she threw in a prayer, wondering as usual, if He only selectively listened to her pleas, asking herself again if she really believed He was there.

I got you this far, didn't I?

Zoe stumbled and Julio glanced back, assured that she'd regained her footing before continuing on. God chose the most inopportune times to speak to her, she decided. Had He really got her this far or had she done it herself? Was the phantom an answer to her prayers to create the financial means to rescue Ben? Or had she merely traded sex for money with no greater hand at work in the act?

The further they climbed, the more doubts crept into Zoe's mind. She trusted Julio solely because she was under the impression that Ben had. Julio had stayed in touch with her, but had he done that in the hopes of luring her here with or without money? She'd had no assurance from anyone but him that Ben's captors were willing to deal with her, to release him if the price was right.

She feared she'd done a foolish thing by coming here alone. And worst of all, she knew why she'd done it. It had been a knee-jerk reaction to

Aaron's refusal to bring her along on his supposed "mission." She hadn't trusted him, but now? She didn't trust herself. Or Julio.

Even if she successfully bargained for Ben's release, she had no idea if he was in any shape to travel. Even getting him back to the village could be impossible. Then what would she do? She'd be trapped and at the mercy of his captors.

Zoe had no answers to her questions. She did know, however, that it would give her great comfort if she could be sure someone who possessed more power than she and Julio combined was at work during Ben's rescue.

Just do what you can, she silently replied to God. In case He was listening.

"Two subjects approaching," came the murmur through the earpiece.

Gonzalez was reconnoitering, making sure they were relatively alone in their position above the mine site. Aaron and his team had arrived as darkness fell the night before. Enough light had remained for them to choose a location to observe the activities below without being seen. The fact that two "subjects" were approaching was not good news.

Aaron signaled to DiPaulo and Jaeger, and as if performing an intricate ballet, the steps studied for years, the three of them drifted back into the forest, to await the arrival of the newcomers.

Aaron forced himself to control his respiration, slow his heartbeat, pay attention. Whoever was coming was as intent on not being noticed by the occupants of the mining camp as he and his team were, for if they were part of the operation they would have approached on the rough track which zigzagged up the east side of the mountain. Instead, these two were approaching from the south, as he and his team had last night.

"Code One," he whispered. The button mike attached to his collar would pick up his words and transmit them to the other's earpieces. Code One meant take them, quickly, quietly, without harm. Disarm and restrain. Period.

He'd worked with the other three for nearly a year. He had nothing to worry about.

"A hundred yards," Gonzalez transmitted.

Aaron readied himself. He knew the other two did as well. Whoever was closest would take them. The third man would assist as needed. And Gonzalez would provide back-up within seconds. Aaron wasn't worried.

From behind a blanket of leaves, he watched their approach, narrowing his eyes to see in the thickening shadows. The individual in the lead was male, a native judging by his dress and the sureness of his footing. The second subject was shorter, and less light of foot. This one made the most noise, alerting anyone in the vicinity of a clumsy approach.

Aaron let the leader pass him. DiPaulo and Jaeger would take him easily. He'd focus on subject number two, with aid from Gonzalez if need be.

The seconds ticked off as the team timed their response perfectly. DiPaulo stepped behind the leader, restrained his arms behind his back, put his hand over his mouth and blocked any further foot movement with his legs. At the same time, Jaeger held a gun to the man's head.

Almost before subject number two realized what had happened, Aaron stepped behind her and executed the same move. Her!

As soon as he had her trapped in his hold, Aaron knew exactly who he'd caught.

Zoe.

He recognized her scent, the feel of her in his arms, even separated as he was from her body by her backpack. Hell, he'd know her anywhere. But her appearance here came as a sudden and rather unpleasant surprise. He'd hoped, he'd thought—what exactly had he thought? Surely he hadn't thought that she'd sit on her ass in New York and wait for him to rescue her brother. When she'd made it absolutely clear at their last meeting that she didn't trust him to do it. Still, he'd half expected to have his mission complete and return Ben Dumont to his sister before she even got her act together enough to complete travel arrangements. Obviously, he'd underestimated her. And once again she had succeeded in surprising him.

She didn't struggle, and that surprised him even more. Had she, on some level, sensed that it was him even though she hadn't seen him?

He needed to have a quick, quiet, private conversation with her, with his microphone turned off. He jerked his head behind him, a signal to Jaeger that he was taking his prisoner a short distance away. Meanwhile, Zoe's companion would be gagged and his hands restrained, incapacitated enough that he'd be easy for three men to guard. Gonzalez stepped forward and Aaron gave him the same jerk of the head he'd given Jaeger, indicating for him to join the others. Gonzalez didn't offer even a questioning look at Aaron and his prisoner before taking up a position next to Jaeger.

Keeping his hand over Zoe's mouth and her arms restrained, no easy task considering her backpack, Aaron frog marched her away from the others, back the way they had approached until he was out of earshot.

"I'm going to take my hand away from your mouth," he informed her. "Because we need to talk. Keep your voice down, because if you scream,

I'll have to silence you and it won't be pretty. Do you understand?"

Zoe nodded once. Aaron removed his hand from her mouth, but didn't let go of her.

"Aaron?" she whispered.

When he released her she stepped away and turned around. They stared at each other for what seemed like a long time, though it may have only been seconds. Aaron couldn't be sure. She was here, exactly where she shouldn't be, and he knew she was going to muck up his mission, knew it deep in his soul. But dammit all, he was glad to see her. Not that he'd let her know that.

He flicked the tiny off switch on the button microphone, but maintained his disapproving frown, his gaze hard. She had to believe he wasn't at all happy about her being here.

"What are you doing here?" she asked, her voice soft and low, as he'd requested.

Aaron decided to go with the reply that would get the most bang for the buck, even though it was only part of the truth. "Rescuing your brother." It was the only part she needed to know.

Zoe stared at him in disbelief. "No. I'm rescuing my brother."

It was all Aaron could do not to burst out in laughter at Zoe's overly confident tone and brash assuredness in herself. Nick Sheppard would eat her alive and spit out her bones. And her friend there would probably be bloodied in the process.

God, he loved her. He was in love with her. Zoe had wrapped herself around his heart almost from the first moment he'd seen her and there she'd stayed, refusing to let go or give up. And God help him, if he got out of this alive, if they all did, he'd find some way to make her a permanent, honest part of his life. Forever.

But now was not the time for romance. He had to get rid of her and her friend. Make her see that she had no place in such a dangerous situation. Make her believe that he'd move heaven and earth to bring her brother back to her. But she had to go. Now.

"Zoe, there's no way in hell you can rescue him. You don't know what kind of shape he's in. You don't know who's holding him."

Her chin came up. "I know he's weak. That he's been starved and beaten, maybe. I know the people who are holding him are evil. I'm not stupid, Aaron."

"I know that," he replied quietly, his heart turning over at her determination, her blatant disregard for her own welfare. Oh, to be loved like that. Did her brother know or care how much Zoe loved him? "But Zoe, I can't let you be involved in this. You have to trust me. My men and I," he inclined his head in their direction, "this is what we do. We're professionals. We'll get your brother out safe and sound." He almost channeled the

Blues Brothers and added "We're on a mission from God," but he caught himself in time. His tendency to verbalize often inappropriate lines from movies during difficult situations wasn't appropriate at the moment.

"What do you mean you 'can't let' me be involved in Ben's rescue? Last time I checked I was a private citizen. I do believe we're on foreign soil at the moment. I, and Julio, for that matter, are, how do they say? Out of your jurisdiction. I'll do whatever I want. You can't stop me. I don't want your help. I don't need your help. And may I remind you, you went back on your word to me in the first place. Maybe you should explain to *me* what *you're* doing here."

Aaron wanted to applaud her speech, she'd delivered it beautifully, but more than that, he didn't want to be overheard. Zoe was good and pissed and it showed in the way her voice was rising with each turn of the conversation. He couldn't afford to goad her and have her end up screaming like a banshee before he could prevent it.

What remained of the light was fading fast. He needed to get back to the others, get set for the night. The four of them had spent all day reconnoitering, planting charges, devising an escape route and a back-up plan, deciding on a diversion that would allow them to slip into the camp and retrieve Ben Dumont. It was all in place, ready to go. In fact, they would have attempted it tonight, except for the arrival of Zoe and her companion.

Plan B, thought Aaron. Adjusting plan A for unforeseen contingencies.

Aaron stepped forward, invading Zoe's personal space. She stood her ground and looked up at him, her eyes light in the growing darkness. Before he knew what he was going to do, before he even thought about it, he cupped her face in his hands and kissed her. Gently, at first, then harsher, rougher, the feel of her in his arms unleashing his need. And she responded, dammit. It'd be easier to let go if she didn't. But her mouth opened beneath his and she returned his kiss as if she wanted to crawl inside of him. *You're already there*, he told her silently.

He smoothed back strands of her hair as he ended the kiss. "God, you're a complication," he whispered as he peered down at her.

"So are you." Her words were shaky. Maybe some of her assuredness had slipped a bit.

"I need to get back to the others. Zoe, this will all be easier if you trust me."

"I'd like to. But I can't."

Aaron sighed and took her hand leading her back to his team. Julio was sitting on the ground, gagged, his hands secured behind his back. The two guards were alert, heads constantly swiveling for any potential threat. The third, Gonzalez, would be slowly circling the camp area.

Jaeger and DiPaulo, glanced at him for a signal when he approached with Zoe, but when he gave none they turned their attention elsewhere.

Aaron paused next to Julio and turned to Zoe. "I need your word, and his, that if we don't restrain you, you won't try to leave, and you won't make any noise."

"What are you saying?" she hissed back at him. "That we're your prisoners?" Her outrage was almost a living, breathing thing. She brought her hand up to slap him. Aaron saw the movement, knew he more than likely deserved it, but at the last moment, he grabbed her wrist.

"Don't push me," he warned, his voice low, vibrating with frustration. "You aren't going anywhere. You can either make that decision for yourself, or we'll make it for you. What's it going to be?"

Zoe jerked her wrist from his grasp. Her eyes shone brightly in the dim light. Please, Aaron, thought. No tears.

"Fine."

"What about him?" Aaron indicated Julio.

"He speaks near perfect English. I'm sure he's understood every word you've said. Ask him."

Aaron hunkered down next to Julio and spoke to him softly in Spanish because he knew Zoe wouldn't understand what they were saying.

Aaron withdrew the gag from Julio's mouth and released his wrists.

Their conversation lasted some minutes and when it was over, Aaron felt quite certain Julio Dominguez had no intention of setting foot outside the immediate vicinity, with or without Zoe, until Aaron gave him the go-ahead. Julio, in fact, might be an asset to the operation. Zoe, he knew, was definitely going to be a detriment.

"What did you tell him?" Zoe demanded as he straightened. Jaeger had directed a narrow beam from his flashlight toward Julio so Aaron could see what he was doing, and now he kept it trained on the ground to alleviate the almost total darkness.

"That's between him and me," Aaron informed her, taking some small satisfaction in turning her ally to his side. Julio rearranged himself, scooting back to lean against a tree trunk. Jaeger offered him water and some of his rations and Julio munched contentedly while Zoe fumed.

Aaron needed to diffuse Zoe's anger before it got out of control. Before she became more of a problem than she already was. To do that, he needed to take her somewhere private and explain what was going on.

He stepped away and said a few words to Jaeger. The other man glanced Zoe's way, but offered no further reaction. One of them would remain on watch, the others would sleep. Aaron badly needed to sleep, as well, but Zoe was going to keep him from it. Fleetingly, he thought of all the nights he'd willingly gone without sleep to be with her. Now, when he wished she weren't with him, she was.

He took her arm, indicating for her to accompany him away from the others. She resisted, trying to pull away from him.

"Where are you taking me?" she whispered. "What do you want?"

"I need to talk to you. And we don't need to be overheard."

"No."

Aaron's eyebrow shot up, though it probably wasn't visible to anyone else. "No?"

He yanked the backpack off her shoulders and let it drop to the ground. Quite efficiently, he gagged her, zip-tied her wrists behind her back, and threw her over his shoulder none too gently. He picked up his flashlight and took off back in the direction they'd come.

She fought him, wiggling mightily, trying to kick, although he restrained her legs. *Should have hog-tied her.* Her behavior seemed all out of proportion to the situation. Didn't she get that he was trying to *help* her?

He walked as far as he thought was necessary to be out of earshot of the others before he set her on her feet. He hooked his light on his belt and gave her a good shake before releasing her wrists. As soon as he did, she removed the gag from her mouth. "How dare you?" Her eyes were blazing, her chest heaving.

Aaron got in her face. "I'll tell you how I dare. I'm trying to help you and all you're giving me is grief. I said I'd rescue your brother, and I'll damn well do it. You don't want to trust me, fine. But I'm here, aren't I? I have men with me, trained professionals who can go in and get Ben out safely no matter what kind of shape he's in. I've got a helo waiting for our signal to get us out of here. You asked for my help. You begged me to help you as I recall. And I said that I would. I'm helping you," he ground out. "What I don't get is why you're fighting me."

"You wouldn't take my money," Zoe reminded him. "And you wouldn't take me with you, even though you told me you would."

"It isn't safe for you to be here."

"I don't care!" Zoe hissed in a high-pitched whisper. "I can't depend on anyone else to do it for me."

"Me, Zoe," Aaron repeated. "You can depend on me."

Zoe lifted her chin looking more determined than ever. "I don't want to. If you fail, I'll have you to blame. If I fail, I'll only have myself to blame."

"I won't fail."

"You can't be sure."

This looked like it might be a long conversation. Aaron gestured for her to sit and dropped to a cross-legged position across from her. Closer to the light it was easier to see her.

"Zoe, I'm going to tell you something I shouldn't. This is top secret, classified information. I can't divulge all of the details, but you need to know, the reason I'm here is because I've been assigned to rescue your brother. The organization I work for is making it a top priority as part of this mission. There are some other objectives as well, but rescuing Ben is part of it. That's why I couldn't take you with me. Originally, I thought we could go in, you and me, and get him out. But then I found out the people who are holding him have interests contrary to those of the U.S. in a big way. We need to close down this operation, retrieve Ben, and get the hell out of here."

"Why didn't you tell me this before? When you came back to the hotel?"

"Zoe, I couldn't. I shouldn't be telling you now, but you're on a need-to-know basis because you're here. You and your friend Julio could single-handedly compromise our entire mission if you don't cooperate, if you don't do what I tell you to do. If you don't trust me."

Chapter Twenty-Eight

Zoe didn't know what to do. From the moment she'd left Aaron in the hotel room, she'd believed herself to be on a roller coaster ride. Alone. She'd pushed Drew away and until she'd made an arrangement with Julio, she'd convinced herself she didn't need anyone, knew she couldn't trust anyone but herself to rescue Ben.

Now Aaron was here asking her to trust him, asking her to let him rescue Ben. Without her. Without her money. Without her input. As part of a larger operation with a different agenda. Another objective.

Julio had essentially abandoned her and seemed quite willing to throw his lot in with that of Aaron and his men. There was no reason why he shouldn't. He had no loyalty to her. He'd refused to accept payment for his guidance to Ben's location. He wanted only to use her and Ben to get into the U.S. Knowing that, she'd be wise to question his loyalty to Ben. If Julio thought he stood a better chance of emigrating by cooperating with Aaron, surely he would do it.

Zoe had to admit Aaron and his men looked impressive in all of their gear and their black military-looking clothing. The way they had stepped out of the trees and captured her and Julio before they'd even realized what was happening was dazzling.

Everyone had an agenda. Upon her arrival in Santa Rosaro she'd learned that Julio wanted out of the country, and he'd do whatever it took and cooperate with whoever gave him the best opportunity to make that happen. Aaron was on a mission. Only part of which was rescuing Ben. Zoe suspected it was a very small part. If the people operating the mine truly harbored "interests contrary to the U.S." on a massive scale, their demise would be Aaron's first objective, surely. If he could rescue Ben in the process, he would. But if Ben became a casualty, so be it. It probably happened all the time in Aaron's line of work, Zoe thought. Innocent bystanders hurt in the fallout from achieving a larger "objective."

Zoe weighed her options which seemed to be shrinking by the minute. She needed to think, but that was hard to do with Aaron nearby. He seemed physically bigger and more aggressive out here in the jungle, in his snug black shirt that outlined every inch of sinew and muscle in his upper body and loose black pants with numerous pockets and zippers and loops. His air of command had increased, his sense of always being on alert was even more obvious. Zoe hated that he made her feel safe. Even when he'd been angry earlier and had hauled her off over his shoulder, she'd never felt physically threatened by him. She knew he wouldn't hurt her. Not intentionally, anyway.

His presence complicated everything. She'd thought, truly believed, she could reason with and pay off Ben's captors and they'd let Ben go. Julio would help her get him back to the Jeep, back to the village, and through Julio's series of contacts, out of the country and on a plane back to the U.S. But with Julio's questionable loyalty, that seemed less and less likely.

"I'll think about it," she told Aaron, keeping her voice down, her tone even.

She thought he'd argue with her. He seemed about to, but then he only nodded, got to his feet with the flashlight in hand and reached for her hand to help her up. He kept her hand in his as they made their way back to the others. Probably only so she wouldn't get lost in the dark, she told herself. Not because he wanted to maintain contact with her. Still, she took what little comfort she could from that connection. A light rain started to fall, the sound of it arriving before the actual drops made their way through the thick branches overhead.

Zoe could barely see anything except the small circle of light cast by Aaron's flashlight. He stopped next to what looked like an oversized duffel bag. He unzipped it and it popped open with barely a sound other than the whoosh of air around it. They must be back at the camp with the others, though she couldn't see anyone.

The rain was falling harder now. Zoe wondered where her backpack was. She thought of all the cash secreted in the bottom of it. She didn't want to lose it. Hoped Aaron's men hadn't gone through it and helped themselves.

"Get in," Aaron whispered. Only then did Zoe realize what had popped open was a small tent.

"Where's my backpack? I need my things."

"I'll get it. Get in. Stay in. I'll be back."

Zoe crawled inside the tent. It wasn't very big, but it was big enough for one person to curl up comfortably inside and stay dry. Her clothes were damp, but there was nothing she could do about that. She'd brought hooded, waterproof, lightweight raingear, but it was in her backpack. Everything was in the backpack Aaron had stripped her of when she'd questioned his authority.

She needed to be smarter. Aaron wanted her to trust him. Maybe what she should be doing is making sure that Aaron trusted her. Perhaps she could lull him into a false sense of security by pretending to go along with his plan to rescue Ben. And then, when he wasn't looking, she'd slip away, make her way to the mine area and bargain for Ben's release.

That was her choice. Trust in herself, in her ability to rescue her brother. Or trust Aaron to do it.

Aaron returned shortly. She barely heard his footsteps before he thrust her backpack through the overlapping folds of the opening, the glow from his flashlight allowing her to see what he was doing. He hunkered down and held the flap to one side. He'd donned black rain gear now slick with rain which made him look even more intimidating,

"Do you have a flashlight in there?" He indicated her backpack.

"Yes."

He directed his flare at her pack. "Find it." He waited until she'd located it and turned it on. "Use it only inside the tent, and don't use it more than you have to. You might need it later. Try to get some sleep."

"Where are you going?"

He smiled, his teeth flashing white in the darkness. "Not far. I've got to take over the watch. I'll be back."

He let the elasticized flap pop back over its twin on the other side, leaving Zoe in complete darkness.

She found a dry tee shirt and traded it for the damp one. Then she pulled on her rain gear even though the tent appeared to be waterproof. Rain continued to drizzle down through the lush forest and the temperature dropped accordingly. Weariness had seeped into her bones long ago and she could feel her stamina slipping away bit by bit. She winced as she tried to ease the tension in her shoulders and upper back.

Ben. That's what kept her going. Whatever discomfort she was experiencing was surely nothing compared to what he'd been through these past months. She would not rest, she would not give up until Ben was safe. She knew if the situations were reversed, he would do the same for her.

She closed her eyes and began to pray, the pleas to that God Ben trusted reverberating around in her head like a panicked dragonfly searching for a way out. *Get me there. Help me get Ben out. Let us get out of this alive.* Some version of those entreaties repeated itself over and over.

She could not rest, for now that she was relatively dry and warm, her bladder needed attention. Immediate attention.

The last thing she wanted to do was get wet, get her raingear wet, and then return to the tent in it and get the inside of the tent wet. But the alternative was to strip down to nothing, leave her clothes in the tent, dry herself off afterward and put them back on. Ridiculous. Not with five men within feet of her. The rain poncho would provide coverage to her activity anyway. She didn't need to go far. She'd take her flashlight and step away from the tent, relieve herself and return. Then, perhaps, by some miracle she'd be able to sleep.

She slipped her wrist through the strap on the flashlight and wiggled her way out of the tent before she turned it on. She'd taken exactly two steps when her upper arm was encased in a steely grip. "Where do you think you're going?"

Again, she hadn't heard him approach. Perhaps he'd been right outside the tent, waiting for her to try to escape. So much for earning Aaron's trust.

"Excuse me, but I have to pee," she hissed back.

She saw the flash of his teeth and was immediately annoyed that he found her dilemma amusing. Men had it easy. Stand up, unzip, do your business. End of story. She'd be wrangling with zippers, trying not to pee on her poncho or her boots or the cuffs of her pants, squatting out in the jungle in the dark.

Aaron's grip on her arm relaxed and his hand slid down to take hers. He turned her flashlight off. "Come on."

She had no choice but to follow him.

He moved a short distance away and she followed, concentrating on the point of light he shown on the slick leaf-covered ground in front of them.

When he stopped, he said, "Do you need your flashlight to see what you're doing?"

"No, not really."

"Then leave it off. I'm going to step away, and turn my light off. When you're ready to head back, turn your light on. I'll come get you."

"Okay." Like she had any choice. She hoped he'd go far enough away that he couldn't hear what she was doing. Although with the patter of rain and the darkness, it was unlikely he'd be able to hear or see anything. And she highly doubted Aaron was the type who would watch. He seemed too honorable for such behavior.

Honorable? Aaron? Zoe adjusted her clothes. How did she know that about him? He probably killed people for a living. Hadn't he admitted as much? Where was the honor in that? But he did it for a good reason, to protect lots of other lives. At least she wanted to believe that about him. Like soldiers in wars. They killed, but they maintained their sense of honor. They did it to protect the innocent lives of the civilians. Aaron was no different. Except his fight wasn't in a war. His fights evidently involved individuals, or groups of individuals with interests contrary to those of his country. She wasn't sure why, but she desperately wanted to believe that about him.

As quickly as she could, she got her clothes back in place and turned her flashlight on. In seconds, Aaron was there, covering her hand with his and turning the light off. He waited a beat, standing there in the dark, the rain falling, his hand over hers, before he turned his light on. Keeping hold of her hand he led her back to the tent.

Chapter Twenty-Nine

She would never go camping, Zoe promised herself as she relived the memory of squatting amidst undergrowth, hoping her tush wasn't touching anything poisonous, with Aaron a short distance away. She would avoid being outside in rain at all costs. She wiggled around in the dark, trying to find a comfortable position on the thin floor of the now damp tent in her damp clothes next to her damp backpack. She would appreciate her bed and being warm and dry and having a roof over her head as long as she lived. She gave up the idea of being comfortable and instead lay on her back with her head on her backpack.

The thought of a bed sent her spiraling back to the room in that awful industrial building. The room where the phantom came and did wonderful things to and with her. She felt the familiar tightening in her gut she did every time she thought about their nights together. It was like he was there, right there. With her all the time. All she had to do was conjure up her imagined images of him above her or behind her or next to her. She could almost feel his arms around her, the way he smoothed strands of hair away from her face, the touch of his lips on her shoulder or her neck.

Involuntarily, she moaned low in her throat. If the phantom didn't know she was gone there might be a stack of white envelopes shoved under her door. Her broken, busted-in apartment door. No. Surely the phantom, clever as he was, had some way of knowing her whereabouts, would know that she had temporarily disappeared. He might wonder why or be worried. Possibly he would miss her.

Ridiculous to think about that now. But in an odd way, thoughts of the phantom helped relieve her misery and her tension, helped her ignore the dampness that seemed to seep into her backside even through the waterproof rain poncho. She closed her eyes, intending to pray. But her prayers were crowded out by memories of the phantom, which she found infinitely more comforting.

Zoe's eyes opened to the awareness she'd fallen asleep. Aaron was halfway through the opening of the tent, his eyes on her as if he'd willed her to wake up. She didn't look away, couldn't. Something in Aaron's eyes held her gaze. He was telling her something, but she wasn't sure what. That he cared about her? That he was sorry he'd gone back on his word to her?

"Did you sleep?" she whispered.

"No, but I will now. Think there's enough room in here for both of us?"

Zoe shifted her position, easing the crick in her neck caused by using the backpack as a pillow.

Her back was stiff from the damp and sleeping on the hard ground.

She curled on her side, making herself as small as possible and Aaron came the rest of the way into the tent.

"It'll be light soon," he informed her. He turned off the flashlight and she heard him shifting in the small space, brushing against her, as he searched for room for his much bigger body to rest.

It occurred to Zoe that were she not here, Aaron would have this one-person tent to himself. He'd have plenty of room.

"I can go outside," she whispered. "It stopped raining, didn't it?"

"Almost, but you're not going outside."

"But—"

"Come here." She felt his hand on her arm. "Lay down right here. On your side." He tugged on her until he got her where he wanted her. He shifted around some more, nudging her in the process, but when he was done, she was surprised to find she was fairly comfortable, her back pressed up against his front, his arm draped across her side.

"How's that?"

"Okay."

She listened to his breathing for a while, until she was pretty sure he'd fallen asleep. Their positions reminded her of waking up in the safe house with him. Which in turn reminded her of the phantom, who often spooned her the same way.

When Zoe next awoke, the rain had stopped, but the cool, wet air had seeped inside the tent. Carefully, she sat up. The light had a thick grayish quality to it but was light enough to see that Aaron appeared to be asleep. Though Zoe wondered if he ever really slept. His facial muscles didn't seem to relax completely. A faint frown line remained between his brows as if even at rest he was puzzling over a problem. Tiny lines radiated out from his eyes, more noticeable now than when he was awake.

Zoe wanted to kiss him. His mouth looked vulnerable and inviting. She craved the heat of his mouth, wondered what it would be like to be with him, to sleep with him, wake up next to him, or wake him up with a kiss.

She was being unfair having such thoughts. To herself. To him. The phantom stepped into her fantasy, and she knew a future with Aaron wasn't a possibility. Not after what she'd done. Sold herself. Become attached to a man she'd never seen. Become addicted to his special brand of invisible lovemaking. Again she asked herself how she could believe herself in love with a man she'd never seen, never met. She had only a vague idea of what he looked like. He was relatively young.

He had a well-honed physique because pretty much anywhere she touched was solid muscle. He had short hair, though she had no idea what color it was. No idea what color his eyes were, either. He wasn't particularly hairy anywhere on his body, which for some reason made her think his hair was light brown. Blond, maybe. Which made it likely that his eyes were either green or blue. Hazel.

Aaron has hazel eyes.

True. She studied Aaron's blondish brown hair.

He's in excellent physical condition.

True. But a lot of men are. What with a gym on practically every corner these days.

Height?

Aaron could be the right height. Could Aaron be the phantom?

She tried to remember how it felt to be close to him during the time they'd spent in the safe house, in bed together, though fully clothed.

Aaron had kissed her. The phantom never kissed her. It wasn't the same. Or was it?

She'd spent the past couple of hours beneath the curve of his arm in close, cramped quarters, layers of clothes and rain gear separating them, but there were similarities between Aaron and the phantom she was finding it harder and harder to discount. The clasped hands, for example. And

Aaron, like the phantom, seemed to have a penchant for running his fingers through her hair, smoothing it over her shoulder, brushing it out of her eyes. She thought of poker players and their tells. Small, instinctive movements and quirks, virtually unnoticeable unless your opponent was paying particular attention and knew what to look for.

It made no sense, though. Why would Aaron arrange to meet her as the phantom? Did it matter who the phantom was or what his reasons were?

Zoe uncapped the lid of her canteen and drank some water. If she kept up this line of questioning, she'd succeed only in exhausting herself again. Or giving herself a major headache. Neither of which would benefit her at the moment.

Besides she had to remember why she was here. And she had to remind herself that she couldn't trust Aaron to rescue Ben. She didn't trust him. That should be her new mantra. *I don't trust Aaron*. Even though his explanation seemed perfectly plausible, it didn't exactly inspire confidence that rescuing Ben was a top priority of his official mission. It seemed more of an afterthought. Ben deserved someone who was there for him and him alone with no ulterior motives other than his welfare. She was that person. Julio wasn't. Aaron wasn't. She had to remember that.

She'd look for a way to slip away from him and the others. She'd find Ben on her own. Somehow, she'd get him out of this jungle and back to civilization. Once she did, she'd never have to see Aaron again. For that matter, she'd have no reason to be with the phantom, either.

Chapter Thirty

Aaron's eyes opened quickly, making Zoe wonder if he'd truly been asleep at all while she'd been watching him. Was he secretly watching her from beneath his lashes? Good thing he couldn't read her mind.

He didn't say anything, but his gaze pinned her and she had the idea his brain was hard at work calculating how best to "handle" her. How to earn her trust and get her to do what he wanted so he could get on with his mission. She tried to rein in her mutinous thoughts and appear compliant, but it wasn't easy.

She probably looked a sight, after tramping through the woods and jungle yesterday, up the mountainside, getting wet from the rain and sleeping in the damp. More than anything she wanted to squelch those thoughts about her appearance, but she and Aaron had been... dating for lack of a better word. He'd been physically interested in her at one time, seemed to like kissing her, and maybe that would have led to more if they weren't here now. And the attraction wasn't one-sided, she had to admit. However, unlike her, Aaron woke looking pretty damn good with his beard stubble, his hair slightly mussed and his vivid gaze.

He sat up, rubbed his hands over his face and parted the tent flap to peer out. Zoe's stomach growled audibly. He turned back, his eyes dancing. "Hungry, are we?"

"I've got granola bars," she countered. She hated being at a disadvantage out here in the mountainous jungle and being fodder for his amusement.

He snorted softly. "You'll need more than a granola bar."

He slid out of the tent and held the flap for her. There were three other tents set up as if in a square, one at each connecting angle, all about 25 feet apart. She supposed that made sense. Were there an attack on one, the others were close enough to be alerted without necessarily being attacked at the same time. She shivered in the cool dawn air.

One of the men appeared, holding a mean-looking gun in his hands. He gave her that laser-like onceover they all seemed to have mastered before looking to Aaron. Aaron walked over to him and they conversed in low tones. Zoe wondered about what. She thought the other man's eyes slid briefly to her once more during their conversation. She could only imagine what Aaron was telling him.

He returned to her with the other man following.

"Zoe Bradford meet Paul Jaeger."

Paul nodded at her and offered his hand. Zoe shook it, hating that he seemed to inspire the same kind of confidence that Aaron did. He possessed that same sense of command, of knowledge. He had the ability to keep a woman, anyone for that matter safe, or die trying.

The three of them moved off to a makeshift kitchen. Aaron unzipped a thick canvas bag to reveal an assortment of foil wrapped packets of military foodstuff. Aaron indicated to her to choose. They were all labeled. "Macaroni and cheese." "Sausage biscuits." "Beef stew."

Zoe shuddered at the thought of eating cold beef stew out of a foil package. Without asking what she'd prefer, Aaron handed her sausage biscuits, then he and Paul made their choices and stood munching while Zoe tried to figure out how to open hers. She seemed to be all thumbs. After watching her fumble for a few minutes Aaron set his packet down and held her hand still, then zipped open a strip beneath the overlap of the seam to reveal two sausage biscuits inside.

"Thanks," Zoe said. He nodded, still holding her hand in his, and time stopped again as she gazed into those mesmerizing eyes. She felt a current of acute awareness run through her, and she almost gasped in surprise. From her peripheral sight it seemed that Paul was looking on with great interest. She felt oddly embarrassed, as if he'd witnessed something intensely private between her and Aaron. She tugged her hands out of Aaron's and picked up one of the biscuits.

She'd eaten about half of the surprisingly edible meal when the others joined them. Aaron introduced her to Jacques Gonzalez and Mark DiPaulo. She got the same keen inspection from both of them she'd received from Paul Jaeger. Julio nodded at her, ducking his head slightly as if in apology. She had nothing to say to him. She couldn't depend on him for help. He'd gotten her this far. Now she was on her own.

After everyone had eaten, Aaron escorted her away from the others, and gave her some privacy to relieve herself once more. In silence, Zoe dutifully followed him back the way they had come.

The others gathered around at Aaron's signal, including Julio. "We're going in today. According to Julio, the mine is virtually deserted on Sundays, because most of the mine workers are with their families. Paul's already done a perimeter check to confirm. There are some guards, and the principals, of course. And the hostage." His gaze didn't flicker in Zoe's direction, although surely everyone here knew who the hostage was and his relationship to her.

"We've got a few problems, though. We've now got two extra people to consider. Since Miss Bradford refuses to leave, even though her presence here jeopardizes our mission, we have no choice but to keep her with us. Mr. Dominguez seems equally obstinate about his role in all of this, although I've done my best to make it clear to him that his participation is of no benefit and that we cannot offer him either transport out of the country or safe haven of any kind."

Aaron looked resigned and rubbed his hand against the back of his neck. "So, we're going to split up into two teams. Jaeger, you'll be with me and Miss Bradford. Gonzalez and DiPaulo, you'll be with Mr. Dominguez. We're going to move into position. On my go, Gonzales and DiPaulo, you'll set off the charges, creating a distraction. Jaeger and I will take out the principals and retrieve the hostage. We'll rendezvous, as agreed. Mr. Dominquez, at that point, you'll be on your own. We'll have a ride out of here as per the original op. Any questions?"

The way he said it made it clear that he did not want to be questioned. Which was just the opening Zoe was looking for. "What do you do if something goes wrong?"

He pinned her with a steely gaze, eyes narrowed. "If everyone follows orders, nothing should go wrong."

"Well, what if you're unable to 'retrieve the hostage' as planned?"

"I don't see that as a probability. All indications are that at the moment, anyway, he's loosely guarded. As I said, the charges will create a distraction. The focus won't be on the hostage, it will be on damage control. We'll retrieve him and head for the rendezvous point. We've got radio contact with our ride. We'll get out as planned."

"It seems to me that retrieving the hostage is an afterthought. If you can get him, you will. If you can't, no big deal."

"I think we need to discuss this in private."

Aaron took Zoe's arm in a none-too-happy grip. "Be ready to go when I get back," he told the others tersely as he marched her away from them.

Zoe didn't care for being dragged off as if Aaron were some caveman and she the woman he'd chosen. For the first time, she felt a little afraid of him. Every muscle in his body seemed to radiate rage and it was all directed at her. He'd probably like to break her in half right about now.

He stalked through the forest like an angry bear, shoving vines and small branches out of his way. She didn't know how far they'd gone before she finally said, "Who died and made you God anyway?"

He stopped abruptly and she ran into him. He whirled on her, his eyes bright with anger. His hands encircled her upper arms and he gave her shake. "Goddammit, Zoe, do you have any idea how you're complicating things? You're actually endangering your brother by being here. Your presence does nothing but jeopardize this mission. Do you want him to die? Do you want us all to die? Is that it?"

"No!"

"Then goddammit, stop questioning my authority at every turn. Why can't you believe that I'll get Ben out alive? That I'll bring him back to you?"

Zoe was sure she detected a note of hurt in his voice. Aaron took her disrespect for his command personally. Before she could even process this new information, she answered his question. "Because I don't trust you. Ben isn't your first priority, and you and I both know that. Rescuing him is third or fourth on your list of objectives. You see him as expendable. If things don't work out the way you've planned, if you can't get to him, I'm afraid that you'll, that you'll—"

Zoe choked up. She couldn't speak. Tears filled her eyes, though she fought letting them fall. They spilled over as she stood face to face with Aaron. God, she hadn't cried in a long time. She wouldn't let herself. Tears were a sign of weakness. She couldn't afford to be weak. She wouldn't be. She had to be strong. For herself. For Ben.

"Oh, God. Don't. Please don't cry."

Aaron sagged as he stared at her. Every ounce of fight went out of him in a physical transformation. Zoe witnessed it, but she was too overwrought to analyze it. He cupped her face in one hand and brushed at the tear track on her cheek, which only caused more of them to spill over.

The next thing she knew she was crushed against his chest, letting him absorb some of her misery and her fear. Oh, God, it felt good to be held. He brushed his lips across her temple. The tears ebbed, but she didn't let go and neither did he. He stayed there, his head bent over hers.

"I'm scared," Zoe whispered.

"Don't be."

She took a deep shaky breath. "Promise me. Promise me you'll get Ben out."

"Do you think I can?"

Realistically, Zoe knew Aaron was Ben's best bet. What she didn't know was how important a successful rescue was to Aaron. Somehow, she had to make it as important to him as it was to her. But how? He'd turned down all of her previous offers.

She stepped back. "I know you can. In my head I know you're the best chance I have to get Ben home. But in my heart..."

"In your heart you don't trust me to do it. You don't trust me."

"I want to. But I can't."

"What if I succeed? What if I do everything I tell you I'm going to do and I get us all out of here alive?"

"Then I'll do anything for you. Anything," she repeated for emphasis.

The light came back into Aaron's eyes, the gold flecks seem to dance in the rays of morning sun glinting down through the trees. He grinned. "Anything?"

Zoe nodded gravely. "Anything."

"Then we're going to find out how well you keep your word because I plan to hold you to that."

He bent and kissed her, lightly at first, but the touch of his lips made her light-headed. She sighed against his mouth, deepening the kiss, wanting to believe he could do anything and everything he said he would. That tingle of awareness, of connection ripped through her again, as he held her close, possessively, his mouth harsh against hers as if searching for something he wasn't sure he'd find. Recognition. That's what it was. Like she'd been here before. A weird sense of deja vu, that wasn't exactly deja vu washed over her. Because she knew for certain she'd never been in a mountainous jungle kissing Aaron before. The feelings that washed through her shook her to the core before Aaron ended the kiss. He bent his head to hers. "We need to get back because we need to get going. Until this is over, I'm the boss, okay?"

"Okay."

"And you'll follow my orders."

"Yes."

"And you trust me to get Ben out."

Zoe hesitated. She leaned back and looked into his eyes. Wrong or right, she had to trust him. She had no choice. "Yes."

"Okay. Let's go."

Chapter Thirty-One

It was still early. Realistically, Aaron knew it could be a couple of hours before they saw any movement in the camp below, but already he felt the hum of adrenaline in his veins in anticipation. His normally alert senses were in super charge mode. Eyes, ears, smell and especially that sixth sense he relied on heavily, gut instinct. It had saved him more than once, sent him in early, got him out before disaster struck. He'd learned to listen to his gut over his other senses.

His gut was nervous. Something wasn't right about the set-up. It was too quiet. He'd been distracted by Zoe's presence. He'd briefly lost his focus. Had the principals escaped? Was Ben Dumont still in that shack? Was he even still alive?

Gonzalez and DiPaulo had been on the last two watches. They'd circled the camp and the mine area alternately, would have been alert to an exodus from the camp. Aaron counted the same number of vehicles at the mouth of the trail as yesterday. Perhaps the rain had kept everyone awake last night. Perhaps they were all sleeping late. The sun had come up barely an hour ago. He told himself to cool it, to focus, and for God's sake not to panic. Patience had been a virtue that had been hard to come by but he'd acquired it. He'd had no choice. Waiting was inevitable in his line of work. Today was no different, he told himself. Only that the entire rest of his life, the future he'd dreamed of depended on the outcome. No extra pressure there. He could do this. He would do this. Do what he'd said he'd do, what he'd come here for. Destroy the mine, eliminate Sheppard, rescue Ben Dumont and get him, his team and Zoe out alive.

A tent flap lifted. Aaron froze, his gaze fixed on the opening. Nearby he knew Jaeger came to attention as well. Aaron put his hand on Zoe's wrist alerting her. She stilled the moment he touched her.

A man emerged, slightly stooped at first and then straightening. He walked with a limp to the blackened embers of what had been a campfire. From beneath a tarp he removed several sticks of wood and kindling. Soon he had a small fire going.

Aaron stared hard at the man who'd once been a trusted co-worker, a member of the team. He and Nick Sheppard had a friendly rivalry at one time, with Nick getting in good-natured digs at Aaron's expertise in the field, which Aaron had occasionally returned with teasing remarks about Nick's shortcomings. He hadn't realized the depth of the bitterness, the jealousy that had taken Nick over the edge, until their mission in Belize. Nick had nearly cost him his entire team by his refusal to follow protocol, by ignoring Aaron's command to withdraw when it became apparent the mission was failing. When Nick went down, it had been because of his own choices. Aaron had made the decision to leave him behind to save himself and the others. That was one of his strengths, which Russell Gannett had pointed out to his superiors more than once. Aaron knew when to break the rules to get the job done, but he also had the ability to judge when a mission had gone awry. He had the highest success rate and the lowest casualty rate of all the Level One team leaders.

Nick had been a decent agent, but his ego often got in the way of his performance. He'd been temporarily demoted from team leader and that had rankled. Being assigned to Aaron's team, when he considered Aaron his archrival had alienated him even further from Level One's objectives. Aaron could see that now, but he hadn't two years ago. He'd thought he could work with Nick, bring him around, talk to Gannett and get him back into a leadership role. But then he'd given them no choice but to believe him dead and leave him in Belize.

Now they'd come full circle. Where once he'd been a friendly rival, Nick was now the enemy. Nick Sheppard and his illegal mining operation stood in the way of everything Aaron wanted. Aaron had no choice but to eliminate the obstacle.

A woman appeared from the same tent behind Sheppard. She threw a dark braid over her shoulder and began to move around the fire, gathering utensils and stored foodstuffs, preparing to cook a meal.

From another tent emerged two of the guards Aaron had seen yesterday. Big burly blonds, expatriated Americans no doubt, probably ex-military as well, recruited from Belize or Costa Rica. They were dressed in fatigues, loose pants and tee shirts and boots. Both removed themselves from the immediate area for a short while and then returned. They sat on a hefty tree log, close to the fire, which had apparently been brought there for the express purpose of seating. Both lit cigarettes and watched the woman prepare the food with avid interest.

Soon the scent of coffee and sizzling pork rose through fresh mountain air. Aaron was thinking it might be best to wait until all the inhabitants were seated and distracted by food, to begin setting off the charges. The two guards were wearing only sidearms, though Aaron knew they had automatic rifles available, for they'd each been carrying one yesterday.

Their demeanor indicated they'd been lulled into a false sense of safety and Aaron was surprised at Nick Sheppard's lax security precautions. Just because no one had discovered or attacked the mine up to this point, certainly didn't mean it couldn't happen. Nick had obviously become overly confident that no one would dare, or that he would know about it in advance if such a thing were to occur.

"We've got company," came Gonzalez through the earpiece. He was speaking in a near whisper but Aaron had no trouble hearing him. He swept his gaze west searching for movement. Though he had a clear view of the mine area from his vantage point, he was far enough back in the tree-lined perimeter to avoid detection. But it also blocked his view to the east and west.

He waited for Gonzalez to report further. "Para-military. Guerillas. Loosely banded. Approaching from the west at nine o'clock."

Aaron swore silently. Where had this band of guerillas come from? It wasn't a coincidence that now, on a Sunday morning they were approaching the mine area. Aaron didn't believe in coincidence.

"How many?"

"Hard to tell. I've spotted three, but I can see movement behind them. They're spread out."

An unpleasant tingle shot up Aaron's spine. He knew bands of guerillas could have as many as a hundred members. If they were fanning out, coming in behind his team, surrounding the circle that encompassed the mine, he and the others would have no place to hide. They'd be forced either to approach the mine head on or try to fight their way through the guerillas to retreat.

"How's your position?"

"Okay for the moment. We're hunkered down pretty good."

Aaron knew Gonzalez. He had a knack for finding excellent cover. An unskilled reconnaissance team could walk right by him.

"What about Dominguez?"

"Under control."

That meant he'd been gagged and bound. Aaron breathed a small sigh of relief. He wished he'd questioned Zoe more closely yesterday. When exactly had she arrived in the village? Julio could have set her up. He could have alerted this guerilla force. Zoe's plan all along had been to bargain for Ben's freedom with all those American dollars she'd collected over the past couple of months. There'd been no ransom demand, yet Julio was her almost direct link to Ben. He'd been calling, giving her reports on Ben's welfare, reports that made her increasingly anxious.

But Aaron was willing to bet Julio had no loyalty either to Zoe or to Ben. He probably had an entirely different agenda. One that involved acquiring American dollars whenever the opportunity presented itself. Aaron had seen Julio's kind before. He was a player. Even in this remote part of the world comprised of mountains and jungle dotted with small villages. He was a free agent and his services were probably available to the highest bidder.

It was no coincidence that Julio was here. Zoe was here. Zoe's money was here. Ben was here. And a band of armed guerillas happened to arrive. He thought it more than likely that Julio had set up an ambush. One that would relieve Zoe of her cash, probably leave her dead and Ben in the same position of captivity as before. Or maybe they'd planned to kill Ben, too, since no one else was likely to step forward with a hefty sum of cash to bargain for his release.

"Let's sit tight," Aaron whispered. "If you have to take them out, detonate the charges at the same time. Hopefully, that'll buy us some time. Jaeger and I will take care of the mine personnel. Once we retrieve the hostage, we'll move out."

Aaron frowned as he ended the communication. He had a problem. Zoe. Once the charges started to detonate, the mine would implode in on itself with a minimum of debris elsewhere. At least that's what DiPaulo had assured him based on their calculations. He trusted DiPaulo, the man was the best when it came to explosives. His original plan had been to detonate the charges, take out Sheppard and the others in the camp, retrieve Ben and have Zoe join them as they made their getaway to the rendezvous point. She'd be perfectly safe staying where she was while everything else was happening. He didn't need her help, and he didn't want her in the fray where she could get hurt. Leaving her hidden would have been the best plan. But with guerillas potentially surrounding the area, that wasn't such a good plan any more. He couldn't spare a man to escort her or guard her. He and the rest of the team would have their hands more than full now with this added threat. He motioned her to move as quietly as possible back from their vantage point.

"I have to go to the bathroom," she whispered as soon as he halted several yards away.

Aaron barely managed not to roll his eyes. *This* is why women were not in combat roles, why they weren't suited for the kind of work he and his all-male team did. There were too many hygiene issues to slow a woman and the rest of the team down or make it more likely they'd be discovered in a situation such as this.

Aaron indicated a medium-sized tree about a foot away from them. "Go. Right there. Don't argue."

He gave her credit. She stepped away. He turned his back, his automatic rifle at the ready, the hair on the back of his neck standing on end. He was used to the heightened state of awareness.

It was a normal state of affairs as one prepared to go into battle. In the Army he'd felt the same way when they'd been called to do bombing raids over Iraq. And many times since when he'd been on a mission, as it came down to the wire, right before execution of the op.

Zoe reappeared and he moved with her another few steps away, behind another tree that was as good a vantage point as any at keeping them hidden but allowed him to see around it. He covered the mouthpiece of his headset with one hand, keeping his finger on the trigger of his rifle, knowing he could shift positions and use it in a split second if he had to.

"We've got a band of armed guerillas moving in behind us from the west." He shook his head. "No. No questions. There's no time. You have to do what I tell you. You have to trust me." Zoe clamped her mouth shut and nodded, though he could see she wasn't happy about it.

"Do you know how to use a gun by any chance?"

Zoe nodded.

"You do?" Aaron tried to keep the incredulity out of his whisper. "Do you have one on you?"

She shook her head, her disappointment obvious.

Aaron took his sidearm from his belt. He handed it to her along with several extra clips of ammunition. "Put this in the back of your belt where you can get to it if you need it. Since you're right-handed put this in your left pocket." She did.

"Once the charges detonate, we're going in. Not you. Us," he explained. Zoe nodded. "I can't leave you here, and I don't want you down there near the action." He stared into her eyes, noting her solemn expression. "I'll get Ben out." She nodded. "I need you to stay as hidden as you can and start moving to the road where those Jeeps are and stay there and stay hidden until you see us coming, understand?"

Zoe nodded.

"Keep an eye out behind you, in front of you, all around you for guerillas. Shoot if you have to. Can you do that?"

Again Zoe nodded. Aaron noted the determined set of her jaw, the light in her eyes. He believed her. But she would only shoot what she could see. If she was attacked from behind—no. He wouldn't go there. He'd have to trust her to take care of herself, just as she was trusting him to rescue her brother.

A sudden thought occurred to him. There was one more thing he could do to insure her safety. Keeping his rifle in his right hand he undid the Velcro straps on his Kevlar vest and shrugged out of it. "Put this on under your jacket."

Zoe tried to shove it back at him. "No. What about you?"

"Don't argue." He hung the too-big vest on her slender frame and fastened the straps as tight as they'd go. She yanked her jacket back on, the set of her mouth clearly indicating her displeasure.

He cupped his hand around the back of her neck and bent close, pressing his lips to hers in a hard kiss. Then came the first unmistakable shots of gunfire. He broke away from her, stared into her eyes for a split second. "Show time," he whispered.

Grabbing her hand, he led her back toward their earlier vantage point, letting go before they reached it. He pointed, indicating for her to start circling the perimeter heading east. He didn't wait to see if she did before he joined Jaeger as the first explosion detonated.

Chapter Thirty-Two

Zoe stumbled through the vine-tangled forest on her own, the handgun Aaron had given her clutched in her right hand. She was glad she had paid attention during the self-defense class's session on handgun basics. Another charge detonated and she could hear gunfire and shouting. She told herself not to panic. She told herself she trusted Aaron. She told herself that he would rescue Ben, that he didn't need her help, that the best thing she could do was follow his orders and get herself to the opening of the track back down the mountain and wait there.

Another charge detonated. More shouts. More gunfire. Zoe's heart raced as she continued on, afraid to look back in case a guerilla happened to be hot on her heels. And what if one was there, aiming at her this very moment, ready to shoot her through her heart?

Another charge detonated. The scent of dust and destruction floated through the dense mountain air. *Please God. Please God. Please God.* She began her silent chant in rhythm to her heartbeat as she stumbled forward, tripping over roots and vines buried beneath a blanket of dead leaves.

More shouting, mostly in a Spanish dialect, reached her ears. She realized she was almost out of breath, more from fear than exertion. She paused, ducking behind a thick tree trunk, telling herself to breathe, to stay calm, to not be afraid. She panted, knowing that wasn't the way to calm herself, but she couldn't help it. She felt like a wild thing, exposed, as if she couldn't run fast enough, hide well enough to escape her imagined pursuers. Surely none of the guerillas had traveled this far, past the earlier vantage point overlooking the mine area. If they had approached from the west, surely Aaron and his team had stopped them before they could encircle the camp.

But she didn't know how many there were. Perhaps others had approached from other directions simultaneously. Perhaps they'd rescue Ben only to be stopped by another force entirely separate from his captors. In which case it wouldn't hurt to be better armed than she was.

Zoe set her backpack down and opened the flap. Digging through, her fingers found the knife she'd buried at the bottom above the stacks of hundred dollar bills. She gripped it tightly and withdrew it with her left hand. She remembered how Aaron and his men constantly seemed to swivel their heads whenever they stopped moving. She did the same, methodically scanning the area on all sides, perking her ears to listen for any human movement.

She couldn't hear anything except gunfire now. She wondered if there would be more explosions. She switched the gun to her left hand and put the knife into her right pocket where it would be easily accessible if the need arose. She was glad she'd worn the black cargo pants, the ones with numerous zippered pockets she'd bought for this purpose. A civilian feminine version of the team's uniform pants.

She took another moment to open her canteen to gulp down some water, telling herself she couldn't afford to get dehydrated and who knew when she'd get another chance to take a drink. Recapping the bottle, she closed up the pack, and slipped one of the straps over her shoulder. As she did, two more explosions came in short succession, rocking the ground beneath her just as she'd been about to rise. She lost her balance and fell backward, losing her grip on her pack. She and it fell down an incline. The pack kept rolling, even when she managed to stop herself, by grabbing onto some thick leaf-covered vines. She'd somehow managed not to lose Aaron's gun, but it shook in her grasp now, as she tried to get her bearings.

The incline was much steeper than she'd first realized, and the bottom, she felt quite sure, would empty out into the bowl that was the mine area. She wasn't sure how far she'd come, how far away the track was. What she did know was that she'd somehow lost sight of her backpack, her backpack with all of her hard-earned money in it. The money that was supposed to save Ben. Even if she didn't need it for that purpose now, she'd spent months acquiring it, had put herself through an incredible amount of emotional angst to get it. She couldn't let it go, leave it in the jungle for some guerilla to find who would use it to overthrow an already unstable government or worse.

She had no idea how much time she had. There was still gunfire. English shouts mixed with Spanish as instructions were called. There might be more explosions coming. Had Aaron rescued Ben yet? They might be making their way to the road, waiting for her, looking for her. If they were being pursued, she was holding them up.

She scrambled to a semi-standing position, crouching low amongst the overhanging limbs and vines. She scanned the area, unable to see the dark green backpack anywhere. She took a couple of waddling steps forward staying low and hanging onto the vines lest she pitch headlong down the incline. Because down the incline meant she'd be right at the edge of the bowl, exposed, in even more danger.

Leave the backpack. No sooner did the thought come into her head than she rejected it. Whether it was her thought or God's, she didn't care. He knew what she'd done to get that money and He knew why. Maybe He'd even been the Invisible Provider of all that cash she'd been sure she needed to rescue Ben. She couldn't let it go that easily. She couldn't walk away from it now. Even if she didn't need it to pay off Ben's captors.

There. There it was. She spotted it at the very bottom of the incline, barely covered by vines and a bit of brushy undergrowth. To get it would put her at the bottom of the incline as well. But if she continued her downward trek, she didn't know if she would be able to climb back up.

Leave the backpack.

I can't! She wanted to shout in frustration. She was so close. She could see it. Almost touch it. If she crossed the incline a few feet, if she laid out flat on her stomach, she'd be able to reach the strap and drag it up to her. Then she could hang onto the vine and crawl back up into the trees and continue on to the road.

She tucked the gun into the back waistband of her pants then tugged the vine as she prepared to lay herself out flat, but the vine had hardly any give. It was thick and already impaled on and twined around other bits of growth. She'd have to let go of it to get to the backpack. Maybe she could hang onto it with her toes. She inched forward over the slanted ground, and hooked the toes of her boots under the vine. But that didn't make her quite long enough to reach the backpack. Another two feet or so, that's all she needed. She tugged on the vine with her feet, but it gave very little. If she kept it up, there was always the chance that she'd yank it off its moorings entirely, that it might snap from above and do her no good at all.

"Oh, God," Zoe cried out in a frustrated whisper.

She unhooked her toes from the vine, certain she could grab the pack and then inch her way backwards on her stomach until she was within reach of the vine. The ground beneath her seemed even more treacherous when she let go. Dirt and leaves slid from beneath her as she inched forward, collecting at the bottom.

Gunfire continued, but it had lessened. An eerie quiet descended in between shots, occasionally punctuated by running footsteps muffled by the leaf-covered ground.

Zoe's fingers brushed the strap of the pack. Almost there. She inched forward a bit more. Wound her fingers around the strap. Success!

Two detonations in quick succession, rocked the earth. The bottom seemed to fall out from beneath where Zoe lay. The incline shifted and she was rolling, rolling, unable to stop, her backpack still caught in her fingers, whipping up and around her and beneath her with each revolution until she came to rest in a rain of gravel and dirt and leaves. An ominous crack prefaced the fall of a tree and Zoe instinctively, cowered, covering her head with her hands as it fell close by, the branches brushing her back, nearly covering her, the trunk only a foot away from her head.

The silence was almost more deafening than the detonations, more frightening than the uprooted tree.

Slowly Zoe lifted her head enough to see over the trunk of the tree, her eyes scanning in all directions. The gravel-lined bowl was littered with still bodies, some in the sort of military uniforms she'd seen on magazine and television coverage of foreign soldiers, dark green army fatigues with canvas caps. A layer of dust floated on the air. Where was the shack that had housed Ben?

One of the tents was completely collapsed, showing only the outlines of whatever objects had been inside it. The other listed to one side, looking as if it too were about ready to deflate. The inverted vee of the mine was buried under rubble. Bits of gravel and dirt and fresh leaves and uprooted plants had tumbled down from above so that it appeared as a swollen river might after a heavy run-off, but frozen with the debris on top of it.

Where were Aaron and the others? Where was Ben?

Had she delayed too long? Had they rescued Ben, perhaps waited for her and then had no choice but to leave without her?

Panic engulfed her. Surely not. Although time had seemed to stand still since Aaron had pointed in the direction he wanted her to take, surely she hadn't taken that much time. Surely it had only been a matter of minutes, a half hour at most since the first shots they'd heard. He wouldn't leave her here, would he?

Stop! She scolded herself. Think. Be logical. Aaron and Jaeger had been behind her, further from the road than she was. Gonzalez and DiPaulo, although she didn't know their exact position, had been even further west of them. She had to have a head start on all of them, even with the time she'd wasted crawling down the incline to retrieve her backpack.

She scanned the pit slowly, forcing herself to focus, to search for even the smallest movement, any sign of life, of Aaron or his men. Any sign of Ben. Goose bumps rose on her skin as the silence seemed to take on a life of its own. She wasn't alone. On some level she knew that. There were other human beings here. Live ones. Possibly uninjured. Watching, waiting, as she was.

Zoe swallowed a gulp of air, hoping to swallow her panic and uncertainty with it. Aaron's instructions hadn't allowed for deviation from the plan. Ducking lower, she looked over her shoulder. The opening on the east side, where the vehicles were parked at the top of the road was perhaps fifty yards away. She saw no sign of life. No Aaron.

No Ben. But that didn't mean they weren't there, waiting for her.

Had she stayed at the top of the bowl and circled the perimeter in an easterly direction, she'd be there now, either joined with them or waiting until they arrived. As it was, were she to try to make it there now, from her current location, she'd have to cross open terrain, even if she stuck close to the edge of the incline. She couldn't hide her movements, her direction, or her ultimate goal.

She didn't have a choice. She couldn't stay here indefinitely. If, by some miracle, they were already there, she was delaying their movement down the mountain to the rendezvous point. If Ben were as weak as she'd been led to believe, every second counted. She didn't want him to die while waiting for her. If she'd blown his survival because she'd retrieved her cash-filled backpack, even when that voice inside told her not to, she'd never forgive herself.

She wanted to scream in frustration, but she didn't dare. She didn't know what to do, but she had to do something. And her choices were severely limited. Stay here or head for the road.

Oh, God, oh, God, oh God.

No voice answered her back. She was on her own.

She looked behind her again, both sides, saw nothing. Once more she scanned the area in front of her. Silence. Nothing. But that didn't mean there was no one there. She couldn't see the entire area. The one remaining tent blocked part of her view. There were bits of foliage on the west end, even down here in the pit, enough to provide cover for someone who didn't want to be seen.

She had to get out of here, had to take a chance that someone or more than one someone was lying in wait. She had her backpack. She could hold it, try to use it as a shield to the side and make a run for it. She still had Aaron's gun tucked securely in her waistband, but she'd save it for when she got to the parked vehicles. Use them for cover, before retrieving it to return fire if it came to that. She wouldn't be able to hit anything while running anyway.

Okay. She had a plan now. That made her feel slightly better. She kept her head down as she untangled her fingers from the strap of the backpack. No need to alert anyone out there to her position before absolutely necessary. With the pack in front of her she took another moment, scanning, focusing, sweeping her gaze slowly across the pit, searching for the slightest movement, listening for a sound that didn't belong. A breeze fluttered across the treetops. Some of the smoke seemed to lift with it, but she saw nothing, heard nothing.

She moved into a crouch position, squatting a moment longer, readying herself, for her intent was to spring up and make a full-out run for the vehicles crowded together at the top of the track. Maybe the keys were in one of them. Or both of them, she thought wildly. She had the sudden bizarre picture of herself careening down the mountainside in one, pursued by guerilla soldiers brandishing firearms, shouting and shooting at her, while she laughed at their feeble attempts to catch her.

A lot of good that would do her. She didn't know where the rendezvous point was. She'd relied on Aaron and the others to get her there. What if Aaron and the others were dead? Bile rose in her throat at the thought and she forced it back down. No. No way was Aaron dead. Not Aaron who was like a life force all on his own. Quick, capable, alert Aaron with his air of command who bent everyone, even her, to his will. Trust me, he'd said. She had. She did. He wasn't dead. He was here. She couldn't see him, but he was here. And he had Ben with him. And his team, too. They were going to get out of here. Alive. All of them. She wasn't going to screw it up. Not now. Now when they were so close.

Fortified by her mental pep talk, she sprang up, turned and darted for the assortment of ancient Jeeps and pickup trucks. No shots were fired. Nothing happened. She sprinted across the uneven ground, slipped once on the gravel but didn't lose her footing. She scooted behind the nearest truck, lowering herself to watch and wait. Nothing moved. She looked down what she could see of the dirt road, little more than a rutted track that led away from the mine area. Nothing. She stared into the trees and jungle growth on the other side of the track, willing Aaron and the others, *someone*, to be there. Nothing.

Through the truck's open windows she looked back at what she could see of the pit. Again nothing. She relaxed marginally, straightened, continuing to scan, to listen. *Where were they?*

Just as she'd decided her best bet might be to cross the track and hide herself in the foliage on the other side, she heard a noise behind her. Before she could turn around, the gun was removed from her belt and an arm locked tight around her neck squeezing off the air to her lungs. An ominous click signaled the gun being cocked, the barrel pressed hard against her skull above her ear.

Instead of the panic she'd expected to feel, she felt a weird sort of calm wash over her. She concentrated on breathing what tiny bit of air managed to get past the vice-like hold around her throat. Whoever had her was male. Taller than her. And definitely stronger. She tossed up another prayer of thanks to the divine inspiration that had led her to that series of self-defense classes, as many of the lessons came back to her. Staying calm was number one. Surveying her surroundings was number two. Was there anything that could be used as a weapon against her attacker? Screaming to alert help was definitely not an option. She knew she could not overpower this assailant. Her workouts had made her stronger, given her more stamina. While they had increased her strength, they hadn't increased her height or her weight. Males, simply by virtue of genetics were gifted with more muscle mass. And this one had a lot of it.

His clothes were dusty and sweaty. The scent of both filled her nostrils.

"You want me, Manning," the man shouted in the direction of the pit. "Come and get me."

Chapter Thirty-Three

Every curse word Aaron had ever heard or knew raced through his head but none of them seemed dire enough for the current situation. *Damn, damn, damn*, was what began circulating through his brain as he assessed his options.

In the end, he supposed it was appropriate that it came down to this. He and Nick Sheppard squared off against one another with Zoe caught in the middle. He'd done almost everything he'd set out to do. The emerald mine was now buried in so much rubble that it would take a small army and a lot of heavy equipment to dig it out. The other three members of his team, after a brief battle with the small band of guerillas and the two guards, had retrieved Ben and were at this moment on their way to the rendezvous point. He'd purposely stayed behind to make sure of two things. That there were no survivors and that Zoe was where she was supposed to be when he met up with her.

Typical Zoe, he thought. Full of surprises. How she'd managed to get from the top of the pit to the bottom was beyond him. All she had to do was follow the perimeter to the end where the trees thinned out and the track opened up. She could stay back in the cover of the forest once she spotted the vehicles and wait, dammit. He'd have been able to get himself out of the bowl and circle around to join her. No sweat.

Instead she'd somehow ended up right smack in the middle of the action. He'd spotted her head above the tree trunk the first time she'd peeked over it, and he was sure Nick had seen her as well, for his view from behind her would have been much better. Unfortunately, Aaron had lost track of Nick during the fight, as he'd focused on eliminating the armed threat and getting Ben out alive. He hadn't seen him go down, hadn't located his body among those lying in the pit. Ergo, he'd assumed him to still be alive. He'd been waiting him out, waiting for him to make a move so he could pick him off and be done with it, meet up with Zoe and get the hell out of here.

Where else would Nick wait, but near the vehicles, ready to make a run for it as soon as the coast was clear. Knowing Nick he probably had millions tucked away from his illegal mining operation. He could go anywhere, do anything, resurface in some other Third World country, running some other operation detrimental to the interests of the U.S. and to whatever country was unlucky enough to have him land there. A good agent gone bad.

Aaron wished he'd told Jaeger to hang back with him. Wished he'd left him positioned at the top of the perimeter with a sniper rifle. Jaeger was an excellent shot. He would find an angle and drop Sheppard before he could pull the trigger and blow Zoe's head off. Cowboy, Aaron thought now. Grandstander. Always had to be the hero. Make sure his team was safe, the objectives reached. Like a captain, he preferred to go down with his ship rather than allow his men to do so. The truth was, he hadn't needed to send all three of them with Ben. Two would have been enough. And it definitely would have improved his odds against Sheppard now. What had he been thinking? That he'd have time alone with Zoe as they trekked toward the rendezvous point? He could tell her he'd gotten Ben out as he'd promised, and be the sole recipient of her undying gratitude. He'd be her hero when they reached the helo and she found Ben and his team safely on board.

Idiot, he chastised himself. Even if he hadn't had those thoughts consciously, they'd probably been lurking there somewhere in the back of his head, clouding his judgment. This is why the agency discouraged romantic entanglements and long-term involvement with a woman. Smart agency. Dumb agent.

It was up to him now. He'd done everything else he'd said he'd do. And there was his reward. Standing right there with Nick Sheppard's arm around her neck and a gun to her head. And

Barbara Meyers

Aaron, the master of improvisation, couldn't think of a damn thing to do. He couldn't move or he'd lose his cover, crouched down as he was behind the few bushes at the west end of the pit. He couldn't get back up to the perimeter and circle around. Nick would shoot Zoe first and him second because he'd be a wide open target. And if he didn't do something pretty quickly, he expected Nick to get behind the wheel of the Jeep he was standing behind and hightail it down the mountain. The only question was would he shoot Zoe first or take her with him as a hostage? Aaron couldn't allow any of those scenarios to occur. He had two objectives. Kill Nick. Save Zoe. How hard could it be?

Zoe was his ace in the hole. Zoe Bradford. Full of surprises. He'd been silently communicating with her for months, wondering if she was picking up his signals both in his role as her anonymous lover and as himself out in the open. He'd been trying to tell her without words who he was, how he felt, willing her to figure out that he'd been there for her all along.

He hoped he could silently communicate with her now and that she'd pick up the signal. He hoped he'd know when she did. Between the two of them they could take Nick Sheppard down and get out of this with their lives.

His options were limited. He'd been insisting to Zoe that she had to trust him and finally, thankfully, she had. Now, without her knowing it, he was going to put his trust in Zoe, in her eternal ability to take him by surprise, only in this case, he hoped she understood that Nick was the one she needed to take by surprise.

Slowly he rose, giving himself a few seconds to let the blood flow back into his limbs after remaining in one position for so long. He'd given Zoe his handgun, the gun that Nick was now pointing at her head. Aaron had no choice but to use his rifle. That was okay, except in a long stand-off, it was heavier and it took both arms to hold it. No problem, he told himself. He was going to get out of this. He hadn't come all this way, risked everything, to die in a damn jungle rock pit on a mountain in Central America.

Slowly he made his way forward, allowing himself to be seen, keeping his sights trained on Sheppard's head.

"Let her go, Nick. You don't need her," he shouted.

Nick grinned, his eyes wild. "The hell I don't. I think this little lady might be my ticket out of here."

"You're not getting out, Nick. Not this time."

"Sorry you left me for dead in Belize? You didn't think I'd survive, did you? I'm like a cat, Manning. Nine lives. I figure I've got eight left."

"Nope. Just this one. And it's gonna end real soon, Nick, so say your prayers."

"Prayers? Hah. Never did me any good. Don't guess it will now."

Aaron didn't like the set up. Nick was behind the bed of a truck which hid fully half his body and left Aaron fewer targets. He'd go for the head, of course, but there was always the slightest chance that Zoe would move the wrong way. In which case, he wouldn't have Nick to blame for her death, but only himself.

"You want to talk Nick? Let's talk. Come out here. You've got a hostage covering you. You're not leaving me too much to aim at."

"I'm fine right here."

"Yeah, well, you always were a coward," Aaron sneered. "Never expected you to hide behind a woman, though."

The attack on his ego worked. Nick edged closer to the tail of the truck. "She's your woman, otherwise she'd be dead by now."

"She's not mine. I barely know her," Aaron lied, hoping Zoe would understand.

"Then why do you care?"

"I don't. Except my objective is to see you dead. Not her."

"Oh, yes. The famous objectives. Too bad you couldn't reach the one set for you in Belize."

"I could have. If you hadn't fucked up the op."

"Liar!" Nick shouted, he seemed tempted to gesture with his gun hand, but instead he moved it slightly away from Zoe's head and then back. "I should have been team leader. The mission would have been successful."

"Yeah, well, Nick, you always were a hothead. And an incompetent hothead at that. That's why you got demoted, remember?"

"That was your doing, Manning. You were always Gannett's fair-haired boy."

"And you couldn't measure up, could you, Nick? You didn't then. And you don't now."

"Oh, yeah?" He jammed the gun more forcefully against Zoe's skull, tightened the arm around her neck. Aaron saw her eyes bug at the loss of air. She clawed at Nick's wrist. Baiting Nick was working to his advantage, but it was also pissing him off and Zoe was paying the price. Aaron backed off. "You're right, Nick. It probably wasn't fair. You had your share of successful missions."

"Damn right I did," Nick agreed, loosening his grip across Zoe's throat.

Zoe stared at Aaron. He could see her gaze locked on him down the sights of his rifle. God he didn't know how long he could keep this up. His shoulder muscles were locking up. Zoe kept her left hand on Nick's wrist, but dropped her right. Although Nick couldn't see her below the waist he thought she was reaching for something in her pocket. In which case his best bet was to distract Nick before he noticed. "It's quite an operation you've got here," Aaron said, thinking he could stroke Nick's ego.

"Took you long enough to figure it out," Nick pointed out, a touch of pride in his voice.

"It did at that. My hat's off. Well hidden, well run. Virtually untraceable, exceptional quality emeralds sold through the black market. You must have made a mint."

"I did all right. Of course, I had help."

"From the villagers?"

"Of course. But also, the missionaries, their assistants. One in particular. Perhaps you know of him?"

"Julio Dominquez."

Nick nodded, his grin widening. "Boy's help has been invaluable. He helped me filter money to the guerillas on both sides, kept them fighting each other. Kept the most recent local missionary in line. Finds parts for the trucks. Julio. Quite the jack of all trades."

"He won't be helping you anymore."

Nick shrugged as best he could given his current circumstance. "That's okay. I don't need his help, do I, Manning?"

"I don't know. You might."

Aaron tried to stop his eyes from bugging out as he saw what Zoe had retrieved from her pocket. A rather large hunting knife. With barely perceptible movements, she gestured her intent to stab Nick with the knife using her right hand. Given their positions, that meant she'd most likely bury the blade in his thigh.

"No, like most people, he'd outlived his usefulness."

"Perhaps. But you never know when something's going to hit you, right Nick? When something might, oh I don't know, drop in on you." He'd given the words the barest emphasis, hoping Zoe would pick up on it and know to drop to the ground after she stabbed Nick to give him a clear shot.

Nick's eyes widened. "Now, Zoe!" Aaron shouted as she stabbed Nick. Aaron pulled the trigger, but he'd waited a split second too long, to make sure Zoe was out of danger. His shot grazed Nick's ear, gave him time to recover and fire his own weapon. Nick's shot caught Aaron below the shoulder, just as Aaron's second shot hit Nick between the eyes.

Nick went down.

So did Aaron.

Chapter Thirty-Four

Zoe was next to him. Aaron noticed she'd had the wherewithal to pick up the gun Nick had used. "Oh, God. You're hurt." Zoe stated the obvious. She yanked off her jacket and pressed it hard against his wound. Aaron steeled himself not to yelp in pain. Instead he managed a much more manly groan.

"We've got to get out of here. Where's the rendezvous point?"

Aaron shook his head. "Never make it. Only on foot."

"No, no. Then tell them to come and get you. Call them on your microphone thingy and tell them."

"Good idea." His words were already beginning to slur. He told himself not to lose consciousness. Not yet. "Help me over to that Jeep. Keys are probably inside. You'll have to drive."

"To where? How far?"

"Don't know." Aaron was feeling goofy and light-headed in spite of the pain. "Plan B."

Zoe helped him up, though God knew how. He leaned on her more heavily than he should, but she got him to the Jeep and got him inside. "Start down the mountain. Just drive. See if I can get a signal."

"Oh God, oh God, oh God," Zoe whimpered softly. But she started the ignition and backed up, turned and pointed the truck down the mountain.

"Jaeger? Gonzalez? You there?" He waited a minute. "Shit."

"What?"

Zoe ground the gears as the truck half-slid down the dirt track. Zoe'd never had a driver's license, but one of her foster parents had been a car nut. He'd taught her to drive cars with both automatic and manual transmissions. Those long ago lessons came back to her now.

Slow down, slow down, she told herself, when every sense she had urged her to go faster. But the muddy track offered little traction for the tires and if she traveled too fast there was a very good chance she'd be meeting another tree up close and personal.

"No signal yet. Keep driving."

"How far away are they?"

"A mile?"

"You don't know?"

"Don't know if they're still there."

"What?"

"Here." Aaron fumbled with the earpiece and the microphone attached to his shirt. "You take it. Keep trying to raise them."

"How? What? What do I do? Yikes!" Zoe nearly ran off the road when she made the mistake of glancing Aaron's way as he undid the radio device.

"In case I lose conscious—consciousness. Just talk into it. As soon as we're within range, they'll answer."

Zoe braked and fumbled with the earpiece, finally securing it in her ear. She managed to attach the microphone to her shirt collar. "What then?"

Aaron did not reply. She chanced a quick glance his way as the truck continued its slip-slide progress down the twisting trail. "Aaron? What then?"

He was slumped against the passenger door. His eyes were closed. Her jacket was soaked with blood and more dripped onto the seat. "Oh, God," she whispered.

"Mayday, mayday," she shouted in the direction of the microphone as she wrenched the wheel of the truck to the left around a hairpin curve. "Jaeger? Gonzalez? Who's the other guy? DiPaulo? Are you there? It's me. Zoe. Aaron's been shot. He's bleeding all over the place. Where are you? Shit!"

She ground the gears some more, although what was the point? The lowest gear was the only one that was going to get them down the steep incline. That and the brakes, which frankly felt a little soft to her.

"Please, God, please, God, please God," she sang in her panicked life-or-death-situation chanting voice. "Gonzalez!" she shouted insistently. "Jaeger, dammit, somebody answer me! Now! Whoaaaaaa." She cranked the wheel left then right. Who the hell had planned this road? Road, ha! Mud track with more curves than a Barbie doll was more like it.

"DiPaulo, I swear to God, if you don't answer me, I'm not going to be responsible for my actions. I've got your leader bleeding all over the place here and if he dies, so help me God—"

"This is Jaeger."

"Oh, thank God. This is Zoe. I've got Aaron. He's been shot. He's bleeding. I don't know where I'm going. Whaaaaaa!" Zoe ducked her head as a low branch slapped against the windshield and brushed her through the open window as she passed by.

"Okay, Zoe. Just be cool," came Jaeger's calm, commanding voice through the microphone. "Where are you?"

"Driving. Down the mountain."

"How far?"

"I don't know! A mile? Two? I have to go really slow because this road's for shit."

"Okay, look, Zoe, we've got the helo. We'll try to pick you up. Keep driving. Once we locate you, we'll find a place to rendezvous."

"Okay, but hurry."

In the distance Zoe thought she heard chopper blades, but it was hard to discern outside noises over the sound of the engine and the tires. She chanced another look Aaron's way. Was he still breathing? Blood still dripped from his wound. She took that as a good sign. If his heart had stopped, the blood flow would, too. Wouldn't it?

"Zoe? We've got you in our sights. Up ahead, about another mile, there's a clearing. It'll be...on your right, okay? We're going to set down there. We'll wait for you. You copy?"

"I—I copy."

"Shit!"

"What?"

"Zoe, we've got company."

"What?"

"Look, keep driving. You've got a couple of vehicles tailing you. Probably reinforcements from the insurgents we took out."

"And they're chasing me?"

"It's okay. We've got it covered. Drive. We've got more firepower than they do."

"Good to know," Zoe said softly enough she doubted Jaeger heard her. She concentrated on driving because there was nothing else she could do. She couldn't give Aaron medical treatment at the moment. She couldn't return fire if the guerillas behind her started shooting. She'd do what she could do. She'd drive.

The clearing came up sooner than she anticipated as the road improved the farther from the mine she got. There was a big military-looking helicopter off to her right, as Jaeger said it'd be, its choppers whirling ready to take off. She braked and jumped out. Gonzalez and DiPaulo ran forward. Gonzalez dropped a medical bag nearby. Between the two of them, they extricated Aaron from the vehicle.

"Chest wound," Gonzalez said.

They laid him on the ground and in short order, Gonzalez had cut his shirt off, packed the opening in Aaron's chest with bandaging material, secured it with tape. They lifted him, keeping his legs higher than his chest and moved him to the helicopter. Zoe picked up the medical bag and followed. Jaeger helped get Aaron aboard then turned to take the bag from Zoe. They heard the whine of engines and gunshots as he tossed it behind him and reached for her hand.

Jaeger brought his rifle up and returned fire. Soon, Gonzalez and DiPaulo joined him. Zoe dropped to the ground, as bullets seemed to zing around her, bouncing off the metal of the helicopter, but seeming too close for comfort to make herself an easy target.

"Let's go, let's go,"

That shout didn't seem to be coming from the radio but from the captain or navigator or whoever was driving the helicopter. She couldn't blame him for wanting to get out of there.

"Zoe, come on," one of the men shouted at her. She scrambled into a crouch and took the hand that had been extended down to her. The rotor blades started whirring more powerfully overhead. She felt the copter lift before she was on board, even as the gunfire continued. She felt something burn her upper arm, but she ignored it. What was a burn when she'd got out with her life? The copter lifted off and shortly they were out of range of the guerilla's guns. DiPaulo slid the door closed and joined Gonzalez and Jaeger who were huddled over Aaron. Gonzalez, apparently was the medic of the group. He was taking Aaron's vital signs, his eyes serious, his expression solemn.

Zoe sagged against the wall. Fear clawed at her, but exhaustion was running a close second. She stared at the parts of Aaron she could see and willed him to live. *Please God please God please God. Don't let him die.*

Then she became aware of another person on board, lying further back, his blue eyes boring into her from a gaunt face.

"Ben?" she whispered through dry lips and a suddenly clogged throat.

"Hey, Sis," he croaked in return.

She scooted across the floor to him, ignoring the burning sensation in her arm. "Oh, Ben." She leaned over her brother, kissed his forehead, smoothed a hand over his thin hair.

"Time for that later. Don't you think you should get one of them to look at that?"

"Look at what?"

His gaze dropped slightly and he inclined his head. "Your arm. You're bleeding."

Chapter Thirty-Five

Zoe paused inside the ICU cubicle. Nothing had prepared her for the sight of Aaron, unconscious, hooked up to tubes and machines. She forced herself to put one foot in the front of the other until she was next to the bed.

He'd survived the helicopter ride to the air base in Honduras with Gonzalez hovering over him the entire time. An immediate assessment had been made to airlift him to Brooke Army Medical Center in San Antonio where he could be treated by a cardiothoracic surgeon.

She and Ben had been flown to the same facility on a separate plane. Ben had been installed in a room in another wing, his condition being assessed by a team of medical experts. For the moment, he was stable.

Aaron, however, was an entirely different story.

She'd killed him. That was her first thought. As sure as she'd taken a gun and shot him herself, she'd killed him.

His normally robust complexion was pale and drawn. He looked weak and that frightened her. She remembered her first glimpse of Aaron in the coffee shop. When he'd gone to the counter to order coffee and she'd made note of his quiet yet commanding presence.

Now he looked like a victim. Her victim. She'd involved herself in Ben's rescue. And Aaron would probably die because of it. Gingerly she slid her hand beneath his, studying the long capable-looking masculine fingers with their blunt nails, the tanned skin, feeling the calluses on his palm.

She swallowed the lump in her throat. What had she done? Ben was safe, but was Ben's life worth Aaron's? Her chest tightened painfully at the thought that Aaron would die. A world without Aaron. Her world without Aaron. He'd become so important to her in such a short time. He'd leave a big empty hole if he died.

Rage engulfed her. Aaron wasn't going to die. She wouldn't let that happen.

"Ms. Bradford?"

She turned at the sound of a quiet voice. It was that man. That man from some government office who seemed to be in charge. The man with no title and no official departmental affiliation. Russell Gannett.

He motioned her out into the hallway. Zoe squeezed Aaron's unresponsive hand and squared her shoulders.

"You had better be doing everything in your power to make sure he recovers," she told Russell Gannett as she approached.

He looked taken aback by her ferocity. "I assure you, Ms. Bradford—"

"Don't use those tired bureaucratic assurances on me," she snapped. "I've heard them all. They usually mean, 'we don't give a shit,' so don't even go there. Let me put it this way, you're obviously in charge, therefore I am holding you personally responsible for Aaron's recovery. If you don't see to it that he gets the best possible care— if he—if he—" Tears filled her eyes at the thought but she refused to let them fall, "dies, I will tell every newspaper, every television and radio station, every magazine, everything I know about your operation."

"Ms. Bradford!" Gannett hissed, glancing around to see which of the hospital staff might have overheard. Grasping her elbow he pulled her further out of range of the nurses' station.

Zoe glared. "I mean it."

He folded his arms across his chest, a study in nonchalance. Zoe didn't fall for his act for a minute. "And what is it exactly that you think you know?"

Zoe smiled bitterly. Russell Gannett didn't like her threat, but he was not a risk taker. He would do whatever it took to cover his ass and that of his operation.

"It doesn't really matter what I know," she told him more kindly. "It only matters how loud I talk and who will listen. I can share my knowledge, or," she emphasized, "my suspicions with my friend Drew Warner for starters."

Gannett blanched at the mention of Drew's name. Zoe tried hard not to show the satisfaction she felt. For the first time in a long time, she felt her sense of power return. No longer was she at the whims of fate, of militant guerillas or kidnappers, of government and church bureaucrats who did nothing but pat her on the head and send her on her way. No more. Never again. She'd done what she'd had to to survive. Ben was alive and safe. Aaron would live. Somehow, he would live. He'd recover. Because she wouldn't let him go. She couldn't let him go.

"Ms. Bradford, Agen—Mr. Manning is of great value to our organization. Please believe me when I tell you that we are indeed insuring that he's receiving the highest quality of care. Everything that can be done for him is being done."

Zoe believed him. "Then we're agreed."

Gannet removed his wire-rimmed glasses and rubbed the bridge of his nose, then put them back on. "I hope you won't find it necessary to share any of your...thoughts with any of the news organizations. Trust me when I say, by doing that you will compromise Mr. Manning in a most unpleasant and potentially deadly way." His unspoken "more than you already have" was not lost on Zoe.

"If he recovers, I'll have no reason to do anything, will I? And if he doesn't, what I say or do will have no effect on him."

They stared at each other, silently taking measure, until Zoe felt herself start to sway. The bravado she'd garnered earlier from her last reserves of rage-induced adrenaline vanished as quickly as it came. She felt faint.

Gannett guided her to a chair in a nearby waiting area and pushed her head between her knees.

"Breathe," he commanded. "Keep your head down." He lightly kneaded her neck. After her earlier words, she felt strangely touched by the gesture.

"Stay there." She sensed him moving away, but her fear of fainting kept her in position.

He returned in what seemed like seconds. "Try sitting up now. Slowly," he cautioned.

She did. The lightheadedness receded. He popped the top on a cold can of Coke and handed it to her. She sipped, then drank more.

"When did you last eat?"

"I don't remember." She gulped more of the Coke.

"Let's go." He took her elbow.

"No. I don't want to leave Aaron." Her gaze went to the cubicle where he lay.

"I'll make you a deal, Ms. Bradford. You let me buy you a sandwich and I'll arrange for you to come back here and keep Mr. Manning company the rest of the night if you'd like."

Something in his voice and manner made Zoe back down. That and the fact that she suddenly realized she was starving.

"How did you meet Ag—Aaron?" Gannett asked once they were seated at a table in the cafeteria with sandwiches on trays before them.

"In a bookstore." Zoe bit into her turkey on whole wheat and almost groaned in satisfaction. There had been many priorities the past several days. None of them had to do with food.

"Ah," Gannett replied, his eyes too knowledgeable for Zoe's comfort.

She swallowed and returned the sandwich to the Styrofoam plate which held a pickle and potato chips. "What?"

Gannett shook his head. "No. Nothing."

"You said 'ah' in a way that sounded like you're not surprised, like you already knew how I met Aaron and were asking to see if I'd tell you the truth."

"Ms. Bradford—"

"You can call me Zoe. If you want." Zoe took another bite of her sandwich. Her stomach growled its approval. She chewed and watched a couple of expressions cross Gannett's face. His eyes behind his glasses seemed far away as if he was debating what or how much to say to her.

"I only meant," he said, "that I wasn't surprised you met Aaron in a bookstore. He's highly intelligent and very well-read. A bookstore would be a logical place for him to meet someone."

Zoe knew there was more he wasn't saying, but since they'd declared sort of a truce, she didn't want to pursue a line of questioning she was certain he'd stonewall on.

"And I'm Russell, by the way." He almost smiled and Zoe noticed how tired he looked. Lines of tension radiated from his brow and around his mouth.

She leaned forward. "He's going to make it, isn't he?"

She'd caught him off-guard with the question, but she needed assurance from someone. The doctors and nurses barely acknowledged her, and they wouldn't tell her what Aaron's chances were if they even wanted to hazard a guess.

Russell shook his head. "I honestly don't know. The doctors seem cautiously optimistic. He lost a lot of blood, surgery further strained his system and now with the infection—"

Zoe gripped the sides of the table, until her knuckles turned white. "I can't lose him. I won't lose him."

"As I said, everything that can be done is being done."

When they'd finished eating, Zoe excused herself and found a deserted waiting area from which to call Drew. He answered almost immediately.

"Zoe? Are you all right?"

"I'm fine. I wanted to let you know we found Ben. We got him out."

"You and Julio?"

Zoe didn't want to withhold from Drew any more than she had to. She'd done enough damage to their relationship already. "No. Julio turned out not to be much help after all."

"Then how? Who?"

"It was Aaron, Drew. He was already there. I'd asked him to rescue Ben, but I didn't think he would."

"Aaron."

"Look, it's a long story, and I'm exhausted. Ben's in rough shape. Aaron was injured. We're all staying at a hospital in Texas for the moment. I wanted to let you know we're safe."

"But—"

"Drew, I know you have a ton of questions. And I'll answer them. But not right now, okay?"

Drew hesitated but then he said, "Okay. I'm glad you're back safe and sound. Thanks for calling."

"Thanks for being my friend."

She disconnected.

Zoe peered around the corner. The corridor was empty. Stealthily she made her way to the chapel door, glancing over her shoulder once more before slipping inside.

Even here in a busy hospital, the place reserved for contact with God seemed hushed and reverent. Perhaps because it was very late. In the dim light coming through the narrow windows, Zoe took a seat in the last row.

She had no idea why she was here. She remembered her last visit to a church. The morning after she'd slept with the phantom for the first time. Same as now, there had been no conscious decision on her part to be there. Yet here she was.

What do I do now, God?

She should probably give thanks. Ben was safe. Whether that was in answer to some prayer she'd uttered or not, someone, somewhere should be thanked.

But Aaron might die. And that didn't seem a fair trade.

Life's not fair.

Was that God? Putting thoughts in her head? Answering her questions? *Tell me something I don't know*, she replied.

I love you.

Zoe sucked in a breath. *How?* She asked uncertainly. *How can you love me after what I've done?*

What did you do?

Slept with a man for money. Surely God already knew that. According to Ben, He knew everything.

Do you want to be forgiven? Do you think what you did was wrong?

Hell, no! I did it for the right reasons.

Well, see there.

Zoe sat in stunned silence. She hadn't expected God to be quite so understanding. She wasn't even sure it was God she was talking to in her head. Maybe she was justifying what she'd done, as she had from the beginning, pushing the guilt aside, reveling in the pleasure her phantom lover offered. And the money. Don't forget the money.

What about Aaron? That's really why she was here.

What about him?

Can you fix him?

She thought she heard God chuckle. *I can fix anything. Or anyone.*

"Will you?" she asked aloud.

Nothing. She felt surrounded by the dim gray light, enveloped by it, as she did in the darkness the phantom created for their trysts.

"Will you?" she asked again, louder this time. "Please? Please, let him get better. Please, God." Tears came and she made no move to stop them. No one was there to see. They splashed from her eyes, and she grabbed the seatback in front of her and bowed her head on her arms. "Please," she begged over and over through her tears. "Please, God, please," she cried until she could cry no more.

When something touched her hair the next morning she woke up, blinking at the bright light. Her eyes were dry and gritty. She was massively thirsty and she ached all over. She blinked again as she picked her head up.

She was sitting in a chair near Aaron's bed, slumped onto the edge of the mattress, where she'd fallen asleep last night.

Her gaze went to Aaron. His eyes were open. It had been his hand that she'd felt moments ago. She stood and peered down at him, sliding her hand beneath his and holding on tight. Her eyes filled with those annoying tears again.

She smoothed her hand along the top of his head. "You look like hell." Her dry throat made her voice hoarse.

He grimaced, though he might have been attempting to smile as his eyes wandered over her. "You, too," he rasped.

She half-laughed, trying hard to choke back the emotion that knotted her throat, tamping down the sob pushing its way forward. Tears continued to spill from her eyes. She couldn't make them stop. She didn't know how.

Aaron's brow puckered. "Don't cry," he croaked. He made as if to brush away her tears, but his arm fell back limply when he tried.

Zoe pressed a kiss on his forehead. "I can't help it. I love you."

She stared down into the murky green of his eyes. She had no idea how he would take her declaration. But whatever happened she knew she'd be able to handle it.

"You—love—me?" Aaron had a hard time pushing the words out.

Zoe nodded. "Sshhh. Don't try to talk."

A nurse came in and seeing that Aaron was awake shooed Zoe away. Reluctantly she let go of his hand. He started to speak but she kissed her forefinger and laid it against his lips. "Shhh. Later."

Chapter Thirty-Six

A nurse approached as Zoe stepped out of Aaron's ICU cubicle. "Ms. Bradford?"

"Yes?"

"It's your brother. He's—"

"Oh my God, what?" Zoe grabbed the nurse's forearms to speed up her speech.

"He's taken a turn for the worse. We think you should come."

"Ben! Oh my God, Ben!" Zoe turned blindly. Which way was the elevator?

The nurse steered her in the appropriate direction. Zoe went along, her mind denying the possibility that anything could happen to Ben now. She'd rescued him, with Aaron's help. After all those months of captivity, all the torture and starvation he'd endured. She'd found him and got him safely to a hospital. She'd looked in on him last night and he'd been sleeping peacefully. Or so she'd thought.

She stepped on to the elevator which didn't move nearly fast enough for her liking. "What happened? I saw Ben last night."

The nurse shook her head. "We don't really know. Not for sure."

Zoe's eyes narrowed. "But you suspect something, don't you? What is it? Tell me."

"I'm sorry. It's not for me to say." The elevator arrived at the second floor. "Please," the nurse indicated that Zoe should precede her. "You should be with your brother."

Zoe arrived at Ben's bedside to find him being attended by two doctors, a respiratory therapist and another nurse. An oxygen mask covered his nose and mouth. The monitors were being watched closely. The nurse held his wrist and one of the doctors was listening to Ben's heart and lungs with a stethoscope under Ben's hospital gown.

"What happened? What's wrong?"

The young doctor in charge of Ben's case shook his head. "We don't know. He's in respiratory failure, but we don't know what caused it."

"But—but," Zoe said helplessly. She approached Ben, edging the nurse out of the way. She picked up his hand and leaned close. "Ben? Ben? It's me. Zoe."

Ben's eyelids fluttered. The corners of his lips twitched. "Ben?" Zoe said louder, panicked.

One of the monitors started to beep. A flurry of activity erupted. One of the nurses dragged Zoe out to the hall. "Ben!" she screamed. "Ben!" She watched through the window as a team of trained medical professionals worked on her brother, doing CPR, intubating him, using the charged paddles to restart his heart. Ben's body jumped in reaction, but the line in the beeping monitor remained flat and the beeping continued. Zoe pounded on the window in frustration unaware that tears streamed down her face as she repeated her brother's name. Eventually, the feverish effort to save Ben stopped. The young doctor looked at his watch and uttered something Ben couldn't hear. The other hospital personnel, nodded or simply walked away in defeat.

When the door opened Zoe launched herself through it and the departing medical staff, like a salmon swimming upstream. "Ben, oh, God, no. Bennnnn!" She collapsed against her brother's lifeless body, holding him as if that would bring him back.

When the doctor tried to get her to release her hold on Ben she lashed out at him, refusing to let go.

Zoe sat in the chapel, her mind a numb blank except for one thought that kept repeating itself over and over. Ben is dead.

No matter how many times it raced through her head like a ticker tape, Zoe couldn't wrap her mind around it.

She'd seen him die, yet the belief that she'd know when he was dead hadn't occurred. Her connection to him wasn't cut off as she'd believed it would be. Somehow, impossible as it seemed, it felt like Ben was still here, of this world, alive. Somewhere.

She had risked everything to save Ben. Everything. She'd put her life on the line in so many ways, starting with that first night, risking that the phantom might not be who he claimed. That he hadn't turned out to be a perverted murderer or worse had been blind dumb luck. Hadn't it?

Or maybe someone was looking out for you. The thought came unbidden into her mind like a special announcement interrupting the regular programming, in this case, her thoughts of Ben's death.

Who? She asked herself bitterly. You, God? This is how you look out for me? By taking away the one person I love? The one I sacrificed everything to save? Tears filled her eyes. The ticker tape started again.

You love more than one person.

Zoe's heart squeezed painfully and she choked on a sob she refused to allow escape. *Aaron. Are you going to take him away, too? Just like you took Tim and Zach? Like you took my parents and my grandmother? That's all you do, God. You take. You take and you take and you take. I've got news for you,* Zoe screamed in her mind. *I don't have anything left.*

She took a deep shuddering breath and bowed her head. She refused to cry, refused to allow God to see how much pain he had caused her.

A hand touched her shoulder. Russell Gannett took a seat behind her and to her right. He leaned over the back of the chair next to her and clasped his hands together. "We think Ben was poisoned," he said.

"Poisoned?" Zoe dashed the tears from her eyes and blinked at Gannett. "How? When?"

"Our best guess is during the rescue. The doctors found a small puncture wound in his shoulder, the kind made by a tranquilizer dart or something of that nature. We're still gathering evidence."

"But if it was poison, Ben would have died immediately. He seemed okay until—until today."

Gannett sighed heavily. "I'm afraid Sheppard or his men may have used a weapon developed especially for us. It's a slow-acting chemical poison that causes the body to appear to die of natural causes such as respiratory failure or heart attack. There are a couple of different strains, used when we need an objective taken out and don't want any foul play to be suspected."

"Is that what you call them? Objectives?" Zoe asked tiredly. "It's so impersonal."

Is that what she'd been to the phantom? An objective? Someone he could have anonymous sex with? Someone he could toy with, watch and observe, have power over? He knew who she was. She had no idea who he was, what he looked like, or if he'd ever contact her again.

Tears welled in her eyes once again. She missed him, her phantom lover. Her heart ached. She longed to be held the way he'd held her that first night when she'd cried on his shoulder. How he'd stroked her hair, offered silent comfort.

Now there was no one. Except thin, angular Russell Gannett who looked about as likely to offer her comfort as a box of broken glass.

"Aaron's taken a turn for the worse," Gannett said into the silence left by his lack of response to her last question.

Aaron's going to die. The ticker tape had been replaced with a new announcement.

"The infection he developed is fairly severe. They're trying a different antibiotic."

Zoe turned to stare at Russell. "No. No more. If he dies, I'll come looking for you."

She stood, turned her back on Russell and left.

"Mrs. Bradford?" Someone was shaking her awake.

"Hmm? What?" She'd been sleeping uncomfortably in a chair in the ICU lounge. She had a crick in her neck and her limbs ached as she straightened them and sat up. A mass of stringy hair fell over her shoulder and she pushed it back impatiently.

"Aaron?" she asked in a panic.

The doctor frowned. "He hasn't stabilized the way we hoped. His fever hasn't come down. The antibiotics don't seem to be working."

"Is he—is he?" Zoe couldn't bring herself to say the words. Aaron had taken a turn for the worse. That's why the doctor woke her from her much needed sleep.

"May I?" He indicated the seat next to her and Zoe shrugged in response. Dread filled her. She braced herself for another death knell.

"I have the results of your lab work here." He tapped a file folder.

"Why would you do lab work on me?"

"Standard procedure. You were brought in with a wound." He indicated her arm, the bandage now hidden beneath her sleeve. "We cover all our bases, especially when patients are brought in under, shall we say, unique circumstances such as yours."

She'd been shot. That burning sensation in her arm had been caused by a bullet. It had torn a chunk of flesh out of her arm but done little damage, according to the doctors.

Maybe she was next on the grim reaper's list. Or she had caught some dread disease. Courtesy of the phantom, perhaps. Or the bullet that hit her had been dipped in poison. "Okay. What about my lab work?"

"Mrs. Bradford, were you aware that you're pregnant?"

"Pregnant?" No way, was Zoe's first thought. Right on the heels of that came a second thought. She and the phantom had made love that one time without protection. Her idea. At her insistence. But the phantom had gone along with it.

"Are—are you sure?"

"We can repeat the test if you want. Or I can do an examination. But blood tests are generally pretty conclusive."

Zoe tried to assimilate this revelation. Pregnant. A baby. The phantom's baby. Joy bloomed in her pain-filled heart. The Lord giveth...

God? Is that you? She looked around the room as if sensing his actual physical presence. Was God smiling at her? Oddly, that's how it felt.

"You need to take care of yourself," the doctor continued. "Get proper rest." His gaze washed disapprovingly over the chair where she'd slept. "Watch your nutrition. Get regular check-ups."

"I know the drill, Doc," Zoe told him dryly.

He smiled. "All right, then. Well, I just wanted you to be aware." He stood. "Best of luck, Mrs. Bradford."

"Thank you."

Chapter Thirty-Seven

"Did you say you loved me or did I dream that?" Aaron asked two days later. His voice lacked its usual air of command, he was still flat on his back in a hospital bed, but Zoe'd been given every assurance he'd recover completely from both his injuries and the infection.

She turned from where she'd been fussing with a flower arrangement that brightened his bedside table.

Their eyes met. "You weren't dreaming," she told him, her voice soft.

He held out a hand to her and when she took it he clutched her fingers tightly in his, then laced his between hers. Unbidden came memories of the phantom. Aaron's eyes that seemed to change with his moods were a smoky green. "You're beautiful," he said, his gaze sweeping her from head to waist.

Zoe laughed. "I made your friend Russell take me shopping." She smoothed a hand down the pink cotton sweater she wore.

She'd also insisted Russell find her a place nearby to get a decent night's sleep, using her pregnancy as added incentive, though she sensed it wasn't necessary. Like the Wizard of Oz, Russell

Gannett possessed magical abilities to make things happen.

"Gannett's not my friend," Aaron said grimly. Then he gave her hand a sympathetic squeeze, genuine sadness in his expression. "I'm sorry about Ben,"

Zoe nodded. "I almost killed you and he died anyway."

Aaron shook his head. "You had nothing to do with it. Don't think it's your fault."

"It is my fault. If I hadn't asked you to rescue him—"

Aaron shook his head against the pillow emphatically. "Zoe—ah, hell."

"What is it?"

"Talk about this later, okay?" Aaron's eyes closed. His fingers relaxed around hers.

Zoe peered down at him, reminding herself of what he'd been through the past few days. His spirit might be willing, but his body was weak.

She pressed a kiss to his lips. "We'll talk later." She sensed he had some things to tell her. Well. She had some things to tell him, too.

The following morning Zoe opened her motel room door to discover Russell Gannet on the other side looking very grave. "May I come in?" he asked formally.

She stepped back trying to read his expression.

"Ah, perhaps you should sit down," he suggested after she'd closed the door behind him.

"It's Aaron, isn't it?"

"I'm sorry to have to tell you this." Gannett sighed painfully, his eyes casting about for something to focus on. Anywhere, except her pleading expression, Zoe supposed.

"No," she whispered. Not Aaron. He couldn't die. She'd warned Gannett. Aaron had to survive. He had to.

"He, uh," Gannett coughed as if choked up by his own emotion. "Took a turn for the worse during the night. The infection...he went into cardiac arrest. There was nothing—" He cleared his throat. "Nothing that could be done."

Something, in Gannett's manner, in his words, didn't ring true. Zoe couldn't put her finger on what it was. Maybe it was nothing more than shock, her own refusal to believe that Aaron was dead.

"I want to see him."

That got Gannett's attention. "Ms. Bradford, I assure you—"

"I don't want or need your assurances. I want to see Aaron."

"But—but, he's dead," Gannett repeated as if she hadn't gotten that the first time.

"Then he shouldn't put up much of a fight, should he?" Zoe said coldly, vaguely aware of the poor taste of her unintentional pun.

As if realizing she wouldn't back down until he gave her what she wanted, Gannett spread his hands in a helpless gesture. "Fine. I'll take you to him. We'll arrange for a memorial service. He'll be buried in Washington, of course."

Zoe remembered what a morgue felt like. Cold. Eerie. Depressing. She instinctively wanted to hold her breath, to keep from inhaling the sanitized scent of death. She'd felt the same way when she'd had to identify Tim. And Zachary.

Dry-eyed she waited on a plastic chair, her arms wrapped around herself, as if that could block out the continuing nightmare that was her life.

What's next? Who's left? Drew? Are you going to take him, too, God? She stared at the white wall across from her, not surprised when there was no answer.

Aaron couldn't be dead. He was too vital, too alive, too present. He wouldn't give up, he wouldn't die. He wouldn't.

"Zoe?"

It was Gannett, speaking to her from an open doorway down the hall. He motioned for her to come. Zoe's stomach did a gigantic flip-flop as she rose from her chair and walked stiffly down the hall, her arms still in defensive mode, protecting her.

She tried to ignore everything, the gray tile, the stainless steel, the equipment, the lights. A man in a white coat stood near a bank of stainless steel refrigerator-looking drawers, his gaze impassive as she approached.

At Gannett's nod, he yanked on the handle of a middle drawer. A platform slid out, a white sheet covering what lay beneath. Zoe gasped. The world around her seemed to tilt. She felt Gannett's steadying hand on her elbow.

"Are you sure you want to do this?" he asked, concern softening the anxiety in his tone.

Zoe nodded. She had to see. Had to know. In order to believe.

Gannett gave an almost imperceptible nod to the other man.

He lifted the sheet, slowly and let it drop back over Aaron's uninjured shoulder.

It was him. No mistaking. Pale. Drawn. Lifeless. Zoe reached out, wanting to touch him one last time. Gannett frowned, but she ignored him. Stepping forward, she curled her fingers around Aaron's forearm. His skin was cold, clammy.

She stared at his face. *Wake up!* she wanted to scream. *You can't be dead. You can't. I love you! I never meant to kill you.* Aaron didn't move. "I'm sorry," she whispered. Tears filled her eyes. "So, so sorry." She leaned forward and kissed his cheek.

When she straightened, her gaze clashed with Gannett's. She lifted her chin, trying to hold back her tears. For some reason she couldn't quite name, she didn't want to show any weakness to this man.

She left the room and he fell into step behind her. Taking her elbow he guided her outside into the sunlight and fresh air. She breathed deeply, trying to rid herself of the stench of death.

Gannett waited until she seemed to stabilize. "I've arranged for an escort back to New York this afternoon. I'm sure you'll want to make arrangements for your brother."

Zoe nodded. Aaron's death somehow eclipsed Ben's. Her mind refused to function normally. Numbness engulfed her and she allowed it, embraced it.

"Wh—what about Aaron?"

"What about him?"

"You said there'd be a funeral or—or a service. Something."

"Oh, yes. Of course. In Washington. Since he's ex-military, he qualifies for a place in Arlington."

Zoe choked on the thought of Aaron being permanently laid to rest anywhere. "I'd—I'd like to be there."

Gannett cleared his throat. "Of course. I'll inform you of the arrangements."

Zoe nodded dully. Surely the numbness of grief had set in, for she felt surprisingly calm at the thought of attending funeral services for the two most important men in her life.

Before she left for New York, the head of Ben's religious order telephoned to inform her that Ben had left specific instructions in the event of his death. The order would arrange a funeral Mass on whatever date she chose. She and Drew put their differences aside and he attended with her. He offered to accompany her to Washington for Aaron's service as well, but she declined. She didn't want Drew to witness the depth of her grief over a man he must have viewed as a rival.

The service for Aaron was painfully brief and lightly attended. The team members were there, and Gannett of course. A few other men in dark suits and sunglasses. Aaron's casket was closed and draped in an American flag, which she supposed wasn't unusual for a military-type funeral. Rote prayers were said by a minister of undetermined denomination who surely had no personal knowledge of the man Aaron had been. Zoe wanted to eulogize Aaron, she had so much she wanted to say. But she realized no one really cared. She was heartsick at the thought that a man as vital as Aaron could be gone with no one to truly mourn him. No one but her. His service to this mysterious agency he worked for might be missed, but his contact with others was limited to his work environment. Apparently he'd had no close alliances with anyone but her and the thought only increased her sadness.

The soldiers who bore the casket to the gravesite and who stood at attention during the service, removed the flag and folded it at precise angles before the casket was lowered into the ground.

Zoe couldn't take her eyes off the glossy wood as it descended. Only when Gannett stepped in front of her did her focus shift. He looked at her kindly. "I think he'd want you to have this."

She stared at the perfectly folded flag he was offering to her. She blinked once. Twice. The finality of death. Aaron was gone. This flag was all she'd have to remember him by. No photos. No gifts. No personal mementos. Her throat worked as she searched for some sort of response, but she had none. She nodded and took the flag from Gannett, clutching it close to her heart.

Chapter Thirty-Eight

Zoe thought she understood the meaning of shell-shocked after her return to New York. Thanks to the phantom, for once in her life she didn't have to worry about money. She had no desire to return to work at the restaurant. She had no desire to do anything. She spent most of her time alone, venturing out only for necessities like food, which she forced herself to eat only to sustain the life growing inside her. The one thing God had allowed her to keep.

Drew came around often, fussing over her, trying to draw her out, but she had no interest in leaving her apartment.

By tacit agreement, they didn't discuss the rescue in excessive detail. She didn't ask Drew to pursue the story about the black market emeralds and Level One's involvement. She found she didn't care whether anyone was exposed or brought to justice. Aaron was dead. Ben was dead. What did it matter? Whether Drew continued working on the story on his own was his business.

One evening Drew lured her to his apartment with the promise of homemade spaghetti and garlic bread. As they cleaned the kitchen together, Drew said, "The night you brought Aaron here for dinner..."

It seemed a lifetime ago, but Zoe simply sighed and said, "What about it?"

"I asked him if we'd met before."

Zoe dried the last plate and put it away in the cabinet, her mind barely on topic. She didn't want to talk about Aaron. It hurt too much. After that night Drew had insisted he'd seen Aaron before somewhere. In connection with her. But he couldn't recall where.

"I remembered where I saw him before that night."

Zoe folded the dish towel and turned to look at her friend. Drew's eyes, behind his glasses were earnest. He was deadly serious. "Where?" she asked, experiencing once again, that feeling that she didn't want to know the answer to her question.

Drew pulled a chair away from the table. His voice gentled. "Sit down."

With an inward groan, Zoe sat so she and Drew were face to face. Drew held her hands in both of his. "He was at the memorial service for Tim and Zach."

Whatever Zoe'd been expecting Drew to say, that was not it. Her mind tried to process the impact of what he'd said, the implication of such a fact.

"Are—are you sure?"

Drew nodded. "I'm sure. He stayed in the background. He didn't speak to anyone, he didn't come with anyone, I'm sure of that. Remember the service, Zo? Most of the people there were people Tim knew from the university. People you both worked with. Teachers from your school, some of the professors and grad students from his, staff from the restaurant. Parents of Zach's friends. But Aaron was there. And he was alone."

Zoe shook her head. "Are you saying he knew Tim...before?"

"I don't know. Not necessarily."

"But why would he come to the service if he didn't know any of us?"

Drew shook his head. "I don't know. Unless he were somehow involved."

"What do you mean? Involved in the accident?"

Drew shrugged.

Zoe shook her head. "No. I can't believe that he had anything to do with it. There has to be another reason."

"And there very well may be. But I wanted you to know, for whatever reason, once I finally remembered, that he was there. I'm pretty sure he came up and shook your hand afterward. Offered his condolences."

"There were so many people and I was in a fog. I don't remember who was there and who wasn't. I didn't know everyone that Tim knew."

"No. I know you didn't," Drew said soothingly, rubbing his thumbs along the backs of her hands. "Maybe it doesn't mean anything at all. It's been driving me crazy all this time, trying to remember, and then it came to me, out of the blue."

"Do you think I should look into it? I could ask Russell Gannett about it. Maybe he'd know something. Do you think he'd tell me if he did?"

Drew shook his head. "I don't know if he would or not. It's up to you, if you want to ask. I thought it was odd that Aaron was at the service, and then you meet him what, a year later? In a bookstore? And he turns out to be someone who can help you rescue Ben. He's with this covert agency. It's a piece of a puzzle that doesn't seem to go anywhere. And as a journalist, you know I like all the pieces to fit."

Zoe smiled. "You need an answer for everything. All the facts."

Drew grinned. "Yep."

"This is a loose end that'll drive you crazy?"

Drew shook his head. "No. But I did something I should have done when Tim and Zach died. The guy driving the car that hit them? Carzoui? He was a suspected terrorist. The FBI had him on a watch list at the time."

"You mean there's a connection of some sort between Carzoui and Aaron?"

Again Drew shook his head. "If there is, it's not a connection that's easy to make. Unless Aaron was assigned to keep an eye on Carzoui."

"But you don't know that."

"No, and there's no way to know. There are a few too many things that don't add up. And you know—"

Zoe gave him a sad smile. "I know. You don't believe in coincidences."

"I thought you should know. That's all. What you decide to do with it, or if you decide to do nothing, it's up to you."

Zoe took a seat on Drew's sofa, cradling a mug of tea. She sighed wearily. "I don't know," she answered. "I don't know anything anymore."

The world was playing a huge joke on her and she wasn't smart enough to figure it out. Tim and Zach. Gone. Ben. Gone. Aaron. Gone, gone, gone. You lose, Zoe. Pay up.

And the phantom? He was gone, too. Had he watched her? Did he know? Had he grown tired of their game, their meetings in the dark? Had he moved on to a new conquest? Set up another series of clandestine meetings with some other woman?

Or had he been in Central America on a covert mission? Had he died from a bullet wound?

Drew set his mug on the coffee table. "You know it wouldn't be the first time a government agency faked the death of one of its own."

Zoe blinked and shifted in her seat. "What do you mean?"

Drew punched a couple of buttons on the stereo remote control. Soft jazz poured forth, barely audible in the quiet of his apartment.

He picked up his mug. "Just what I said. It's sort of like a witness protection program. Say one of your operatives becomes a liability. His cover's been blown, or he wants out. He's been relatively valuable to your organization, possesses a lot of knowledge you don't want known. Or maybe he's disabled or less useful than he once was. You need to get rid of him but save face.

"Look, Zoe, if a terrorist organization knew Aaron's true identity, if they came after him as part of a vendetta, they wouldn't stop until they'd taken him out. He'd never be safe and neither would you. What's worse, as a spy, an operative, an agent, whatever it was he did for our government, he's compromised.

"But you can make pursuit of him end if you kill him off. You make everyone believe he's dead. Killed in the line of duty. You have a very public memorial service. You plant an obituary in the Washington papers. Maybe even a couple of news stories about the circumstances surrounding his supposed death. You take him out before your enemies can.

"The pursuit stops. Everyone associated with him is safe once again. Eventually, he could conceivably resurface without anyone connecting him to who and what he once was."

Zoe listened avidly as Drew continued talking. Hope began to form in her heart, but just as quickly she squelched it and slumped back into the cushions. "You're forgetting. I saw Aaron. In the morgue."

Drew shrugged, took a sip of tea and said nothing. His unspoken skepticism reverberated through the wailing notes of the saxophone.

"Are you saying Aaron was in a morgue, but he wasn't dead?" Zoe tried to wrap her mind around the possibility. That seed of hope sprang to life again, and she tried unsuccessfully to stamp it out.

"I'm just saying it's possible," Drew said mildly.

"But—but I touched him. His skin was cold. He looked *dead*. I thought he was dead."

"Of course you did, Zoe. That's what they wanted you to think."

"And I fell for it."

"It's hard sometimes not to believe what you see."

"But how could he look dead and feel dead but not be dead?"

"There are drugs that slow the heart and respiration so that they're almost unnoticeable. They might have actually refrigerated him long enough to cool his skin, dampened it maybe, to give it a clammy feel. You only saw him for a couple of minutes, right?"

Zoe nodded, Drew's skepticism infecting her.

"Zoe, I don't know, obviously; I honestly don't know whether Aaron is alive or dead. They could have staged his death for a lot of reasons that suited them at the time. And it was very important for them to convince you of his death. They probably know your history with Ben, trying to find him after he disappeared. They knew if Aaron disappeared, you'd ask too many questions, make a nuisance of yourself. Perhaps mention it to the wrong people."

"The wrong people being you, of course." Zoe smiled at Drew.

"Of course," he replied good-naturedly.

"You're saying it's all some big conspiracy."

"I'm saying it could be. We may never know."

"Never knowing," Zoe said. "That's the worst part." Aaron would be relegated to the same section of her heart as the phantom. She'd never know what happened to him. Who he was. What might have been.

"I'm going home." She got to her feet and put her mug in the sink. Leaning down, she kissed Drew's cheek. He held her a little longer than usual, his touch evoking sympathy rather than passion.

That night she lay awake for a long time, thinking of the possibility that Aaron was still alive, that she'd see him again. Then she brutally reminded herself that she couldn't live on hope. She'd done it for too long. She wouldn't any more.

The next day Zoe sprang into action refusing to give in to the doldrums that had plagued her since her return to New York. The Ben as captive/phantom as lover/Aaron as rescuer phase of her life was over. She had only herself left. And she had a child to think of and plan for.

She made a doctor's appointment. Cleaned her apartment. She began to research the New Jersey suburbs, making a list of elementary schools and day care centers. With her previous teaching experience, she should be able to find a job at a day care center, where she could bring the baby, and also earn money. She wouldn't have to be separated from her child all day. When the child was old enough for pre-school, she could return to teaching kindergarten. She dug out her resume to update. She was going to move forward with her life. Even if it killed her.

Chapter Thirty-Nine

Determined to take action and move forward Zoe did not allow herself to wallow in grief and guilt as she had after Tim and Zach's deaths. Within days Zoe had put a down payment on a house in Markham, New Jersey. She felt almost content with the knowledge she was pregnant. *The phantom hasn't contacted you since you left with Aaron. Not since Aaron died.* Was Aaron the phantom? Some days the idea seemed ludicrous. But other days, the similarities between them and her sense that Aaron and the phantom were one and the same was hard to deny.

Was she carrying Aaron's child? Or the child of a stranger?

In some part of her mind, she continued to reject the fact that Ben had died. She still felt connected to him, still found it difficult to believe he was not alive. Sometimes she stared at the urn containing his ashes, questioning whether it truly held his remains. Was he really dead? Why couldn't she accept it? If indeed, the *agency* had faked Aaron's death, they could have faked Ben's as well. There could be a reason. Especially if Ben was also some sort of spy.

She smoothed her hand over the slight curve of her stomach. She'd have her baby, at least, even if she had no one else. Her baby. Her family. Her lips curved into a smile at the thought of a new life, someone to share her life with.

A knock sounded at her door, startling her from her thoughts. The buzzer for the street door had not sounded. Other than Drew she rarely had visitors. She peered through the peephole, startled to see a man who looked almost exactly like Aaron. Leaving the chain on she opened the door, staring at him through the narrow opening. He was thinner, but otherwise looked almost as fit and in charge as Aaron ever had.

She stepped back as if he'd pushed her and tried to absorb the fact that he'd come back to life and now stood in front of her. "Aaron?" she whispered, afraid to believe it was really true, that it was really him. Alive.

He nodded, his eyes locked on hers. Feeling as if she'd been sucker punched, she closed the door, fumbling to release the chain. She wanted to launch herself at him, twine her arms around his neck and hold on tightly as his arms came around her. At the same time, she was so stunned by his appearance that she felt rooted in place, unable to move or respond. He closed the door behind him, backed her into the apartment and kissed her feverishly as if he couldn't get enough of her. And then he held her.

"Marry me," he whispered into her hair. "I don't think I can live without you."

"What?"

He lifted his head and looked into her eyes. "Marry me?" This time it was a question tinged with uncertainty. "Would you?"

Zoe shook her head as if that would help her accept the reality of his sudden appearance.

His face fell. "Is that a no?"

His arms around her felt real enough. He was looking at her, his green eyes flecked with gold, intent, piercing. Alive. But how could that be?

Aaron kissed her again and Zoe's mind shot back to that first encounter with the phantom all those months ago. How lonely she'd been, how deprived of physical contact with another human being. He'd made her realize how much she needed to be touched, and she'd become used to the phantom's touch. That and a steady supply of satisfying sex. Satisfying, ha! Mind-blowing was more like it.

But how much of the mind-blowing aspect was caused by the mystery surrounding the phantom? If she'd met him as she had Aaron, would it seem so special?

Well, one thing was for sure. Aaron knew how to kiss. He'd proven that before the trip to Central America. And he hadn't forgotten any of his technique. He ravaged her mouth, his fingers buried in her hair. Zoe tingled all the way to the tips of her toes. Her breasts, especially sensitive due to her pregnancy, ached for his touch and she pressed herself hard against his chest, savoring the contact.

When he stopped kissing her, they were both breathing hard. His eyes were smoky green with sensuality, the gold flecks blurred and dusky. He brushed the back of his knuckles against her cheek. "God, I missed you."

"I thought you were dead."

Aaron's gaze softened. "I know." He kissed her. "I'm sorry. I'll explain everything." He held her close and Zoe allowed it, even as fritters of uncertainty hummed through her veins. His death had been a fake, but he'd allowed her to believe it. Against her better judgment, she'd reluctantly given him her trust back in the jungle-covered mountain, before Ben's rescue. But she didn't see how she could trust him now when he'd obviously been a party to the lie about his own death.

She'd fallen in love with this man even though she'd tried not to. It wasn't fair when she was deeply emotionally and physically involved with the phantom. Yet Aaron was here now, ready to fulfill every need the phantom didn't. She had a million questions for him, but he was real and alive, thank God. And he wanted to marry her.

Her brow furrowed. She was pregnant with the phantom's baby.

At the thought, she pulled away from him to put distance between them. She had no right to be in Aaron's arms. No right to enjoy his kisses, to want him the way she did. No right to be his wife.

Unless Aaron was the phantom.

She broke his embrace completely and stepped away. Reluctantly he let her go. She didn't know what to do. Not with Aaron right there watching her. "What's wrong?" he asked. "Is it me? You don't know enough about me? Ask. I'll tell you anything I can."

Of course she had questions she wanted answered about his supposed death. She wanted to ask, Are you the phantom? But if Aaron was the phantom, she'd never forgive him. If he wasn't, he'd never forgive her for what she'd done. Even if Aaron could explain himself to her satisfaction, even if she could give him her trust again, she had no future with Aaron.

She felt as though she'd been given a wonderful gift, something she'd longed for and never expected to have. Aaron. Back in her life, wanting her, wanting to marry her. And just as quickly the gift had been snatched away.

Pain at the thought knifed through her. She turned away from him as tears filled her eyes. She walked blindly into the kitchen where she could conveniently keep her back to him as she made coffee. Familiar territory, filling the carafe with water, scooping the grounds into the filter. Even after her part in creating coffee was complete she stayed where she was, watching the coffee drip into the carafe.

Aaron came up behind her dropping his hands to her shoulders. She flinched at his touch, but he ignored her reaction and began kneading her neck. She dropped her head forward while he massaged her with his thumbs and his strong fingers. He moved closer behind her. Thoughts of the phantom flashed through her mind. She felt Aaron's strength and his heat. He kissed the back of her neck and she whispered, "Stop," in a choked voice. He lifted his head. She could tell he was surprised by her reaction. He slid his arms around her from behind, his cheek next to hers.

"What is it? I know it's a shock, seeing me like this, but I swear I can explain."

"I'm pregnant," she blurted.

Aaron froze, his arms still around her, his cheek touching hers. She breathed in the clean male scent that was uniquely his. I'll miss this, she thought. The way Aaron held her, kissed her. The way he smelled, his touch. What would be worse? To think she'd lost him in death, that she'd never see him again? Or to know he was alive, out there somewhere in the world, and she'd never see him again?

He turned her around and she forced herself to meet his eyes. He didn't seem angry. Just surprised. He'd shocked her with his sudden return from the dead. And she'd shocked him with her own announcement. "Pregnant," he repeated.

She nodded. He stepped back and took a good look at her. "How far along?"

"A-about three months."

"Do you want to tell me about it?"

Why wasn't he walking out the door, Zoe wondered. He'd asked her to marry him and she'd told him she was pregnant with another man's child. Yet there he stood. Unless he knew how she'd come to be pregnant. Knew because he was there.

"Does it matter?" she asked lightly.

"It does to me," Aaron said.

She pulled mugs from the shelf and poured coffee. "You won't like it," she warned. "You won't understand. You may not even believe it."

"Try me."

She handed him one of the coffees. "It's decaf." They settled on the sofa.

Calmer now, Zoe managed to tell him the story of the phantom as succinctly as possible, including her own desperation, leaving out the depth of her feelings for her unknown lover. Leaving out also the fact that she'd instigated unprotected sex.

The coffee remaining in their mugs had gone cold by the time she finished. Aaron had listened virtually without interrupting. When she finished he said, "That's quite a fantastic story."

"You don't believe me." Who would? It sounded like the most outlandish fiction even to her own ears.

"I didn't say that. But it's an incredibly unusual situation."

"I'll say." Zoe picked up the mugs and went to the kitchen to refill them. She handed Aaron his and resumed her seat, tucking one foot beneath her. She leaned back in the cushion and gazed at the ceiling holding her mug in both hands. Even here now, with Aaron, knowing he knew everything, she felt oddly comforted. Unburdened. He was the first and only person she'd been able to talk with about the phantom.

"Are you still seeing him?"

A humorless chuckle escaped Zoe. "You're forgetting. I've never actually seen him. But to answer your question, no I haven't. Not since I left with you that night. He hasn't contacted me."

"Because he knew you were away?"

"At first I thought so," Zoe admitted. "But I've been back here. Alone for over a month." She shrugged unwilling to admit to Aaron that she'd been disappointed at the lack of contact. Unwilling to admit that she'd thought Aaron was the phantom.

"So...where do you go from here?"

Her gaze connected with his. His eyes were bright, alert, as if he were hunting.

"I don't know."

"Do you think he'll be back? That he'll want to see you?"

"I don't know."

"And if he did?"

Zoe shrugged. "I'm not sure I can answer that unless it actually happens."

Aaron set his mug down on the coffee table between them and approached her. He hunkered down next to her and set her coffee aside as well. "Zoe."

"Yes?"

"I still want to marry you."

"You do?"

"If you'll have me. What you've told me doesn't change how I feel about you."

"Really?"

"So we get started early on a family."

"Aaron, are you sure? Absolutely sure?"

"More sure than I've been about anything in my life."

Chapter Forty

The words burst out of Zoe. "You know, all this time I've been thinking about all that I've lost. First Tim and Zach. Then Ben. Then you." *And the phantom.* She wondered, as she often had in the past, if Aaron knew what she was thinking. "I loved you. I don't know why. I don't understand it. I didn't think I could trust you, but I made myself do it when you promised you'd rescue Ben."

Aaron said nothing. It seemed as if he was barely breathing, though he seemed to be listening intently. "And you did rescue him. You did exactly what you said you'd do. You got him out. You risked your own life, but you got us all out. It wasn't your fault Ben died."

When Aaron didn't respond, not even bothering to agree with her, Zoe plunged ahead. "And now you're here, and you say you want to marry me, even if I'm pregnant with another man's child. You appear after all this time of letting me believe you were dead, *faking* your own death, and I wonder if I wouldn't be a fool to trust you again. Because I'm afraid I'll always be wondering what's next, waiting for the other shoe to drop. I don't think I could survive losing you again."

Aaron reached out, trailing his fingers through strands of Zoe's hair. His eyes darkened, the gold flecks no longer glinting. "Zoe." Abruptly his hand dropped away. A look of resignation crossed his face. "You're right. I've given you no reason to trust me. To believe in me. I think it's asking too much for you to forgive me for what I've done."

Was that it, Zoe wondered, panicked at the thought. Was he going to get up and walk out now, leave her wondering what the hell was going on? Not in this lifetime. She put a hand on his forearm. "I'd still like to know whatever you want to tell me. Why you let me believe you were dead. You owe me that, I think. Otherwise, I'll never know if I can forgive you or trust you. Not without all the facts."

"You won't like it."

"I didn't like thinking you were dead, either."

Aaron tilted his head in acknowledgment of that truth. "To put it simply, my identity was compromised. That night we were attacked here? That never should have happened. Someone who had access to classified information shared it.

"Once your identity is known, you're virtually worthless as an agent. I'd been looking for a way out of the agency anyway, but when there's a price on your head, it's not conducive to relaxation. I made a deal with Gannett. Run the op at the emerald mine, take Sheppard out, bring Ben back, and I get my life back. A life outside the agency. There's only one problem."

"That terrorist group is still looking for you."

Aaron nodded. "And they're not the type to give up easily. Plus, we don't know who the mole is within the agency. Or we didn't then, I should say. There's no way to guarantee, if I'm still alive, that information won't be passed along again."

"You're saying the agency faked your death."

"It was the only way."

"And you went along with it."

"I had to. I had no choice. Not if I wanted a future. Not unless I wanted to always be looking over my shoulder. It had to be done and it had to be believable. To everyone."

"Including me."

"Most of all you."

"You were in the morgue...I touched you. Your skin was cold. Clammy."

Aaron nodded. "Drugs. Refrigeration."

"Were you awake when I was there?"

"No. But Gannett told me about it. Zoe, if I could have spared you that, I would have."

"It was so...surreal. I couldn't believe you were dead, yet all the evidence was there."

Aaron picked up her hand, rubbed his thumb along the back of it. "I'm sorry. I can't undo it. But I'll spend the rest of my life making it up to you. I promise. If you'll let me."

Zoe said, "Aaron, I can't think about that right now. This is—it's almost too much to absorb. Drew suggested the possibility that your death had been faked, but I dismissed it. I'd seen your body in the morgue. I had the flag from your coffin. I attended your memorial service. How could I not believe?"

Aaron looked positively grim. "I know. It's hard not to believe what's right in front of you. But it was the only way."

"What about Ben?"

"What about him?"

"Is he really dead?"

"I don't know."

Zoe gave him a look, clearly not convinced he was telling the truth.

He sighed. "Zoe, I'm going to tell you something I shouldn't. I trust you, even though I know you don't trust me." At Zoe's look, he held up a hand. "I know, I know, you have good reason not to trust me or believe anything I say."

Zoe squeezed his fingers. "The sad thing is, I want to."

His expression softened at that. "There's a small group that works in conjunction with U.S. intelligence organizations. Mainly what this outfit does is recruit missionaries and aid workers, people like your brother, to gather intelligence in Third World countries."

Zoe sat up straighter, staring hard at Aaron. "You're saying Ben was a spy."

Aaron nodded somewhat reluctantly. "Essentially, yes. We know he was recruited by this group prior to his arrival in Guatemala. It was at their request that we made it part of our mission to rescue him."

"Ben was a spy," Zoe repeated. "I find that hard to believe. Ben wasn't the type to do anything...covert, underhanded, whatever you want to call it."

Aaron nodded. "Exactly why he was recruited. It's actually fairly common, believe it or not. Missionaries and relief workers are, or they were at least, fairly innocuous. Their organizations are always in need of funding. Operations like this one can offer money, grease the wheels with Third World governments to get the missionaries in place. All that's asked in return is that they turn over any interesting information they gather."

"Ben never said a word."

"He wouldn't. Doing so would endanger you and compromise him. Most likely he never thought he'd stumble across anything worthwhile anyway. It's an attractive offer. Missionaries like Ben get badly needed money for their mission, their orders, the church itself. More often than not, they don't have to do much of anything to earn it."

"But this time was different."

Aaron nodded. "The priest that had been stationed in that village before Ben disappeared more than a year before Ben arrived."

"Coughlan."

"Right."

"Was he one of these...recruits?"

"Classified information." Aaron smoothed Zoe's hair. She heard the smile in his voice. "It doesn't really matter, does it?" She wiggled closer to him.

"What followed his disappearance is what's really important. There were rumblings in that village before Coughlan disappeared. Then some odd things began to happen in the area. We were still trying to piece it together when Ben was captured."

"But Nicholas Sheppard was involved."

"Right," Aaron agreed bitterly. "But we didn't know that then. Nick was very clever, but the coincidences began to add up. Gannett suspected, but we needed more evidence. Sometimes gathering intelligence is a slow and tedious process. We could hardly charge into the area guns blazing until we knew what and who we were dealing with.

"After we were at the safe house, after you asked me to rescue Ben," Aaron explained quietly, his fingers sifting through the silk of Zoe's hair.

"And you agreed," Zoe reminded him.

Aaron nodded. "I did. Right before Gannett essentially asked me to do the same thing. I made a deal with him. I told him I wanted this to be my last mission. I was sick to death of what I was doing. I had no life except for my work. I wanted more. I wanted you," he told her softly.

Zoe was drifting in an almost dream-like state. "Mmm," she murmured at Aaron's admission. "Me too."

"I wanted out, but Gannett didn't want to lose me. Too valuable to the organization. But I had an ace in the hole. My identity as an agent had already been compromised. I couldn't continue working undercover even if I wanted to. We had an agreement. I destroy the mining operation. Take out Sheppard and Coughlan. Get Ben out. And I'm home free. I get reassigned, get to work regular hours, no more traveling. I get to have a life. That's all I wanted. A normal life."

Aaron's voice had grown soft, almost wondering, as if he could hardly believe all he'd wanted was something that simple, something easily achievable by a large majority of the earth's population.

"You know the rest of it. They had to fake my death. There was no other way. If I could have spared you that, I would have, believe me. But I had no choice. It was the only way out. Nick blamed me for a mission that failed, for being left for dead in Belize. He still had contacts. He's the one that sent information to that terrorist faction, told them when and where to find me, sent them after me. And Zoe, I'm sorry about Ben. I never got to tell you. I'm sorry you had to go through that alone."

Zoe didn't reply. Her gaze was fixed on something across the room. Aaron followed her gaze, to the bookshelf. On the shelf below the shrines for Tim and Zach a rectangular wooden box was surrounded by framed photographs and what looked like small bits of memorabilia. He realized what it was. A shrine of sorts to her brother.

On the shelf below that was an American flag, folded into a neat triangle, and nothing else. The flag from his funeral.

Abruptly her gaze swung back to him. "Are you sure he's dead?"

Aaron shook his head. "I honestly don't know."

"That means it's possible his death was faked the same way yours was. It's possible Ben's still alive."

Aaron frowned.

"This group, these people you say Ben was working for, are they as underhanded as your organization? Do they use the same tactics to throw someone off the trail?"

Zoe rushed on while Aaron considered the question.

"What if Ben's identity was compromised in some way? But he still had value to the organization. Like you?"

She jumped up and crossed to the shelf. Reverently she picked up the box and held it in her hands, looking down at it before she turned and crossed back to the sofa. Standing before Aaron she lowered the box, encouraging him to take it from her. "I need to know," she told him softly. "I have to know for sure."

"Zoe—"

"Please," she whispered. "If there's any chance that Ben's alive, if he's out there somewhere, I need to know."

Aaron accepted the box from her, a look of grim resignation on his face. He looked up at her. "Are you sure you want to do this?"

"Yes."

Aaron settled the smooth wooden box in his lap. It was surprisingly heavy. He lifted the lid. Inside, surrounded by foam inserts was a cremation urn with a dark coppery finish. He glanced up, catching Zoe's gaze. She nodded, indicating he should continue.

Aaron hated this, but he understood Zoe's need to know. If Ben was still alive, it was only fair that she know. And if he wasn't, well, she deserved to know that as well.

Using both hands he lifted the urn and set the box aside. He set the urn on the low table near the sofa, glancing once more at Zoe. Her gaze was on the urn. He unscrewed the lid, feeling dread build inside him. When he could delay no longer he averted his gaze and removed the lid, allowing Zoe the first look inside. He took note of her confused expression before he looked for himself. He stared for a moment, then tilted the urn a bit to make sure. "Is that—?"

"It looks like—"

Their gazes clashed. "Sand," they both said at the same time.

They stared into the urn again. Zoe bit her lip. "It looks like ordinary sand. The kind you'd find in a children's sandbox." Her brow furrowed. Aaron tilted the urn again, the grains of sand moving with the motion.

"Does this mean...?"

"That Ben's still alive?"

Zoe nodded, her eyes pleading for confirmation.

"It would seem so, wouldn't it?"

"But why? I understand the need to make everyone believe you were dead. But why fake Ben's death?"

Aaron sat back on the sofa. "Coughlan?"

"Coughlan?" Zoe echoed. "What about him?"

"He was involved. He was the other principal. But we didn't get him. We took out the mine, Sheppard and the others. But Coughlan got out. I don't know how, unless he left in the middle of the night. Ben might be the only one who can identify him as the other major player."

"Where's Coughlan now?"

Aaron shook his head. "I don't know. And I have to be honest with you, Zoe, I'm not privy to the ways and means of the organization that recruited Ben. But what seems likely is that if Ben is alive, they may have needed him to pursue Coughlan, to draw him out so he could be captured. They may need to use Ben to bring Coughlan to justice."

Zoe glanced back down at the grains of sand. "But do you think Ben's alive?"

"I think if he were dead, we wouldn't have found sand in that urn."

Zoe lowered herself to a nearby chair, covered her face with her hands and mumbled something unintelligible. Aaron got up and tugged her hands away from her face. "Come on." He drew her to her feet and walked her into the bedroom.

Except for their narrow escape through this room some weeks ago, he'd never been in it. He planned to marry Zoe, yet he'd never been in her bedroom. Hadn't been in her bed. Well, he had. Just not as himself. He frowned as he stared at her double bed.

Of course he'd have to tell her the truth. But not tonight.

He drew back the covers and maneuvered Zoe to the edge of the bed. "What are you doing?" she asked.

He bent and slipped her shoes off. "Lie down." When she did he drew the covers over her. Dropping a kiss on her forehead, he gazed at her for a long moment. "I think you need some time to think. And you need some sleep."

"You could stay," she told him.

Aaron shook his head. "I'd like to. But not tonight. I want you to be sure." He kissed her again. "I'll call you tomorrow."

Then he left.

Chapter Forty-One

The blood drained from Zoe's face as she stared at the envelope that lay on the floor.

She picked it up, feeling the familiar weight of the hundred dollar bills inside.

Tonight. That's what the envelope meant. He'd returned from the dead yesterday, and he expected her to meet him tonight.

Zoe closed the door and took the envelope with her as she sank into a nearby chair. How could he?

If she hadn't convinced herself before that Aaron was her phantom lover, she knew it now. She stared at the envelope, adding up coincidences, remembering similarities and listening to what her gut instinct had been telling her for a long time. Aaron was the phantom.

She opened the envelope and withdrew the money and knew what she had to do.

Zoe lay in the dark wide awake.

She heard the door open and close. Every nerve ending she possessed tingled in anticipation. She turned toward him as he approached the bed, and listened to the sounds of him undressing. Shoes slid off, material rustled as he shucked shirt and pants. A belt buckle hit the floor with a muffled thud.

He came to her and she welcomed him into her arms. Holding him tight, tamping down the lump of emotion. He was the phantom, but he was thinner, just as Aaron was. Her arm brushed against the puckered skin on his side and chest. Aaron would have a scar in the same place.

His lips were buried in her hair and he remained still until she finally relaxed her grip on him. Then he kissed her, her hair, her temple, her ear, jaw and throat.

She knew every nuance of his lovemaking, responded to each touch and kiss and returned them. But tonight there was something different, something indefinable. It was as if he wanted each touch, each kiss to leave a lasting impression. She felt his heat and his intensity, the same yet not the same.

When he entered her in one quick thrust, she gasped in reaction, feeling him fill her everywhere. Everything she felt and wanted to say lodged in her throat, and she desperately feared he'd never know how much he meant to her.

His lips burned a path along her throat to beneath her ear. His hands tangled in her hair as he rocked against her. She wanted to speak but she couldn't find her voice. And if she didn't say something soon, it would be over. He'd be gone. He'd never know.

His lips moved along her jaw. Taking her by complete surprise, his lips touched hers. Just a whisper of a touch at first.

Zoe held his head in her hands. Her eyes were wide open but she could see nothing. It didn't matter. She knew he was there. She knew who he was. Whatever she said or didn't say, he'd always be with her, and somehow she was sure he knew that.

She kissed his mouth, feeling his reluctance slip away as he pulled her even closer beneath him. His kiss felt familiar yet exotic. Her concentration slipped away as she gave herself up to the purely novel sensation of kissing him while they made love. Fully and completely made love. Became for all time a part of each other.

How could she give him up? How could she ever trust him? Tears leaked from Zoe's eyes as their lovemaking concluded. Silent tears fell into her hair and onto the pillow in the dark. "I love you," she whispered before he withdrew.

He didn't respond, at least not in words. But he stilled above her. Zoe could feel him peering down at her in the darkness, every sense alert in case she was going to continue. But she'd said what she needed to say. She'd leave here soon and never return. Never be with the phantom again.

His lips touched hers in a series of tender kisses. Then he did what he always did. He lay on his side and held her close.

Chapter Forty-Two

Rolling away from him, she flipped the flimsy covers back and left the bed, maneuvering across the ancient linoleum to the wall by the door. She got her bearings, her hand fumbled for the light switch, groping in the dark.

"Don't."

Zoe froze. Her mind fragmented into a thousand pieces at the sound of his voice. He'd never spoken to her before, yet she knew his voice. She tried to lessen the restriction of her suddenly tense throat muscles before she spoke. "A-Aaron?"

Her mind rebelled at this final, definitive confirmation, telling her it couldn't be, he wouldn't do this to her. At the same time every coincidence, every suspicion, every intuitive nudge she'd had that Aaron and the phantom were one and the same collided in her brain. It was as if she saw her life since that first night with the phantom flash before her eyes, a thousand pictures at lightning speed, all telling her it was true. *It's true. It's true.*

"Yes."

She flipped the switch and the overhead light came on. Something like hatred flared inside her as she saw the room, the chair, the bed, and the man from her peripheral vision. She was naked and the light was on. He could see everything about her now. In exposing him, she'd forgotten she'd also be exposing herself. She stared at the floor, willing this not to be happening, feeling the room tilt and her vision blur. She willed herself not to faint.

No. She would turn. She would face him. And she would finally have the truth.

She brought her chin up, shook back her hair, and turned. He was sitting up in the bed, sheet pulled to his waist, staring at her, probably trying, through force of his will, to make the light go out before she saw him. *Too late, Aaron. Phantom in the dark. I've caught you now.*

Emotions battled within her as they stared at each other, eyes locked for what felt like hours. She loved Aaron. She loved the phantom. They were one and the same. She was pregnant with the phantom's child. Which Aaron had been willing to accept as his own. Because it was Aaron's child. And he knew that.

He'd tricked her, playing from both ends. He'd made a fool of her and she'd gone along with it willingly, ignoring the signs, ignoring her own instincts.

She'd been so incredibly stupid, seeing what she wanted to see. Seeing what Aaron wanted her to see. Or not see as the case may be.

He'd chosen her, set her up.

She hated him. She was almost sure of it. Hated him as much she loved him. Them. Him.

She could feel tears filling her eyes, but she didn't know why. She was angry, wasn't she? No. Maybe she was hurt. Crushed. He'd tricked her, fooled her. He'd been laughing at her. Yes. She was pretty sure what she was feeling was hatred.

He moved from the bed. She thought she made a sound in her throat, warning him off, but he ignored it. She watched him stalk toward her, naked, gloriously naked, that body of his that had given her such pleasure, such passion. Never again. She'd never reach those heights with another man. And never again with him.

He wrapped his arms around her. All that warm male skin surrounded her and she didn't react. Maybe she was in shock. The circuitry in her brain overloaded. So much to process at once, she couldn't think.

"I'm sorry," he said.

Those words galvanized her into action. She knocked his arms away and slapped him, hard across the face. It must have stung, for her hand throbbed, but he didn't move away.

He knows he deserves it.

She hit him again and again, his biceps, his scarred chest, until she was wildly pounding on him with both fists, not caring if she damaged him or not, but unable to stop. He should feel some of her pain, shouldn't he? One of her blows glanced off the jagged scar along his side and that did it. He subdued her quickly and easily by virtue of his greater strength and weight and bore her back to the bed, holding her when she flailed beneath him. "Let me go. Let me go!"

"Stop it. You'll hurt yourself. Or you'll hurt the baby."

She stilled. She wouldn't endanger her unborn child. Even if it was his. Her breathing was ragged from fighting him and she felt helpless as she had all those months ago when she'd first come here. She'd become strong because of him, because of his money, because he showed her who she was, who she could be, here in the dark. She'd taken some of his strength for her own. But now it had all been stripped away. She was a fool and she'd gone on a fool's errand, prostituting herself to save her brother. She'd allowed herself to be used and she hadn't saved him. He hadn't needed her to save him.

Tears welled in her eyes. She wanted only to be out of here, away from him, the phantom. Aaron! And to never see him again.

"Please let me go." Her tears leaked into her hair.

He stared down at her. "No way. Not until you let me explain—"

"You can't explain this! You used me, made a fool of me, tricked me, lied to me, and I, and I—" She began to cry in earnest.

"You what?"

"Loved you, damn it. Fell in love with you. I didn't even know who you were, who you are, and I fell in love with you."

"You know me, Zoe," he told her quietly. "You've always known me."

She refused to believe, rejected the ring of truth in his words, for wasn't that exactly what she'd told herself almost from the beginning?

She turned her head away so she wouldn't have to look into his eyes and see the sincerity there, the truth, the genuine regret he felt for causing her pain. He couldn't make it right, no matter what he said. He'd gone too far, done too much, for any woman to forgive or understand. Hadn't he?

"Zoe, please."

She turned back to him. "I hate you."

She could see the words affect him, wound him. "No, you don't."

"I hate you. I'll never forgive you. Now let me go."

"No. Let me explain. Let me make it right."

"I *hate* you!" Zoe struggled beneath him, but he didn't budge.

He bowed his head and when he picked it back up there were tears in his eyes. He shook his head as if to clear them, as if they were annoying foreign objects filling his eyes, but they kept coming.

"Please don't leave me. Please don't hate me. I can't stand it. Please, Zoe, please." He buried his face in the crook of her neck and his whole body started to shake. In typical male fashion he was trying desperately not to cry, to hold his emotions at bay. The sound only a man can make when he's completely broken escaped and took all of the wind out of Zoe's sails. He was no longer restraining her, she could have slid out from under him, she was sure of it, and he wouldn't have stopped her. But he clung to her, and as his tears wet her shoulder, and her hair, and the sheet beneath her, she felt oddly at peace.

Gently she stroked his hair, his back, murmuring inconsequential words of comfort until he quieted, but she still continued the stroking.

"You're still here," he croaked.

"I know." She hated the harsh overhead lighting from the ancient fixture. She'd never realized how comforting being in the dark was.

He shifted a bit away from her. "I'm sorry." Whether for his outburst or for everything else, Zoe didn't know or care. Perhaps she didn't hate him quite as much as she thought.

Phantom

Chapter Forty-Three

The following morning, when Aaron arrived, he rang the buzzer at the downstairs door and Zoe let him in. He'd wanted to spend the day with her yesterday, stay the night, also, Zoe was sure, but she'd let him buy her breakfast and sent him on his way.

She needed to sort out how she felt about what he'd done.

She dodged his embrace when he entered the apartment, but he didn't push.

"I thought of bringing you flowers," he told her as they moved further into the room, "but I figured no gesture is going to be big enough."

"You're right." She picked up a roll of tape and started taping the box she'd packed.

"What are you doing?" Aaron asked.

"Packing."

"Why?"

"I'm moving."

"Moving where?"

"Markham, New Jersey."

"Just like that? You're leaving?"

"No, Aaron, not 'just like that.' You've been gone for over a month. I thought you were dead. I have a child to think of. I'm not raising him or her in the city. Thanks to you I had something I never had before. Money. Enough to buy a car and put a down payment on a house. Not a big house, but a house, in a place where my child can grow up and I can, I don't know, maybe go back to teaching." At Aaron's look, she rushed on. "I checked out the school system and it's one of the better ones in the area. I'm not going back to work right away. But maybe in a year or so." Zoe turned to construct another box.

"What about me?" Aaron asked. He'd folded his arms over his chest and adopted a wide-legged, you're-not-getting–by-me-or-around-me stance. Even though he'd lost some weight, he'd lost none of his air of command.

"What about you?" she returned lightly.

"This is my child, too."

"Of course. I'm sure we can set up an amicable arrangement. I won't keep you from him. Or her."

Aaron grabbed her so fast it startled her. She dropped the tape. His grasp on her arms was light but firm. "I'm not going to be a part-time father. I asked you to marry me, dammit."

"And I said I'd think about it! You can't just show up and mow right over me and expect me to forgive and forget everything you've done. You can't expect me to forgive just because I know the truth. If it is the truth."

"I never lied to you, Zoe."

"Lies of omission are still lies," she returned sullenly.

"You never asked me. Not once, in all the time you knew me since I arranged to meet you in the bookstore. Even if you suspected, you never asked."

"I couldn't," Zoe told him softly.

He eased his grip. "Maybe you didn't want to know."

"Maybe so." She fixed him with a look. "Drew told me he saw you at the memorial service for Tim and Zach. But I don't remember."

Aaron's gaze never wavered. "I was there."

"Why?"

He glanced away for a moment before looking into her eyes once again. "I was at the scene of the accident. I saw it happen."

"What!" She tugged her hands away from his and he let go. She stared at him.

"We'd been following the man who was driving the car that hit Tim and Zach. He was part of a terrorist cell. We had intel about a plot to blow up... some significant parts of the city. He knew we were after him when he stole that car. We were in pursuit." Aaron lifted a hand and let it drop. "You know the rest."

"But why would you attend the services? You didn't know Tim or Zach. Or me."

"Your name was the last thing Tim said." Aaron's words fell like individual drops of rain into a placid pool.

"How do you know that?"

"I told you. I was there."

"But—but…" Zoe didn't know where to go with her questions.

"I felt responsible, okay? If we hadn't been chasing Carzoui, he wouldn't have panicked, wouldn't have stolen that car, wouldn't have killed your husband and your son."

"The money. That was you."

"It was me. I couldn't change what happened. I didn't know how else to help."

Zoe covered her ears, then her mouth. What he was saying was almost too much to absorb, but she couldn't look away from Aaron.

He said, "When I saw you in the restaurant a year later, which was not planned, by the way, but completely coincidental, something clicked."

"And you decided to set me up."

Aaron chose to ignore her choice of words. Maybe he was right to. No one had coerced her into the relationship with the phantom. No one had forced her to accept that money. "I know, believe me, I know it's asking a lot for you to forgive. Maybe you'll never forgive me for the past. But that doesn't mean we can't have a future, does it?"

"I don't know." Zoe picked up the roll of tape and fiddled with it. "I honestly don't know."

"Do you remember the day you said you'd do anything for me if I rescued Ben? Anything at all. Do you remember, Zoe?"

"I remember. I can't believe you're bringing this up now. That you expect me to—"

"I don't expect anything. All I'm asking is that you give me a chance. Because I'm not going to disappear. I'm not going to give up."

Zoe nodded. She'd known Aaron wouldn't walk away. She'd have been massively disappointed if, after everything he'd said yesterday, he'd been willing to bow out of her life and that of their child completely. And she *had* made that promise.

"Okay."

Aaron smiled as if he knew something she didn't. She wasn't sure she liked that smile. "I'll let you get back to work." He bent and kissed her. Then he was gone. Again.

ONE MONTH LATER

She missed him. It hadn't taken her long to figure out that she wanted Aaron in her life permanently. She wanted a father for her child and whether or not Aaron was exactly ideal husband material given his past, if he asked her again to marry him, she knew what her answer would be.

The problem was, even after his promise not to disappear, Aaron had disappeared.

Zoe had managed her relocation to Markham all on her own. She hadn't heard from Aaron since the day he'd walked out of her apartment, and she didn't know if she ever would. She had Gannett's phone number. For that matter she still had Aaron's phone number. Unless he'd changed it. But she couldn't bring herself to call.

If Aaron wanted her as much as he supposedly did, then he could find her. He could come and get her.

She hated feeling that he was once again playing her, that he somehow knew what she needed better than she knew herself. Maybe that's why he'd left her alone, to give her time to miss him.

His absence also gave her time to thoroughly sort through the boxes she'd brought with her. In one, she'd tossed a bundle of letters she'd received from Ben after he'd left for Guatemala. In her letters she'd poured out her grief and her guilt, what she saw as her own part in Tim's and Zach's deaths. Ben's replies had been filled with words of God. He'd talked of love and forgiveness, most of which Zoe'd skimmed over, unwilling then to forgive herself or allow anyone else to.

Now she pored over the letters, seeing the truth in Ben's words, allowing herself to believe. As she reflected on the events since then, she thought perhaps she had been forgiven. For what was this child she was carrying if not a second chance? A chance to do it right, make it right. And if she forgave herself, didn't Aaron deserve that as well? Didn't he deserve a second chance?

She gritted her teeth. If he ever called, that is. If he ever asked her again, she'd say yes. Marriage to Aaron would be a constant challenge, she decided. But never boring.

Her stomach growled and she realized it was almost time for lunch. She'd kept herself busy, cleaning and painting the rooms in her new house. On weekends she browsed yard sales and flea markets for bargain furnishings and decorative touches.

If she carefully budgeted the money she had left, she thought she might be okay for a year. Until she'd opened her bank statement last week to find that a $50,000 deposit had been made earlier in the month.

Assuming it to be an error, she had called the bank. But the bank could find no error. The money had been wired from a bank in the city and was most definitely intended for her account.

Aaron.

She tried to be surprised, but she wasn't. She tried to be angry at his manipulation, but she couldn't quite manage that, either. The money was Aaron's way of telling her he would take care of her and their child.

Just as Zoe decided on a tuna sandwich for lunch her doorbell rang. She'd met a few of her neighbors, but she thought most of them worked and were away during the day. Through the peephole she could see only a huge bouquet of flowers.

"Who's there?" she called through the door.

"Flower delivery, ma'am," came a man's voice.

"From whom? From where? I can't see you."

"That never bothered you before," came the reply.

"Aaron?"

"If you don't want these flowers, I met a lovely red-headed divorcee earlier. Maybe she'd like them."

Zoe knew exactly who he meant. Jessica Hoveland lived two doors down. She'd come over to introduce herself shortly after Zoe moved in. Word on the street was she was gunning for a new husband, and she wasn't too picky about the applicants.

Zoe unlocked the door. The gigantic bouquet preceded Aaron inside. He set the flowers down before presenting her with a covered casserole dish.

"What's this?"

"I'm not sure. When I moved in this morning, my new neighbor Jessica brought it over as, let's see, how did she put it? Just a little something to welcome me to the neighborhood. She promised to stop by later because she knows how lonely it can be for us single people."

"Moved in?"

"Next door."

"I didn't know that house was for sale."

"It wasn't. But I bought it anyway." Aaron grinned at her. "Aren't you happy to see me?"

"I'm—I'm surprised is all. I'm sure I'd have noticed if there was a moving van around this morning."

"I travel light." Aaron stepped closer. "I missed you. I couldn't stay away any longer. I

460

figured this is the perfect solution. You don't have to forgive me. You don't have to marry me. Just let me be around. Let me help you raise our child. Let me love you."

Zoe stared down at the glass top of the casserole dish. Silence stretched between them.

"What do you say?" he asked, when it became apparent she was at a loss for words.

She lifted her head and looked into his eyes. "I think we should heat up this casserole because I'm starving." She turned toward the kitchen and Aaron followed. "And I think," she told him over her shoulder, "I'll inform your friend Jessica that she's got some serious competition."

Epilogue

"What's this?" Zoe asked, when Aaron set a package on the table in front of her.

"I don't know," he said. "It was next to the door. UPS must have delivered it." He dropped a kiss on her lips and moved to the counter to pour himself coffee. He had indeed purchased the house next door to hers, but he spent little time there. He'd refused to put it on the market, however, until she set a wedding date.

In theory she'd agreed to marry him and he'd promptly given her a ring. Not diamonds and certainly not emeralds. But a stunning sapphire in a platinum setting.

"I didn't order anything," she informed him. The return address was a fulfillment center in Dallas. She tore the seal of the padded envelope and peered inside at a bubble-wrapped object.

Aaron leaned against the counter watching as he sipped his coffee. He stepped closer, brows knit as they both studied what she'd unwrapped. It was a cross fashioned from wooden building blocks painted in primary colors. The kind of wall decor suitable for a child's room.

Zoe glanced up at Aaron. "I don't know where this came from."

"Neither do I." He took the cross from her and turned it over, examining it for a clue.

"It's not the kind of thing Drew would send. And even if he did, there'd be a card or something."

"I agree," Aaron said, handing it back to her. "It's not exactly Drew's style."

"I don't know anyone who would send me a cross, except..."

"Ben?"

Zoe nodded, her gaze pleading with his. "Do you think he's alive? That he knows?" She gestured at her now significant baby bump.

Aaron took the chair across from her. "What do you think?"

She'd never told Aaron that she'd been asking for a sign when praying to that God she'd begun to believe in. She'd never truly believed Ben was dead even before they'd found that his urn was filled with sand. If she'd learned anything at all, she'd learned making a fake death look convincing wasn't hard. She knew now to look beneath the surface instead of seeing only what others wanted her to see.

Aaron stood and picked up the cross. He reached for her hand. "Show me where you want this in the baby's room."

The MANUSCRIPTS UNDER THE BED Project

Dear Reader,

I wrote this story early in my writing career. Probably 15-20 years ago. I couldn't see a way to get it traditionally published back then, and so the many pages I'd labored over, the notes, the revisions and the rejection letters, went into a box and found a home under the guest room bed.

I continued to write and eventually my work was published by small publishers. After 30 or so years of writing, I no longer have the inclination to wait on a decision by someone else to determine whether my work should be published, seen and read.

Writing a novel is a time-consuming process for me, but God reminded me that I have quite a few novels already completed. They are stories I love, and I hope readers will as well.

Thank you for giving one of The Manuscripts Under The Bed a chance, because in the end? Your opinion is the only one that matters.

--Barbara Meyers

About the Author

Barista by day, romance novelist by night: When not writing fiction, Dr. Seuss-like poetry (for adults) or song lyrics, Barbara Meyers disguises herself behind a green apron and works part-time for a world-wide coffee company.

Her novels are a mix of comedy, suspense and spice and often feature a displaced child.

Barbara is still married to her first husband and has two fantastic children. The most recent addition to her family is Winner, a rescued black lab mix. Originally from Southwest Missouri, (she blames her roots in the Show Me state for her somewhat skeptical nature) Barbara currently resides in Central Florida.

Visit her at barbarameyers.com

Look for these titles by

Barbara Meyers

<u>Now Available:</u>
Misconceive
Scattered Moments
Not Quite Heaven
Cleo's Web
White Roses in Winter
Training Tommy

The Braddocks Series:
A Month From Miami
A Forever Kind of Guy

I Never Thought I'd See You Again
(Novelists, Inc., Anthology)

The Red Bud Series:
If You Knew

Coming Soon in this series:
If You Dare
If You Stay

Barbara Meyers

If You Touch
Coming Soon:

A Family for St. Nick (Christmas Novella)

The Manuscripts Under the Bed Project:

Phantom
The Color of Nothing

Barbara Meyers writing as AJ Tillock
The Grinding Reality Series:

The Forbidden Bean (Book One)
Cool Beans (Book Two)

Acknowledgments & Thanks

As always, I thank God for every bit of writing talent and ability He gave me, and for the daily inspiration and assistance He sends me.

And also to:

Bill, for everything he has done and still does for me.

Ellen Holder, patient proofreader and copy editor, who allows me to pay her in Panera Bread gift cards.

Kathy Haffner, the best ever beta reader, proofreader, fan and friend.

Stephanie Cunningham, assistant extraordinaire.

Margaret Velasco, the "final word" proofreader and beta reader.

Gaylene Atkins, Sandy Carmouche and Donna Kelly. They know why.

Cover artist Steven Novak, Novak Illustration.

My Facebook, Twitter, Instagram and newsletter followers and friends for their support and feedback on everything from research to covers.

Lakeland Writers, Novelists, Inc., Florida Writers Association, and Coffee & Quill friends for their assistance and support.

And finally, to all the strong, courageous women I've been privileged to know throughout my life.

Dear Readers,

I hope you enjoyed reading about Zoe and Aaron's journey as much as I enjoyed writing about it.

If you did I hope you will leave a brief review on the site where you purchased it or on Goodreads.com. Reviews are so helpful to authors, especially indie authors. I also hope you will tell others about the book.

I love hearing from readers. You can contact me, follow my blog and sign up for my newsletter at barbarameyers.com. All my social media links are on the following page

All the best,

Barbara Meyers

www.ingramcontent.com/pod-product-compliance
Lightning Source LLC
Chambersburg PA
CBHW021118260626
47169CB00005B/1341